The Cleanup Committee

ISBN: 978-1-7358497-0-6

www.cordeliarains.com
Published in the USA.

For Dad

Prologue

1978

Jonah Bernard Stoneking poured his first cup of coffee. Holding it carefully, he shuffled in slippered feet to his richly appointed living room. Seating himself by a softly crackling fire, he picked up a white telephone, punched in a number, and listened to the recorded message. When the message was finished, he replaced the phone and smiled.

From beside his chair, Jonah picked up a leather briefcase and extracted a sealed envelope from it. He broke the seal, pulled out a pamphlet, and began to read. The lines on his face stood out in concentration. It was a highly confidential report prepared for him by an associate. It was the only copy. When Jonah finished reading, he stood, opened the glass door of the fireplace and tossed the pamphlet inside. He stepped back upon the pamphlet catching fire, and smiled up at a portrait of a young man in a University of Oregon football uniform. From his place on the mantle, Jonah Junior smiled at his father.

Jonah the senior was 59 years old, and a still healthy 6 foot 2 inches and 200 pounds. His finances were as healthy as his body as he cared well for both. Jonah was Owner and CEO of Stoneking Enterprises. He controlled a vast empire of finance, transportation and retail outlets. He could also be credited with the creation of the Cleanup Committee.

Three years ago, Jonah B. Stoneking Junior had been a highly rated young quarterback for the University of Oregon football team. They had gone to the Rose Bowl. A victory party followed when they defeated Washington State. Young

Stoneking was found dead of a drug overdose. His death shocked the state and the nation. Their shock was nothing next to the grief of Jon and Beth Stoneking, and young Jonah's twin sister, Dot.

In the trying days after the funeral, it was young miss Dot who kept her parents' collective sanity in place. It was during that time the idea for the Cleanup Committee had first come to Jonah Stoneking. The idea had developed and was about to become a reality. The best financed and best trained private army was recruited and ready to begin training.

Jonah walked to the master bedroom where Beth slept. He had no need for lights as he dressed in the day's suit. As he knotted his tie the bedside light came on. Beth sat up and rubbed the sleep from her eyes, then started in surprise upon seeing Jonah.

"Hey you, what are you doing up early on a Saturday?" Beth asked.

"Good morning beautiful," Jonah answered. "I tried not to wake you. I've got a meeting this morning about that airport job down south." He hoped she couldn't see his guilt over the lie.

"Why didn't you say so? I could've gotten up and fixed your breakfast."

"You need your sleep", Jonah said gently. "Besides, it's a breakfast meeting. I'm sure there'll be something. I can only hope it's palatable." He crossed the room and sat on the bed by Beth, drawing her in and holding her close. "I'll bet there's no woman in all or Portland, or all of Oregon, who looks as good as you do."

"Flattery will get you everything," she answered coyly.

"I have everything a man could want," Jonah answered with a smile. "I have since I found you 24 years ago."

"I sure didn't look very good then," Beth said. It was true, she hadn't looked well...but people who had just been in traffic accidents don't usually look all that well.

Jonah had encountered Beth when she rear ended his car at a stop sign. Although she came out of the car bloody and dazed, Jonah had fallen for her immediately. He got her bleeding under control and helped her to calm down. After speaking with the police and refusing ambulance transport, Beth allowed Jonah Stoneking to take her home. They got married that June.

If Beth had known about the Cleanup Committee she would have insisted he abandon the project. Jonah knew he couldn't abandon the idea of avenging their son's death. Thousands of other sons and daughters, hundreds of other parents even, had been killed or maimed by drugs and those who pushed them. For the distributors, the dealers, the pushers, Stoneking planned death. Quick and merciless death.

Jonah stood and turned the light off. "Get some more sleep," he said.

"Did Dot make it home last night?" Beth asked while laying back down.

"Yes,I heard her come in around 3."

"I wish she'd quit running around in the winter. Those roads are slick. I worry." Beth looked anxious.

"I know, dear, I do too. She's young, and does what makes her happy. I'll be home by 4, maybe sooner. Why don't you and Dot join me for lunch?"

"Where?" Beth asked.

"I'll pick something and call you later." Beth snuggled back into the covers, and Jonah headed out.

It was a cold January morning as Jonah Stoneking drove his Cadillac west. He was meeting the other founders of the

Cleanup Committee. The others were men like himself; successful men who had lost children to drugs. It had not been hard to tell them the idea of the Cleanup Committee. Stoneking had not achieved his situation in life without the ability to make people see things his way. One by one, they had agreed. One by one, they had given freely of their time and money.

Stoneking nosed the Cadillac into the basement garage of the warehouse where the meeting was being held. Once inside he crossed the cold concrete floor to the freight elevator. On the second floor, among the crates and merchandise, was a large semi truck. Past the truck was a back office. Stoneking started the coffee brewing and waited for the other 7 men to arrive.

The first two to arrive were William P. Rodgers and Edwin Colley. Rogers was a trucking magnate, and Colley was the computer man. Rodgers had contributed one million dollars and the use of his trucks, along with reliable drivers. Colley, along with his million dollar contribution, had designed a computer system to steal information from the Law Enforcement database. Each of them greeted Stoneking and went for the coffee.

Next was David Braun, the export/import man. Fred Ritter, owner of a large sporting goods chain, was right behind him. Ritter and Braun were securing the Crew's weapons. Al Fielder and Jay Smith were next to arrive. Fielder owned a large flying service. He was to supply the private jets and pilots for the Crew. Smith owned a wholesale food company that supplied hospitals, schools, and developing countries. He had recently added the Cleanup Committee to his list of customers, under an assumed name.

Keith Brown, of Brown and Stone Construction Company, would be building a school . Gerald Lewis, last to arrive, owned a printing company that would supply paper and literature.

The men were old friends and chatted as they arrived. Some of the relationships extended clear back to World War II. Stoneking called the meeting to order.

"Gentlemen," he began, "Thank you for attending. We have a lot of business to cover and not a lot of time. I'll tell you what I have, then I'll take your reports. First, I got a message last night from Doctor Fish. He is the one member of this crew not in attendance and known only to me. That will change soon. You'll all be in for a surprise. The Doctor reports that the last of the recruits has been located. He is a 17 year old who looks promising. The Doctor will let me know for certain later today if the young man will work out. Now, I'll take your reports." Stonelake looked them over. "Fred, do you have everything in?"

Fred Ritter stepped forward. "Got them all, Jonah. 40 Browning 9 mm pistols, 40 M-16s, and 40 Uzi 9 mm's. We have 20 thousand rounds of ammo for each gun type, with more on the way." Fred waved his hand at several crates stacked nearby. "Ready for transport."

"Did you secure the weapons from the military?"

"We did, and completely on the up and up" Fred replied.

"Congratulations to you and David for a job well done!" Stoneking said. "Next!"

Smith reported that the food supplies were ready and the delivery system was in place. Fielder had a helicopter and reliable pilot ready to transport personnel and supplies.

Lewis showed each crew member a card he had designed. It was a small, ordinary looking, common business card. Yet in a few short months it would be one of the most famous cards to ever be printed. Finally, Brown stated the school would be ready for the students when they arrived next month.

"What do our teams know of this?" Stoneking asked.

"They think we're working on a project for the CIA," Brown answered.

"Excellent. Doctor Fish will be assisting the teams and working with security." Stoneking looked at Bill Rodgers, then the parked semi truck. "You have a good man for this truck, Bill?"

"Sure do," Rodgers replied. "He's one of my best. He'll be here at 2 p.m. I'll meet him and let him know where he's going. We'll need to load the truck, though."

"Then I suggest we get to it," Stoneking said. They all removed the coats and ties they'd worn for the benefit of their wives. They changed into coveralls one might expect a mechanic to wear. Four hours later, under Rodger's direction, the crates were placed in the semi, expertly placed for equal weight distribution. Stoneking checked his watch. 10:53 a.m. Time to call Beth for lunch.

One by one the men made their way to the back office, washed up and changed back to their expected corporate look. Each man left the warehouse looking just like they entered. The last men in the building were Stoneking and Rodgers. They stood by the truck and looked at each other.

"Well," Rodgers said, "the fat is on the fire."

"It sure is," Stoneking replied. "Shortly it's going to start splattering."

"Let's just hope it doesn't splatter on us."

"If everyone's done their jobs, it won't."

"Are the recruits coming in on Monday?"

"Some are here now, but by Monday they'll all be ready for school."

Rodgers took a breath. "It's a big adventure, Jonah. I hope we're successful."

Chapter 1

It was a cold, wet January night in Eugene, Oregon. John Clay Redwine, 17 years old, left his sporty orange Mustang and ran. He sped across the parking lot toward the big EMERGENCY sign, ignoring the rain. Electric doors opened automatically, and he left wet footprints in the hospital lobby. He stopped at the counter.

"I'm Johnny Redwine. I got a call at work that my sister's here."

"Just a moment, I'll check for you." The nurse was pretty and had a soft voice. Johnny unzipped his raincoat and took out a pack of Camels. He lit one and waited nervously while the nurse made her calls.

"Thanks for waiting," the nurse said as she hung up the phone. "Brenda is in the emergency room. Doctor Ellis will speak with you there. Head to your right and just follow the signs."

"Thanks." Johnny's path brought him to some swinging doors. The sign over them said EMERGENCY ROOM NO SMOKING. He dropped his Camel on the floor and ground it out while pushing open the doors. The place was jam packed. Doctors and nurses rushed around, people were all over the place. It was chaos. Johnny wondered how the hell he'd find Doctor Ellis in this crowd.

As if to answer his question, a young doctor with sandy colored hair materialized out of the crowd. "Are you Johnny Redwine?"

"I am. Where's Brenda? What happened?"

"Follow me," the doctor said as he turned and started walking. The noise level dropped as they entered a small exam room. It was empty.

"Brenda's not here. Where is she?"

"Johnny, I'm sorry to tell you Brenda is dead."

He stood looking at the doctor. Somehow he had known this was coming, but hearing it still didn't make it seem real.

"What?" He needed to hear it again.

"Brenda came in about an hour ago on an ambulance. She seems to have died from a drug overdose."

Johnny and Brenda had shared an apartment since their drunken father had killed himself and their mother in a car wreck 2 years ago. Johnny had been 15 at the time. Brenda was 19. He'd stayed in school and worked part time. Brenda had tried but then fell in with the wrong bunch. Watching his sister slide downhill had been tough on Johnny. They'd had several arguments. Recently he'd come home and found Brenda with one of her suppliers high in their living room. The supplier was a fat little pig-looking creep called Fat Freddy Zeis. In a rage, Johnny had beaten the stoned pusher up and tossed him out of the apartment. Then he and Brenda had another argument. He loved her in spite of it all. He knew who she was before Fat Freddy and others had changed her. A tear now found its way out of Johnny's eye and started down his face.

"I'm sorry, son," the doctor was saying. "I'm really sorry. Such a waste."

Johnny pulled a wrinkled handkerchief from his pocket, and wiped away the only tear. "It's that bunch she was hanging out with. I know who supplied her."

"Tell the police, son. Someone is guilty of murder." The doctor shook his head in sorrow.

"Fuck the cops!" Johnny yelled. "The useless pigs would have that filthy dealer back on the street in half an hour. I'll deal with him myself."

Johnny turned to the door. The doctor put a hand on his arm.

"Why don't you let me get you something? Then you can go home and rest."

Johnny shook the hand off. "Put your drugs in your ass, Doctor. I don't need your pills."

"Violence won't bring her back," the doctor said. "It'll just land you in jail."

"Yeah, but it'll stop them from killing anyone else." Johnny opened the door and stepped back into the chaos. Crossing the room toward the exit, he hardly noticed the activity around him. He didn't notice the uniformed patrolmen entering the ER. Johnny's mind was on one thing only: Fat Freddy.

The rain was still pouring outside. Johnny reached the car, and gunned it out of the parking lot. He was headed for a joint on 13th Street called The Rainbow's End. For a minute, he was tempted to go by the apartment for his .22 that he kept under the mattress. Screw it, he thought, I'll beat the little bastard to death with my bare hands.

Johnny was 6 foot 3 and 180 pounds. At 17 he'd seen a lot of life. He had not known real happiness except for those few short months after his parents had been killed. For that time, it was him and Brenda against the world. For just a little while he thought they might make it. Now, he had nothing left to lose. Now it was a murderous heart that drove him.

Parking the car a half block from his target, Johnny slid out into the cold rain. He checked the cars parked along the street for Freddy or his thugs as he walked. He hadn't spotted anyone as he pushed open the dirty glass door of the Rainbow's End and stepped in.

Acid rock screamed at him from the jukebox. Marijuana smoke filled the air. Teens and twenty-somethings sat or moved to the music. When his eyes adjusted to the dim light he moved over to the bar and took a stool.

The Rainbow's End was licensed as a restaurant. It was obvious that someone downtown was not doing their job,or they were on the take. This place should've been shut down long ago.

Taking the chance on his health, Johnny ordered a cup of coffee. He dropped a quarter on the counter when it arrived. He was halfway through his second cup when Fat Freddy walked in.

Freddy stood by the door as his little eyes adjusted to the light. He was dressed in ragged Levi's that looked as though they were last washed in 1946. His fat gut hung over the waistband, exposing a black tuft of hair. Over his dingy white t-shirt hung a black raincoat.

"Hey Freddy!" someone yelled. "Back here!"

Freddy waddled from his spot at the door toward the back of the room. Johnny watched as he sat himself next to a black man and a scruffy looking white girl. As Johnny slowly finished his coffee and watched the situation, he did not notice the brunette staring at him. She didn't want to be seen. Not yet.

Leaving the stool, he covered the 25 feet to where the trio were seated. He wondered why he hadn't popped the little scumbag the moment he'd come in. Johnny wasted no time as he got to the table. He gave the leg of Freddy's chair a vicious kick. The leg snapped, tipping Freddy out onto the floor. Johnny had his foot back, ready to kick Freddy's face in, when the black man jumped up.

"Fucker, what the hell you think you're doing?"

Johnny whirled on him. "Keep out of this. My fight is with him."

"Well, suppose I decide to make it my fight too!"

Johnny rammed a swift right into the man's midsection. He dropped to his knees, hands over his gut, mouth open in pain. The disheveled blonde girl stood up.

From the floor, Freddy said: "No, Barbara, let him be." It was too late. Johnny's left fist caught her as she stood. His punch knocked her back into the chair that toppled over and took her with it. By this time Johnny was seeing nothing but red. Two down, one to go, he thought. Freddy was on all fours, struggling to get his feet under him. The toe of Johnny's right boot connected with his right side. The wind rushed out of his lungs and he rolled to his back, gasping for air. Someone with more fighting experience would've stopped right then and looked around. All Johnny could see was his enemy on the floor, laid out and ready for punishment.

The brunette who had been watching this closely had to fight back the urge to shout a warning to the young man. She also resisted the stronger urge to pull out the 9mm Browning in her waistband as a large man approached the situation with a baseball bat. Johnny had his foot drawn back for another kick when something hit him on the head. He was out before he hit the floor.

The brunette left her seat and was out the door before anyone could notice. The black man was the first to speak. Still holding his guts, he looked up to the man with the bat. "Thanks, Harman. Thanks a lot."

"Shut up, Willie. Get on your feet. Who is this kid anyway? What's his problem?"

Willie struggled to his feet then started extracting Barbara from the chair.

"I don't know, Harman," Willie answered. "Maybe Freddy burned him on a deal. He said the fight was with him."

Harman fixed Freddy with a cold stare. "What about it, Freddy?"

Freddy was on his feet, one hand pressed to his side. His little eyes were scrunched in pain. "I know him. I took care of his sister. He's still mad."

"What do you mean 'still'?" Harman asked. "You've had other run-ins with this kid?"

"Just one, a couple weeks ago. His sister Brenda came to me earlier today. She was in bad shape. I gave her something. He must've found out. I gave her the good shit."

"I know your stuff is good when you get it. I don't know what you do with it. That's not here or there. Get yourselves out of here before this kid comes around. I'll have a talk with him when he does."

Harman watched as the battered trio got themselves together and out the door. The kid at his feet had done a lot of damage in less than a minute. Harman looked him over and figured the kid would have a headache but nothing more. Harman knew where and how to hit. If he had wanted the young hellraiser dead, he'd be dead.

Harman looked out at the crowd. They'd mostly gone back to normal. He was looking specifically for the brunette. She'd been hanging around a lot lately. She tried to look like part of the crowd but didn't succeed. He suspected the well dressed woman was some kind of cop.

Johnny came slowly out of the fog. His head throbbed.The noise was awful. It took him 30 seconds to remember where he was as he slowly sat up. His right hand found the knot that had begun to form where he'd been hit. Johnny looked around and then up as he spotted the man with the bat, who was staring down at him.

"You want another lick on the head?" the big man asked.

Johnny started to shake his head but damn near passed out. "No I don't," he muttered.

"Then get up and get out. You ever come in here again I'll split your head open…and take my advice: leave those three alone."

Johnny got to his feet slowly and looked around. He then started for the door with Harman a few steps behind. Johnny stepped out into the rain. He took a deep breath and turned to walk toward his car. Halfway there he stopped under an awning and leaned against the building. The wind felt like it was right out of the arctic. It brought the rain under the awning where Johnny stood, hands in his pockets, head throbbing. He let the wind blow the fog out of his mind as the rain washed the grime off his face. After a few minutes he continued to the car.

Johnny decided it was time to get his gun. He would come back to this slop bucket and show the big man how to hurt people. He started the car and turned the heater to full blast, shivering in his wet clothes. After taking a minute he put the car in gear and drove slowly down 13th.

He made a right turn, and immediately dropped the idea of the gun. His targets had been delivered into his hands once again. About halfway down the block his lights picked up three figures in the middle of the quiet street. Giving no thought to what he was about to do, he gunned the Mustang. The Cleveland 351 engine responded and the car leapt forward.

The three heard the motor roar and saw what was coming. Willie reacted by standing his ground and pulling a gun from his hip pocket. Barbara and Freddy scrambled for the curb. Johnny stepped down on the accelerator. Willie registered too late that he would lose this game of chicken and tried to get out of the way. Johnny got him in a blow that broke his left leg and dropped him to the street. Willie's gun flew out of his hand and skidded away.

Johnny leaned on the brake, skidding to a stop in the middle of the street. He got out of the car and ran back past Willie, then spotted the gun. He grabbed it up, thumbed the hammer back, and looked for Freddy through the falling rain.

A car rounded the corner and bathed Johnny in its headlights. They also revealed Freddy, who had fallen in the gutter 30 feet away. Johnny applied pressure to the trigger and tripped the hammer. The car came to a stop on his right, as the gun clicked.

"Shit!" Jonny shouted. He squeezed the trigger twice more. Two more clicks. He felt robbed. He sensed movement to his left. Barbara was rushing towards him, knife in hand. Johnny stepped back and she rushed by. Johnny brought the barrel of the gun down on her head as hard as he could. He could hear her skull crack. The knife clattered to the street as she fell like a rock.

Johnny tossed the gun away and took off running after Freddy. Had the situation not been so serious, he could almost laugh. Freddy bounced like a ball as he attempted to run. His blubber would not allow for more. Johnny was in hot pursuit and would have had him in another 10 feet. From somewhere behind him, a female voice called out "Cops coming!" Sure enough, the sound of sirens pierced the night.

Johnny stopped. "You're a dead man, Freddy. It's just a matter of time." He turned and ran back to his still running car. Freddy continued his bouncing run. Johnny slid into the front seat and started moving before the door could even close. Two blocks later he made a right. The lights that were coming up fast behind him made the right also. "Cops? No, they'd have their lights on by now," Johnny thought. He was doing 60 in a 25.

During the next few seconds, several things occurred to him. First, he realized with some shock, he had tried to commit murder with a witness watching from another car. Second, the witness had done nothing to help or to hinder him. Third, whoever it was had probably been the one to shout the warning about the cops. Confused by all of this, he decided to try and lose the lights behind him. Without further thought Johnny put his foot to the floor. Even at 60 miles per hour the 351 engine still delivered enough thrust to throw him back against the seat. Wild, unexplainable joy took him as he watched the speedometer climb to 70, 80, 90. He knew he was crazy, taking a wild chance, but Johnny just did not care.

Fortunately this was a 4 lane street and traffic was thin. He sailed through 2 red lights and caught a 3rd as it changed from red to green. Realizing he was running out of room, he slowed down. The lights were still there.

Without signaling Johnny made a left onto a narrow street, and slowed again as he prepared to make a right, but the Mustang slid on him. He saw the parked car coming at him and fought down the panic that was screaming "Brake!" in his mind. Desperately, he tried to fight the car against the slide by steering toward and it willing it to straighten. Johnny was saved by a mixture of skill, luck, and radial tires that had cost him a fortune. The Mustang came to the end of its slide, caught and straightened.

Johnny resisted the urge to get out and run. Instead he killed the headlights and made a left. There were no lights behind him now. The residential street was empty. Johnny drove slowly, trying to figure out who was behind the headlights and why they had followed him, as he headed home.

Chapter 2

The street in front of Johnny's apartment was empty.
There were usually only a few cars at night anyway. As he
stepped out of the car, it was still cold and wet, but Johnny
barely noticed. The apartment complex's lobby had a
threadbare carpet and stained wallpaper. The whole place
smelled. For the first time, Johnny wondered if there might
not be something better.

The apartment he shared with Brenda was on the second
floor. Out of habit, he stepped over the 3rd step from the top
because it squeaked. There were two dangling light bulbs in
the hallway, no doubt in violation of fire codes. His
apartment door was the third one on the left. The door was
ajar and the light was on. This was not unusual. The door
was never locked. He stopped worrying about it a long time
ago when he figured out he and Brenda had nothing worth
stealing.

Johnny pushed the door open, stepped in and froze. In
the living/ dining room in front of him, a woman sat at the
table, facing the door. What struck him first was the gun
pointed at him. It was rather large, and her hand was steady.
Johnny knew from his boss at work that if a gun was pointed
at him he should do as he was told and take no chances. With
Mr. Paddock's advice in mind, Johnny remained where he
was until the girl behind the gun spoke.

"Come in, John. Close the door." Surprised to hear his
name, Johnny did as he was told. "Come sit down. We need
to talk. There's not much time."

"Talk about what?"

"Why did you try to commit murder? Why did you try to beat those guys up?"

"Try?" Johnny sat down. "I think I did a pretty good job. I would've done even better if it hadn't been for the guy with the bat."

"What did they do to you?" the girl asked.

"What business is it of yours?"

"Look," she sighed, "believe it or not I'd like to help you. I also want you to help me."

Johnny looked at the gun. "Is this how you help people?"

"This is how I make sure you won't try to bash my head in before we can talk. I'll put this away when I'm sure I don't need it." She smiled.

"Were you in the car when I found those guys in the street?"

"Yes. By the way, I believe the girl you hit is dead. The others are just hurt. Did you mean to kill them all?"

"Well, I guess, I mean..." Johnny stammered.

"Stop," the girl ordered, lowering her gun. "We don't have all night. The cops are likely to be here any time. So let's get back to the point. Why are you intent on murder?"

"The fat one, my fight is with him. He's a drug pusher. My sister died of an overdose."

"When did she die?"

"Tonight. A few hours ago. Her name was Brenda. Brenda Redwine. If you know about me why don't you know about her?"

"I'll explain later," she replied. "Right now, we need to get out of here. Come with me."

They both stood. "Where?" Johnny asked.

"I know a place in Springfield. We can sit and talk there safely. We won't be found." She looked at her watch with a sense of urgency.

"This isn't some kind of trick is it?" Johnny asked.

"No tricks. I'm here to help you. Don't bother to bring anything. If you like what I have to say, someone will get your stuff for you." Her eyes narrowed as she holstered her gun and Johnny touched the knot on his head. "The big guy got you good, didn't he?"

"I'll say. I'm gonna kick his ass for that."

"I hope you get the chance." She stepped past him and opened the door. As they went down the stairs she said "My name is Dot. Get in your car and wait for me to get in mine. I've got a blue Oldsmobile. Follow me. Close, but not too close."

The drive to Springfield took about 20 minutes. Springfield was a small town of 40 thousand next to Eugene, the home of the University of Oregon. They wound through neighborhoods and backroads until they settled at a warehouse. It was in an industrial area and the street was lined with trucks. Everything seemed to be empty this time of night. Dot turned into the warehouse driveway and opened the door with a remote from inside the car. The giant door slid up and the lights came on. Theirs were the only cars he saw as they drove in.

Johnny got out and looked around.It was about 200 feet wide and every bit as long. It was probably designed for trucks. The sound of the car doors and their footsteps echoed. Johnny followed Dot toward the back of the place. He noticed the sway of her hips as she walked. Dot wore tan pants, brown boots and a matching jacket. She had neat, short dark brown hair. He guessed her age as 21-ish.

Dot unlocked a door at the back of the warehouse. The lights went out behind them as they entered a small room. It was an entry to something else. Another door fit perfectly into the wall across from them. Instead of a key, this door had a series of buttons. Dot entered a code and the door slid open on quiet runners.

"Come in. This is our hideaway," Dot said. "I'll give you a tour."

Johnny entered and the door slid shut behind him. He found himself in a comfortable apartment. The living room was about 20 by 15, with expensive modern furniture. They entered a spotless kitchen that featured gadgets he had only seen in magazines. Each bedroom had its own bathroom and a color TV.

"Quite the place," Johnny said.

"Thank you. We can talk here and be comfortable." Dot led Johnny back to the kitchen.

"You got anything to eat here?"

"Of course," Dot replied. "What would you like?"

"Steak and eggs would hit the spot," he said jokingly.

"Steak and eggs it is," Dot replied. "I'll have them done in nothing flat."

"I was kidding," Johnny said, taken aback.

"I'm not." Dot pointed to the hallway. "Go wash up. I'll cook. We'll eat then talk. It'll be easier on a full stomach."

The meal hit the spot. Johnny had not realized how hungry he was until he took the first bite. Finished, Johnny took his dishes to the built in dishwasher while Dot sipped a coffee. He returned to the table, took out a Camel and accepted the light Dot offered.

"Feel better?" she asked.

"Oh yeah," he said. "Thanks for the food."

"You're welcome. Now, tell me about Brenda."

Johnny sighed and looked at Dot. "She was my big sister. My only family. She was good and I loved her. She got in with these guys and they hooked her on drugs. It started as just an occasional party, then she started taking pills, then the hard stuff. I tried to keep her away from them. Tonight I got a call from work to go to the hospital. When I got there a doctor told me she'd died of an overdose. I went looking for those assholes who got her hooked. You saw when I found them. I didn't see you, though."

"You weren't looking. You were too focused."

"So, who are you?" Johnny asked.

"Like I said, I'm Dot. I represent an organization that's getting ready to put people like Freddy out of business. Forever."

"How can you do that?" Fred looked at Dot in disbelief. "The cops can't control drugs. What's your group going to do?"

"The cops are handcuffed by rules," Dot answered. "Plus the lawyers and the press get in their way, screaming about the rights of criminals."

"So what are you going to do? Just go around blowing people up like terrorists?"

"Not quite." Dot looked serious. "Indiscriminate killing doesn't solve anything. It just frightens the survivors and maybe calls attention to the cause. The group I represent believes there's just one way to solve the drug problem. Kill the pushers. Kill them off carefully and in an organized manner."

Johnny had never thought of an organized campaign like this, but he believed her. "Did you say you're just getting started?"

"Yes. We're well advanced in our plans. In fact, we think you might like to be part of our organization." Dot smiled.

Johnny looked unsure. "You want me to just go around killing people?"

Dot said his name gently, though she seemed to have a shadow across her face. She was starting to lose patience. "If you say yes, and pass a few tests, we'll send you to training.

You'll go to a school with people from your age group with similar backgrounds. Like you and me, they've all lost someone to drugs. Some of them are recovered addicts themselves. They all have a desire to do something positive."

"What kind of tests? Where's the school?"

"Say yes and find out."

"What if I say no? Are you going to shoot me?"

"No," Dot said while laughing. "If you say no I'll take you back to your apartment and leave you be. Of course, it wouldn't be long before the cops came around. Hey, don't worry about the tests. We have some people you'd think were too dumb to spell their name. The important thing is your will. Your commitment."

"Are you Mafia or something?"

"Good Lord no. It's just a group. We're called the Cleanup Committee."

"Ok. You said you want to help me. How is this helping?"

"Your training program lasts 6 months. During that time you'll be paid $600 a month. You'll have room and board. At the end of that time you'll work for us for a year."

Johnny thought for a minute. "You guys are for real? Not some half-assed bunch with crazy ideas?"

"We're people with a cause, and millions of dollars to work with. I can only give you so much information right now. Say yes."

He looked around the modern, well appointed apartment. "Will I be able to get a place like this?"

Dot smiled. "After training, yes. Your service will earn you $100,000 a year." Johnny's eyes grew large and his mouth dropped open, speechless. "You can buy an awful lot of stuff with that."

He was convinced. "I'll do it."

Dot breathed a sigh of relief.

"What now?" Johnny asked.

Dot rose to her feet. "I'm glad you've decided to come along. Since that's settled, I need to get busy. Time is short. As for you, you'll be staying here for the night. When you get up in the morning, a man will be here. He'll explain some things to you."

Johnny could see that Dot was in a hurry. He was getting too tired to care. The bang on the head, the fight, the driving, it all seemed to fall on him at once and he felt drained. Remembering the comfortable looking beds he asked "which room do I use?"

"The one at the end of the hall. You must be exhausted." Dot walked around the table and stood by Johnny's seat. Her face softened as she looked down at him. Brenda's face used to soften that way when he was tired or worried....back when it was them against the world. "I'm truly sorry about Brenda," Dot said sincerely. "I lost my twin brother a few years back. I'm sorry you won't have time to mourn her properly. We must move quickly. Her final expenses will be covered by the organization, so you have nothing to worry about. Would you like to be involved in her funeral?"

Johnny thought for a minute before responding.

"No, I think not. I'd rather just get on with things. She's gone. Nothing's bringing her back. I don't have any relatives. There's no point." Johnny looked at his boots.

"It must be terrible to be alone," Dot said. "I've never been alone."

Johnny simply said: "I'll get used to it."

Chapter 3

An hour later, Dot silently opened the door where #36 had gone. She found exactly what she expected: a young man sound asleep and likely to stay that way for a while. Closing the door, she returned to the living room. She double checked to make sure everything was spotless and in its place, then let herself out into the big garage.

Five minutes later she drove through the dark, rain-slick streets on the way to an appointment. The appointment was with two people, known only to her as Doctor Fish and Boxer. Dot knew they were just nicknames. She didn't really care. All that mattered now was her orders were to report directly to the Doctor. Dot had called him as soon as she was sure Johnny was asleep to give a complete report. He had given her the address of the office where they were to meet.

Dot parked in a predetermined space. She put the Oldsmobile keys in her pocket, secured a bandana over her hair, and removed her Browning 9 mm from beneath the seat. She would not be returning for this car. She got a different one for every assignment.

Walking along the dark street, she noticed the vehicles and buildings. Her glances were nervous around the edges, to look like a girl alone at night might be expected to look. In Dot's case, she was looking for people. She looked for anything that might suggest she was being watched. She stopped in front of a large building, looked both ways, and entered the lobby.

It was warm and dry. Dot stood for just a moment, letting the rain fall from her coat. She removed the bandana from her hair and dropped it in her pocket. The building held offices and apartments. To her right was a bank of elevators.The lobby was empty save for a white haired janitor watering some plants. He took no notice of her as she passed on her way to the 4th floor.

Dot paused at room 418 and knocked twice. The door was opened by a tall man who appeared to be in his late 40's. His dark brown hair had streaks of gray that came off as distinguished. He was dressed in a brown suit with shoes polished to a high gloss. Stepping back with a wave to invite Dot in, he said "Good evening."

"Good evening, Doctor Fish. Hello, Boxer."

The large office held a beautiful oak desk in the center of the room. A file cabinet stood in the corner. Boxer sat in one of the guest desk chairs drinking a cup of coffee. He was about 27 years old, 5 foot 9 with sandy hair and steel gray eyes. His features were plain; the kind of guy you could pass then easily forget. He gave what passed as a smile and indicated a chair for Dot to take the seat next to his. The Doctor took his seat behind the desk.

"I did some checking, Dot. Our young #36 has one dead girl in his wake, and the black gentleman has a broken leg and skull fracture. He's still out and is likely to remain that way for a while. The police are treating this as a hit and run traffic accident, since they have no other leads. It's a lucky break for us. Dot, what did you do with the gun that 36 hit the girl with?"

"I dumped it in the river on the way here," Dot replied.

"Good, then I won't worry about it," said the Doctor. "I have Boxer filled in on the current situation. Now I want you two to go back to that Rainbow dump and erase Fat Freddy. Of course that's been the idea all along, but while you're there, take out whoever's seated with him. Take out that slob Harman, too."

"With pleasure," Dot said. "It was all I could do to not shoot him earlier."

"I'm glad you managed to restrain yourself, my dear. That could have been unfortunate."

Not certain what the Doctor meant, Dot said nothing and waited. He continued: "In this operation, Boxer is the field boss. He has prior experience, Dot, this is no discredit to you. I'll leave the details to you two. Call me here when it's done. I'll then pick up the car you left, Dot, and you get your own car and head home."

"Yes, Sir."

Boxer went to a coat rack in the corner of the room and took down two long black raincoats. He handed one to Dot, saying "There are plastic gloves in the right pocket. Go ahead and put them on now."

Dot put on the coat and gloves, and followed Boxer out of the office. The carpeting in the hall muffled their footsteps. Boxer moved quickly and quietly. Dot was impressed at the smooth way he seemed to glide along. He made an intimidating figure. Reaching the end of the hall, Boxer opened a steel door that opened to a stairwell, then a fire escape. They stopped to make plans. Boxer questioned Dot closely on the layout of the building, as he'd never been in it. They checked their weapons and exited into the rain.

They carefully made their way down the iron steps of the fire escape to an alley. Parked near the alley exit, which opened to a street behind their building, was a dark green Chevy sedan. Boxer handed Dot the keys. The car started easily and the engine sounded smooth. Driving east from their meeting point, Dot kept her speed down and turned on the radio. Boxer immediately turned the radio off. Dot gave him the side eye but said nothing.

Boxer was a quiet man. Even though the pair had been through months of highly specialized training together, she knew nothing about him but his code name, and that this was not his first time in the killing business. Dot had done extensive training and surveillance, but this would be her first sanctioned hit.

"Turn right at the next block," Boxer said. "Circle the place once. Let's check for any last minute patrol cars or watchers." Dot made the right and cruised slowly down the street, making the loop around the Rainbow's End.

"Double park in front," Boxer instructed. "Leave the engine running but turn your lights off. When we come out, you take the car. You know what to do with it. I'll take care of myself."

Boxer pointed. "Here's good for the double park. Good. Get your gun out, keep it low till we're in place."

Boxer slid out of the car and quietly closed the door. Dot set the hand brake, turned off the lights, and joined Boxer. They gave a final look up and down the street. It was devoid of traffic. They crossed the lot and pushed open the same door Johnny had opened earlier. Just like him, they stopped just inside to let their eyes adjust to the dim lights and smoke. The joint was just as crowded and loud as it had been earlier. The smoke still burned Dot's nose.

"Christ," Boxer muttered. "A guy could get high just standing here."

Fat Freddy was sitting at the same table in the rear where he'd been before. Two guys were with him. Dot recognized them as regulars. One she knew to be another dealer. She'd seen him make deals right in this spot a few times.

Boxer raised his gun and sighted on the back table. Dot looked left and saw Harman looking down the counter toward them. He had some cash in his left hand and a burning joint in his right. Harman saw the two black clad figures and thought it was a stick up. He tossed the money aside and made a dive for the sawed off shotgun he kept under the counter. Dot was faster.

The 35 caliber bullet moved at 1300 feet per second. It hit Harman one inch above his left eye. He died instantly. The force of the slug knocked his body back where it crashed into a rack of cups and glasses. The glass made a wonderful shattering sound as it fell to the floor.

The sound of the shot was even louder than the rock and roll screaming from the jukebox. It drew everyone's attention. Fat Freddy looked at the black clad figures at the door, and right at the barrel of Boxer's gun. He opened his mouth to scream but it never got out. It died in his throat as Boxer's bullet struck him in his open mouth. Blood splattered across the wall behind him. He toppled out of the chair to land with a thud.

The men next to him were up. Dot killed the other dealer with one shot directly through the heart. His fall knocked chairs and tables aside. As the other man drew a gun and started to raise it, a table that had been moved by the dead dealer struck him and spoiled his aim. Boxer's fire just missed the man as he fell. The man tried to get the table between him and the killers. Dot fired. The bullet slammed into the floor, 2 inches from the man's head. As she adjusted quickly and sent a round through his neck, Boxer fired again and the bullet tore through his center mass. The body jerked and fell to the floor.

Boxer turned, gun raised, and looked out at the crowd.

"Freeze, every one of you. Listen up." He looked around to ensure compliance.

"We're the Cleanup Committee. Remember us. We're leaving now. Don't follow. The first person to stick their head out the door before 5 minutes is up will get their head blown off."

Dot had the door open and was backing out. Boxer passed her and walked left down the street. He holstered his gun

and donned a baseball cap. Dot pulled the building door shut
and ran to the idling Chevy.

Chapter 4

Johnny woke up and wondered where he was. Then he looked around and remembered. The light he'd left on in the bathroom was still on. He checked his watch. 8:05. Surprised he had slept so long, he sat up. A knock sounded on his door.

"Come in!" he called. He was hoping for Dot, but then saw a tall man at the door and remembered what she had said.

The tall man had glasses and a little ponch that didn't quite fit him. He stood very straight. He gave off an air of authority. "Good morning, Mr. Redwine. I trust you slept well."

"Yeah, I did. Thanks."

"If you would like to shower and shave, you'll find fresh clothing when you return. Breakfast will be in 30 minutes."

"Thank you," Johnny said, as the tall man left and closed the door. Johnny sat thinking for a moment. He realized he'd just been given orders. It had been done in a neat way. It had also been done so as not to need repeating.

He got up and stretched. It had been a good sleep. One of the best he ever had, in fact. For a moment he wondered if he'd been drugged. He went into the bathroom and dumped his dirty clothing in a hamper. He wondered, as he stepped in the shower, what they were going to do with him, and where his new clothes were coming from. Seventeen minutes later he stepped out of the bathroom, showered and shaved. Surprisingly, the clothes fit beautifully. He checked himself in the mirror before exiting the room.

He stood by a chair and looked at the man who sat at the far end of the table. The man was reading a newspaper and had not acknowledged his approach. It reinforced Johnny's first impression of the man. He held authority and was fully aware of it, and knew how to wield it. The man felt Johnny's eyes on him and lowered the paper, smiled and stood.

"Good morning," he said while extending a hand. "You can call me Doctor Fish."

Johnny reached out and took the hand. The grip was strong and the hand was warm.

"Nice to meet you," Johnny said with uncertainty. He wasn't used to shaking hands with people, especially authority figures. He hadn't really had the chance to. His life had been limited to school and work. He had little to do with the kids in school and work was always hurried. In the few resting moments of work people wanted to bitch and complain, not shake hands.

"Are you hungry, Mr. Redwine?"

"You can call me Johnny if you want. I'm not too hungry. That gal Dot fixed me a good meal last night. Steak and eggs." He stopped and looked around in the kitchen.

"Dot went home after you fell asleep last night," Doctor Fish said, "but I'm a good cook."

"I'd just like some coffee."

Doctor Fish indicated the coffee pot and said "the cups are in the cupboard to the right of the sink." When Johnny grabbed a cup he continued: "I'll join you in a cup. I take it black. If you desire, sugar is to the left in a marked canister, and there's milk in the fridge."

Johnny's mind was jumping around as he fixed the coffee. Questions crowded themselves in with memories of his sister. He wondered where Brenda's funeral would be held, and what it might be like. He wondered why the organization would pay for it when they didn't even know her. Maybe Doctor Fish knew...but then why would he? He wondered if Dot really went home, and if he would feel better if she was still there.

Johnny took the coffees to the table with a thanks from the doctor, who was now smoking from a pipe. He sat down and looked at his cup, feeling uncomfortable. Actually, he wasn't sure what the feeling was. Fear? Sorrow? His mind just wouldn't let him name it. All he knew for sure was that with Brenda gone, he felt alone. Johnny looked up and saw Doctor Fish watching him.

"I'm very sorry about your sister, son. I wish my being sorry could bring her back for you." His voice was low and soft, and his eyes were sincere. The smoke from the doctor's pipe rose slowly toward the ceiling.

Johnny couldn't stop the sudden tears from falling. He didn't want them, but they came anyway. Regret piled in and forced the tears to fall harder. He cried silently, the tears dripping down from his chin to fall lightly onto his t-shirt. Doctor Fish got up and came around the table. He silently handed Johnny some napkins from a holder. Johnny, still sniffling, squeezed his eyes shut. He was starting to feel shame for crying in front of this man he didn't even know. His mind told him if he just kept his eyes closed long enough, when he opened them everything would be ok. This had been a game he had played with Brenda years ago... but now it wasn't a game. When he opened his eyes Doctor Fish would still be there, Brenda would still be dead, and the bastard who killed her would still be getting away with it.

He opened his eyes and let the last of the tears fall. It was only the third time in his life he could remember crying. He told himself it would be the last.

Doctor Fish had a low, quiet voice as he asked if Johnny was okay now. Johnny nodded, and the doctor sat back down. "Crying is necessary at times, son. It's nothing to be ashamed of. It's the people who cannot cry who have the real problems."

Johnny looked at Dr. Fish with curiosity. "What kind of doctor are you?"

"The correct term is psychiatrist, but the common term is shrink, or head doctor."

"Are you part of that committee Dot was talking about?"

"Yes. The Cleanup Committee. Did she talk with you about what the group hopes to do?"

Johnny took a long drink of his coffee, remembering the serious look on Dot's face when she talked about their mission. "Yeah. She said something about shooting dope pushers."

"It's not quite that simple," Fish said, "but basically, that's what the Committee is about."

"How can you get away with just running around shooting people?" Johnny asked. "What about the cops? Murder is against the law."

"You're right," the Doctor replied. "The police won't like it at first."

"What do you mean at first?"

Doctor Fish relit his pipe and dropped the match into an ashtray. "We're getting ahead of ourselves. I think it would be best if I explained some things to you. I won't give all of the details now, but I think I can set your mind right about a few things."

"I'm going to need more coffee," Johnny said.

Doctor Fish stood up. "I'll serve this time." He refilled the cups and returned to his seat. "Dot contacted you because she felt you would fit into our organization. I respect her judgment. First we have to make sure that we're a good match and can help each other. We have a process for our potential recruits."

"How many are there besides me?" Johnny asked.

"Plenty," Dr. Fish replied. "They're in different places, in various stages of preparation."

"You're really serious."

It was a statement, not a question. Fish let it stand a moment before he answered.

"Yes, we're serious. We're not just another bunch of zealots. We are well financed, we're organized, we have a good intelligence system, and we have well defined goals."

"What am I supposed to do?"

"Maybe nothing. Maybe everything," Dr. Fish said. "Right now, if you feel up to it, I'd like you to fill out some papers for me. You'll be answering questions that will help me determine if we can work together. "

"What happens if I fail the test?"

"You can't fail, Johnny. In any case, you're putting the cart before the horse. I don't believe this will be a problem for you. Shall we begin?"

"I'll fill the papers out," Johnny answered, "but first I'd like to see about my sister's funeral."

"That won't be necessary." Johnny's eyes widened. "Don't worry, son. My associates are taking care of the arrangements. She'll have a funeral service that you'll be able to attend if you wish."

Johnny had no way of knowing this, but while they were speaking Boxer was entering the funeral home dressed in a business suit and a wig. He carried a briefcase which held the money that would pay for the funeral and burial. If any questions came up later, the mortician would only be able to say the funeral was paid for in cash by a man who represented the family.

Dr. Fish saw the questions in the young man's eyes and offered a reassuring smile.

"For the time being, son, don't worry. Just let your mind relax and concentrate on filling out the papers I'm going to give you. When they're finished I'll answer more questions for you."

Johnny took 2 hours to fill out the forms. The first one was some kind of personality test. It had 100 statements that he had to answer as true or false. Some of the statements seemed mighty stupid and he was tempted to pass them over. Then he figured he should answer every one of them no matter how silly they seemed because there must be a point.

When he finished Dr. Fish was nowhere to be found. Johnny figured he must have slipped out while he was focused on the test. He wondered where the doctor had gone, then decided he didn't really care. He went to the kitchen and poured a glass of milk. He was standing by the sink when he heard the entry door open and close. He looked over and saw Dr. Fish standing in the living room, briefcase in hand.

"Hello again, Johnny," said Dr. Fish. "All finished up, I see."

Johnny kept looking at him. Something was different. He realized the doctor was dressed differently. He was now in slacks, a sweater, and a yellow raincoat.

"While you were busy I went to my place to pick up more paperwork. I decided to change while I was there. Would you like some lunch before going on?"

"I could stand to eat something," Johnny replied.

"Let me store my briefcase," said Dr. Fish, "and we'll go to a little cafe I know near here. They make a splendid hot roast beef sandwich."

Twenty minutes later they were seated in a booth at the cafe 3 blocks from the warehouse. Dr. Fish seemed to be well known here. A pretty blonde waitress took their orders.

"Where's my car?" Johnny asked.

Dr. Fish smiled."I wondered when you'd ask about that. Your car is being looked after by a friend of mine. If all goes the way I think it will, you won't be needing it for several months. When you get it back it might be a different color, but it will be in tip-top shape."

"Why-" Johnny started to say, but Dr. Fish held a finger to his lips for silence. The waitress approached and set salad dishes on the table. Johnny dropped his questions and concentrated on eating. He wondered silently about one thing, then another. If Dr. Fish was being honest, this group knew exactly what it wanted and how to go about getting it. He decided that whoever they were, they were not fools. So far, they had demonstrated organization and good personnel. He decided that, for the time being, he would follow the doctor's advice and try to relax. Let things fall where they may. He didn't have anything to do for a few days, anyway.

After lunch they walked back to the warehouse under a drizzling sky. The wind was cool, but after being inside for so long it felt refreshing. Dr. Fish had insisted the fresh air would do them good, and clear his mind for more papers.

"How many more papers do you have for me?"

"Quite a few, actually. There's still a lot I want to know about you. In fact, I want to know everything." They stopped at a light and Fish busied himself packing his pipe while they waited. He lit it right as the signal changed to walk. Once at the warehouse, Dr. Fish opened the door with a remote he'd removed from his pocket. Did everyone on the committee have remotes, Johnny wondered? He got another surprise when the door opened to a green and white Dodge two door with a woman looking at them in the rearview mirror.

When the door closed the woman stepped out of the car. "Good afternoon, Dr. Fish."

"Good afternoon. This is the young man I called you about. Johnny, meet Linda. She's going to take you over to see another doctor, one of my friends, at his office. He's going to make sure you're physically okay. While I'm capable of an exam myself, my friend has the equipment. Linda will get you where you need to go and bring you back. I'll be here when you return."

Johnny looked at Linda. She was maybe in her early 20's, about 5 foot 5, with what appeared to be a good build under her heavy coat. She smiled at Johnny and waved. Johnny walked to the passenger side of the Dodge and got in.

Dr. Fish opened the door and Linda backed the car out. The sun had gotten through the clouds and cast a bright light over everything. Linda picked some sunglasses up off the dash and put them on. As she drove, Johnny tried to watch her profile without being obvious. She had pretty brown hair that hung just past her shoulders. She smelled heavenly. Johnny felt like he should say something but wasn't sure what. He started with his name.

"I'm Johnny."

"I remember. Dr. Fish told me" Linda replied with a smile. She turned left. Springfield was fairly busy with afternoon traffic and shoppers doing their thing.

"Do you work for them too?" Johnny asked.

"For who?"

"The Cleanup Committee."

"I don't know what you're talking about," she said.

They drove the rest of the way in silence. Johnny got the feeling Linda had been instructed not to talk to him. He figured he may not get the time of day from anyone until he passed all those tests Dr. Fish had planned.

"I don't like waiting around at the doctor's office."

"Neither do I. You won't have to wait for this one. He's expecting you." Linda replied. She parked the Dodge in a lot next to a large building. The lot was empty except for one other car. Inside the large building a directory listed the names of several doctors. Linda led the way to an elevator and pushed the button for the 5th floor.

Johnny turned to face Linda in the elevator and noticed that she had taken off her sunglasses. She had beautiful soft brown eyes that he suddenly couldn't get enough of. He had met plenty of girls before but never had time for them. He decided right then he'd make time for her.

"When you're in the exam room, don't volunteer any information" Linda said. "The doctor will only ask you what he needs to know. I'll be in the waiting room. When it's over I'll take you back to Dr. Fish."

The elevator stopped and the door slid back. He followed her out, wondering if he would ever see her again after today. Did she have a husband or a boyfriend? Would she give him a chance? These things and more ran through his mind as they stopped at a door that read "Dr. N. McDonald, M.D."

Linda entered first and went straight over to a seat. Doctor McDonald stepped out from behind a partition, looked at Johnny and indicated a door. "This way, son." As they walked down a hall Johnny speculated that this doctor looked a lot like Doctor Fish. He had no way of knowing they were in fact related. The physical took half an hour. McDonald poked and listened. He thumped Johnny's knees and elbows. He took X-Rays. Finally, he told Johnny to get dressed and be on his way.

Linda was in the waiting room as expected. She was reading a magazine. The doctor had not followed Johnny out. Twenty minutes and a half dozen words later, Johnny was standing in the living room of the warehouse hideaway. The ride had been a downer. He knew no more about Linda than the moment they met. This, combined with other reasons he couldn't quite grasp, left him feeling pissed off. Fuck them, he thought. I don't need this run around.

"My, you look fierce. Did that young lady make you mad? Or perhaps the other doctor?"

Johnny looked to his left and saw Dr. Fish standing in the hall. "Sorry" was all he could think to say. He walked into the kitchen and sat at the table. Dr. Fish followed and sat at the opposite end, looking at Johnny with a frown.

"I'll explain something. Linda was told to be cool with you and discourage questions. She's in no position to give you answers anyway. As I said this morning, I'll have more answers for you when the tests are finished."

"Fair enough," Johnny said with a grunt. "Where's the rest of the paperwork?"

Dr. Fish brought his briefcase up from the floor and placed it on the table. He opened it and brought out a stack of papers. "These are general knowledge tests. Each test is 50 multiple choice questions. Do them quickly, but pay attention to each question. Take a 10 minute break between tests. Don't worry about your scores. I know you haven't had time to study. I'll be in the other room. Bring me each test when you've finished."

Johnny worked until 4:30 p.m. He felt like he'd been beaten with a rubber hose. The tests, the whole day in fact, had tried his mental strength. He didn't know it, for nobody had ever told him, but Johnny was a very bright young man. Had his life been normal, had he been able to concentrate in school, he would have been an honor student. Doctor Fish had seen his intelligence from the start, and the tests proved he was both bright and quick.

Johnny carried his last test, a History exam, into a room Fish was using as an office. He dropped the test on the desk and left the room. He went to the bathroom then brewed a cup of coffee. When he entered the living room Doctor Fish was waiting for him. The doctor sat in a chair with his feet up, puffing thoughtfully on his pipe. He motioned toward another chair and Johnny sat down.

Doctor Fish looked at Johnny thoughtfully. "You've done very well."

Johnny waited. He wasn't sure what to say. He wondered if he would finally get answers to the questions that had been running through his mind all day.

"Does that news make you happy?" Dr. Fish asked.

"Yes, it does. I like to do well at whatever I try."

"That was my impression of you. Now, do you need a rest or are you ready for some answers?"

"I want to know the score. I'm tired as hell," Johnny admitted, "but I want to know."

Dr. Fish picked up a newspaper from the end table next to his seat and tossed it over. Johnny caught it with a questioning look. "Read the front page. I'll admit I'm interested in your reaction."

Johnny turned the paper around and saw that it was today's issue of the Register Guard. The headline jumped out at him. "FOUR DEAD IN EUGENE RESTAURANT SHOOTING." He read on. 'According to Eugene police investigators, two persons, one of them female, had entered the Rainbow's End near 13th Street.....' Dr. Fish watched as he read.

Johnny lowered the paper. "Did you do this?"

"I ordered it to be done."

"For God's sake! What if they figure out who did it? What if they come after you?"

"They have no idea who was behind this. It's not likely they ever will. A dimly lit place with loud music, pot smoke and chaos is unlikely to produce a reliable witness."

Johnny's forehead wrinkled in concern. "I don't understand. What did they do to you?"

"When Dot found you last night, you were in the street, ready to commit murder. You had no plan, no training, and high emotions. If you had been allowed to make the kill, you would have been caught in no time flat. Those people were on our list before they made yours. They would've died whether you came into the picture or not. They were all drug dealers and pushers. We've been on them for several weeks, just waiting to get them all in the same place at the same time."

Dr. Fish paused as Johnny looked between him and the newspaper. "In a nutshell, that's what the score is. Killing off dealers. They murdered your sister and hundreds of others like her. They're filthy slime that ruin thousands of lives. They get people hooked and it only leads to death or life-long disabling illness. These monsters lead good people to commit armed robberies to get their fix. What I ordered last night, young man, wasn't murder. It was rodent extermination. Justifiable homicide."

Johnny was dumbfounded by it all. He had been ready to kill last night. Left to his own devices, he very well might have... but it was personal. He'd been damn good and mad. The doctor had ordered the shooting of 4 people with what seemed to be cold-blooded ease.

Dr. Fish saw the turmoil in the young man's eyes. He leaned forward and said:

"Johnny, listen to me, son. We are in a war. We're fighting with a highly organized and well financed army. The stakes are absolutely huge. Billions of dollars are made in drug sales every year. More people are sick and dying because of drugs every day. The police just can't cope. The situation is completely out of hand. Think about it. How many of the kids you went to school with are hooked? Think about the kids who have been ruined in the prime of life.

Your sister would be alive today but for people like Fat Freddy. Our organization will deal with these people on their level. We're going to give them the only thing they understand: justice from the barrel of a gun. We want you to be part of our army. It's a worthy cause. It's every bit as important as anything you've ever done.

We call ourselves the Cleanup Committee because we're going to completely stop the flow of drugs in this country, starting right here in Oregon. Our plans are made and our goals are set. We want you as part of the private army doing this job. The 9 men who formed the Cleanup Committee have all lost sons or daughters to drugs. They believe they have a responsibility to do something. They've each pledged their time and money. You and the others will be trained by the best people money can hire. You'll be trained on how to kill with the least possible risk to yourself. We need your help. We need you just like America needed everyone's help in World War II."

Johnny looked at Dr. Fish. The man was sitting forward in his chair, fists clenched and his face completely serious. His pipe was forgotten, resting in an ashtray. To his surprise, Johnny found himself saying: "OK, Dr. Fish. I'm with you."

The doctor visibly relaxed. "You won't regret your decision, son. We'll take care of you." He sat back in the chair and picked up his forgotten pipe. Johnny could feel the tension go out of the room like draining water. He was tempted to ask what would have happened had he said no, but decided against asking. Instead Johnny asked:

"What happens to me now?"

"I'm finished with you here. In a few minutes, Linda will come back and she'll drive you to Portland. You're going to see Dot again, this time at her home. Linda will explain the drill on your way up there."

"What about my job?"

"You will just disappear. Your boss will be told you decided to take a powder for a while."

"Take a powder?"

"It's an old expression, meaning you're just gone and no one knows where."

"Where's my car?"

"It's on ice. In other words, it's stored away. You won't be needing it for a while."

"Where am I going from Dot's house?"

"Linda will explain more to you on the drive."

"What's Linda's job?"

"Linda is a recruit, just like you. She is from the Grants Pass area. She's been living and working here in the Eugene area for the past few weeks while we get some details straightened out."

"Can I talk to her this time?"

Dr. Fish smiled. "Of course. She'll tell you as much as she knows. I'm going to call her now and let her know you're almost ready to go. She isn't far away."

"I had a bag in my car with some clothes, an album and my .22 pistol."

"That's all in storage too. All your things will be returned to you at a later time. For the next few months we'll supply you with everything you need." Dr. Fish turned and picked up a phone by the chair and quickly dialed. "Your package is ready. Please pick it up in 15 minutes."

He hung up and turned to Johnny. "Your ride is on the way. We'll hear a buzzer when she arrives, and we'll be able to watch her arrival too."

"How are we going to watch it?" Johnny asked, wondering what else they could watch.

"Closed circuit TV, of course."

Dr. Fish got up and walked over to the TV. He flipped a switch on the side of it, and a picture of the street in front of the warehouse appeared. Cars and pedestrians moved along the street in the afternoon drizzle. Fish moved something and the scene changed to a different street. Probably the one behind the warehouse. This street was lined with trucks and loading docks. Men could be seen moving about, pushing carts in front of them. Johnny was impressed.

Dr. Fish returned to his chair and picked up a little box from the table. He held it up for Johnny to see. "This device permits the viewer to lock in on a picture for better viewing." The scene on the TV kept changing. It was clearly a rotation covering all sides of the building. The doctor continued: "It might be that you or some of our other people will want to use this area for a place to cool your heels. You might as well know if you're going to have company."

The green and white Dodge slid into view on the screen. Fish saw it at the same time. He pressed a button and locked the camera onto the car. He followed its progress through the trucks and around to the front of the building. He pressed another button as the car entered the driveway,and the door opened for Linda. He pushed a different button and the screen changed from the camera outside to one inside the parking area. He watched the door shut behind the car and saw Linda get out.

Dr. Fish went to the door. He pushed an intercom button and said "We'll be right there."

He turned to Johnny, who was already standing, and held out his hand."Best of luck, Johnny. We'll be meeting again sometime."

Johnny shook hands with the man and realized he liked him. He was a nice guy. He seemed honest and was passionate about his beliefs. They walked out to where Linda was waiting.

Chapter 5

Dorothy Marie Stoneking woke slowly from a sleep that she had fallen into immediately after getting into bed at 3:30 a.m. She was tired, bone tired, from the crazy night. From chasing that wild kid and the shooting at Rainbow's End, to dumping the car and clearing town, it had been intense. She had driven home in her own car, resisting the urge to floor-board the gas and put as many miles between herself and Eugene as possible. She'd driven home in the pouring rain, quickly but not fast enough to attract attention.

She turned to look at the nightstand clock. 9:30 a.m. She felt well rested for only having 6 hours of sleep. From downstairs she could hear her mother moving around. The smell of fresh brewed coffee drifted up the stairs of the big house. She stood and padded across the carpet to her private bathroom. She dropped her nightgown in the hamper and looked in the mirror. At 22 Dot was in excellent shape due to an active and adventurous lifestyle. She stepped into the blue and white tile shower and turned up the hot water. As the steam rose she contemplated the events leading up to last night.

At one time, Dot could have been referred to as the average American girl. Her interests had been fun, friends, shopping, clothes, nice cars, and cute boys. At one time she wanted to become a medical technologist. She'd even gone so far as to spend two years at the University of Oregon studying the subject. Then the death of her twin brother, coupled with the unspeakable grief of her parents, changed all of that. The funeral was barely over when Dot started planning ways to get at the people who had been responsible for hooking Jonah on drugs. For months she had contemplated one plan then another, yet all of her ideas came to an end against brick walls.

Then 5 months ago, she had accidentally discovered what her father was doing. She caught him making some phone calls when he thought no one was home. Feeling no shame, she eavesdropped on her father until she had enough of an idea of what he was doing to offer her help in the project.

Jonah Stoneking Senior had been shocked to his very core when he discovered his daughter knew what he was up to and had been thinking along the same lines. At first, he tried to talk her out of participating. His main concern was for her safety, and he was concerned for her mother. He argued that he and Beth could not possibly handle it if their daughter was hurt or killed. Finally, after her father realized he could not stop her from planning on her own if she was excluded, he was convinced to let her in. Dot made it clear to her father she wanted an active role. She insisted on getting the same training as everyone else. He sent her to Eugene where Doctor Fish trained her and 3 others, one of which being the vicious Boxer she'd just worked with.

Dot turned off the shower and stepped out. She dried off with a blue and white towel and walked back into her room. She mused over the fact that to this day she did not know the connection between Doctor Fish and her father. She made a mental note as she dressed to ask him sometime.

During training, Dot had learned right away that questions about her associates were not permitted. Boxer was just Boxer, and the other two were young black men codenamed Cain and Abel. In those few months they formed a loose union based on the others' abilities. Doctor Fish had instructed them in physical conditioning and mental resilience. He taught them how to field strip and shoot the Ingram Model 10 machine gun, the Israeli made Uzi, M-16's, and the Browning 9 mm pistol. They had also learned the fine art of killing quickly and silently, using wire. They had also been taught the science of recruiting; meaning how to spot future soldiers for the army of the Cleanup Committee.

Now, as Dot pulled on her slacks this weekday morning, she examined how she felt. Not even 8 hours after shooting 4 people, she decided she felt good. The first blow in the war had been struck. She buttoned her blouse and thought about last night being nothing more than a dress rehearsal for what was to come. When all of the soldiers were trained and working, no dealer would be safe. No pusher would be able to sleep at night.

Dot made her bed and went downstairs to join her mother. She found her mother in the kitchen, reading a newspaper and drinking coffee. She walked up from behind and kissed her mom on the top of her head.

Beth Stoneking looked at Dot and smiled. "Good morning, Dear. How are you today?"

"I'm fine, mom. How are you?"

"Just fine. Your father left early this morning so I slept in."

"Good for you. You should sleep in as much as you can! I'm going to get some coffee. Do you need more?"

"Yes, thank you dear. How was your ski trip?"

"Just fine," Dot fibbed and walked over to the coffee pot. Dot did no like lying to her mother, but it was best this way. Beth was not the kind of woman who could live with the knowledge that her husband and daughter were murderers, no matter what the cause. With her back still to her mother, Dot said "We went down to Mount Ashland. It was fun. The skiing wasn't all that great because the wind was pretty strong, but we spent time sitting at the lodge having hot chocolate by the fireplace, and that was nice."

She knew she was safe in this story, because her mother would never check. She had no reason to. However, just in case, Dot had called and checked the ski conditions at Mount Ashland from a payphone on her way out of Eugene.

She carried the cups over to the table and sat with her mother. They discussed the expected guests for the coming evening, and their overnight stay. As far as Beth was concerned, the 4 guests were skiing friends who were coming up to ski at the famous slopes of Mount Hood. They would stay the night at her house then go on to the lodge tomorrow.

The 4 people expected tonight were in fact the group that would be Dot's responsibility until they were shipped out to school in March. Tomorrow would not be spent skiing, but getting them situated with housing and clothes for the next few weeks. They would be arriving around 7 p.m. from different points. Each would be briefed in advance of what to say, and what not to say. Following the dinner with their "good friend" Dot, they would be hustled off to the basement for some movies. The films were there to keep them entertained and reasonably quiet. All Dot could do was hope they paid attention and pray for no slip-ups. Trying to keep 4 strangers interacting like old friends and entertained might be difficult.

Dot realized her mother was speaking and asked her to repeat the question.

"My goodness, Dot," her mother said. "Where is your mind this morning? I asked how many of your friends were coming."

"3 for sure, mom, possibly 4. One wasn't sure but he'll call about 11 or so to let me know for sure." The one that she wasn't sure of was that wild kid Johnny. Dr. Fish was supposed to decide on him this morning.

The conversation moved slowly forward. Beth talked about the party she and Jonah had attended over the weekend. They talked about the weather. Beth offered breakfast; Dot said she had a late dinner as the reason she wasn't hungry. Finally, Dot excused herself in order to write letters. She actually did have a letter to write, so that at least wasn't a lie. "Thank you though, Mom. I could join you for lunch."

"I was thinking we could have lunch with your father," Beth replied.

"Good idea mom!" Dot said. "If he's free please let him know we'll both join him."

Dot went back up to her room and sat at her desk. She got a pen and paper out, but was not able to concentrate enough to write. She kept looking at the phone on the desk. It was her private line, and when it sounded she would know if Johnny Redwine was going to be her guest tonight or not.

She abandoned the idea of writing and set down the pen. She thought about the operation. The committee was bringing 36 people to Portland from all over the place. She did not know exactly how they recruit that many, or the details for getting them all to the city. She did know that her home was the only home of a committee member that was receiving them. Jonah Stoneking was the only committee member these particular 3 or 4 recruits would meet. His cover and home were being used for the simple reason that Dot and her father were putting up a smoke screen for Beth. Security, not only so her mother wouldn't know, but so no one else would know. That was the order of the day, every day. The other 32 people were being temporarily housed in a warehouse that had been converted into a dorm. Tomorrow she would take her small group to join the others. When they were all under one roof, they would all be her responsibility for the next several weeks. Dot knew what was expected of her, and she hoped she would meet all expectations.

To her relief, the phone rang. She quickly picked it up. "Hello?"

"It sure is foggy here," said Doctor Fish.

"Yes," Dot replied. "The fog is pretty thick here too."

"In spite of the fog, all four of your packages should arrive."

"Will they arrive at the house or do I need to go to UPS and pick them up?"

"They will arrive at the house. Please keep track of the container."

"Of course, sir. Anything further?"

"Not at this time."

"Thank you, and have a good day." Dot set down the phone and relaxed.

The container Dr. Fish had referred to: the car they were arriving in. Whichever car Linda was driving today, Boxer or one of the others would claim it tomorrow. The committee had several cars, all large and fast and well kept. The talk about fog had simply been code to identify each other. Well, she thought, at least now I know how many I'll be expecting. Johnny, Linda, Ronald Dill from St. Helens, and Charlotte Matson from Astoria. She barely knew them. She hoped they were good actors.

Dot went back downstairs and informed her mother they would be having 4 guests. She then idled away a few minutes while her mother changed for going out. They joined Jonah Stoneking for lunch at the Yacht Club. They used her mother's Pontiac Grand Prix. It had several upgrades. Custom wheels, tinted windows, vinyl seats, and a souped up engine. Compared to her little Saab Sonnet III, Dot felt like she was driving a tank. She adjusted easily and got to the Yacht Club without issues. She exited the car with relief.

Jonah met them just outside the door. After exchanging greetings Dot followed her parents into the restaurant. They were met by a white coated waiter who led them to the Stoneking table. Jonah asked Beth to order for him while he went to the men's room. Dot had slipped him a note in the parking lot so he took the opportunity to take a look.

Dot watched her father walk across the room and said to her mother: "He hasn't changed in all these years. He still looks just like he did when I was little."

"What about me, dear? Do you think I've changed?" Beth asked.

"Only a little, mom. I hope I look as good as you when I'm your age."

"Let's not discuss my age, dear."

"Still, mom," Dot said, taking her mother's hand with a smile, "you look really good."

"Thank you, dear. I'm sure you will always be beautiful yourself. I just hope you'll settle down a little and quit running from one end of the state to the other." Beth set her hand down.

"Mom, it's my running around that keeps me in shape," Dot said with a smile.

Beth's next question changed the subject. "Are your friends driving up from the south tonight?"

"Two of them are but two are getting rides from other people." Damn it, thought Dot, I wonder if I said anything about this before that I don't remember. The worst thing about lying is remembering all the details.

Dot became aware her mother was looking at her oddly. "Are you alright, dear?"

"Yes, mom. I'm fine."

"You looked worried for a moment."

"Not really, I was just thinking about the weather. I hope it's not too rough on the drivers. I wonder if the fog will set in."

"Goodness, I hope not," said Beth. "You'd better allow for a late dinner just in case."

"What about dinner?" Jonah asked as he returned to the table.

Dot was relieved to see her father take his place next to her mother. It would save her from more questioning.

"Welcome back, dear," Beth said. "We were just discussing what to do for dinner. The kids might be late if the fog sets in."

"Unfortunately that's exactly what the weatherman is calling for," said Jonah. "You girls plan accordingly. By the way, Dot, are they all arriving together?"

She was tempted to kick her father in the shin. He knew damn well they weren't, this was his show. Was she supposed to know something more?

"No, Dad. Johnny and Linda are driving up in her car. Ron and Charlotte are coming with someone else."

"Ok," Jonah said. "Nothing to worry about. I'm sure they'll all get here in one piece."

The waiter rescued them from further conversation when he arrived with soups and salads. Dot concentrated on her food and mulled over the coming evening. She hoped that Fish and whoever else had briefed the guests thoroughly and they would play along easily. Dot found herself wishing the pretense could be dropped and her mother could just be told the truth. If it was Dot's choice, that's exactly what would have happened. She didn't believe her father gave her mother enough credit for having good sense... but then he had always treated Beth as though she were made of the most fragile type of crystal. Dot had never wasted a minute of her time trying to show her father that policy was wrong. She hoped they would not have to do too many of these cover shows for mother. Anyway, even if the cover story fell through, the odds were nil that Beth would connect her daughter with killings 80 miles away.

She made a mental note to get her father alone sometime to review the story they were going to give her mother regarding her absences upcoming in the next few months. That shouldn't be much trouble, though, as she was often gone for several days at a time. By now Beth was used to her daughter not being always at her fingertips. Beth had adjusted quite well, actually, and didn't pry too deep into her daughter's activities.

This time when the waiter returned, he was carrying a phone. "Apologies for the interruption. Your office, Mr. Stoneking. They said it couldn't wait." The waiter plugged the phone in near Jonah then withdrew.

Stoneking put down his knife and fork and picked up the phone. "Yes, what is it?"

The two women listened as Jonah said "yes" and "no" and "why not." As is usually the case with one sided conversations, they learned nothing.

Jonah set down the phone and looked at his family. "Sorry about that, girls. Business, you know. Sometimes they can't function on their own for even a minute."

Dot felt her heart skip a beat. Some sort of hitch had developed.

Beth said "You really should start thinking about retirement soon, Jonah. It's time you relaxed a little."

"I'll relax when I die, Mother," he teased. He dismissed the subject by signalling the waiter to remove the phone and bring the check.

In the parking lot a few minutes later, Jonah held his wife for an extra long hug before she got in the car. Then he came around to the drivers side where Dot was. She pushed the button to roll down the window and allowed her father to kiss her cheek. He took the opportunity to whisper to her: "Only the ones from Eugene."

To cover the relief she felt, Dot looked at her father and said, "I love you, Old Man."

"Who are you calling old, young lady?"

"It's the modern age, dad. I'm 22 and you're a lot older than me!"

"It's a good thing you're a cute kid," Jonah replied with a smile. He started walking back toward his car. "See you two later."

"Have a good afternoon Dad!" Dot said while rolling up the window. As they drove away from the Yacht Club, Dot couldn't help but feel relief. The odds of anything going wrong had just been reduced by 50 percent. Two would be easier to manage than 4. Besides, she knew enough about Linda to fake it really well and Johnny shouldn't be a problem. With her mind at ease, she drove through the afternoon traffic toward Safeway. The air was getting colder and starting to show the mist that would turn into fog.

By letting her know she would have 2 guests instead of 4, her father had solved one problem and presented another. Beth was expecting 4 guests. Dot decided that would be easy to cover. At an opportune time she would stage a phone call from her "friends" about the change. Mentally she patted herself on the back for figuring it out quickly. Her planning was almost her undoing, though, as she lost focus on traffic and almost rear ended a VW bus at a stoplight.

Beth looked at Dot. "You'd better quit daydreaming and watch your driving, dear."

Chapter 6

Johnny and Linda were northbound on Interstate 5. They had left Eugene, and a worried Dr. Fish, just before 5 pm. When they left the warehouse a fine cold rain was falling, as was the temperature. Both recruits had lived in Oregon long enough to know that the rain and cold would turn into sleet, and that would make for a miserable drive. Linda had briefed him on the parts they were to play while they endured rush hour traffic.

"Now let me get this straight," Johnny said. "We're going to Dot's house in Portland. We'll spend the night. Then we're going up to Mount Hood for some skiing tomorrow. The whole thing is so her parents won't guess she's involved with the Committee. Instead of going to Mount Hood we'll be joining the rest of the group in Portland."

Linda nodded. "You catch on quick."

It seemed the fog thickened as the traffic thinned. Now, as they were approaching Albany, visibility was reduced to about 50 feet. Suddenly, Johnny felt the rear of the big Dodge slip a little.

"Ice!" he called out. "Damn. As if the fog wasn't enough, now black ice."

Johnny had been anxious since leaving Eugene. However, he hadn't panicked about the ice and gone for the brakes like some people do. He eased off the gas and let the car kind of slide back into line.

After driving for miles, his arms and shoulders hurt. His eyes ached from looking at the fog. Linda was curled up on the seat beside him, sound asleep. He didn't know if that was a compliment to his driving skills or not, as before she fell asleep Linda was delighted in catching him in a mistake. Like a fool, he'd been so focused on getting used to the feel of the car he had not gotten around to changing the headlights. He sulked at having to be reminded by a girl, and she had fallen asleep.

Linda moved a bit in her seat. Johnny threw a quick glance and saw that she was still asleep. He turned on the car radio on low volume and dialed around till he found a radio station. They identified as KUGN Eugene and went into some news.

"Eugene police report no new leads in the Rainbow's End shooting. 4 men, including the establishment owner, were killed last night when 2 people opened fire. Police say the murders have the earmarks of a Gangland style killing. The investigation is ongoing."

Johnny kept changing stations until he found music. After a while, Johnny found himself wanting coffee and food. He reached over and poked Linda on the arm. She jumped like she had been bitten.

"What? What's happening?"

He grinned. "Where can we get something to eat around here? I don't know the area."

"Where are we? What time is it?"

"We just passed through Salem and it's 6:15."

"Shit, we were supposed to be in Portland by 7."

"We'll never make it," Johnny pointed out.

"That's a brilliant deduction!" Linda replied sarcastically. "Woodburn is just up the road, maybe we can find something to eat there."

"Good grief, I just remembered, I don't have 10 cents to my name. I don't even have my drivers' license. Dr. Fish said they stored my stuff. My wallet was in there."

Linda opened the glove box and dumped his wallet on the seat by him.

"Well, I'll be. Where'd that come from?"

"I put your stuff in here while you and Dr. Fish were at lunch. You won't need your money, though. We have an expense account for the trip. Dr. Fish gave me a credit card. We can use it for anything," Linda said.

"Awesome," Johnny said. "I suppose you'll tell me next we have suitcases in the trunk with ski clothes?"

"Yep. If anyone asks we're renting gear at the lodge."

"This is all so far out," Johnny mused with a shake of his head. "It's all hard to believe."

"Surely you've been in the program long enough to know the Committee likes to have all their bases covered?" Linda asked.

"God no," Johnny replied. "24 hours ago I'd never heard of any of this."

Linda's eyes widened in surprise. "You're putting me on."

"The hell I am. Dot found me last night after I tried to kill those creeps that got shot at the restaurant later." Johnny told her what happened and why. She listened without comment until he was finished.

"Well, that's interesting," Linda said. I thought the recruiting process was all over. Excuse the pun, but you must be a Johnny-come-Lately if ever there was one."

"I have no idea. So far this whole thing sounds like it was dreamed up by Hollywood."

"It's no movie," Linda said. "It's for real and we're playing for keeps."

Johnny was silent for a minute. "What would have happened to me if I failed the tests? Or refused to go along?"

"I honestly don't know. I'm sure they have a provision for people who don't work out."

"I'll bet they do," Johnny answered, wondering if it involved murder.

The ice and fog were not lifting in the slightest. Johnny was starting to think he couldn't stand another mile of this when a sign loomed up out of the fog announcing Gas, Food, and Lodging in 1 mile. At the exit, he eased the big car down the icy ramp. They found a restaurant near the freeway and Johnny felt like he'd aged as he turned off the engine and lights. He put the keys in his pocket and looked at Linda. "Do you usually lock it up?"

"No, there's nothing in here that's super important. Besides, the locks might freeze."

Johnny realized right then how tired he was. The tests, the drive, last night, it had all just drained him. He wished with all his heart Brenda was still alive. Linda reached out and took his hand.

"Listen," she said. "I know you've been through a lot. God only knows just how much. Hang in there. After we get some food it will all look a little better. If you want, I can drive when we start again."

Johnny removed his hand and opened the door. "Let's eat." He saw the restaurant clock as they entered. 6:35. "Maybe we'd better call Dot."

"We're only supposed to call in case of dire emergency. This doesn't qualify."

"Whatever floats their boat," Johnny said, and led the way to a table.

Linda excused herself to the restroom. The waitress approached with menus. She was about Johnny's age, and looked like she'd rather be anywhere but here.

"We'll order in a few minutes," Johnny said. The waitress retreated without a word. Linda looked much more at ease when she returned. "Did everything come out alright?" Johnny asked with a mischievous grin.

"Don't be crude", Linda said, but she smiled as she said it.

When the waitress returned they ordered cheeseburgers and a coke, then a coffee. Linda took out a pack of Winstons and offered Johnny one. He took it and she held out a fancy silver lighter. They smoked and watched the small crowd in silence while they waited.

They were seated facing the door. A group of 4 entered, 2 guys and 2 girls. They were sloppily dressed and were loudly laughing and hooting. One of them peeled off and headed for the jukebox. He stuffed in some change and filled the room with hard rock. His companions occupied a nearby booth. By doing so they effectively blocked the path to the door. Johnny was not immediately aware of what was happening. He looked away from the jerk at the jukebox and saw Linda's face and realized something was wrong.

Linda had put out her cigarette and was watching the guy at the jukebox intensely.

"That one is a speed freak," she said. "The other 3 are spaced out too but probably on grass or something else. This is a setup."

The waitress arrived with their orders. She was uncensored with the group that just entered as she took her time setting everything in place. By the time she retreated, Linda had lost interest in eating. Johnny was too busy watching her to think about his food.

"What do you mean it's a setup?" Johnny asked quietly.

"We're obviously travelers. They probably saw us get out of the nice car. They'll start taunting us soon. They expect us to get mad and try to leave. If we don't handle this right, we won't make it to the car."

"How the hell do you know all that?" Johnny asked.

"While you were busy watching music man I had my eye on the other 3. They pointed us out to each other then grabbed that booth." She'd been talking over the din of the music while keeping her eye on the jukebox man. She leaned closer and said "Keep a close watch on the 3 in the booth. If trouble starts, I'll handle it. If we leave the booth, stick to me like glue. Don't let them get between us."

Linda turned her attention back to the music man, who was now half dancing, half swaggering in their direction. He approached the table trying to be cool. It was obvious he was nervous.

Johnny looked at the booth. The 2 girls were seated with their backs to him. The other guy was facing them. He then sized up the music man quickly. 6 feet tall, skinny as a rail. Ragged blue flannel and brown pants. Long, dirty brown hair and a beard that was probably home to half the bugs in the state. He had a smirk on his face as he dance-stepped closer. Looking down at Linda he said "Hey baby, what do you say you shed fancy pants and you and me get it on?"

"Thanks," she said, but I'd rather not."

Johnny started moving things in where he could reach them quickly. He had a sugar bowl, a ketchup bottle, a glass ashtray, salt & pepper shakers, two paper cartons of coke, and two cups of coffee. The sugar bowl, he decided, would be best for the music man. The ketchup bottle and coffee cups would be for the heads in the booth.

"Aw, come on, baby," the music man continued. "I could outscrew your lover boy any day of the week."

Johnny felt Linda moved and realized she had picked up her purse. He kept an eye on the booth.

"Thanks anyway, but we're in a hurry." Linda edged toward the end of her seat.

"Come on, honey. Let's do it. We could make beautiful music together," Music man said, prepared to grab her when she stood.

Suddenly, the music man let out a screech and toppled backwards to the floor. Linda was on her feet and Johnny quickly followed. She caught the other guy coming out of the booth with the ashtray. Johnny stood ready to bust heads with the ketchup bottle.

"Let's split," Linda said.

Music man was still groaning on the floor, clutching at his manhood. The second man was trying to clear the ash from his eyes. Johnny gave him a swift kick in the knee as he passed toward the door. They hurried out toward the Dodge. Then Linda grabbed his arm and stopped.

"They might have friends out here. If they do they could be waiting in the car. Let's go easy. You open the rear door on your side, I'll open the passenger side. If someone's there let's deal with them fast."

They approached the car from the rear and split. Johnny went left, Linda went right. He watched to time his door opening with hers.

To their relief, the car was empty. They got in quickly and got the car started. In the short time they'd been gone the ice had started building up on the windshield. They had to wait for the heat to clear the windows. It took real concentration to resist the urge to speed away, but Johnny knew the ice would not permit the speed he wanted. He was relieved to find the I-5 northbound on ramp had been sanded by the highway department. The trucks were now working on the freeway itself.

"Just how did you know those clowns were after us?" Johnny asked.

"They were too strung out to not be obvious. I've had some experience with people like them and the games they play."

"You sure did a number on that poor bastard by the table."

"Maybe a knee in the balls will teach that jerk some manners," Linda replied.

"Think anyone will put the cops on us?"

"It's not likely they'll bother. They probably get situations like that all the time. It's just that kind of place. You can bet," she continued, "if those bastards had gotten the upper hand on us no one would have helped."

An hour and 15 minutes later, Johnny nosed the Dodge into the driveway of the biggest house he had ever seen. It was also the house he thought he would never see or find. Linda had the address, but he sent what seemed like forever looking up one street and down the other. They'd gotten turned around and detoured, all through fog and ice. When they finally arrived Johnny turned off the motor and lights, then rubbed his eyes.

"God I'm tired," he said. "This is the damndest town I've been in."

"Yeah, it's pretty confusing," Linda agreed.

Johnny looked at Linda, knowing he liked her better than any girl he had known in his young life. He then did something he'd never done before. He leaned in and reached his left hand up to touch her cheek. She leaned in and they kissed.

"Linda, I'm sorry for griping about the drive."

Linda smiled. "I know it was tough, Johnny. Now let's go see what's in store for us."

Johnny removed the keys and opened the door. He and Linda took a long walk to the front door of the big house. It was large and imposing. Even after dark it reflected money through its yard lights and decor. Neither of them had been this close to money before. They were both a bit apprehensive.

Before they had a chance to ring the bell, the door was opened by a stately looking white haired man. They didn't know it yet, but they were looking at the man who would direct their young lives down a bloody road.

"Welcome, welcome!" he said, holding out his hand. "You must be Johnny and Linda. Come on in, Dot's been expecting you." He stepped back for them to enter. "We've all been worried about you driving in this weather."

"It's something else out there," Johnny answered.

They followed the white haired man they assumed was Dot's father down a short hallway and 3 steps into a sunken living room. Dot greeted them, and Johnny was immediately struck by the change in appearance between this Dot and the one he had met in his apartment. She was dressed in a long flowing dress of a type he'd never seen in person before. It struck him that she was an extremely good looking gal.

"I'm so glad you made it!" Dot said. "You two must be beat."

"We are, "Linda replied. "That drive is tough on the nerves."

"I can just guess what you've been through."

Johnny was looking around the sophisticated living room when he saw a woman, obviously Dot's mother. She entered from a door to the right of the fireplace, over which hung a picture of a guy in a football uniform. The guy looked familiar for some reason. Dot's father stepped forward from where he'd been standing near Dot and put an arm around his wife.

"People," the man said. The girls stopped chatting and the new arrivals looked. "I'd like to present my wife, Beth Stoneking. My dear, this is Johnny Redwine and Linda Smith."

Johnny stepped forward and took the soft warm hand she held out. He looked in her eyes and saw something he couldn't identify. Sadness? Loneliness? He wasn't sure, for now she was smiling and saying "Pleased to meet you, young man. Welcome."

"Thank you," he said, hoping to get away soon. The house, their clothes, their manners... it was all overwhelming. He wasn't sure what to do or what to say. Beth turned to Linda.

Dot's father noticed Johnny's distress and said "Let's go get the bags from the car, young man." They walked out without saying anything further. Johnny had the feeling Dot's father wanted to talk. He didn't realize he had a striking resemblance to the late Jonah Stoneking Jr., and while Mr. Stoneking had been warned and had time to adjust, Beth had not.

"I sure got turned around trying to find this place," Johnny said.

They were at the back of the car, and he was horrified to discover he didn't know which key opened the trunk. He had a choice of 3 keys, and while he swiftly tried one in the lock he tried to think of what else to say.

"I understand," the man replied. "Portland can be confusing to the visitor, like any big city. Is the key giving you trouble? Oh, there you go, that's the right one."

To Johnny's relief, the last key opened the trunk. The trunk light came on and revealed 2 suitcases side by side. They were the same except for color. He had no idea whose was which. Johnny's nervousness spiked, still thinking he had to fool Dot's father into thinking he was a friend. Shit, he thought, this old man's no fool. He'll figure out something's rotten for sure. He reached in, grabbed both suitcases and pulled them out.

"I'll carry one of those if you like," Dot's father said.

"Thanks, sir, but I can make it. I wouldn't mind if you opened the door though."

Stoneking led the way back up the walk. Johnny hoped Dot or Linda would be paying attention when he came in. He had no idea which suitcase to offer Linda. When they entered the big house, the living room was empty. Stoneking walked down the steps into the living room toward the fireplace. Realizing he shouldn't just stand there, Johnny followed. Stoneking looked back and said "Put them right over here by the chair. The girls must be in the kitchen. You're welcome to join them for food or coffee."

Johnny set the suitcases down by a large rocking chair near the fireplace. He saw Mr. Stoneking look at the portrait above the fire. For the first time Johnny really looked at it, and realized the face looking back at him was remarkably familiar. It also looked like a younger face of the man standing next to him.

"My son," Jonah said, "Dot's brother. He passed away a few years ago."

"I'm sorry," Johnny said, and he meant it. They stood for another minute looking at the photo, saying nothing.

"Well, you must be hungry as well as tired," Jonah said. "I'll show you where to get washed up and then we'll join the women."

Johnny was saved from too many questions at dinner by the fact that Dot and Linda kept a running conversation. They knew each other enough to go through subjects like skiing and boating. Dot's parents occasionally asked about one slope or another or commented on what great exercise skiing can be.Johnny ate like the ravenous person he was. He had really needed the sandwich he'd been cheated out of earlier. Mrs. Stoneking watched him but resisted asking questions. Growing boys need lots of food, she thought. Besides, she was too well mannered to distract guests as they ate.

Finally the meal was over. Johnny retired to the living room with Mr. Stoneking while the women cleared the table. The suitcases were gone. They sat by the fire, Stoneking in the big chair and Johnny on a sofa. Dot came in with coffee and retreated after some banter with her father. Jonah looked at the young man. He knew all about this kid. Fish had filled him in during a 30 minute phone conversation. Now, he was thinking of what to bring up without giving too much away. There were things the young man didn't need to know yet. The need to speak first was relieved by Johnny.

"My sister died last night."

Jonah was taken off guard. He was aware that the young man had lost his sister, but he had not been told it was so recent. It was not fake when he said "Oh Lord! I'm so sorry, I didn't know. Is Dot aware?"

Jonah waited patiently for an answer. He did not like surprises.

"Linda may have told her. I came up here to get away from it all… but I miss her, Mr. Stoneking. I miss her a lot."

Jonah, still at a loss, fully understood how the boy felt. He looked at the young man and his heart went out to him. Johnny was kicking himself mentally for what he had said. It had just come out. He was tired, and sitting with this old man he somehow knew he liked him. The Stonekings and their house fit an idea of parents and home that he had dreamed about as a child. He never allowed a dream to take hold of him in real life, but it would sneak up on him sometimes just for a minute. In his dreams he had a mother who looked at him with admiration and a father who was there for him in tough times. They were just dreams, though. Now, faced with a new reality, he had instinctually blurted out the statement to catch the attention of the father figure sitting next to him. It led to a feeling of embarrassment that made him wish for a place to hide.

"I'm sorry I made you feel bad," Johnny said to his host.

Jonah looked at him with a soft face that looked just a bit older. "Young man," he said, "When we lost our son, we felt the same way. In my case, the grief was shared by my wife and Dot. Perhaps it was easier because of that. Obviously you're alone or you'd be with family right now instead of here. Don't feel bad about anything you say. I feel honored that you shared. If I can help you in any way, please let me know. Speaking for my family, we'll be glad to help in any way we can."

"Thank you," Johnny said. "I'm sure things will work out somehow." He wished he could say Dot was helping, but he didn't. He believed this man could not know what his daughter was doing.

Beth entered the room and stopped. She saw the way the two men were looking at each other and she did not want to interrupt whatever this was. However the moment had passed and Jonah sensed his wife's presence.

"Hello dear," Jonah said as he stood. "Please join us." He gestured to the chair next to his. As she sat down Jonah went to the fireplace, opened the glassdoors, and set fire to papers under carefully stacked woods.

Beth turned to her guest. "Do you like the fireplace, Mr. Redwine?"

"Yes," Johnny said. "I haven't been around them much. I just have an apartment."

Jonah resumed his seat and asked "where are the girls?"

"Dot is showing Linda her room. They should be here shortly," Beth said. She looked back at Johnny, who was just setting down his cup. "Would you like more coffee?"

"No, thank you, though."

Linda and Dot appeared from the hallway to Johnny's left. They crossed the room with Dot leading the way.

"Hi girls. Did you get situated?" Beth asked.

"Sure did," Dot replied. "I'm going to take them to the basement to watch movies."

"Try not to stay up too late, honey," Beth answered. "Our guests look quite tired."

"Mom, please, it's Johnny and Linda. You don't have to be formal."

"Go on, then, dear."

"We'll be back up soon. No need to wait up," Dot said, as she started to go to the hall.

Johnny got up and said "Thank you for dinner. See you in the morning."

"Goodnight," Linda said.

Dot had led the way downstairs to a large basement. It held a pool table, a color TV, a shuffle board game, and bean bag furnishings. She passed the games and went into a small home theater capable of seating 10 people. She pulled the door shut and dropped into a seat.

"Pull up chairs, you two."

Johnny wondered as they sat if they were really going to see a movie.

"Thank you both for a job well done under difficult circumstances. I apologize for putting you through that, but it was necessary. Now, I owe you an explanation."

"Johnny, Linda has been in the program for 3 months. She knew a week ago that she'd be coming here and why. However the original plan was for her to come in quite a different way. With your late arrival we had her motor up here with you, so she did not have enough information to give you a full briefing. Nevertheless, you came through in fine shape considering just how much your life has changed in the last 24 hours.

Linda, I didn't get a chance to tell you this. Johnny lost his sister just last night to a drug overdose. When I found him, he was trying to murder Fat Freddy and two of his friends on a downtown street. He damn near got them, too."

Johnny looked at Dot and said "Someone did get them. Would you know anything about that?"

Something crossed Dot's face, and her eyes grew cold. She said icily: "I'll forgive you for that question, because you're new. It's something the others have already learned. Simply put, it's none of your business. Certain questions are not permitted. You'll learn what to ask and what not to ask. One of the things not to ask is who does what job."

Johnny was partly irritated, partly nervous. "You said you were ready to answer questions."

Dot softened. "It's ok. You couldn't know. Go ahead and ask questions. If something isn't allowed, I'll tell you. I won't jump your case any more tonight. Before the questions, let me tell you about tomorrow." She looked at both new recruits. "We'll leave here at 8:30 a.m. tomorrow to join the others. My dear mother and father, God bless them, think we're going to Mt. Hood for a week of skiing. In fact, we'll be going to a place in northeast Portland. It's an old 40 room inn that sits on 7 acres. At one time, it was probably the biggest, nicest thing in the city. It was allowed to fall into a sad state of disrepair. The committee bought it, fixed it up nicely, and for the next 6-8 weeks it will be your home. At the end of that time, you'll be going to yet another place for more specific training."

Linda asked, "How many more of us are there?"

"34," answered Dot. "You'll get more details tomorrow when we're all together. The others are at the house now, getting acquainted under the watchful eye of a committee member."

Johnny was tempted to make a few inquiries but decided against it, opting to wait. He was getting too tired to care. He did ask one question he deemed harmless:

"Can you tell us anything about the others?"

"Sure," Dot said with a smile. "They're all from similar situations. They're relatively close to your ages. To be specific, Johnny, you're our youngest at 17. The oldest is 27 or 28. In terms of numbers, there are 10 females and 26 males. We would've liked 18 and 18, but it's not super important."

"Why are there 36?"

"Generally, for all of this will be covered in more detail later, it has to do with the number of counties in the state."

"Thanks," Johnny said. "I'm ready to get some sleep."

"I'll show you to your room."

Dot led him to a room with a night light on. The covers of the double bed were pulled back. It was the most inviting thing he'd seen in his life. He dumped his clothes in the bathroom hamper and took a good hot shower. He'd been told that his clothing for tomorrow would be found in the mysterious suitcase, which had been placed at the foot of his bed.

Now, he was reaching the point where he felt that sleep would finally come. He rolled, situated his head on the pillow, and drifted off.

Chapter 7

As was his practice, Jonah Stoneking was up early on a cold Tuesday morning. He got the coffee started and then went into the living room to start the fire. He liked having morning coffee by the fireplace. Usually Beth would join him and they would plan the day together. At the moment she was in her shower, and Jonah took the opportunity to make a phone call. He confirmed everything was in order at the Big House.

Dot joined him and quickly reviewed some last minute details. Then she went to awaken her guests. When that was done she returned to the kitchen and started breakfast. Jonah moved restlessly between kitchen and living room until Beth joined him. Dot brought her parents their coffee then set the table. Linda appeared first, then Johnny, both looking well rested.

Breakfast was served in the dining room. When the meal was over, Jonah excused himself to get ready for an early meeting at his office. He didn't really relax until he was in the garage starting the car. He eased a little knowing Beth couldn't see him here. He pushed a button on the dash that opened his garage door and slowly backed the blue Cadillac out into the icy morning.

It had cleared during the night, leaving a sheet of ice over everything. Long icicles hung from the trees and the eaves of the house. The green and white Dodge was iced over. The kids are going to have a scraping job this morning, he thought. Once on the road, he headed toward the Big House, not the office. He drove carefully on the slick roads. Anyone observing him would not have guessed that he was in a heightened state of expectancy. Months of planning and careful recruitment were finally about to start showing results. When Dot delivered Johnny and Linda this morning, all candidates would be in place and the first step in forming their private army would be underway.

Each candidate had been approached through various methods. If they indicated an interest in joining, they were screened and then turned over to Doctor Fish and associates. They had arrived in various states of physical and mental distress. In twos and threes, Fish had put them in shape in his little specialized school. Stoneking did not know his methods, and he didn't really care. All he cared about was the results.

He slowed for a stop sign then turned right. He thought about the fact that Linda Smith was at his house, right now. She had been the product of poverty. Mother drunk, father gone who knows where. Her little brother, who was only 12, had gotten into the same rut as his sister. She had been a user and a pusher; a first class juvenile delinquent. When it finally dawned on her what was happening to her little brother, it was too late. The kid was hooked. He financed his habit by beating up or threatening other kids at school for their lunch money. They always paid. Linda tried to cut off his resources by telling the other dealers not to sell to him. They refused, and when she threatened to turn one of them in she was beaten as an object lesson.

One night last summer, the kid was in need of a fix but didn't have the money. Somehow he got his hands on a .38 Colt Revolver and used it to stick up a grocery store. At the age of 13, he was probably one of the youngest major felons in Grants Pass history, if not Oregon history. Someone in that store had triggered an alarm. The kid ran out of the store only to run into 2 policemen in the parking lot. The officers were not expecting a 13 year old suspect. They made the mistake of hesitating.

Officer Pete Tibs died standing by his vehicle. The second officer was hit as he was rounding the back of his car. From where he lay on the ground, that officer killed the 13 year old with two shots from his service revolver before dying. The young man, or rather the child, had only gotten $19 for his efforts.

Three lives were suddenly and viciously snuffed out. In her grief, Linda had gone wild. For two days and nights, she roamed the city with a double barrel 12 gauge shotgun. She shot 3 different pushers on sight. One of them was shot in a busy parking lot in broad daylight. She was finally run to earth and taken into custody.

Dot had been in Grants Pass at the time. Somehow, and Jonah had no idea just how, she had managed to get Linda released into her custody. She had taken her to Dr. Fish and hired two of the best lawyers in Oregon to defend her in court. It never got that far. Charges were dropped.

Not all of the candidates had been received under such wild circumstances. Yet all had lost relatives to drugs, and they all had loose family units with no close friends. Nevertheless, it had been necessary for each candidate to have a solid cover story to circulate around their communities to explain their absence. None of them would see their hometowns again for quite some time.

When he arrived at the Big House, Jonah met privately with the two men known as Cain and Abel. They had been responsible for the arrival of personnel. They were in an office near the front of the building. It had, at one time, been a reception area for guests.

"Good morning, gentlemen. Is everything in order?"

"Good morning, Mr. Stoneking. Yes," replied Abel. "Everyone is situated and adjusting quite well. They're a friendly lot and seem to have taken to each other easily."

"Good. Any last minute issues or material shortages?"

"No, sir."

"Excellent," Jonah said with palpable relief. "I understand that you two will return to Eugene this morning and Dot will take over for the next few days."

"Yes, sir. Next Monday I'll be back to spell Dot. Then this SOB with nothing to say," Abel said as he indicated his partner, "will relieve me." Cain flung a paperclip at Abel.

"Do you know of the car you need to return?"

"Doctor Fish called about it yesterday. He also said we'll be getting a new man. One we haven't met yet."

"Yes, he'll be arriving with Dot and Linda. He's a good kid. He has what it takes." Jonah stood up, satisfied that all was in order and ready. He opened his briefcase and took out an envelope. He placed it on the desk within easy reach of Abel. "That's a small bonus for a job well done. I appreciate your work, gentlemen."

"Thank you sir." Abel opened the envelope to ten $100 dollar bills for himself and Cain. The Committee believed in rewarding its people.

Jonah shook hands with them at the door and wished them well. Outside, he looked up and down the hill but saw no one. He heard voices coming from a room somewhere down the hall. He heard laughter and assumed someone was telling a joke.

Chapter 8

Johnny Redwine looked at the ice covered car and shook his head. This is going to be a job, he mused while walking to the passenger side. He pulled the cold door handle and was thankful when the door came open. He slid in on the cold seat. He opened the glove box and looked for a scraper. He found it behind a couple of maps, a flashlight and a first aid kit.

By the time he cleared the windshield, his hands were frozen. He put the scraper down and shoved his hands in his pockets. His fingers came in contact with the keys and it dawned on him to start the car. With the heater system on it would warm the rear window as well.

He stayed by the idling car once the scraping was done. It wasn't that he had any fear of it being stolen; he just wanted to get out of the house. Beth Stoneking was unfailingly polite. He liked her. However, she had a way of making him feel uncomfortable. He figured it had to do with the fact he looked like the son she no longer had.

Soon Dot and Linda came out with their suitcases full of "ski clothes". Beth trailed behind offering advice on how to drive and how to behave when they arrived. Johnny put the scraper in his pocket and stepped forward to take the suitcases. While getting the keys to open the trunk, the girls continued chatting. He couldn't help but wonder how Dot and Linda were putting on such a great act. One might believe they were actually going on a ski trip.

Finally, the bags were stashed and they were all in the car. Johnny had gotten behind the wheel automatically. It occurred to him that he had no idea where he was going, but it didn't matter. Either Dot would navigate or they would switch places once away from the house. Beth wished them good luck and turned for the house.

Johnny backed out into the street. Once out of sight of the house Dot said "Pull over, Johnny. I'll do the driving from here on." He pulled into an empty lot and traded places with her. He saw Dot adjust the mirror and ease back into the still icy street. He was glad for the car's studded tires.

"Ok," Dot began, "we're going to join the others. They have already gotten a chance to know each other. They don't know you're coming. I'll introduce you to the group."

Most of the drive was silent. Johnny busied himself watching traffic flow by and looking at the long icicles hanging from trees and buildings. This was a pretty section of town. He relaxed into a "wait and see" attitude. He figured these people would provide for him, so there was no sense in worrying. He looked to his side and saw Linda looking at him. She smiled.

"Did you sleep well last night?" Linda asked.

"Sure did. How about you?"

"Very well. Thank you."

Twenty minutes later, Dot drove up a long driveway to the Big House. Johnny and Linda watched its approach. It was so big as to be a little bit eerie. Maybe it was the unknown events waiting for them that seemed scary. Johnny felt butterflies in his stomach. The top of the driveway turned into a large horseshoe shape. There was a covered parkway in front of the large porch and entry doors. In front of the parkway were several tall columns that went all the way up to the roof. He didn't know what this type of building was called. He'd only seen buildings like this in movies. It was the type of house extremely rich people had built around the turn of the century. There was a massive lawn and trees which must have been there forever.

Dot stopped in the covered parkway. "This is a come as you are party," she said while getting out. "Don't bother with the suitcases in the trunk. Climb out and come on in."

They followed dot up the steps and across the porch. The large heavy doors opened to a large entry hall. A winding staircase turned up and out of sight. The floor was made of hardwood that was polished to a shine. The lights were soft and warm. The tile ceiling meant the hall did not echo. Dot led the way in toward the sound of voices. Two large black men appeared from a room to the right and the trio stopped.

"Cain and Abel!" Dot said with a smile. "Good morning! I would like you to meet Johnny Redwine and Linda Smith. Linda has been with us for a little while, and Johnny is new to the program."

Johnny stepped forward and held out his hand. The two men shook hands with him and said "Welcome to school."

Dot asked, "Will you be taking your leave now?"

"Yes, ma'am," Abel said. "The group is all yours. We have the rest of them corralled for you in the Day room at the end of the hall."

"I can hear them," Dot replied. "They sound like they're having a good time."

"They've been cutting up all morning. We just let them take this chance to relax. These two will have to carve themselves a niche."

"I'll help them," said Dot. "They helped me, so I owe them. See you next week. Drive easy, guys."

Dot flipped the car keys to Abel. He said, "Good luck. See ya." Then he and Cain disappeared out the doors.

"Those guys look mean," said Johnny.

"Gentle as kittens," Dot said, "unless you get them mad. Come on you two."

Dot led the way to the day room. Johnny walked beside Linda, butterflies in full tilt. She gave his hand a quick squeeze before they entered. He told himself it was just another classroom.

The trio entered and stopped by a large desk. The room was about 30 by 30. The floor was covered in a dark blue carpet. The windows had heavy, expensive looking drapes. There were 9 tables, each with 4 comfortable looking chairs. Along one wall there were easy chairs and end tables holding ashtrays and lamps. People were seated all across the room.

One of the girls noticed them. The pretty blonde girl was seated at a table with a tall lean guy. She poked his arm. When he looked up from the paper he'd been poring over she pointed to the three new arrivals. He said "Hey people, we've got company!"

Everyone stopped what they were doing and looked toward the front of the room. Johnny figured this must be what it felt like in a fishbowl, with all eyes turned to him and Linda. They all said "Hello Dot!"

"Hello yourselves," she replied. "Good to see all of you again. This is Johnny Redwine and Linda Smith. They are here last because they've been on assignment. Make them welcome. They're part of our team."

The pretty blonde Johnny had noticed stood up. "Welcome you two! Come sit with us."

Linda joined the table where they had been invited, and Johnny went to another table. As soon as he was seated, Dot called out: "Everyone, land at a table. For now it doesn't matter where. No smoking during class time. Move it. Now!"

The people along the wall quickly put out their smokes and headed for tables. Dot walked to the front of the big desk and sat down on it. Everyone fell silent.

"It's time to answer some of the questions you may all have. For security reasons we had to wait until you arrived.

You're now on an estate purchased and fixed up for our purposes by the Committee. It will be your home for the next 6 to 8 weeks. While you're here, starting in the morning, you'll have all clothing provided for you. You have freedom to move about the building and the grounds. However, no one is permitted to leave the grounds alone. All activities outside the grounds will be done as a group. During the time you are here you will learn a variety of subjects including advanced first aid and cooking. If outside instructors are brought in, they will be told you're Forest Service Wildlife Firefighter trainees. Be careful not to do or say anything that might let them think otherwise.

Among your group is one registered nurse, several cooks, and some Vietnam vets. By the end of the week, you will be broken down into 9 groups of 4 personnel each. The group formations have already been planned out. The only thing left to determine is who the group commander will be. The groups will consist of people whose counties border each other.

Tomorrow morning your first classes will begin. You will learn about the human body and how it functions. You'll have films, discussions and reading. At 4 pm you will all report to the local YMCA where you will swim, play basketball, lift weights, etc. Questions?"

"Where are we going from here?" one guy asked.

"You'll attend combat training in Eastern Oregon. Where you're going is desolate and we will be largely dependent on ourselves. That is why all of the training you receive here will be so important. We're going to prepare you for survival in the high desert."

"What if one of us decides this program sucks and we want out?"

All eyes turned to the questioner.

"You can quit. However, if you say one damn word to anyone about what we're doing, one of us will run you down and kill you. Do I make myself clear?" Dot asked in all seriousness.

"Yes ma'am. You sure do."

"Good. As stated, no smoking during class. Lights out at 10 pm weekdays, and midnight on weekends. Ladies and gentlemen, you will not be cavorting, dating, or in any way engaging in romantic activity. We can't have anyone turning up in the family way."

A snicker passed through the room. Dot's eyes turned to ice.

"It's not an amusing subject. If anyone is caught violating this rule you will be gone. You're all healthy people. You're also sensible. That's why we picked you. You're going to have to curb your impulses for the next few months. We can be forceful in making sure this rule isn't broken if needed. However, I imagine you're all going to be too damn tired anyway."

The room was silent for a moment. Then someone asked "how are team leaders being picked?"

"The team leader will be responsible for ensuring his or her group is on time, in order and carries out assignments. For a team member who is late for class or does not complete an assignment on time, the consequence will be 50 pushups for each minute late. The team leader will be doing them right alongside the violator." Dot smiled.

"Are we going to be here 7 days a week?"

"No. In fact, for anyone who wants them, we have tickets to all the home Trail Blazer games while you're in town. For those who don't care about the ball games we'll get you to the movies or the disco for dancing. We have trips scheduled to the Oregon Zoo and the Oregon Museum of Science and Industry. You should find the trips fun and informative.

You'll be allowed to use cars, but God be with any of you who causes an accident or gets a ticket." Dot paused. "Any more questions?"

Her gaze moved around the room. She finally slid down from her seat on the desk.

"All right, since there are no more questions let's move on. Right now, each of you will stand up and state your name, age and hometown. This will get everyone identified to everyone else. Johnny, you're the youngest and newest, so we'll start with you."

Johnny felt like throwing something at her. The last thing he wanted was to get up and stand like a statue in front of all these people. Slowly he got to his feet, hoping his knees wouldn't fail. He gave his name, age and hometown as ordered then quickly sat down. He watched as one by one the others were on the spot. He discovered the long lean kid was Roy Errickson from Salem and he was 26 years old. The pretty blonde was Amanda Dail from Roseburg and she was 21. A lovely redhead near the back of the room identified herself as Carolyn Post, 25, of La Grande. A tall brown haired girl stated she was Charlotte Matson, 24, of Astoria. A gorgeous black woman named Paula caught Johnny's eye. So it went, 26 boys and 10 girls. They all felt better when it was over. Johnny expected the personality of each would start coming through after this.

The rest of the morning was used to give information such as room assignments and meal times. Finally they were given a tour of the building. It featured, among other things, 2 fully equipped game rooms, two lounges with easy chairs and color tv's, and a fully equipped modern kitchen. There was even a laundromat in the basement. When they had passed through the kitchen a man and woman had been there busily preparing lunch. They had not stopped to greet the students.

Back in the day room, Dot said "Starting Monday, all kitchen duties will be assigned to teams. One team will cover one week, then it will move to the next team, and so on. Team leaders will be responsible for ordering supplies and seeing to it that the work is kept up."

"What if someone gets sick?"

"As stated, we are fortunate enough to have a nurse in our midst." Dot looked at the tall brown haired girl. "Charlotte, please stand."

"She can be my nurse anytime," some guy said, and laughter filled the air. Dot visibly fought a smile, but said in all seriousness, "unacceptable. The women on your team are your colleagues, not your dates."

"Yeah, try to stay healthy," Charlotte said, and sat down.

"We have medical reports and know you are all in good health. If you do get a cold or other illness let your team leader know. Stay in your room so you don't infect others and rest. Anything else?"

Johnny brought up something he figured might be on everyone's mind. Money.

"I understand we're on the payroll. How much and when do we get paid?"

"Everyone starts at $600 a month during the time you're in training. You'll have little need for money. Pay day is the first of each month. We encourage you to take out only a small draw. Save as much as possible so when training is over and you head out to communities you'll have a healthy stake. You'll be given the opportunity on Fridays to submit requests for pay, which will be brought to you. While we're talking about money," Dot said while looking around, "gambling with cash is strictly forbidden. We know there are some damn good card players among you, and we're not about to have people losing their paychecks in card games."

"When do we eat?" asked the tall lean guy.

"You're not going to starve," Dot replied. "Lunch is in half an hour. You're all on free time until then. Be back here at 1 p.m.

Chapter 9

Johnny opened another package of steaks and handed them to Linda.

"Thanks," she said. "Can you make sure the milk supply is still good please?"

Johnny walked toward the huge walk in freezer at the other end of the room. He passed Roy Erickson who was busy preparing a salad. Johnny pulled his apron strings loose and quickly jumped away.

"Hey ya bastard!" Erickson said, and threw a piece of carrot at him.

"If I find a finger in the salad I'm kicking your ass!" Johnny replied as he kept walking.

"Keep messing with me and it'll be your head in the salad."

The two men in group 3 were grinning at each other. They were in the third week of training, and all routines were now established. Erickson and Johnny had gotten to be close friends. Erickson was 26, and a former marine with combat experience in Vietnam. He had some interesting war stories to tell.

"I have to go check the milk supply for Linda," Johnny said. "Finish your salad."

Johnny opened the big door and walked into the cold room. He hated this place. He had dreams of the door closing and finding himself trapped. Death would be slow and miserable. He remembered that he'd be missed pretty quickly and someone would come check on him. Preparing meals for almost 40 people was a job that required teamwork.

He found and counted the milk cans. They got the milk delivered 10 cans at a time and 6 remained. While there he noted that there were only 2 crates of eggs left. He made a mental note to tell Linda so she could order more. Linda had been named team leader. Amanda Diall rounded out the group.

Johnny came out of the cold storage room and closed the door. He walked back up past Erickson, who eyed him suspiciously as he passed. He made the report to Linda then busied himself helping Amanda set the tables.

Amanda was 21. She was the blonde he noticed when they arrived. She had a pleasant personality that made her easy to work with. Johnny felt sorry for Roy, who was hopelessly in love with her and nothing could be done about it. They were both firmly committed to their work. However, Roy had said more than once if he got a chance, to hell with the rules, he would take it. At this moment, Johnny observed Roy talking to Linda, and he smiled thinking of their prior conversations. Amanda noticed the smile.

"You got a thing for Erickson, Johnny?"

"Oh for Pete's sake," he said.

Amanda laughed and passed him more plates. He took them and quickly got out of the area. Amanda loved to catch him off guard and embarrass the daylights out of him. He didn't mind too much, because she wasn't vicious about it.

He walked around the tables placing the plates. He thought about his companions on the other side of the wall in the kitchen. They were the closest thing to a family he had. They also thought of this team as family. He had no doubt that in the coming months individual feuds would develop. He had been in this world long enough to know that was always possible in a close knit group. However, he had reached the point where he'd be willing to give his life for any of them. He knew they felt the same way. So, knowing a sort of happiness like he had not known before, had strolled back into the kitchen and presented himself to Linda for his next assignment.

"Get rid of the garbage, Johnny, then we can eat."

The kitchen crew always had family meals prior to everyone else. That way, they were free to serve when the others arrived. Naturally, they bitched about the cooking or the service. The kitchen crew gave it right back to them.

This was the Wednesday evening meal. They only had 4 more days on kitchen duty. The rest of the candidates were in physical training at the Y. They would be back soon from their basketball games, weight lifting, swimming, etc. and ready to eat.

Johnny finished with the last garbage can and washed up at a washroom off to one side of the kitchen. He came out to find the team already seated at the table. He grabbed up his equipment and served them from the bar. Johnny had never been a big eater, but the routine of daily drills had given him the appetite of a horse. He speared a large steak with his fork, then helped himself to a liberal helping of mashed potatoes and gravy. He shoveled on peas and corn, then grabbed up 2 slices of toast. He carried it to the table and poured a glass of cold milk from a pitcher. In the time he had been there, like all the others, he had gained weight. With the exercise and healthy eating he knew it was muscle instead of flab.

"What do you think of that guy Cain?" Amanda asked Linda.

"Rougher than hell," she said.

"That's the way with those Marines," Johnny offered. "They claim they build the best fighting force in the world."

"Marines are also the best lovers in the world," Roy said.

"What would you know about it?" Amanda teased.

"Give me half a chance and I'll be happy to demonstrate."

"Half a chance wouldn't do it, Roy," Amanda teased. "You'd only get the job half done."

"Marines are half-assed lovers," Linda said.

Erickson looked incredulous, then looked at Johnny for help. Johnny grinned at his friend. "You're not getting me into this," he said, then kept on eating.

Roy shook his head. "Sometimes I think you're helpless, boy. Stick with me and I'll straighten you out."

They had hardly finished with family meals when they heard the sound of their classmates returning.

Linda said, "I hear the sound of the thundering herd. Let's hit it gang. I fear what they might do if the food isn't here when they land."

Group 3 got busy and stayed that way for the next 45 minutes. Dinner was at 5:30 sharp. The first group roared through the door at 5:29. The drill was for Roy and Linda to serve plates as everyone came by with their plates. Johnny and Amanda made sure extra platters of meat were passed to the servers as needed. When all were served, they got busy storing leftovers, leaving out a bit for those wanting seconds.

It didn't take long, it seemed, until the trays and dirty dishes started coming back. Now, Johnny and Amanda started scraping plates, pouring out unfinished liquids, and stacking dishes for their trips through the big industrial dishwashers and dryers.

"I sure hope we have equipment like this wherever we're going," said Johnny.

"That would be nice," Amanda said. "Even if we don't, we'll make it somehow."

By 7:00 p.m. the last dish was done and put away. The last tray was stacked and the leftovers were wrapped and stored. Leftovers were tossed on the weekends, or eaten by the kitchen crews snacking. Occasionally, groups held ice box raids late at night. The last group caught doing that had to work off the extra weight by doing 50 pushups for Cain in the hallway.

Johnny and Amanda fell into chairs by the table. They drank coffee and planned for the next morning. Breakfast was due at 6:30 a.m. The kitchen crew started at 5 am to get everything ready and have their own meals. Kitchen duty meant they were excused from morning exercise class at 5:30 in the day room. In order to shower and get their rooms straight they had to be up by 4 a.m. Cain had a policy that was carried out by all instructors of holding morning inspections. God help anyone who was caught with a sloppy room. Not only would the candidate suffer, but the team leader as well. It had only happened once, and word had gotten around fast.

Amanda exclaimed "Damn! I'll be glad when this week is over and group 4 takes it."

"I second that," said Roy.

Linda looked up from her notepad. "Alright, gang. Here's your assignments for the morning." She tore off slips of paper and passed them around. The first morning, they had run into some confusion when they hadn't assigned work in advance. As a result, breakfast was 15 minutes late. It was an elemental mistake but they learned and had no plans to make the same mistake twice. Johnny put his paper into his shirt pocket without looking at it. He would just forget anyway.

Linda looked around the group. "Any gripes? Suggestions?"

This was the time to bring up any gripe that one may have had during the day. It was also the time to make any suggestion that might streamline the work. For team 3, things had gone amazingly well after that first error. Tonight, no one had gripes or suggestions. Linda stood up. "Thank you for a job well done, gang. See you in the morning."

They all got tiredly to their feet and trudged toward the door. Linda followed them out and shut off the lights. Johnny climbed the stairs behind Roy and headed for his room. The group members roomed next to each other. They had private rooms here. However, they had been given notice that private rooms would not be available where they were going next. Roy's room was next to Johnny's. They both stopped in front of Roy's door and watched Amanda walk by. She knew they were watching her. She stopped at her door and turned around.

"Goodnight men," she said, and passed through her door. They heard the bolt close.

"Damn," said Roy. "One of these nights she's going to forget that bolt."

Linda stopped at her door a few feet away. "Unacceptable, boys. You are too damned horny for your own good. Amanda is your colleague. Take care of yourselves and leave her alone."

"Want to help us out?" Roy asked.

"Not a chance," Linda replied.

Roy turned back to Johnny as Linda disappeared into her room.

"I'm going to read awhile, then hit the rack," he said.

"Likewise," Johnny answered. "See you in the morning."

"Goodnight, kid. Watch out for the wet dreams," Roy teased.

"Screw you," Johnny replied, and turned to his own door. He went in, closed the door and fell on his rack. He reached over and turned on the lamp by the bed, picked up the alarm clock, and wound it. He sat up and removed his boots, dropping them by the foot of the bed. He placed his clothes on a chair and stretched out on the bed. He pulled a book out from under his pillow and opened it to the marker.

Reading was a new habit he had picked up. He had borrowed this book from Linda, after she mentioned how much she enjoyed reading. It was an adventure novel called "South by Java Head" by Alistair McClean. He hoped she had more adventure books stashed somewhere. He found reading one of the most enjoyable things he had ever done. He read 3 chapters, placed the book on his night stand, and got under the covers. He switched off his light, and was sound asleep in 2 minutes.

Chapter 10

Luther Sherman halted his Jeep on top of the hill. He turned off the engine and climbed out into a cold, raw February wind. The weak afternoon sun held little warmth. He reached back into the Jeep and brought out a leather case, put it on the hood of the Jeep and brought out the telescope. He stepped around the front of the vehicle and brought the scope up. He adjusted the focus and then locked in on the big truck working its way along the road a few miles away. He saw instantly that it was a transport rig built for hauling cars. Its cargo was not visible because they were covered with canvas.

The truck left the narrow road that ran along the lake and came slowly toward a cluster of buildings. It traveled for another mile and a half before halting near a large building where some other vehicles were already stored. He knew they were there because he had seen them arrive. For 2 months now, he'd been checking on the progress of this development. He had quickly deduced that this was a military base camp probably organized by the National Guard. He could think of no other reason why the regular army would want to do anything way out here.

Sherman was standing on a hill in Lake County, Oregon. He was west of Summer Lake, looking across at the camp. Slowly, he lowered the scope and speculated on the cargo. Judging from the size of the individual covers, they were probably Jeeps. What he wanted to know was whether or not these Jeeps were equipped with the heavy 50 caliber machine guns he had used in Korea. If so, he was going to set up a complaint. He didn't want Jeeps running around this country blowing the hell out of everything in sight. He was too aware of how some soldiers acted with that kind of weapon. He had done it too many times himself. He had two thousand beef cows to look out for. He couldn't promise that one of them might not wander into whatever range these people planned to use. He was not anxious to have his cows used as targets.

When Sherman raised his scope again, he saw that two men were now up on the rig loosening the canvas covers. He watched as the first cover came away, exposing the military Jeep with Oregon National Guard markings and no machine gun. He breathed a sigh of relief.

He'd first become aware of activity here a few weeks before Christmas. He'd been up here looking for one of his prize bulls that had wandered off. He'd been standing in this very spot, actually, looking around with his scope when he had seen the men working on the old Rockwell home. Curious, he'd watched until the cold December wind that was sweeping over the hilltop forced him back into his Jeep. He'd found the bull a few minutes later. Two days later, he had driven purposefully back up here for another look. They were still working away, and he was amazed at the progress made in only a few days.

The old house they were working on had been deserted for years. The last person to live in it was old man Rockwell who had died in 1956. At one time, the Rockwell place had been a small but productive ranch. It only covered 400 acres, small by some standards but nice around here. Far off relatives wanted nothing to do with the place, but they had priced it so damn high no one else could afford it. For 21 years the land went to weeds, and the house was falling apart. Sherman had been in it many times. He and Bobby Rockwell had shipped out to Korea together. Bobby had died within 2 weeks after they arrived. One month later, Sherman had lost a leg when his Jeep hit a landmine. He had returned home to Summer Lake in 1953 and remained on the family ranch. He still worked it with his aging parents and his wife, Susan.

All of the Jeeps stood exposed on the carrier. The two men were now running down a ramp to unload. Sherman returned his scope to its case, then got back into his Jeep out of the wind and left the hilltop. He would make another inspection in a few days.

At the camp, Boxer drove the last Jeep into the garage and parked it with the others. This building held the five newly-arrived Jeeps, a large transport for troops, and two four door sedans. He got out of the Jeep and walked over to the pegboard where he hung the keys. He turned to a man who was inspecting the papers on each rig.

"Everything in now?"

Doctor Fish put down the papers he was looking at. He picked up his pipe from the desk and started packing it. "Yes, it's all in. By tomorrow the final electrical work should be done, and the day after that the painting should be finished."

"Did all the bugs get worked out of the water system?" Boxer asked.

"Yes, water should be no problem."

"Alright. I'll bum a cup of coffee from the kitchen and then get that damn truck back to Eugene." Boxer looked tired.

"You're going to try and drive all the way back?" Doctor Fish asked.

"I'm going back over the Diamond Lake cutoff, so I'll probably grab a room in Roseburg tonight."

"OK. When you get to Roseburg call the Portland number and let them know all is in place."

"Maybe everything's in place," Boxer replied, "but all is not well. Ronsen told me some guy's been watching us through a telescope from across the lake." Ronsen was an electrician and had noticed the man some weeks back. He'd reported the situation to Fish and was disturbed that nothing had been done about it. Boxer had arrived while Rosen was in the shop filing a report . While Fish had been up on the truck, he had taken Boxer aside to point out what was going on.

"Ronsen worries too much," Fish said. "He told me several weeks ago we were being watched. I checked him out and he is just a concerned rancher."

"What's he concerned about?"

"He's worried the soldier boys are going to be running around the countryside blowing the hell out of his cows with 50 calibers," Fish said.

"You contact him?"

"No. I'm known in the little Summer Lake town as Major Howard. I seldom go there for anything, but when I do that's my alias. The store owner and the gas station owner expressed concern. I let the word get around that we wouldn't be using any heavy weapons and that any shooting would go on near Wildcat Mountain. Apparently he hasn't gotten word yet."

"Any chance some local might check to see if we're real Guardsmen?"

"It's a small risk," Fish replied. "Very small. This place is a long way from anything."

"I hope to shout," Boxer replied. "I had no idea Oregon had so much empty space."

"Fly over this area sometime and take a close look, Boxer. You'll be surprised. A man could stash 4 fully equipped divisions in this damn county alone. The people around here are not likely to say anything unless we're so brazenly stupid as to get their suspicions up."

"Will the candidates have any contact with the locals?" Boxer asked.

"Not if we can help it. I wouldn't want one of them to let something slip. I can't guarantee 36 people will keep quiet."

Boxer moved toward the door. "I'm going after that coffee. You coming?"

"I believe I will," Fish said.

Boxer walked out the big doors with Fish trailing along behind. Boxer stopped by the fender of the transport and looked down the road he had arrived on. "That's a pretty lake down there."

"Sure is. The candidates will get to use it this summer for swimming and boating."

Boxer shivered in the cold wind. "You mean they have summer in this God forsaken place?"

Fish said, "You'll be here in July and part of August. Tell me about summer when you get back."

They proceeded to find coffee.

Chapter 11

Doctor Fish, now acting as Major William Howard, drove the green Chevy sedan carefully along the dirt road that skirted Summer Lake. It was a cold clear day with a winter sun hardly showing. They had freezing rain most of yesterday, but the puddles in the road were iced over. He was beginning to wish he had brought one of the Jeeps. They were marked, and this car was not. Impersonating a National Guard officer was one thing, but driving a plainly marked Jeep on a state highway was too far.

He did not look like a Major, but he had the ID of one ready to show any rancher or townsmen who wanted to see it. He was dressed in olive drab coveralls with no markings, and would've passed inspection anywhere if it wasn't too close. His knowledge of human behavior told him that nobody around here would be doing any inspecting.

It was one week until the candidates were due to arrive. All that could be done at the base camp was done. All electrical and sanitation problems were worked out and settled. The water supply was working. His tests had determined it to be safe. Today he was on a public relations trip. He was going to make a couple of contacts in the little town of Summer Lake, and then pay a visit to some ranchers who had concerns about having the Guard in the area.

Fish turned right off the lakeshore road onto state route 31. As he gained speed, dirt flew off the tires and clattered against the insides of the fenders. The lake to his right was about 3 miles wide, with marshland to the north. To his left were hills and fields. He marveled again at the beauty of the land. While working on something at base camp he would stop and listen to the land. Mostly he heard wind, and marveled that this must be what the Natives also saw and heard hundreds of years ago.

The remoteness could also be unnerving to a city man. He turned on the car radio. He dialed around until he picked up a far off station. He hoped the candidates could handle it. It was up to Cain, Abel and the others to prepare them.

The station identified itself as KBND out of Bend, Oregon. It went into an ad for a local Ford dealer. He half listened, for his mind was not on new Fords. It was on the task that lay ahead. Simply put, the task was to reassure the locals they had nothing to worry about. A year and a half of careful planning had gone into this camp. The site was probably not the best they could find. The ideal place would have been completely secret. Yet in a free society where people had freedom of movement, even in a remote place it would have been impossible to keep secret.

The committee had chosen this spot with several factors in mind. Food, water, and a place for the candidates to let off steam on their one day off. The lake would be good for swimming, fishing, and boating. It had some risks, but Dr. Fish, now posing as Major Howard, would minimize the risk as much as possible.

Fish came to a stop in the graveled parking lot of Effie's Restaurant. He had only been in the town of Summer Lake a couple of times, but he knew that the original Effie was not involved in the business anymore. The little restaurant, the Union 76 gas station across the road, and the General Store were all owned by Billy Pratt. Pratt was a blowhard who loved to talk, and was kind of a spokesman for the locals. So, whenever Major Howard paid Summer Lake a visit, he saw Pratt and his friend John Wilson. They mostly got into bullshit sessions.

One other rig was in the parking lot. It was a late model Ford Ranger pickup, property of some rancher from out in the sticks. Fish got out of the Chevy, and noted it was just as cold here as it had been at base. He walked across the gravel, his footsteps loud in the morning quiet. It was 10 a.m. this February morning, and all he could hear was the sound of the wind, and a dog barking far off somewhere.

He opened the dirty glass door and went into Effie's. There was just one customer seated at the counter, the probable owner of the pickup. Ellen Pratt, the pretty 19 year old daughter of Billy and his wife Thelma, was seated in a booth reading a magazine. As he came in, she looked up and smiled.

"Good morning Major Howard," Ellen said, and stood up.

The guy at the counter turned and looked. He was a weather beaten man, one of the outdoorsy types he'd seen around here. These folks were mostly ranchers who spent little time indoors.

"Good morning, Ellen. I need a cup of black coffee and a couple of those maple bars your Mom makes." Fish walked over and sat down near the rancher at the counter, who was polishing off bacon and eggs. "Good morning. I'm Major William Howard from the camp on the other side of the lake."

"Marlin Thomas," the man replied, and they shook hands.

Ellen put his coffee and maple bars on the counter in front of him. Howard put a dollar on the counter and said "Keep the change."

"Thank you," Ellen said. "Let me know if you need anything else."

"Thanks, I will," he replied. Fish turned to the rancher. "Where's your place at, Mr. Thomas?"

"Oh, I'm back down toward the lake a couple of miles. Little place on the right as they're going out. My sign says XYB Ranch."

"I saw it," Fish replied. "Darn fine looking place."

"We try to keep it looking good," Thomas said. "Me and my wife, we've worked at that place now for 25 years." He looked at his now empty plate. "My wife went to help our daughter out this morning and I was too lazy to cook."

"I understand," Fish replied.

Thomas took out a pack of Camels and offered the doctor one. He shook his head no thanks. "Mind if I ask what you soldier boys are up to over there, Major?"

"I'll be glad to answer any questions you have, Mr. Thomas."

"Well, I was in the Army for 4 years during World War II. Damned if putting a military camp in a place like that makes any sense. It's so damned far from anything, and that country is so broken back there you couldn't have a decent firing range."

Fish hoped his answer would sound reasonable. He'd designed it knowing the people here were politically conservative. "I can't say much, but I'll tell you one thing. This isn't a run of the mill bunch we're bringing up here."

He had them. Even Ellen had lowered her magazine and was all ears. Fish paused for the effect to sink in. He took a bite of his maple bar and chased it with a swig of coffee.

"Well, go on," Mr. Thomas said.

"My bosses are darn good military men," Fish continued. "However, the military in this country is run by civilians. Sometimes that's good, sometimes it's bad. The military men often see things long before the politicians who run them. When the military finds things, they can have a hell of a time convincing the politicians who control the money to see it their way. When the politicians are convinced, then there's a vote. Well, a few years back some forward looking men got together and decided this country was on a downhill slide. They could see the day when another depression would happen. It was obvious to them that the day would come when it would be necessary to our national survival to go in and take other nations' oil wells by force. A full scale invasion would be just plain silly. They'd blow the wells up before one man had time to make footprints in the sand."

Fish paused, took a bite and drink, and gathered his thoughts. He had them. They were hanging on every word he said.

"These men knew our forces were in no shape to fight a desert war. They were fresh out of the jungles of Vietnam. All of the training and equipment for years had been geared to jungle fighting. To retrain the whole military as desert fighters was not reasonable. They got recruits from the military schools. They decided to train and equip a small but highly elite force who could be dropped over a desert and be totally trained in how to support themselves."

Thomas had put out his Camel, now he took out another. "I had some West Point officers in World War II, and they impressed me. What I hated were those damn 90 day wonders."

Fish replied, "Unfortunately the 90 day wonders were somewhat necessary. We had a critical shortage of officers. These people are young and professional. I can't go into specifics about the training program. What I can tell you is there are several bases being established around the country for just this purpose. To save money, the National Guard is being used in individual states. That's why I'm up here building a school."

"How come I ain't heard nothing about it on the radio or TV?"

"That should be obvious, Mr. Thomas. The liberals in Congress and the press would have a fit and fall in it."

"Well how do they plan to keep those nosy committee members in Congress from finding out?"

"The military has ways of running things and keeping it quiet. All of us as taxpayers know that. It will be found out eventually, but by that time they will have their tracks covered."

"What about the governor and his people? Do they know about this?"

"Only a few people in Salem know about it. Very little Oregon money is being used so they don't have to talk about it much. When the camp is finished, I leave, my crew leaves, and Oregon is finished with it. They have their own instructors. They're using some of our Jeeps and one of our helicopters."

Fish saw a look of disappointment cross Ellen's face. It was obvious she would've liked to see some soldier boys. Probably the more, the merrier.

"One more thing I want to ask you about, Major."

"Go right ahead, Mr. Thomas."

"What kind of weapons are those boys going to be training with?"

"Boys and girls, Mr. Thomas. Even the military is co-ed nowadays."

Ellen spoke up. "How many girls are there?"

"I couldn't say," Fish replied.

"Well, I hope there's a girl shortage."

Fish made a mental note to have this one watched. One girl like this could raise hell. He turned back to Mr. Thomas. "To answer your question, submachine guns and semi automatic rifles. In my experience, it's not reasonable to load down a quick strike force with heavy weapons. We learned that painful lesson from the Viet Cong. They fought 90% of the war with rifles. Their best anti aircraft gun was a 50 caliber machine gun."

"I heard you were going to be doing all your shooting back around 10 Mile Butte and Wildcat Mountain."

"That's about right," Fish answered. "We've laid out a couple small ranges. On that note, Mr. Thomas, pass the word that if anyone has a gripe with the base or its personnel to contact the base commander. They don't want anyone calling Salem or Washington with a complaint." He slid off the stool and held his hand out to the rancher. "It's been a pleasure meeting you, Mr. Thomas."

Thomas took his hand and shook it warmly. "The pleasure's mine, Major."

Fish turned to Ellen. "Tell you folks hi for me, and I'm sorry I missed them. I'll be back in a day or so."

Chapter 12

Dot leaned back in her desk chair and looked at the candidates in front of her. They were all gathered in the Day Room knowing that today they would find out just where all this was leading them. They were a lean looking bunch, as the many weeks of training had made them fit. Johnny Redwine, for example, had grown an inch taller and gained 15 pounds. He filled out his 6 foot 1 frame quite well. Linda and Carolyn had never looked better. Dot smiled at them, for she was pleased at all they'd accomplished so far.

"Alright gang," Dot began. "It's time I clue you in on a few things. One week from today you'll rise bright and early at the usual 5 a.m. Weather permitting, we'll bus you out to the airport where you'll board a Huey 53 helicopter and fly to your new base. You Vietnam vets will know that bird. You're going to a place that's close to a large lake and not much else. All of the things you're used to will be absent. No TV. The nearest hospital is 150 miles away. Now you know why we made EMT 2's out of you. Be careful at all times, because serious injury could result in death. In the event of a major disaster, which we hope to God won't happen, we will do our best to evacuate you. Phone service will not be available to us. All communications will happen by radio. With no phone, you won't be able to call the fire department, so be careful with fires at all times. You do not want to burn down the whole damn base. You'll receive further instructions when you arrive. Questions?"

Charlotte the RN asked: "You said this place is near a lake? Will we be allowed to swim there?"

"Yes you will. Also, there will be fishing equipment and boats available."

Rodger Davidson, a 21 year old from Ontario, asked "How long does it take to get there?"

"About two and a half hours by helicopter," Dot answered. She waited for more questions, and when none were forthcoming she stood up. "Today you're starting classes on some of the tools you'll be using at your camp. We'll start with the Browning 9 mm handgun. You'll each be issued one and will carry it at all times. Your rifles will be the M16, which is standard issue in the American military. Finally, you'll learn the Uzi 9mm machine gun. It's manufactured in Israel and is a fine weapon. It's standard issue in about 5 armies. Let's start with the Browning."

Dot produced one from her desk. She walked over to the nearest group and placed it on the table. "Take a look and pass it around. When you've all had a chance to examine it, we will field strip it and put it back together again. We'll practice until each of you can do this in your sleep."

Everyone had a chance to examine the gun. Then class began in earnest. Dot started by drawing a detailed picture of the weapon on her blackboard. She then took the weapon apart, showing each part in detail so everyone could familiarize themselves with its look outside the gun. This process would be repeated until everyone could identify each part at a glance.

From an instructor's viewpoint, it was slow and boring. Yet it was necessary in the forming of a fighting force. Over the next week, Dot would repeat the process with the M16 and the Uzi. When they boarded the helicopter each of them would be fully familiar with all the weapons. Then, over the next few months at Summer Lake they would learn how to fire them. Cain, Abel, Boxer and herself would be their teachers. She was certain they would excel. Then they would be unleashed on an unsuspecting bunch of death dealers who would start feeling the sting of what real justice should be. Dot's only regret was that their deaths were going to be too quick. Quick death was better than nothing at all, though. Next week, she and Boxer would pay a visit to a house in Roseburg. The world would again hear of the Cleanup Committee.

Chapter 13

"No breakfast will be served here, except coffee and pastries," Abel had said. "Departure is 0530 sharp. You'll bring nothing but the clothes on your backs. New clothing will be issued upon arrival. When we arrive, breakfast will be waiting. It will be prepared by the people serving the construction crews. They will leave on the bird when we arrive. You are to have no conversations with them. They will not approach you. Any questions?"

Kyle Zimmer, a 23 year old from Baker City, was in group 9. "Can you tell us where we're going?" he asked.

"You'll be advised of that after boarding." Abel looked around the room for more questions. When he saw none were forthcoming, he dismissed them for the evening.

When they had arrived at the airfield early this morning, Johnny had climbed down from the bus, taken one look at the helicopter and wished he were anywhere but there. It was sitting on its pad looking like a giant bug, lit up like a Christmas tree in the mist. Reactions varied in the group from "Groovy!" to "Good God!"

"Hush your talk and form up!" Abel shouted.

Abel had relieved Dot last night. She had told them goodbye for now and wished them success. She promised to see them again in a couple of months. Abel had given them the drill for the next morning.

Abel formed them up in two lines and marched them to the helicopter. They were seated in order of groups. Johnny, still wishing he was anywhere but here, turned to Linda.

"Have you ever flown before?"

"No," Linda replied. "Have you?"

"No, and I'm not among the happier people in the world right now."

"Don't worry, kid," Roy Errickson said from behind him. "We'll be alright. Unless the Jesus Screw comes loose."

Johnny turned slightly and looked at Roy in the cabin lights. He was trying to tell if this was one of Roy's jokes, but he wasn't sure from the look on his face. "Alright, I'll bite. What is a Jesus Screw?"

"That's the bolt that holds those big blades in place. If it flies loose, it's curtains."

Linda threw Roy a side eye. "You're just bubbling over with good cheer this morning."

"I do my best to please at all times, ma'am," Roy replied.

From across the aisle someone asked, "You putting us on, Errickson?"

"Me? Would I do something like that?" Roy asked. "Ask old Terry Stout, he flew on these things with me in Vietnam."

The pilot started the helicopter, and further conversation was impossible except with your closest neighbor. It clattered and rattled until Johnny and a half dozen more would've given anything to get out and walk. By that time it was too late. The chopper was 50 feet up and rising fast.

They had been airborne for about 20 minutes when Abel stood up and walked forward. He picked up a mic and they heard the public address system click on.

"Listen up you scaredy cats," Abel said. "You're going to a place most of you have never heard of. It's called Summer Lake. It's in eastern central Oregon. As we've said before, it's not close to anything. You folks are going to be on your own.They've built a nice camp for us. When we land, we'll be on the lake side of the motor pool area. Don't anyone get anxious and charge for the door when we land. We will disembark in an orderly fashion. Remember, keep your heads down. We don't want any blood on the blades. They might gum up and quit working."

Something resembling laughter passed through the chopper. Most people ignored it. Abel had an odd sense of humor. He continued: "After you've all had a chance to feed your faces, we'll meet in a predetermined area and discuss what we're going to do here. You'll be issued new threads. Get ready to look like soldiers."

Cat calls and boos greeted this announcement by the former Marines in the crowd.

"I know, I know," Abel said. "This is what the powers that be want. By the way, if any of you scaredy cats can somehow manage to look to your left, you'll see the 11,200 foot Mount Hood sticking up there. Let's hope the pilot doesn't hit it. That would sure be messy."

Abel put down the mic and returned to his seat. His last attempt at humor fell on its face. Some of them looked, but for the most part they ignored it and settled in. This was a rare chance to get some extra shut eye. Even those who found the noise offensive in the first few minutes now accepted that they were too far up to step out, so they settled down too. It was a quiet flight from there on out.

Toward the end of the flight Abel stood up and walked to the mic again. "In about 2 minutes, we'll be passing over Summer Lake. 4 minutes to touchdown. Remain seated until you're told to move."

"Deer!" Johnny said when he saw the buck.

Linda woke up with a start. She had somehow slept through Abel's announcements. "What the hell?" she said.

Johnny pulled back from the window. As he did so, he heard Amanda saying "Watch that, Roy." Johnny grinned. Errickson was still trying.

"We're about to land," Johnny told Linda. "I saw a deer as we passed over the lake. Looked like a big guy."

"Hey, we're coming in," Amanda said.

The helicopter swept in low over the lake. Its blades set up a breeze that made the water under it choppy, sending out thousands of little ripples in every direction. An early morning sun reflected off the chopper's whirling blades and silver paint. If anyone had cared to watch they may have found it to be a pretty sight, but on this particular February 28th, no one was out to watch. There was only a lone mule deer getting himself an early morning drink from the lake. As the noisy machine passed over him, he bolted. In his 4 years he had never heard such a sound.

From 300 feet up, several anxious people looked down at the lake and breathed a sigh of relief. They were more than happy to see the lake, for they knew now in a few short minutes they would be on the ground and out. One of those who looked and sighed was Johnny Redwine. He was leaning over Linda Smith, who was sound asleep, and looking down at the blue water of the lake. He caught a glance at the big mule deer as it bolted and ran. They watched the ground come up at them at what seemed like an alarming rate. When the chopper sat down on its pad, it was a surprisingly easy landing. The pilot shut off the engine and they all sat listening to the big blades slowly winding down. Johnny wondered if he was ever going to be able to hear again. Finally, the blades fell silent. The silence was just as deafening. Abel stood up.

"Welcome to Camp Summer Lake," he said. "Behind you is a gravel road that leads from the lakeshore road and passes here to where our firing ranges are near 10 Mile Butte. To your right is the motor pool area. On the other side of that is the building where you'll eat and sleep, and not much else. Past that is the camp arsenal. You'll all get a chance to see it later. Now, get off this bird the way you came on. Team 1 first. Keep your heads down until you are clear of the blades. Team leaders, form your people up on that gravel road. Face them to what is now your right. Wait for me at attention. Dismissed!"

They were all off the bird in 5 minutes. Linda double timed her team to the road and formed them up with the others. They stood in the road and waited while Abel spoke with the pilot. They stood in a cold, raw wind. The sun was up but it gave little warmth. Frost covered everything. Except for the quiet voices of the pilot and Abel it was almost silent. It was the kind of quiet these people had never known before. Like Doctor Fish before them, they now heard it and tried to understand it. They waited, listening, and occasionally shivered.

Abel ended his conversation and slowly approached the group. They stood at rigid attention with eyes forward, blinking against the sun. Abel walked onto the road and stopped a few feet in front of teams 1 and 2.

"Damn!" he shouted. His voice echoed off the nearby hills. It was terribly loud in the early morning. "You people are the sorriest looking bunch of so-and-sos I have ever seen."

Here we go, thought Johnny. This was part of the drill and discipline of the Marines. They knew how to react, for they'd been doing this for several weeks.

"No Sir!" they shouted back.

Abel put a hand up to his ears. "What say?"

"No Sir!" they shouted again, their voices shattering the air.

"Are you arguing with me?"

"No Sir!" they shouted.

"Well I think you are," Abel shouted back. "50 pushups here and now. Go!"

Not one person stopped to think about the cold gravel, and how uncomfortable it was going to be. They got down and did the pushups, for failure to comply would have meant 50 more. Instead of worrying about gravel, they thanked their lucky stars Abel didn't say 100. Abel saw that they went at the same pace. When they were finished, he ordered them up and at attention. "Double time to the front of the second building and wait."

They double timed to a covered area that ran across the front of a white painted building. The concrete area where they now stood was about 60 feet across and ran the length of the whole building. It was about 25 feet from the gravel path that led from the road. The area between the road and the covered area was planted in new grass that was just beginning to show. As they waited for Abel to give his next series of orders, the smell of breakfast reached them.

"Are you people hungry?"

"Yes, sir!" they shouted back. Johnny felt sure the combined noise in that area would break a window.

"Very well, then. Go eat."

Nobody moved. They stood waiting, ready to go.

"Dismissed!" Abel shouted. They ran for the big doors.

Chapter 14

On March 2nd, it started to snow. At first it was small flakes that slowly fluttered to earth. Now they were bigger and falling much faster. Boxer watched through the windshield of the same Dodge that Johnny and Linda had driven to Portland a few years back. Now, it was a different color, black. It was Dot who sat in the passenger seat. They were now waiting for a light to change from red to green in downtown Roseburg. Boxer turned on his windshield wipers.

"This snow could be a blessing," he said.

"How do you mean that?" Dot asked.

"People being people, it'll keep the cops busy working traffic accidents." Boxer eased the car away from the light, making a left turn. "People are asses. Instead of taking it easy when the snow starts falling, they speed up in order to get out of the snow quicker. Fifteen more minutes of this type of snow and these streets are going to be slick as snot on a doorknob."

Dot said, "Let's hope we don't find one of those accidents. It would mess up the schedule."

They were in this city to make a hit by the Cleanup Committee. They were acting on information stolen from the state by Ritter's computer. This would be the first hit where literature from the Cleanup Committee would be found.

It was 8:45 pm and they were now only 5 blocks from the home of Rafael Zorella. Zorella had a long record of narcotics arrests. He had been convicted only once and served a light sentence. His confidential file disclosed that Roseburg Police suspected he was behind most of the hard narcotics in this area. Zorella was being hit now because he was an important job to the committee, and it was time to put him out of business.

Around October the hounds would be unleashed, and the statewide campaign against pushers like Zorella would be in full swing. It was important that killing pushers and the accompanying publicity started now in order to avoid attention to the training school. Rafael Zorella was going to die now so the few ranchers around the camp wouldn't be curious if hits started 6 months from now. It was believed that someone would figure it out if publicity started after camp ended. There were 2 more hits scheduled in the next couple of months designed to receive maximum media coverage. The plans were already worked out. The only uncertainty in this puzzle was whether or not Zorella would be home. If he wasn't, there would be a surprise waiting when he arrived.

Boxer looked at the falling snow and said, "If he isn't home, this should bring him in sooner."

Zorella's file had disclosed that his very nice house was occasionally under surveillance by the Douglas County Interagency Narcotics team. They had no way of knowing if the surveillance was active at this time. They also didn't know what methods the watchers were using.

In order to protect themselves the Committee had taken certain steps. First, Roseburg police had received a telephone tip that a large narcotics scale was expected to go down that night in another part of town. The information was just complete enough that it couldn't be ignored. Secondly, the Dodge was painted black, the plates were changed, and the numbers were splattered with chemicals to make them look muddy. No officer behind a hidden camera would be able to get a clear reading on the plate. They assumed that Roseburg would not take the bait entirely and would leave at least one surveillance van in the area, and information on any vehicle in the area would be noted.

They drove around the block twice looking for any cars with people in them. They also looked for vans parked where an observer could aim a camera at Zorella's house. They saw none. They had no way of checking for surveillance from inside another house, but no evidence existed that the watchers had gone that far.

They had solved one uncertainty the first time through. Zorella's car, a late model white over red Ford LTD, was parked in front of his house. They knew it was not in the garage because a 14 foot boat was stored in there.

Satisfied that no surveillance was on, Boxer parked two doors down from the target. They got out, the snow helping to muffle the sound of the car doors. They were dressed in dark clothing. When they got out, both of them put on black rubber raincoats. Those coats kept them dry and concealed the Browning 9 mm pistols they both carried. Boxer led the way. He and Dot stepped carefully on the already slick sidewalks. The houses here were modern ticky-tacky with adjoining lawns and only a few fences dividing them. They could see the greenish blue reflection of TV's through the windows. The locals were all settled indoors, unaware of what was going on.

While they knew Zorella was home, they did not know if anyone but his wife and two kids would be with him. The plan was to take Zorella out as quickly and quietly as possible. The family was to be left bound and gagged. The Brownings were silenced. Little consideration was given to the feelings of the wife and kids. If they didn't already know he was a pusher, they soon would. With so many unknowns, no perfect plan could be made for approaching the house. They decided in a whispered conference that Dot would go knock on the door. When someone answered, they would force their way in, guns drawn. While one covered the people, the other would cut the phone cords. They hoped the children were asleep and could be left alone.

Dot walked slowly up to the porch, the snow muffling her approach. It was falling hard enough to cover any tracks within a few minutes of them being made. She stepped up to the door, freed her Browning from under her coat, and pushed the doorbell.

Zorella opened the door dressed in a red and white robe and matching slippers. She was on him before he had time to react. Dot rammed the big Browning into his gut, pushing the air out of him in a huff. He fell back, and Dot stepped by him quickly as Boxer came in. He gave the off-balance Zorella a shove that made him fall heavily on his butt. He started to open his mouth and yell, but Boxer stopped him.

"Say a word and you'll die where you sit!" Boxer hissed.

Boxer shut the door behind him. Mrs. Zorella, an overweight and scruffy looking woman was sitting in a recliner chair. She opened her mouth to protest when Dot put her Browning right in the woman's face.

"Stop. You and your children will not be harmed. We're after your husband. I'm telling you once, and only once, to keep quiet."

Boxer kept them covered while Dot took out a knife and cut the phone cord. She found another phone in the kitchen and put it out of order. Returning to the living room, she looked at the shaking Mrs. Zorella.

"Are the kids asleep?" Dot asked.

"Yes! For Christ's sake! You're not going to...."

"I told you, our beef is with him."

From the floor, a nervous Rafael stammered, "What...what the hell do you people want?"

"You. Just you," Boxer said. "On your feet and be quick about it."

Rafael looked at the face of the man behind the gun and scrambled to his feet.

"Turn around!" Boxer ordered.

Zorella did so, fearing he'd be hit over the head. He was surprised when he heard Boxer's next words. "Hands behind your back." He complied, then felt himself being handcuffed. It wasn't the first time in his life, and a smile crossed his face.

"What are you smiling about?" Dot asked.

Rafael said, "I swear you fucking pigs never give up, do you? This time you've gone too far. I'll be out and back home in an hour, and tomorrow I'll sue your asses. I'll have your jobs."

"No you won't," Dot said, "because we're not cops. We're from the Cleanup Committee, and you're going to die."

Before Zorella could say anything, Boxer rammed a gag in his mouth.

Dot turned to Mrs. Zorella, who was breathing shakily with fear. "Out of the chair! Get yourself over on the couch."

She either wouldn't or couldn't move. Dot stepped over, grabbed her by the arm, and jerked the weak-kneed woman to her feet. She stumbled over to the couch and fell heavily. Boxer took some bailing wire from his pocket and tossed it to Dot. She caught it and told Mrs. Zorella to lay down. The woman did as she was told. Dot had her bound and gagged within minutes, then turned to Boxer.

Boxer reached out into his pocket and took out a business card. He flipped it onto the rigid form of Mrs. Zorella.

"Did you touch anything in here?" Boxer asked Dot.

"No, sir. I was very careful. Will that wire show any prints?"

"No. Let's go."

Boxer turned to Zorella, who was standing where they had left him watching the happenings in his living room. His eyes were as big as dinner plates. Gut wrenching fear was in his face. "Zorella," Boxer said with ice dripping from his voice, "you are a dead man. You're going to die for all those people you have killed over the years. You're going to die for all the people you've crippled with drugs. For the sake of your wife and children, we'd prefer not to shoot you here."

Boxer put on plastic gloves and put his gun out of sight. He walked past the condemned man and opened the door. "Refusal to cooperate won't save you," Boxer told Zorella. Dot followed Zorella out with her gun to his back. He went, moving with a kind of stubborn pride. Dot put her gun away, put on plastic gloves, and closed the door behind them. Boxer walked beside Zorella with one hand on his elbow.

The snow was coming down just as hard as it had been when they entered the house 10 minutes ago. They were halfway to the car when Boxer suddenly stopped, dragging Zorella to a halt behind him.

Dot stepped quickly to Zorella's right, her hand in her coat. She saw a man approaching through a screen of snow. He had a large dog on a leash. He spotted them and slowed his walk.

"Good evening," he said. 'Isn't this some kind of weather."

"Yes sir," Boxer replied. The man immediately saw something was wrong.

"Hey," he said. "What's going on?"

"Read your papers tomorrow, sir," Boxer replied.

"Oh, you're cops. I see. Is this man under arrest?"

"You could say that," Boxer replied. "Now if you'll please let us by sir, he doesn't have to stand out here in the snow, and we'd appreciate it."

"What's wrong with his mouth?"

Dot could feel Boxer's patience starting to slip.

"Sir, if you don't mind. We need to observe this man's rights."

The man gave a tug on the dog's leash, and he and the beast stepped aside. "I know what you mean," he said. "Violate one little right and they beat the whole damn case."

They walked by the man, both supporting Zorella. For a moment he must have thought he was saved, but now that hope was gone. He sagged so that his killers had to practically drag him the last few feet to the car. Dot opened the back door and heaved Zorella in. She went in behind him, and Boxer closed the door. Boxer started the car and noted that the man was still standing with the dog, watching them.

"Damn him," Dot said.

"Don't worry," Boxer said. "His type are the world's worst witnesses."

The next morning, Mr. Frank Asher waded through 10 inches of snow to get his newspaper. He saw this article in the Roseburg News Review dated March 3rd:

Local Resident Found Shot to Death

A passing motorist found the partially snow covered body of Rafael M. Zorella of Roseburg, age 37, handcuffed to a mile marker on route 42 at approximately 7 a.m. He had been shot twice through the back of the head at close range with a large caliber weapon. An accurate time of death has not been determined due to weather conditions.

According to the police report, Zorella was taken from his home by 10 pm on March 2nd by an armed male and female. His wife was found this morning by one of the

As soon as Frank read it, he called the police. "I have important information on the killing that's in the paper. Please send someone over to see me."

On March 12, Astoria Police faced a killing similar to the one in Roseburg. This time, the suspect was described by witnesses as a lone female. That was the best description anyone could give. The victim had been contacted in a bar. The female had coaxed him to go outside with her by telling him she had an important, confidential message from some friends. Twenty minutes later, when the victim had not returned, a friend went to check and found him in his car. He had died of a single gunshot wound through his head. A card from the Cleanup Committee was found on his dashboard.

Six days later, a man walked into a night spot in Pendleton at 12:30 a.m. The place was full as a hot band was in town that night. He approached a table where two men and two women were seated. He dropped two cards on the table, then stepped back and produced a short double barreled shotgun from beneath his blue overcoat. He gave each man a barrel, turned, and walked calmly out. The best description anyone could give was that he was tall.

On March 26th four men and one woman were found shot to death on a boat drifting 7 miles off of Brookings. The Coast Guard found 500 pounds of Colombian gold, a valuable strain of marijuana, in the cargo holds. They found machine gun rounds and believed the shooters were on another boat.

In all cases, the police admitted the victims were known dealers.

In the early morning of March 29th, Patrolman Bill Crockett of the Eagle Point Police found a car parked alongside the road east of the city. He stopped to investigate and found the driver slumped over the wheel with the top of his head missing. The inside of the car was covered in blood. The investigation determined the man had been dead for at least 24 hours. The Cleanup Committee left a card on the dashboard. A one word note was found on the bloody seat. It said: "Trunk".

Officer Crockett opened the trunk and found 50 pounds of marijuana, 5 thousand red devils, and 5 thousand blues, both of which were powerful downers. It was a considerable take. When questioned by the press, Patrolman Crockett had referred them to the Chief of Police as required by department policy. The Chief declined to comment.

By the time the bloody month of March was over, The Cleanup Committee had become a household name. Husbands and wives, parents and kids, all started discussions over it. Editorials started appearing. Law enforcement agents discussed it, wondering when and how the Committee would strike again. The targets of the Committee did business as usual. Clearly, they hadn't yet gotten the message.

Chapter 15

Luther Sherman was up on his hill again. It was a clear, crisp April morning. He was sitting on the hood of his Jeep, his telescope trained on the camp of those army people across the lake. Out over the lake, Sherman saw an eagle. He quickly brought it into focus. It was circling as though it had not a care in the world. The sun reflected off the large bird as it drifted lazily in the air currents. Sherman watched it and let the sounds of nature and the smells of fresh air sink in. Damn it's a lovely day, he thought. It made him want to pick up a bat and go play baseball.

The eagle had spotted something below on the lakeshore, or perhaps in the water. Luther wanted to look and see what it might be, but he didn't want to take a chance on losing sight of the bird. Eagles were rare. Sherman wondered where its nest was, thinking it was probably back on Wildcat Mountain or the northwest ridge.

With no warning whatsoever, the Eagle dropped. The swiftness of his descent made Sherman catch his breath. The Eagle went out of sight behind some trees, only to reappear a minute later with a large snake. It flew away from him, heading east. He lowered the scope in awe.

The sound of a helicopter brought him back to reality. He brought his scope up and found the copter. It was coming fast from the south. He had heard the choppers before but this was the first time he'd been on the hill when one landed. He watched it come down, waiting to see if it brought people or cargo.

He still felt unsure about these people, and the idea of the Army being so close. It wasn't that they were bothering anything, they just made noise. When the wind was right, he could hear the rapid firing of their weapons from the range by 10 Mile Butte. The helicopters made more noise than anything he had ever heard. It was coming down on its own pad a few miles away. The giant blades made a chop, chop, chop sound as it descended.

He refocused the scope after the chopper landed. He watched 8 people, all dressed in military uniforms, run down the gravel road from what he called the barracks area. They lined up by the road and waited for the signal to approach the helicopter, then began the unloading process.

Johnny Redwine was in the group that Luther Sherman was watching. He was unaware of his distant audience of one. Like the others, he was just ready to get this over with. This was food, ammo, and 5 gallon cans of gasoline. The chopper would be taking away big plastic bags of garbage.

The pilot stepped down and signaled them to get busy. Two hours and 10 gallons of sweat later they had the job done. "Damn," declared Roy, "that was hot work." He wiped the sweat from his face.

Linda replied, "If you think that's hot, wait until July gets here. I'm going to check on the possibility of night flights."

"Good idea," said Amanda. "We'll never make it when it's 100 degrees."

"A couple months ago we didn't think we'd make it through this," Johnny offered. "I think we'll make it through any kind of weather."

They stood in front of the covered exercise area in front of the barracks. They called it that at Abel's insistence. They were taking a short breather before joining teams 6 and 8 at the firing range 3 miles away.

Abel had left them at the end of March, and Cain had taken over. If anyone at Camp Summer Lake thought the going would get easier, they were sadly mistaken. Cain did not run them more, but he certainly didn't run them any less.

He was a man of few words, and despised having to repeat himself. He made sure he was heard the first time.

"Come on, people, let's move it before Cain has us running the 440."

Linda stepped out into the ever-warmer sun and led the way up the 3 mile road. The group could trot, jog, or run it now without even breathing hard. It had taken work with all of them, but Abel knew they would make it. Cain took over a well prepared group who had been run, exercised, and run some more. When they weren't exercising they were in class studying guns. They were now experts on the weapons they would be using before they ever fired a round. That was where Cain came in. Now they were ready to shoot. On even number days, Cain had the even numbered teams at the range, and odd teams on the odd numbered days. They spent the morning shooting, then spent the afternoon picking up spent brass, patching targets, and cleaning weapons.

Cain had introduced a new element to their training. On days when they were not at the range, the teams were watching films on drugs and addiction. Each evening there was a written test about what they had seen. Discussion was encouraged. Cain appointed a "teacher" each day to run the movies and lead discussion.

"You may be instructors someday," Cain said. "You might as well learn how it's done."

Linda's group arrived at the range to find teams 7 and 9 on the firing line. Terry Stout, leader of team 5, turned and watched Linda's group approach at a trot. "Pull up chairs. 7 and 9 just started." Terry was going to say more, but whatever it was got drowned out by the sudden roar of gunfire from the line.

Team 1 was on kitchen duty, so team 3 waited with 5 for their turn on the firing line. Johnny dropped onto a bench beside Roy and leaned on the table. These tables were picnic type, but in this case they held weapons and loaded magazines. No one was permitted to have a magazine in the weapon until they were on the firing line.

Sidearms were required to be carried at all times, but Cain had not seen fit to issue ammo for them yet. Cain had said "Get used to them first. Carrying a gun doesn't feel natural. When you start to feel undressed without it, then we'll see about ammo."

"Look at that," Roy said. "She's the best looking girl here. Outside of Amanda, of course." Roy indicated a girl named Paula from team 9. It had not been necessary for Roy to point her out, becaused Johnny had already spotted her form, specifically her ass, before even sitting down. She had turned and was walking back from the line with a rifle held high. She was smiling, and she was looking at Johnny. His young heart was singing with all the music ever composed. He didn't have to wonder if he was in love, he knew it. He had been since the first time he laid eyes on this woman months ago. The problem was, he had no idea if she had feelings for him. She was sweet, kind, and he thought at times she might be interested. Yet each time he thought he might find out, something came up and they were off and running to the next thing.

Paula walked up and set her rifle on the picnic table next to Johnny's group.

"Good mornin', 3," she drawled. "How's the helicopter duty?"

Paula had given her hometown as Bay City, Oregon. It was barely a town, let alone a city, on the northern Oregon coast. She had an accent that suggested she had spent more of her life in the south. Nobody could say exactly which state. She was also the only black person that had been recruited in his class.

The point of race had been brought up only once during a discussion. Teams 3 and 2 had been on laundry assignment. Linda had said, "I'm surprised the Committee didn't recruit more people of color."

"Oh hell," Roy had replied. "They probably had a hard enough time finding any of us. I'm sure no one was rejected because of their race."

"I should hope not," Amanda had said.

Now as Paula approached, Roy said: "Good morning, beautiful. How's about you and me going skinny dipping in the lake?"

"No thank you," she replied. "It's much too cold for swimming." Paula's grin was mischievous.

Johnny looked at her and thought he wouldn't notice cold, heat, or anything else if he had a shot with her. Paula looked away from Roy and turned to him.

"Good morning, Johnny. You look like a cat that caught the bird. Are you having delusions, too?"

"Get your mind out of the gutter," Roy teased.

Linda interrupted that banter. "Our turn. Get your weapons, team 3."

They picked up their rifles and magazines, walked forward and took their places in line. They waited on Cain's commands before loading, bringing their rifles into position, and firing. The teams continued to rotate and went through two magazines of 18 rounds each. Then they rotated through with their hand guns.

Cain, Roy and 2 others guys collected the targets. Everybody had a chance to see how he or she had done. Each person hoped to find improvement of their overall score from the prior session. Johnny found he had not improved one bit with the rifle, but his score with the Browning had increased. He was now the top shooter among the teams currently on the range.

One Jeep was kept at the range for transporting weapons and for emergency use. They loaded the weapons and prepared to head to the barracks for lunch. Cain drove the Jeep while the recruits ran. They got back in time for a quick shower and change. Lunch was served promptly at noon. They had 45 minutes to eat, and 45 minutes of free time afterward. It was during the time after lunch a lot of discussions developed, and some romances.

In spite of the warning Dot had issued in the first part of training, Johnny knew some people were making it into other peoples' beds. He had not. He only wanted Paula, and she had not invited him. He wasn't quite sure how to go about getting an invitation. He had brought the problem up to Roy a few weeks back.

"Well kid, I thought you would never ask," Roy said with a smile. "The first thing you have to do is let her know how you feel. Then let nature take its course."

"What if she likes someone else? I don't want to get slapped, or get into a scuffle with some other guy."

"Use your eyes kid! Have you seen her messing around with anyone else?"

"Well, no," Johnny answered.

"Then don't let fear or the anchor in your ass hold you back."

"What if we got in trouble? Or what if I brought her some trouble?"

"Don't worry about it. Somehow, Charlotte got pills for all the girls who want them. Hell, kid, sex is going to happen no matter what. Attempts to restrict it were bound to fail. I'm glad Charlotte came through. Hell, Dot probably helped her. The girls just have to remember to take the pill."

"Whatever, Roy. It's not like you've been making it with Amanda."

"Well shit, kid. I bunk with you, she bunks with Linda. There's no way Linda's going to let it happen. Besides, I think she has Amanda convinced to wait or something. I don't get it."

"Want me to ask Linda about it?" Johnny asked.

"Sure, good luck. Hey, what's with you and her anyway?" Roy asked.

"We're just close friends. We met under some strange circumstances."

"Oh yeah? Tell me about it." Roy was curious.

"I'll tell you sometime," Johnny answered.

Johnny had been watching closely since that conversation to see if Paula had formed any relationships. He didn't see any forming, but on the other hand, she treated everyone the same. Polite, but nothing more. Today he decided to try and start a conversation. He found her reclining in a lawn chair out by the exercise area. Paula was alone, wrapped up in reading a novel. She didn't seem to hear the thud of his boots on the concrete as he approached.

"Hi, Paula," Johnny said. "Want some company?"

Paula lowered her book and looked up at him. She had a strikingly beautiful face. Her features were delicate, like a work of art. She was 5 foot 4, maybe 130 pounds. She was built small but her abilities were as good as any of the other recruits.

"Why not?" she answered. "Pull up a chair."

He drug one over and sat down next to her. It was cool under the covered patio, and they were still wearing their winter uniforms. "What are you reading?"

"The Foxes of Harrow," Paula replied. "Do you know it?"

"I don't think so. Who wrote it?"

"Frank Yerby. It's about a guy in New Orleans before the Civil War. The book covers many years, explores plantation life, and treatment of my people. I'm not making a great book report here, but if you like to read I recommend it. It's good reading. Linda says you're a reader."

"You're from the South, aren't you?" Johnny asked. Her drawl sounded like music.

"Yeah. I'm from Georgia. I haven't seen the place in years."

"Do you have family there?"

"I'm the youngest of 9 kids. I have 5 brothers and 3 sisters."

"I remember at the other school you said you're 20," Johnny said. "You seem older. That is, you don't act like some other 20 year olds I know."

Her eyes, a lovely dark brown that were usually shining, clouded over.

"I didn't mean to hurt your feelings," Johnny said quickly.

"You didn't," Paula said. "I was just remembering. The fact is that none of us here act our age. We're a special bunch of social misfits who randomly got picked to work for some rich folks with an axe to grind. It's a legit axe, don't get me wrong. We're going to make a lot of noise, and kill a bunch of people, but I don't think we'll succeed with their ultimate goal."

"Do you think we'll get caught?"

"I doubt it. Most likely we'll end up dead. We'll buy it in ones and twos. Eventually we'll all be memories." Paula stretched lazily.

"I've gotta say, you don't paint a bright picture. I plan on staying alive." Johnny had to make sure he wasn't drooling. Paula's every move was smooth and graceful. He bet she could run to the range with a glass of water on her head and never spill a drop.

"What brought you here from Georgia?"

"It's a long story, and not a very nice one," she answered. "You might think I'm a bitch if I told you."

"I doubt that," Johnny replied. "You probably didn't do anything I wouldn't do."

"Law enforcement might disagree with you on that."

"I'd still like to know," Johnny said sincerely.

"My mama died when I was 12. Daddy disappeared. We hadn't seen much of him anyway. I was sent to live with my oldest sister in Atlanta. The guy she shacked up with was her pimp. He let me know I was going to have to work for him if I wanted to stay there, so I ran away. I lived where and how I could. I was hooked on drugs within 3 months, and locked away in Juvie in 5. They released me to my sister but I promptly ran again. I hitchhiked west, mostly with truckers. I lived in Mississippi for a few years, then New Orleans, Tucson, and finally landed in LA.

After living in LA for a while I got pregnant. I gave the baby away. Then I went north. I ended up in Bay City broke, hungry, and desperate. I tried robbing a woman outside a bar. She knocked me on my ass, picked me up like I was a ragdoll, and tossed me in the back of her car. It was Dot. She took me to Eugene. That's where I met Doctor Fish. He got me through withdrawal and nursed me back to health. He also helped me get better with reading, writing and math. I made a deal to string along with this group. Now here we are." Paula looked at Johnny, unsure what he would say.

"Paula," he said, "I don't care what you've done. I think you're amazing. I like you very much."

Paula smiled. "I like you too, Johnny. I hope life is good to you."

"Paula, I tried real hard to kill some people. That's when Dot found me. I was seeing red. I did kill one person, a girl. She wasn't my main target."

"I've killed one person too," Paula replied.

"Sometimes I wonder if I'll be able to do all the killing assigned to us after leaving here."

"I think you can do it," said Paula. "You'll do it because we have to. The process has already started and can't be stopped. It's like when you throw something and you can't change the trajectory while it's sailing through the air."

"Yeah, I get it. I heard about the hits in March on the radio. Are we all crazy?" Johnny asked.

"I don't know," Paula answered. "Maybe we're normal and the rest of society is crazy. I try not to think about it much. When Dot found me I was on the downhill slide going nowhere. She slowed down that slide and put off the final end, at least for a while. Sure, I'll kill for them. If I survive, I'll come out with some money, and in my way of thinking I'll have done some good. If we do stop the flow of drugs like the Committee wants, that'll be quite an accomplishment. This is war, and we know people die in war. We're just mercenaries."

Johnny sat thinking, looking at Paula. She talked like someone closer to 40 than 20. He was completely taken with her, and with what she was saying. He'd heard things like it before, but never as well as she'd just said it.

Paula smiled.

"Damn, you just cleared up any doubts about what I was doing here," he said.

Paula stood up, and he joined her. Then he pulled her close and held her. He felt like they were alone in the world. All thoughts of killing or wrongs and rights slipped away. Her skin was the softest thing he'd ever felt, and smooth as butter. Paula held onto him just as tightly. For one precious moment their young hearts beat together. Then it was shattered by the ringing of a bell. It was time to report for afternoon assignments. They walked back to the barracks together.

Chapter 16

Editorial- Portland Journal- May 21

*On the night of May 14th, two Portland police officers
and one civilian were shot to death. They had been sitting in
a Portland police cruiser by a bar on NE 82nd Street.*

*The Office of the Chief of Police confirmed that the two
dead officers were involved in illegal drug trafficking. They
also confirmed the rumor that internal affairs had been
investigating these two officers for a while. The Chief has
promised a full report of his investigation when it's
complete.*

*Please do not condemn the Portland Police Bureau
because of this extremely unfortunate situation. The Chief
has reassured your editor that this is not a widespread
problem in his department. The record of the Portland
Police has been historically remarkable. Unfortunately,
they must recruit from the human race. No matter how high
the standards, no matter how good the screening methods,
a bad apple is bound to get through.*

*This newspaper condemns the fanatics who did this.
Given time, justice would have taken its course for the
officers that were killed. Fanatics with guns have never
solved a problem. They only increase them. The Cleanup
Committee, whoever they are, will eventually be brought to
justice.*

The governor of Oregon was a worried man, to put it
mildly. On this lovely May morning he was standing by his
office window in the Capitol building. Below him, workers
and tourists were moving in and out. He didn't see them as
people, though. He saw them as voters, and they were only
one of the reasons for his worrying.

He turned from the window without noticing the lovely spring day and returned to his desk. The private poll that he had conducted laid on the desk in front of him. It said that if the election were held today he would lose. Big time. Frowning, he picked up the poll and dropped it in the shredder pile. It wouldn't do for the press to get wind of the fact he was conducting polls right now.

The governor's other reason for worry was that damned Cleanup Committee. During March, it looked like they would shoot everybody who had ever so much as touched narcotics. In April, it slowed down a little...up until the murder of the 2 cops and their supplier. The Portland killings had shaken not only the city but the whole state. The shockwaves had extended right up to his office. Now he was going to have to take some kind of action. He was awaiting the arrival of the state Attorney General and the Superintendent of the Oregon State Police.

Attorney General Tom Blakely was a good looking, fast talking country lawyer. His charm had gotten him elected. The man wasn't truly qualified to be the state's top lawyer. If it wasn't for an excellent staff that covered his ass he would've been recalled by the voters some time ago. Whenever he thought about Blakely, the governor was consoled by the fact he was elected, not appointed, so he was not responsible.

On the other hand, Richard Brownwell of the State Police was a good man. Some of his ideas were a little far out, though. For example, at some social events he said: "Every baby born in this state should be fingerprinted at birth." A secretary heard it and remarked that if it were up to Brownwell everyone would have a number on their forehead. He replied that the forehead would be too obvious; he'd put it on their ass.

His pet project was a drive to make every police officer in Oregon a state trooper. Record systems, radio codes, uniforms, pay, and most things would be standardized in Brownwell's opinion. That way If a cop wanted to move across the state, all he'd have to do is transfer. He could talk for hours on the subject and would put down any arguments as silly. The governor had to remind Brownwell more than once to cool it. The press might think he was speaking for the state.

The governor's intercom buzzed. His secretary informed him that his guests had arrived. He stood up, and put on a smile. You could never tell when the press might be lurking nearby. The door opened and Blakely led the way in, also smiling. Brownwell followed and closed the door behind him.

"Good morning, gentlemen. Please be seated." The governor let his smile fade.

Blakely strolled across the thick carpet and sat down at the governor's right. He was tall and tan. He looked like a cowboy that had just parked his horse and come in for a cold drink. He had a brown suit tailored to fit like a glove.

Brownwell was in his fifties, about 5 foot 11 and 170 pounds. He had iron gray hair and striking bright blue eyes. He wore his uniform proudly, with the gold buttons and badge highly polished. Others in his position might have worn a business suit, but Brownwell never had. He took the seat to the governor's left and lit a cigarette.

"What's the matter Paul?" Brownwell asked. "You don't look so good."

The governor leaned back. "It's this damned Clean Up Committee."

"They sure have been raising hell," offered Blakely.

"Brilliant observation, Tom," Brownwell said with a smirk.

The governor looked at both men with a frown. "That's why I called you two in. What does the state know about these people?"

"Nothing that's not in the papers," Blakely said.

"I'm afraid he's close to being right," said Brownwell. "All of these killings, except for the one on the boat, happened inside a city. They're being handled by the city or county. Half the time the city and county can't get together on any evidence they've found. For example, it took 3 weeks for the handcuffs found on Rafael Zorella to make it back to the Roseburg PD. It took them another week to find out those handcuffs were reported stolen from an Eagle Point policeman during a bar fight over a year ago."

"Are you trying to sell me your state police idea again, Rick?" asked the governor.

"No, not this morning."

"The idea is ridiculous anyway," Blakely offered.

"Never mind," said the governor. "We'll argue that another time. At this point, do we have anything?"

"I'll tell you what we have, and it isn't much," said Brownwell. "The State Crime Lab has seen just about all the evidence at one time. The different agencies have recovered numerous bullets and lots of spent brass. We've lifted one thumbprint off one of those business cards they leave around. Of course the print's not on file, or we'd have had a warrant out already."

"How about the recovered bullets and brass? Do they show anything?"

"Only the types of weapons used. We know that the same gun was used to kill Rafael Zorella and the guy in Astoria. That doesn't give us much." Brownwell leaned forward and put his cigarette out.

"Maybe it's the mafia doing it," suggested Blakely.

"Well," said the governor, "as Attorney General I expect you would know if the mafia were present and what they're up to. Do you have any evidence that organized crime is behind all this?"

"No," Blakely replied, shifting his weight nervously. "It just seems hard to believe anyone other than the mafia could do all of this. They've covered their tracks perfectly so far. It's obviously well organized. Every person they've hit so far has been a known drug dealer."

Brownwell added, "The only one of these killings that look like a mafia hit at all was the shooting in Pendleton. In that case, the guy walked in, blasted his victims and walked out. Another card was found at that one, but the only prints on it were the dead man's."

The governor asked, "Why would the mafia want to cause such a fuss when they're used to killing quickly and quietly? They've left witnesses. They leave calling cards. This is something else. The only resemblance to the mafia so far is that they're organized."

"Well, maybe the CIA is behind it," said Blakely.

The governor looked as though he might choke. "Tom, for God's sake! Be serious."

Brownwell cleared his throat. Blakely looked a bit hurt. "I am serious!" Blakely protested.

"I was afraid you might be," replied the governor.

"Paul, you know as well as I do that the CIA have been behind some strange things. It's been shown that the CIA conspired with the Mafia to knock off Fidel Castro. There's a theory that the CIA and the mafia knocked off the President in 1963. In 74, the CIA spent millions of dollars trying to raise a sunken Russian submarine off the floor of the Pacific just so they could look at its secret computer. God knows what other unexplainable happenings they've been behind."

Brownwell got up to get a cup of coffee. When he returned to his seat he said, "I've got to admit the same thought briefly crossed my mind."

"Why, gentlemen?" asked the governor. "Why would they do this?"

"It would sure create confusion," said Brownwell.

"It would have us looking anywhere but the CIA," offered Blakely.

"Alright," said the governor. "I'll grant that what you're saying might hold water, but I find it too far-fetched. I just can't believe it. I want both of you back in here next week at the same time. Give this some serious thought. I want a proposal on how to find out who these people are. Meanwhile, if anything else develops in this case, be sure to let me know."

The governor stood up, indicating the meeting was over. He had developed a headache. Brownwell stood up and drained his coffee.

Blakely stood up, looked at the governor, and asked "Are you eating right, Paul? You don't look so good."

"Yes, Tom, I'm eating fine."

"Perhaps you should get married again. It would do you some good to have a woman around to cook for you," Blakely said.

"Perhaps you should move from Eugene to Salem and quit wasting all that gas driving," the governor said testily.

Blakely looked hurt. "Paul, I think you need a vacation. You've been working too hard."

"What would you know about that, Tom? You're never in town long enough to know what I'm doing."

"I read the papers. You're a busy man."

Brownwell was already at the door, hat in one hand and doorknob in the other. "Come on, Tom," he said. "The

governor is a busy man. Let's go get into our own mischief
somewhere." He opened the door and they both went
through it.

The governor sat down. He thought it would fit
Brownwell perfectly to mount a big white horse and ride off
down the hall yelling "Hi Ho Silver!" Paul took his head into
his hands, wondering why he ever wanted this job.

Chapter 17

While the governor was having his meeting, Jonah B. Stoneking was attending a meeting of his own. This was a board meeting for Stoneking Enterprises. It was being held in the large boardroom next to his private office. As chairman, he called the meeting to order at exactly 10 a.m. Old topics were handled quickly. Then the board heard a proposal from the chairman himself.

Stoneking proposed that they buy out a certain car dealer who was anxious to sell and retire. As one of the city's most respected dealerships, it was not only a good investment, it was a much needed resource for the Cleanup Committee. The board knew nothing of the Committee, of course. Furthermore, they wouldn't care. It was a wise investment. It would do no harm to the Stoneking stock. A half hour after the meeting was called, Jonah had his proposal approved. The board then drafted a letter to their retrained law firm authorizing them to enter into immediate negotiations for the purchase of the dealership.

Another 10 minutes was taken up with discussion of updates. The meeting ended with each member passing by and shaking hands with Stoneking before exiting out the side door. They dispersed to their offices to call their stock brokers. When the last man had gone, Stoneking locked the door behind them. He returned to his seat at the head of the table to think and take notes. Ten minutes later he was back at his desk, checking his appointment calendar. His next task was to dictate two letters. When his secretary left, Stoneking picked up a private, unlisted phone on his desk and dialed a number in Salem. It was answered on the second ring.

"This is the Chairman calling," Jonah said.

"Good morning," the voice replied.

"The proposal was accepted. We should have final results in a few days."

"I've just returned from a meeting myself. The man I met with was very worried. If your schedule permits, I'll drop in this afternoon and tell you about it."

"Not this afternoon. However, I think it's time that you met with the other members and let them get to know you. It won't be long until the cargo is available, and it would be good if they see its manufacturer."

"When and where would you like the meeting to take place?"

"The usual place. Meet me there at 7:30 tonight. Come as the Doctor."

"It's a date," the voice said, and paused.

"Do you have a question?" Jonah asked.

"Nothing that can't wait until tonight."

"That's fine. 7:30 it is." The voice hung up.

At 12:15, Stoneking left his office and walked 3 blocks to the Imperial Hotel where he had lunch in the dining room. He ate alone. After placing his order he requested that a phone be brought to him. When it arrived he plugged it in and called Beth. He explained that the meeting mentioned a few days ago was still on for tonight.

Beth was silent for a moment, then asked, "Do you know what time you'll be home?"

"Around 9:30. If it runs any later I'll call you."

"Will you have dinner first?" Beth asked.

"Yes, I'll be there at 5:30. Is Dot home?"

"Yes, would you like to speak with her?"

"No, but please tell her I would like her to attend this meeting with me. I think it's about time she starts learning about the business. After all, I'm going to have to retire someday."

"I like that idea," Beth said. "I'll suggest strongly that she go with you after dinner."

"We'll keep the meeting short if possible. I don't like leaving you alone."

"Don't worry about me, Jonah. Barbara Colley and another wife who will be left alone by this meeting are coming over."

"That's good," he said, and meant it. "I'll see you for dinner then. I love you."

He hung up, then picked up the phone again. He punched in a number that was only covered by an automatic answering unit. It was Dot's voice on the machine instructing the caller to leave their message after the tone.

"Game on for 7:30. An extra chair will be needed."

He replaced the phone, sat back and waited for his lunch. The number he had dialed was attached to the back office of the warehouse where meetings occurred. Every day a member of the committee would take a minute and dial the number. Any messages left were kept short and vague just in case.

The other members of the committee were not familiar with Doctor Fish. Stoneking had decided the time had come for them to meet him. He accepted that they would be shocked, just as he had been last spring when they discovered each other.

By 1:15, Stoneking had finished his lunch and was back in the office. He spent a long afternoon in meetings and signing documents. He left his office and walked to the Cadillac parked in the basement garage.

He arrived home to find Beth and Dot relaxing by the pool. It was a warm afternoon. He greeted his family, then retreated to shower and change from a business suit to a polo shirt and slacks. He then went to sit with Beth by the pool while Dot made dinner. The family ate at 6:15. Afterwards, Dot and Jonah Stoneking left for the final meeting of the Committee before the hounds were unleashed.

They drove in silence toward the river. They arrived for the meeting at 7:23. Ritter, Colley and Rodgers arrived within a minute of each other. Jonah had Dot take the others upstairs. He then walked to a corner of the garage area where Doctor Fish was waiting out of sight. He had a quick word and then rode the elevator to where the others were waiting.

"Gentlemen," Stoneking began, "thank you for coming. Tonight I would like to introduce you to a man who has been of tremendous help to us. He has given countless hours of his time, at considerable risk to himself. He's prepared our recruits, organized training, and handled the locals near the camp. You have heard of him numerous times. Some of you may know him personally. Without any further ado, gentlemen, I give you Doctor Fish."

The elevator opened, and every eye was focused on the tall man now stepping forward. He removed a wig that nobody had realized was not his real hair. He took off a perfectly fitted false mustache. He slipped off a light jacket, and unbuttoned his shirt, removing a small roll of foam rubber from his waist that had made him look heavier than he was.

Tom Blakely, Attorney General of the state of Oregon, stood before them. The committee members' faces showed shock, amazement, and disbelief. After a moment, Colley was the first to speak.

"I didn't even vote for you!" Colley said. "I thought you were the dumbest son of a bitch ever to seek public office."

"Well I'm a monkey's uncle," said Rodgers.

Fish, or rather Blakely, grinned and produced the pipe that was so well known for both his public and private personas. Then he spoke.

"Jonah and I thought it was best to delay this meeting as long as possible. You've all been busy. So have I. Now that things have almost reached a state of readiness, it's time we all know who is who."

"Where did this doctor routine come from?" Colley asked.

"I dreamt the idea up last spring. What I'd like to do is explain my story to you in detail, then take questions. I'm sure you have a lot. Get comfortable, men. Dot, please make sure the coffee is on."

"Yes, sir," she said, and headed for the back office.

The members started dragging out anything they could find to sit on. Mostly, they used empty packing crates. Blakely remained standing, declining the offer of a crate. He waited, puffing on his pipe, until all were seated with cups of coffee.

Blakely laid his pipe down carefully on a huge packing crate, and started to pace slowly in front of the waiting members. Finally, he stopped, hands behind him, and began to speak.

"As you know from my campaign, I am a former military officer with some considerable financial means. What isn't commonly known is that I spent many years in the Intelligence service. It was during this time I learned a lot about people, how they act and react, and most importantly, how to make someone believe you are someone other than yourself.

Two years before I was scheduled for retirement, my father died and I inherited a considerable fortune. I entered law school immediately after leaving the service, as much to protect my own interest as anyone else's. With my law degree in one hand, a checkbook in the other, and a whole lot of luck, I managed to get myself elected Attorney General. I know that some of you gentlemen worked to defeat me. I could hear your moans and groans all the way to Eugene when the election results were announced."

Laughter spread throughout the room, coupled with a few sheepish looks.

"At any rate," Blakely continued, "I went to Salem with some mighty big ideas. I dreamed of cracking down hard on crime, particularly drug trafficking. I meant to make a name for myself as the toughest Attorney General the state had ever seen. Well, it took me about a year to realize it was a lost cause. Between an overwhelming amount of crooks, the liberal courts, and an overcrowded prison system that just doesn't work, I decided to take more direct action.

I moved slowly and carefully. I had to establish a new identity, and also change the image my staff and the public had of me. I created Doctor Fish for the purpose of starting my own type of Cleanup Committee. I recruited Cain and Abel on my own. I found Boxer by accident. You haven't met the men I've just named. They are instructors and hit men."

Colley asked, "Do you mean they're the ones who've been raising such hell?"

"Them, and Dot."

They looked at Dot in astonishment. Most of the men had known her since she was a child. They knew she had assisted with recruiting and training, but this was the first any of them had heard of her being involved in a hit.

"God almighty!" declared Rodgers. "I can't believe it. Is it true, Dot?"

"Yes Mr. Rodgers," she replied. "I personally shot those two cops and their supplier, along with the guy in Astoria. I also assisted Boxer with the hit on Zorella, and that boat off of Brookings."

"Sweet Jesus!" exclaimed Ritter.

"Gentlemen," Blakely said, "Please control yourselves. This isn't a picnic. It's a war. Dot is qualified and she has done an excellent job. However, with the recruits soon to be on the loose, she may not be as active. I understand your shock. Just remember, Dot's brother, Jonah Junior, died because of drugs. She has a personal stake in all this, same as you.

To continue, one day last summer I got a little careless and was recognized by Jonah. Those details are not important. Suffice it to say, we talked, compared notes, and decided to join forces. Hence, I was a latecomer. Due to my public office I decided to keep my real identity secret as long as possible.

We've now reached the point where Doctor Fish will be available by phone to our people, while as Attorney General I'll remain as close to the center of things as possible. For example, I was at a meeting this morning with the governor and our noted State Police Chief, Rick Brownwell."

"Now there's a son of a bitch we'd better watch out for," Colley said. "If there is a man in this state who's capable of tripping us up, it's him."

"My thoughts exactly," Blakely replied. "I plan to keep a close eye on him. The governor wants us back in his office next week with some proposals on how to run down the Cleanup Committee. I presented the idea this morning that the CIA might be behind the whole thing. The governor is considering it, but isn't quite convinced."

"To hell with him," said Braun. "What about Brownwell?"

"I'm not sure what he was thinking. He's a hard man to read. Gentlemen, I'll now take any questions you have."

Louis, the public relations man, asked: "How did you get away with the Doctor routine? How did you keep the Medical board off your back?"

"No one excetp a few cleaning people in the building where I keep an office knew Doctor Fish. He had no signs or phone listings for the public to get a look at. His clients came in with the help of either Cain, Abel, Boxer or Dot. There was no risk of them recognizing Fish as my public persona. Hell, some of them wouldn't have recognized the President himself. They were the only people Fish ever saw."

Smith, the food man, asked: "How have you managed to avoid detection of your double role by your legal office?"

"As you know from reading your newspapers, Attorney General Blakely has gotten to a bit of a screw off. Half the time he can't be found. Judging from some of the editorials I've read about me in the newspapers, I think I've done a more than adequate job of convincing the public I couldn't possibly be involved in something this organized."

"I'll say," said Smith.

Braun, the import-export man, asked: "Can you explain more about what your role will be from here on out?"

"As I stated, Doctor Fish will remain active remotely. He's given notice at his medical office space, and the lease expires at the end of this month. The lease was signed in a completely different name. My immediate plans are to remain as close to my Salem office as possible. I'll still be hard to find occasionally, as I can't change colors overnight."

The committee members nodded. No one had more questions.

Blakely continued: "I want you to know the training program is going well. I get weekly reports from the instructors. The reports are available from Jonah upon request. Please be careful to burn them when you're through reading. If they should ever fall into the wrong hands, it would be curtains for all of us."

"Now gentlemen, I'm going to take my leave. Dot has some things she is going to explain. They have to do with the way our troops will be used after they've completed the school. The plans were worked out over several months by myself, Dot, and the other instructors. We hope they meet with your approval."

Blakely began putting on his wig and mustache. He replaced everything, and his transformation was unbelievable. It was just as shocking as when he had arrived. He then went among the members and shook hands with each, giving them a personal thanks for attending.

At the elevator door, he stopped and looked back. "If any of you need me, or if I can help you in any way, please tell Jonah. He knows how to find me."

Blakely, now dressed as Doctor Fish, stepped into the elevator cage. The doors slid shut and he was gone.

The elevator door had hardly clicked shut when all of the men started talking at once. Their voices sounded irritated. It was clear what they were saying, as they looked from Jonah Stoneking to his daughter.

Dot, who had been standing near a packing case, stepped forward and addressed the men where they stood. She was clearly offended.

"Gentlemen, listen up!" she said.

They fell silent.

"I was as badly hurt as any of you when you lost your children. I lost my twin brother. Just because I'm not a parent doesn't make me any less immune to pain and grief. When Jonah died, I not only lost my brother, I lost my best friend. I had to absorb that loss while watching my parents go through hell. I promised myself those sons of Satan responsible for Jonah's death were going to pay.

For more than a year after that I looked with determination for revenge, but had no idea how to get it. When I found out what Dad was doing, I hounded him until he gave in. I made him promise to let me take an active role. He reacted the same way you all just did. He was shocked, and couldn't stand the thought of his little girl shooting someone.

When he realized I would not take no for an answer, he sent me to training with Doctor Fish, where my group and I learned how to do it right. You've been seeing in the newspapers that we learned well. You men are like most other men- living behind the times. Women do a lot of things now that weren't even possible a few years ago. Hell, you're all businessmen. You should know the rise of women is here. In business, government, medicine, and even the military. It's only a matter of time until the United States has women in its combat ranks. Israel realized it years ago. The PLO, the PLF, all have women in combat roles.

I'm in a combat role as well as being an instructor at the school. You gentlemen will have to get used to it. Furthermore, when this is behind us, I plan to step into Dad's shoes at the business. You gentlemen are far from seeing the last of me."

Dot turned and walked back to stand by her father. The others remained silent with downcast eyes. Stoneking faced the men.

Al Fielder, owner operator of Fielder Flying Services, was the first to speak.

"Jonah, I'm sure I speak for the others when I say, I apologize for questioning your judgment in this matter."

"Thanks, Al, but I also owe you men an apology. Important policy matters such as this should've been made known to the rest of you from the start. As fellow businessmen, I'm sure you can appreciate that sometimes decisions must be made on the spot."

Jonah smiled. "Gentlemen, you have just been told off...but not half as bad as I was. This little hellcat used every weapon in her arsenal to get her way. When logic, tears, swearing and stomping didn't work, she threatened plain old blackmail. It may have been a bluff, but I didn't dare to call it. By that time she had stopped looking at me as a father, and just saw a man in her way. Now we're here, and it's time to move on. Do any of you have any other business you'd like to bring up at this time?"

Keith Brown said, "I think that we should continue to refer to our departed guest as Doctor Fish."

"I second that," said Colley.

"I agree," said Louis.

Once agreed, they proceeded to questions about the progress of the training. Supplies were reviewed, and slight modifications were made to a few items.

Stoneking said, "I think this should be our last meeting here. Ed tells me this place is too big to ensure an electronic listening device couldn't be put in without our knowing it. I'll look around and see what I can come up with. If I find something that looks reasonable, I'll get word to you all to look over."

The men talked it over and left it to Jonah and Dot to find a new meeting place. With that, the meeting ended. Jonah and Dot remained behind to pick up cups and empty ashtrays. Finally, Dot turned off the lights and followed her father out.

Chapter 18

It was a warm afternoon in late June. Luther Sherman drove his Jeep up to the top of the hill, this time for a better look at the doings across the lake. He parked his Jeep and slid out. He brought out a pair of new binoculars he'd picked up on a shopping trip with his wife. They had gone 100 miles away to Lakeview, a town just shy of 3,000 people.

Watching the doings, as he called them, had become a hobby to Luther. He placed the leather case carefully on the warm hood of the Jeep and slowly lifted the binoculars. They had set him back 70 dollars so he handled them with care. He'd found the expense hard to justify to his wife. Finally, he'd said he needed a better view for finding strays. After all, he didn't want to miss a cow that's hurt, and have it die from lack of help.

When Susan had thought of an injured cow, that ended her objections. His wife could not stand the thought of any animal suffering. Luther didn't enjoy using that information to lie, but if she knew his real purpose she would have had a fit.

As he took up his position and prepared to spy on the trainees, he realized for the first time he was not proud of what he was doing, but couldn't help it. He wanted to know. He felt wrong in spying, but it was like hiding any other addiction. He just couldn't stop.

He brought up the new binoculars and saw at once they had been worth it. Hell, he thought, compared to my old telescope these things are like nice new glasses. Luther observed at once that the trainees were on r & r. This was the first time he had seen them in actual relaxation. All of his previous views had been while they were on some kind of drill. They had always been too far away for individual features to show.

Three widely separated boats, all belonging to the army, were on the lake. He knew they were Army property because he had seen them arrive on the transport some months ago. He had also been an eyewitness to part of the dock construction across the lake where the boats were kept tied. He shifted the binoculars and brought the dock into focus.

"My,my,my," Luther said. "This is too much."

Over there on the dock, in plain view, 3 of the prettiest girls he'd ever seen were sunbathing. Something else caught his eye and he made a slight re-adjustment to the focus. Looking again, he let out a slow whistle.

"By God, she is black...but what a fantastic sight. Lord, why couldn't I have been born a few years later, and be in this man's army?"

Now Luther saw, with some grief, that there were 3 guys with the pretty girls. Naturally, he thought. No way chicks like that would be alone. The 3 couples had blankets spread out on the dock and were taking in the afternoon sun. These binoculars were so good that he could even see the bottles of suntan oil and a portable blue radio next to the girls.

He watched, bug eyed behind his binoculars, as the lovely black girl left her blanket beside the good looking white boy and walked to the edge of the dock. She stood in magnificent splendor. She was so close in the sight of the binoculars that Luther thought he might reach out and touch her. She was even looking right at him.

Before he had time to wonder if she could see him or not, she raised her left hand and gave him the middle finger. She then disappeared into the lake with a graceful swan dive. Luther was so surprised he almost dropped his new toy.

Shit, he thought, lowering the binoculars. I've been caught. He stepped back, feeling ashamed and belittled. He thought, where does she get off doing that to me? Bitch.

He raised the binoculars for another look. What he saw this time made him quickly lower the binoculars and hustle back to his Jeep. One of the guys had some binoculars of his own and was looking right back. Not only that, he had plainly seen a telescopic lens in the hands of one of the girls.

Luther tossed his binoculars into the Jeep and climbed in behind them. Damn it, he thought, they've gone and spoiled it now. Angry with himself, angry for being caught, and angry with the army for catching him, he started the Jeep and turned around. He took off down the hill, anxious to put some distance between himself and the people on the dock.

The odd numbered teams had the afternoon off. 10 of the 16 recruits were out on the boats, either fishing or just relaxing. One or two had even tried their luck at water skiing.

On the dock, Johnny Redwine shared a blanket with Paula. On his right, Roy Errickson was sprawled out alongside Amanda, who was reading a book. On the blanket next to them, Linda was on her stomach while Terry Stout rubbed suntan oil on her back. Linda had brought her radio along, and it was tuned to the only station they could find. It was not the music they wanted, but it would do. Charley Pride was currently on, singing about burgers, fries and cherry pies.

"Hey," Roy said to Paula, "that's your kind of soul music, isn't it?"

Paula stopped humming and looked at Roy. "Sure is white boy, and sung by one of my own kind."

Roy laughed. "You sound just like one of them, Paula."

"I should," she said. "I am one of them."

"You are not," Roy said. "You're one of us."

"Well," Paula replied, "as nice as it is to be one of you, I'm still one of them too."

Amanda looked up from the book she was reading and said, "Change the subject, Roy."

"Don't worry, Amanda, I'm thick skinned," Paula said.

"I know you are, honey," Amanda replied. "I don't think of you as anything but the beautiful woman you are. Neither does anyone else. Roy sounds off before he thinks."

Paula smiled. "I'm going for a swim. Anyone else want to join me?"

"I'm too tired," Johnny said.

"Roy is going to put some suntan oil on me," Amanda said.

"First I've heard of it," Roy said. "Maybe I'd have more fun swimming with Paula."

"You probably would, dear, but I need you here."

Johnny grinned at Roy. "She's got you already, and you're not even married."

"Whatever," Roy answered, and reached for the bottle.

Paula walked over to the edge of the dock. Johnny watched her. At that moment, his thoughts were similar to those Luther Sherman had when he first saw Paula. My, but she is something special.... Then he saw her flip someone off before diving into the water.

"Hey, what the hell is up?" Johnny asked. He got up quickly and picked up the binoculars he had brought to keep the boats in view. Linda was on her feet, a camera in hand. The other three had rolled away from each other and were now stretched out flat, facing the lake, Browning 9mm pistols in their hands. Johnny raised the binoculars and scanned the lake, observing that all boats were turned away from them. It was by accident that he saw the guy on the hill.

"Linda, up on that hill," he said. They saw the man on the hill bring his binoculars up, then quickly lower them and back away. Johnny kept him in view until he disappeared behind a tree, then lowered his binoculars. "Did you get him, Linda?"

"Sure did, several good ones."

The other three were now slowly rising.

"Who the hell is up to what?" Roy demanded.

Linda sat back down, and Johnny walked over to the edge of the dock to look for Paula. She was floating on her back about 50 feet out. He waved to her, then turned and walked back to the others.

"Some son of a bitch was spying on us," Johnny said. "Paula saw him and flipped the bastard off."

Amanda looked at Johnny and asked, "Did you get a good look at him?"

"Not really. Linda's camera should tell us a few things."

They were silent, each with their own thoughts. Margo Smith sang on the radio about only hurting a little while.

Johnny scanned the hilltop again, but saw nothing except trees and a few birds. "He's gone, whoever he was. I bet he won't be back now that he's been spotted."

"Nevertheless," Linda said, "I'll see to it that Dot gets these pictures."

Johnny sat down on the blanket to wait for Paula. Since that first conversation a few weeks ago, their relationship had slowly blossomed. They enjoyed each other's company. They had deep admiration and respect for one another. Neither of them had used the word love, for neither of them was truly sure what the word meant. He knew what lust was, though, and he felt that for Paula all the time. He also knew that what he felt for her was based on more than lust alone. She had a certain quality, a special kind of way about her, that he'd never known in any other girl. She was all he'd ever dreamed of in a female.

"Black really is beautiful, Roy," Johnny had told his friend one day.

"It certainly is in her case, kid. She is a real doll. I'd keep her close if I were you."

It hadn't been hard to keep track of her here. She knew that Johnny looked at her whenever he could. She always had a smile or a wave. Then, a week ago, he'd finally had her.

It happened during the free time after lunch. They had run into each other outside the room she shared with Kathy. Paula simply opened the door, and he followed her in. It was one of those situations that might not have worked had it been planned. This was fate. She locked the door and proceeded to get undressed. Johnny, with no prior experience with a tryst like this, had fumbled with his own clothes until Paula finally came to his rescue.

They went at each other with all the abandonment of two young people who had nothing to lose. It was wild and imperfect, yet perfect for both of them.

Afterwards, he had laid beside her for the few minutes they had left, reflecting on the fantastic experience. He had no words, and neither did she. As if on cue they got up and started dressing. At the door, they paused for a breath and to enjoy a long kiss. Then Paula opened the door, scouted the hall, and slipped out. Johnny walked down the hall the other way.

As he was remembering now, Terry Stout was standing by the edge of the dock. Johnny hadn't even heard him get up. Something about the way Terry stood made Johnny get up and walk over to ask what was up.

Terry was a stocky kid of around 22 with brown hair and brown eyes. His left arm sported a tattoo that proclaimed

"This Earth Sucks". That left arm was now pointed toward a small figure in the water. Johnny looked beyond Terry's hand to see Paula at least 150 yards out from the dock, swimming along like she didn't have a care in the world.

"I don't think Paula realizes how far out she is," said Terry. "She's a great swimmer but I don't know if she's good enough to swim all the way across this thing."

"I don't know either," Johnny said. "When she comes back she could get tired before reaching the dock."

Linda had walked up to join them and also saw how far out Paula was. She went back to her blanket, picked up the portable two way radio, and turned toward the water. The nearest boat was at least a mile north of the dock. Johnny and Terry figured out what she had in mind.

"Tell them to be careful," Johnny said.

All of the boats, Jeeps, and cars were equipped with two way radios. When Cain had put them through the radio course he had insisted the radios only be used sparingly. They were to say what they needed to without too much detail and be done. To that end, they had spent hours talking to each other on practice radios about mythical situations.

"Team 3 to 7," Linda said.

Wesley Keeler, leader of team 7, had answered promptly. "Team 7, go ahead team 3."

"We have a swimmer in the water about 150 yards off our location. Please head this way and be prepared to make a pickup in case they get into problems coming back."

"Roger, 3. En route."

They saw the boat turn and speed up. Terry speculated on the waves from the boat. Linda spoke into the radio again. "3 to 7, slow on your approach."

Paula had now turned and was swimming back. She was still about 100 yards out and her swimming had developed what Johnny could only describe as a limp. "Oh shit, she's cramping!" Johnny said.

"Do either one of you swim well?" Linda asked.

"I swim like your average rock," Terry said.

"I'm even worse," Johnny said.

Linda handed the radio to Terry. "Keep an eye on the boat," she said, and dove in. Amanda followed her. Terry and Johnny looked at each other.

"Hell, I feel useless," Terry said.

Johnny heard a sound behind him and turned to find Roy, who was just returning from a nature call and wondered what was going on. Johnny turned back to the water and said, "Paula got out too far and is having trouble. Linda radioed team 7 in the boat, then she and Amanda jumped in to help."

Linda and Amanda were strong swimmers. They were closing the gap fast. Paula, now obviously having problems, saw them and tried to relax. Amanda reached her first. Linda got on Paula's right, and they started back to the dock. That's when things started going wrong.

Team 7 was coming in too fast.

Terry grabbed the radio and shouted, "Team 7! Slow down!"

The guy operating the boat made the simple mistake of going the wrong way on the throttle. Instead of slowing the boat, it increased speed. He caught his error, but by that time they were close to the swimming girls.

Clarence Moore, a kid from Lakeview, was at the helm. The guys on the dock saw him turn the boat in a hard right. He succeeded in missing the swimmers, but the backwash from the boat caught the girls full force.

"Damned fool!" Roy said.

Johnny was beside himself. He would have given a million dollars right then to be an Olympic swimmer. They watched as the girls reappeared and fought to stay together against the waves that were still buffeting them.

The boat made another turn, and this time it slowed to a snail's pace. It came up alongside the swimming trio. Rather than try to pluck them out of the water, they stayed close and got out ropes.

"What the hell are they up to?" Roy asked.

"Life lines," Terry said. "Someone on that boat has a brain. If they'd tried to reach over and lift them out, they could've tipped the boat over."

As it turned out, the ropes were not needed. Amanda and Linda, with the limp Paula between them, were still making steady progress toward the dock. They were angling toward the end of the dock where the ladder was.

Johnny ran down to the ladder with Terry and Roy right behind. He climbed down to water level and waited. He tried with force of will to send more strength into the swimmers as he watched their slow approach. It was clear they were all starting to tire. The boat had dropped back in order to not cause any waves to the dock area.

They were 20 yards out, then 15, 10, 5. Johnny reached out and grabbed Paula by the back of her swimming suit with one hand and lifted. Amanda got one hand on the ladder and assisted Paula. Johnny got her into a fireman's carry and started up the ladder. Terry and Roy helped him over the top. He carried Paula a few feet then gently laid her down. He heard the others coming up behind him, and the boat slipping into its tiedown spot.

Linda said. "Get her on her stomach, Johnny."

He got her turned over and started artificial respiration by pushing down on her back, then lifting up on her arms, then pushing down on her back again. The treatment had speedy results. Paula was very lucky and had not swallowed much water. She sputtered, groaned, and rolled. She sat up, still coughing.

"Damn!" Paula sputtered. "What a hell of a day." She gave her rescuers a weak smile.

Clarence Moore climbed up out of the boat he'd been piloting. He came over to where they were all gathered around Paula. "I'm so sorry," he said.

"It worked out this time," Roy said. "Paula's still with us."

Clarence turned and looked at the lake. The blue green water was reflecting the sun. He said, "I've lived within 100 miles of this lake all my life and never saw it until we came here. The name of it is pretty, almost sounds harmless. Now we know it isn't."

Johnny helped Paula to her feet. She leaned against him, raising and lowering one leg.

"Are you going to be ok?" Johnny asked.

"Yeah, I'll be alright. Let's go sit somewhere."

Johnny walked with Paula to the blanket they'd been sharing. She sat and stretched her legs. He sat down beside her and looked out at the lake. The two remaining boats were now headed for the dock. They were no doubt curious as to what had happened.

Clarence walked over to where they sat. "You alright, Paula?" he asked. His suntanned face was full of concern.

"Yes, I'm fine. Come sit down and tell us more about this lake."

Clarence looked at the incoming boats then sat. Tom T. Hall was on the radio singing about coffee and old pickups. The others were talking quietly. "I'm ashamed to admit it, but I don't know much more about this place than you guys do."

"Who named it Summer Lake?" Johnny asked.

"You got me there," Clarence replied. "All I know for sure is that it's big as lakes go. It's at least 12 miles long and 5 miles wide. I think the marshland to the north keeps it full of water."

He stood up. "I'm going to help the other boats tie up. Again, I'm sorry, Paula. Let me know if I can help at all."

The boat carrying the remaining members of group 9 docked first. Paula's team mates came over with their questions. She smiled at them from her now prone position on the blanket. "Sure guys, I'm fine."

Linda and Terry came over and sat down.

"It's been an exciting afternoon," Linda said.

"Something else happened?" Terry asked.

"We had a spy," Roy said. "Paula flipped the bastard off."

Linda told the story. Tom Stevens, leader of team 9, was a 20 year old from Tillamook. He asked about the pictures.

"I'll give them to Dot as soon as we get back."

The story of the spy and the drowning was repeated when the team from the last boat came over. After everyone had heard it, Tom Stevens called out that rest was over and it was time to head for the Jeeps.

They gathered up and headed to each team's rig. Johnny bid Paula so long and got behind the wheel of team 3's Jeep. He was today's designated driver. Engines revved, and one by one they drove up the hill toward the barracks with team 9 in the lead.

Linda looked over her shoulder toward the lake, reflecting on how pretty it looked. "Well, it was more exciting than Urban Warfare School," she mused aloud.

"I hope to shout," Roy replied.

Tomorrow they would be in school while the even numbered teams had rec time. Dot was the instructor for this term, and she was good. Still, they agreed, class wasn't as much fun as sitting around the lake in the sun.

There was so much dust kicked up from the Jeeps that Johnny did not see the Ford truck near the barracks until he parked. Team 9 was already talking to their guest. Team 3 got out and walked past 9 toward the building.

Paula walked over to join them. She gestured to the truck and said, "That guy is from the little town named for the lake. He's on a committee that's planning a 4th of July party. He's up here to see the base commander and invite us all to attend. Tom told me to bring Dot on the double." She double timed ahead and the others kept walking at a slower pace.

"Hey," Johnny said, "it'd be fun to go to a party like that. I'll bet these backcountry folks really know how to put on a show."

"Don't count your chickens," Linda said. "We might not be allowed to go."

Dot Stoneking was tired. The building was hot, and her class that day had been long and uninteresting. The nice weather made everyone want to be outside. She was currently in a small room used as an office. The instructors would hide here for a quiet minute, or use the space to take notes and write supply orders. It didn't have the usual office equipment, because this organization did not keep records.

Right now she was sitting back in her chair, bare feet up on the desk. Her light green summer dress was hiked up in a way she wouldn't have it in public. She really wished the committee had paid for air conditioning.

Dot heard the out of class recruits coming back from the lake. She lowered her feet and her dress, and found her shoes. She opened the blinds that covered the only window and slid it back. The fresh air felt good. She looked through the wire screen over the grass to the stand of Sugar Pine trees 50 yards away. The trees looked cool and inviting. She was considering going for a walk among the trees when she heard a knock on the door, and bid whoever knocked to enter.

Paula opened the door and stepped in. Dot smiled at her. This was one of her favorite recruits. The strong, lovely black girl in the swimming suit was a far cry from the skinny, half nuts weakling that had tried to mug her several months ago.

"Hi, Paula. What can I do for you?"

"There's a man outside wanting to see the base commander. He says he represents the town of Summer Lake, and they want to invite us to the 4th of July festivities."

"He does? Well, I guess I'll just have to talk with him," Dot said, and she pulled a hairbrush from the desk.

"You don't need that," Paula said. "You look just fine the way you are. I would love to keep your schedule and manage to stay as pretty as you do."

"Well, thank you Paula. Flattery will get you nothing though. Is someone keeping an eye on our guest?"

"Yes. The rest of my team's with him."

"Well then, if you'll excuse me, I'll go see him. By the way, you are very pretty yourself. If you stand around in that swimsuit long I'm sure all the boys here will tell you the same."

"Thank you." Paula smiled as she left.

Dot found the visitor standing by his truck, talking to team 9. They weren't saying much as they didn't know what to say. The visitor was a stout man in his 50's. He had gray hair, brown eyes, and a long scar down the right side of his face.

Dot walked up and addressed the team. "Thank you, guys. Dismissed." She then addressed the visitor. "Good afternoon, sir. May I help you?"

"Excuse me ma'am, but I was looking for the base commander."

"You're looking at her."

His eyes widened as he stammered, "Oh. Oh, well, excuse me, I was kind of, well…"

Dot smiled. "I know. You were expecting a man."

The visitor looked relieved. "Yes, ma'am. I was."

"Next month, or last month, you would have found a man. This month I'm in charge."

He held out a big hairy hand. "My name is Billy Pratt."

Dot took his hand and shook it firmly, then let it fall. She did not offer her name.

"I represent the entertainment committee. We're planning the 4th of July festivities for the town of Summer Lake. We thought since the military was present, it might give the show something extra if you could participate."

"In what way?" Dot asked.

"Well, we always have a parade, not much you know, maybe a speech or two, then the rest of the day is eating and drinking. That night we always have a big dance."

"Tell me, Mr. Pratt, do people come in from a long way off for this affair, or is it mainly locals?"

"It's hard to say for sure. Folks sometimes come from Lakeview, sometimes Paisley has some folks over, nothing too far off."

Dot carefully considered what she had to say next. Doctor Fish had warned her to be extremely careful in what was said to the locals. He had briefed her extensively on their Army National Guard cover he had built. "Mr. Pratt, as you have no doubt heard, we are a classified unit. I cannot permit any official representation because of that. Of course those of you who live nearby know we're here. However, Washington is not prepared to widely advertise our presence. Do you understand?"

Pratt nodded.

Dot continued. "It is possible some of our people could attend, but it would be strictly unofficial. I hope that our decline of your offer will not be viewed as a snub by your committee. My orders come from much higher up."

"Of course," Pratt said. "I understand, and I know the others will. I was in the Army and remember what it was like."

"On behalf of my troops," Dot said, "thank you for considering us. It's nice to be remembered, especially when you're a long way from home during holidays."

Pratt turned toward his pickup. "Well, I'd better get back to town. Thanks anyway." He opened the truck door and looked at Dot with curiosity. "I do have one question while I'm here. Why are all you people so heavily armed?"

The question took Dot off guard. "Well, this is a training base, Mr. Pratt. Guns are part of military life." The answer felt lame, but it was the only thing she could think to say.

"Well, you're right," he said, and stepped into the truck. "Thanks again, ma'am. Good luck with your school here."

Dot watched him disappear in a cloud of dust down the road toward the lake. Pratt bothered her. Was this really an invitation to visit, or was he using the excuse to look around? She turned and walked toward the barracks. Her mind was working fast. Some kind of security system had to be devised to stop people from just driving in. She and the other instructors should have figured that out a long time ago. She wondered if Pratt had time to wander before he was discovered.

She entered the building and caught the smell of dinner cooking. She realized she was hungry, looked at her watch, and saw she still had 45 minutes to wait. She found Linda and Johnny waiting by the office door. Linda was holding a camera.

"Hi," Dot said. "What can I do for you?"

Linda held up her camera. "We had a little excitement at the lake today."

They entered the office with Dot in the lead. Linda put the camera on the desk. Johnny brought over 2 chairs for them. He explained about the spy, including the bird Paula flipped him before diving into the lake. Next, Linda and Johnny related the happenings of the near drowning. Dot listened with a frown. When the story was finished Dot picked up the camera and removed the film.

"I'll develop this after dinner," Dot said. "We'll see what we have here. As far as the lake, it sounds like everyone reacted well enough. Let's hope everyone learned from it. It would be a shame to lose any of you that way."

Johnny grinned. "What if we get shot?"

"Can it, smartass," Dot answered. "It would be bad to lose any of you in any way at all. Now, both of you get going. I have something to do. Also, pass the word, I want everyone to meet in the Day Room at 7:30."

When they left, Dot pulled off her shoes and sat back in her chair. She was going to have to explain to the recruits why they wouldn't be allowed to attend the festivities. They wouldn't like it. Some would be more upset than others if they had a case of cabin fever. She reached left and picked up a clipboard. She began making notes for the upcoming meeting.

When Dot was finally done with notes and other tasks she stood and noticed the smell of the pine trees. The cool evening breeze brought the summer air in. She realized this was as close to nature as she had ever been.

Dot put her shoes back on and went to the dining area. She chose to sit with Team 3 this evening. It was a different team every night. She used the time to get a feel for how people were doing.

"Linda, how is it you happened to have a telescopic lens on your camera?"

"I enjoy taking shots of deer, birds, and just about everything else," Linda answered. "I only had 2 or 3 shots left when our spy showed up. The rest of it will just be wildlife."

"That's okay," Dot answered. "You want to help me develop them?"

"Sure," Linda said. "I've wanted to learn about developing anyway."

"I'll make sure you get a complete course in photography before you leave here. Cain is an expert in the field."

The small talk continued, mostly centering around base activities. When dinner was over, Linda accompanied Dot to the dark room the committee had furnished them with. It didn't take long for the photos to be developed. There were several shots of deer, one of an eagle, and one blurry photo that appeared to be an elk.

"These are very good, Linda. Very good indeed. Is that last one an elk?"

"Thank you. I think it's a bull," Linda replied.

The pictures of Luther Sherman were excellent. One of them even caught the look of surprise on his face.

Dot smiled. "This must be the result of Paula flipping him off."

"How did she see him from that distance?" Linda wondered.

"Must have just been the way he was standing or something," Dot mused. "I want to keep these two snaps of our spy."

"Fine with me," Linda said.

Dot dropped them in an envelope with the negatives. She would send them to Doctor Fish on the next helicopter. Funny, she thought, I still think of him as Fish. She dropped the envelope into a box of outgoing things, and gave Linda her wildlife pictures. They left the room and headed for the 7:30 meeting.

Chapter 19

Boxer drove a blue Buick up Lancaster Drive in Salem. This morning of June 25th was warm and clear. Traffic was heavy with people preparing for the upcoming holiday. He checked his watch. 11:42 a.m. He was right on schedule. The destination was a small town of around 5,000 people called Silverton. The next road ran that direction. It was a wide rural two-lane through farm land. The fields were green and farmers were out on their machinery.

On the seat beside him, with its box of ammunition, lay a .357 Magnum. This was Smith & Wesson's model #19. It had a six inch barrel with adjustable rear sights. Boxer had chosen this weapon because he would be firing from inside the car. He planned to drop the target on the sidewalk as he came out of the house. With a six inch barrel he was sure of better aim.

Abel had been watching this target for two weeks. Every afternoon between 12:30 and 12:35 the target left his house, never earlier. The target was a Lutheran minister who, for some time now, had been doing an excellent side business peddling narcotics.

The minister was a well respected man in his community. The police had no suspicions about him. The Cleanup Committee had not known of him until he was named by Wesley Keeler, a recruit from Albany. When Keeler had been recruited by Cain, he named more than one person from different respected community positions. The others would be left for the recruits to finish off after their training. Today the minister was Boxer's.

The shock value had factored into the selection of this target. The deaths of those Portland cops had shaken everyone. The city was still reeling from it. This would be the first shooting since the two cops and their supplier, and was bound to send even more shockwaves through the state.

Once in Silverton, Boxer turned onto a quiet street. The houses were older but well kept, with lots of flowers and cherry blossom trees. He mused that if he ever settled down, he might like to have a home just like one of those. He drove around the block once to size it up. Abel had given him an excellent briefing, including the best escape route. He found several children playing at a school on the next street to the north of him. Other than that, no one was out.

Boxer chose a spot diagonally across from the target's house. He had a clear view of the front yard and sidewalk. The target's white Chevy wagon was parked in front of the house. Boxer decided the man would die the minute he opened his front yard gate.

He checked his watch. 12:32 p.m. He looked around and thanked God most of the women in America were now working, so there were no prying eyes from the neighboring homes.

Boxer saw the minister go out his front door. He stopped in the yard, picked up a hose and put it to one side. He was dressed in a white buttoned up shirt and tan slacks. The target straightened up then continued toward the gate. Boxer had the .357 up and was sighting down the barrel. The minister opened the gate. Boxer had the hammer back. Then he applied pressure. The gun roared and bucked upward. The target was struck in the heart. His body fell to the sidewalk as Boxer started rolling the Buick away.

Boxer didn't realize there was one woman watching him. Alice Pitcher, 83 years of age, was reading on her front porch. Mrs. Pitcher had been widowed when she was 66 years old. For the past 17 years she had lived in this house and enjoyed being the neighborhood Grandma. Kids had grown up on this street and gone off to bigger and better things, but they always remembered her. Many of them brought their own children to see her.

From her vantage point on the porch, she could see many things. At 83, she was still sharp as a tack and her eyesight was very good. Not much got by her. Thanks to a thick tree with a screen of leaves, the man she was now watching could not see her. She could see clearly what happened at the preacher's house.

Boxer made a few turns, crossed the Silver Creek Bridge, and continued on while keeping the speed limit. He was about to turn left onto the highway when an old man stepped off the sidewalk right into his path. It was too late to avoid him. The impact knocked the old man sideways, throwing him like a rag doll to the street. He died from a broken neck. Boxer swore twice and put his foot to the floor.

Patrolman Jack Hawkins was one half block behind Boxer when the pedestrian went down. Hawkins reached for his overhead lights and siren. At the same time, his radio started broadcasting an APB on a shooting that had just occurred. The suspect vehicle matched the one that he was following.

Hawkins took the microphone in his hand and keyed down.

"511 in pursuit of the suspect vehicle on Mt. Angel road. Suspect vehicle just hit an elderly pedestrian at Waters Street intersection with said highway. Pedestrian appears deceased. One half mile from city limits. Speed 80, unable to read license plate at this time."

He hung up the mic and concentrated on the fleeing Buick. It was obvious he was going to have a run for his money. The Plymouth patrol unit climbed to 85, 90, then 95. They were heading for Mount Angel, and the next 5 miles were straight with lots of driveways and side roads.

Boxer had his foot firmly down on the gas, but he wasn't yet to the point of panic. All he could do now was drive like hell and hope the cop ruined his engine or wrecked. From what Abel had said, he doubted the small town police force could react in time to put up a roadblock.

Boxer sped up to 100. This was not a road meant for this kind of speed, but he was desperate now. The patrol car was hanging close, siren screaming. A sign indicated he was one mile from Mt. Angel. Cars were streaming by in the other direction. Boxer wished he had not had to do this in the middle of the day. Night hits were so much better. He entered the town of Mount Angel praying for luck.

He dropped his speed to 90, which still looked insane for the people in the business district that saw him pass. Quick as a blink they were out in farm country again. Perhaps the priests at the Abbey on the hill heard his prayer for luck.

The patrol car was still on his rear. He had the Buick up to 100 again. He reviewed the upcoming highway in his mind. Abel had told him it was a narrow stretch of road with lots of curves. He had also been warned that farmers here often hogged this road with their tractors. He saw the sign warning of the first corner with a recommended speed of 45. He took it at 80. He was almost through the curve and accelerating when he saw a hay truck coming at him. It was on the wrong side of the road.

Boxer never stood a chance. He slammed into the front of the hay truck at 86 miles an hour. Both car and truck exploded on contact. The engine of the Buick landed 400 feet away from the point of impact in a corn field.

Hawkins then came through the corner, his car under control. It was only luck that got him through the accident site uninjured. Parts and hay were flying through the air.

When he finally skidded to a stop, some 200 feet beyond the accident, everything was in flames.

"511, reporting an accident 3 miles from Mt. Angel. Likely fatalities. Suspect vehicle hit a hay truck head on. Send fire department, both units in flames."

Hawkins jumped out and started flagging traffic. The funeral fire burned hot and bright behind him, fueled by hay and gasoline.

Chapter 20

The police were having trouble identifying the charred remains in the smashed Buick, but the three men in the safe house were not. Cain, Abel and Doctor Fish were in the living room of the Committee's apartment in Eugene. Fish was pacing, visibly upset. Cain and Abel sat on the sofa. Fish had been involved in risky things long enough to know that you couldn't win every time. Still, when you lost a man, especially a good one, it hurt.

Two days had passed since Boxer had carried out his assignment and been killed. Fish had wanted to meet with Abel and Cain sooner, but had delayed the meeting until he could check out the investigation. He stopped pacing and faced the two men.

"Well, we've lost a good man."

The others were silent. They had not expected Fish to say anything.

"Abel, was standard procedure followed in this operation?" Fish asked.

The former Marine drill instructor had no emotion in his eyes as he answered. "Except for the fact this was a daytime hit, yes. It had to be done in the daytime for practical reasons. The target must have read about the other killings and took safety measures at night. He didn't think we'd hit in broad daylight."

"Was normal security followed as far as the Buick was concerned?"

"Yes. They'll trace it eventually, but all the owner will be able to tell them is that it had been paid for in cash."

"When was the car bought?"

Abel looked at Cain, who answered: "Five weeks ago."

"I know that Boxer was observing the other rules," Abel said. "I talked with him just before he left. He was packing a fake ID, and the gun was picked up from a guy in a bar several weeks ago. If it came through the fire it's highly unlikely they'll be able to trace it."

Fish resumed his pacing. Cain and Abel waited in silence. After a few minutes, Fish stopped and took out his pipe, filled it and puffed it to life. He thought for another minute then said: "Abel, I'd like you to take the chopper to camp tomorrow and relieve Dot. Boxer was scheduled. Cain, how good a burglar are you?"

It was a foolish question. Fish was well aware of Cain's qualifications.

"The best."

"Boxer had a dentist here in town," Fish continued. "As far as I know, he hasn't been there in a long time. Either way, get into that office as soon as you can and get those charts."

"Excuse me," Abel said. "If that dentist finds he's been robbed he's going to yell for the cops. It probably won't take them long to figure out whose file was taken and why."

Fish felt foolish. "You're right, Abel. Cain, use the shotgun method. Grab everything 4 or 5 letters on each side of Boxer's file. Mess the place up good. You know the drill."

"Consider it done," Cain said.

While Fish was meeting with Cain and Abel, another meeting was taking place in a city 200 miles south.

Ashland Police had received a teletype requesting they contact Mr. and Mrs. Jay McFarlen. They were asked to find out if the couple knew the current whereabouts of their Buick Sedan. The message included the license plate and ID number.

An officer visited the residence with the teletype in hand. The following statement was recorded:

"On or about the night of May 20th of this year, at around 8:30 pm, a man came to our house. He wanted to know if the car we had advertised in the paper was still for sale. We told him it was. He asked to see the car, so we walked with him to the garage. He looked the car over and took out his wallet. He did not haggle about the price listed in the paper. He took out seventeen $100 bills. We gave him the papers to the car. He got in it and left. We don't know how he arrived. All we can remember about him is that he was tall, well dressed, and black. His voice was soft and sounded slightly southern. We didn't notice any scars or marks."

The officer took the statement to his office. The statement was put on teletype in its entirety and sent to the Oregon State Police office in Salem. The message sped north electronically. When the dispatcher on duty got the teletype from the machine, she tore it off and carried it down the hall to Chief Richard Brownwell.

Brownwell read the message and looked at the dispatcher. "No reply." The dispatcher left the room. Brownwell picked up his phone and dialed the Silverton Police Department. He asked for Chief Putnam.

"Putnam here, what did you turn up?"

Brownwell read Chief Putnam the message.

"Balls!" the chief exclaimed. "That's no help at all."

Brownwell answered, "I think that we're dealing with more than just a few fanatics looking for some publicity. This bunch is organized, whoever they are."

"I agree," Putnam said. "My people turned up a witness here that saw the shooting. An elderly gal who lives down the street from the preacher. From what she says, the guy who did the shooting seems like a professional. She also said she knew the victim was pushing drugs, but declined to say anything because she was afraid no one would believe her. The worst part is, she's right."

"If this minister was above suspicion, how in the name of all that's holy did this Cleanup Committee find out?"

"That's the question of the week," Putnam replied.

Brownwell looked at the teletype again. "Chief, do you have any doubt in your mind that this Cleanup Committee was behind this shooting?"

"I'd be more convinced if one of their little business cards they like to leave was found. None have shown up on this one yet."

"Well, good luck, Chief, and let us know if we can be of any help."

"Good luck to you too," Putnam said. "If we turn up anything here in Silverton, we'll let you know."

Brownwell hung up the phone and sat thinking. After a few minutes, he picked the phone up again and dialed the private home number of the governor.

"Paul, Rick Brownwell speaking."

"What have you found out?" the governor asked anxiously.

"Not much, but I do have some ideas. I'd like to stop by and bounce a few of them off of you."

Brownwell thought the governor waited just a little too long before he said "Sure, Rick, come on over. Any idea right now beats no ideas at all."

"I'll be there in 30 minutes," Brownwell said.

"Fine," replied the governor. "I'll be by the pool.

From the Silverton Appeal, June 29th.

Identity of Dead Man Remains a Mystery.

Silverton City Police, in cooperation with Oregon State Police, are still trying to identify the charred remains of a man killed yesterday. The car he was driving slammed head on into a loaded hay truck 3 miles east of Mount Angel. At the time of the accident, the car was being pursued by Silverton Police Officer Jack Hawkins. The vehicle had failed to stop following a pedestrian collision on the corner of Waters Street and Silverton Highway. In that accident, 84 year old Theo Amberg of this city was killed.

Silverton Police are also investigating a fatal shooting that occured around 12:30 pm yesterday, at 223 Falls Street. It is not known at this time if there is any connection with that shooting and the subsequent events. Two other persons died in the fiery collision near Mount Angel. Elmer Schmitts and his 19 year old son Richard were in the hay truck. Both were lifetime residents of Mount Angel. Funeral services are pending.

Chapter 21

It was the morning of July 2nd. The weather at Summer Lake was cool and cloudy. The chopper carrying Abel and the camp supplies landed promptly at 8:40 a.m. Dot was waiting anxiously as Abel stepped down.

"Is it true?" she asked.

"I'm afraid so."

That was all they said near the chopper. They walked together to the office for a briefing. The teams busied themselves unloading supplies. Dot closed the door behind Abel, and they sat down at the desk.

"What went wrong?" she asked.

Abel filled her in as quickly as possible. Having no phone or television here, Dot had only been able to guess based on what she heard in radio newscasts. She listened silently until Abel had finished.

"I don't think that he had any choice but to run," Dot said quietly.

"Neither do I. I know it seems heartless, but we have no choice but to carry on. Now, young lady, let's wrap this up. The chopper pilot wants to get out of here."

Dot reported that everyone had passed their last month of classes with flying colors. Everything was normal except one afternoon.

Abel's eyes narrowed. "What happened?"

"The recruits caught a guy spying on them with binoculars while they were swimming. Linda got a couple pictures of him. I'm sending them out to Doctor Fish. I don't think the spy will be around anymore."

"Fish might make sure the spy regrets his actions. Anything else?"

"Yeah, we got an invitation to attend the 4th of July celebration in town."

"Oh hell. I hope you turned them down."

"Of course," Dot replied. "The troops didn't like it, but I reminded them that since some of them are from this county, the last thing we need is for one of them to bump into an old friend. I've also put the lake off limits until the holiday is over. The risk is high enough during regular days, I figure it's doubled over a holiday weekend. That lake is going to attract people like flies to sugar."

"I'm afraid it's going to be a rather dull 4th for the recruits," Abel said, "but it's the only safe way. They'll just have to accept it."

"Oh they understand," said Dot. "They won't cause any problems."

"Good." Abel stood up. "If that's it, let's get you on board before the pilot has kittens."

"One other thing," Dot said as she stood. "Starting today I've posted 24 hour guards on the road coming up from the lake. The odds of someone just driving on up here is too high."

"Did the guy with the invitation from town drive up here?"

"Yes he did. He did not get a chance to poke around. Team 9 occupied him right away."

"Good for them! You've done well."

Dot picked up her purse and Abel picked up her suitcase. The pilot was in his seat when they got to the chopper, clearly ready to go. The team assigned to loading and unloading stood at attention at a safe distance. Dot waved at the two teams then boarded the chopper.

Abel stood with the recruits and watched the chopper lift up and out. As soon as the noise cleared enough, he barked: "Day Room! On the double!"

Team 3 double timed it to the day room. Johnny was following Roy.

"I hope he tells us what's been bugging Dot," Johnny said. "As a friend of mine used to say, she's been like a sore tailed cat in a room full of rocking chairs."

"Yep, something's been bugging her," Roy agreed.

In a few short minutes, everyone was assembled and waiting. Abel stood by the desk at the front of the room. He told the recruits to have a seat. Abel started with the bad news, given the only way he knew how- simple and direct.

"Boxer is dead."

The news shook the recruits. However, these recruits were not as upset as other people might have been, because they'd each witnessed unexpected or unusual deaths in their young lives

The first question came from Johnny Redwine. "How did it happen?"

Abel took his time explaining the details. It wouldn't be long before these people would be out doing the same thing. Perhaps hearing what happened to Boxer would help them somehow in the future. He answered questions as they came. The room finally fell silent. The final remark was made by Linda Smith.

"Boxer was a good man. We'll miss him....but we've got to keep going."

Chapter 22

Team 3 was reclining under a large pine tree. It was a warm summer night, and team 3 had the midnight to 8 am guard shift. They were 50 yards from the intersection of the lake road and camp road. It was silent except for the quiet music coming from Linda's radio. The breeze from the lake rustled the pine tree above them. A silver moon reflected off the lake.

Johnny was sitting up straight with his back against the tree trunk. The others were asleep. Each team member took a 2 hour part of the watch. It was just after 1 a.m now, and Roy would take over at 2. Johnny lifted the weight of the M16 on his knees, and shifted his back to reduce the tug of the holstered Browning. Far off somewhere he heard the sound of a motor. That was not unusual as the highway was only a few miles away. He listened some more and figured in a few minutes he would see the lights of the car he was hearing across the lake.

This was the night of July 4th, technically the 5th now. Traffic was a little heavier than usual. Johnny couldn't help but wish he was out there somewhere celebrating. Everyone was getting cabin fever. Tempers were short. Abel kept a close rein on them and stopped any fights before they really started. Team leaders were also responsible for keeping their teams in line, since Abel couldn't be everywhere at once.

Johnny stood up slowly, and walked over to the road. The sound of his boots on gravel was loud. He heard the others stir. He stepped back off the road and stood quietly. The breeze shifted slightly, and Johnny smelled the lake. He took in a deep breath, let it out, then stiffened.

The motor he had heard was not out on the highway. It was on the lake road and it was coming this way. He walked a few paces to the left. Sure enough, back down the road a couple of miles, he could see the twin beams of headlights.

Nothing had happened since guard duty started. No cars had come up the road, night or day. If this one stayed on the lake road it would be no concern of his. However, if it turned and started up toward camp, they were to turn it back. Abel had briefed them on how to handle the situation if one developed.

"Be firm but polite," Abel had said. "Explain this is a military area that's closed to the public. If they get nasty, point guns at them. That usually makes people listen up. Hope and pray you don't have to take it any further." Abel had also ordered full military uniforms while on guard duty. They were uncomfortable but necessary should anything occur.

Johnny watched the lights as they came up slowly. He hoped they might stop or turn off somewhere....but they didn't. When they were 100 yards from the intersection, Johnny called out: "Up and at 'em you guys! We might have company!"

The team was with him in 30 seconds.

"What's up?" Linda asked.

"The car coming up the road might be heading here."

Linda took a look. The lights were very close now. "If they come up here, you guys put your flashlights on and stop them. I'll wait here with Amanda. With luck they'll take one look and scat. If they get nasty, Amanda and I will approach and assist."

The car stopped at the intersection. It sat still, the occupants debating what to do. They were loud enough for the team to hear. They also heard a bottle shatter.

"Damn it Billy!" a female voice said. "Watch what you're doing!"

"Up yours," Billy replied.

Linda scoffed. "Great, a bunch of drunks."

Before they had time to plan, the car turned right. The girls stepped back so they wouldn't be picked up in the headlights. Johnny and Roy stepped out into the road, flashlights on. The car ground to a halt 20 yards in front of them. They approached the car, one on each side.

"Holy shit, it's the fucking army!" someone said. "Of all the unluckiest things."

Johnny had his light on the driver. "Sir, Shut off your motor and lights," he said.

The driver, a kid of maybe 16, did as he was told.

"What the hell is this?" asked the female voice.

"This is restricted military property," Roy stated. "This is as far as you go."

From the back seat someone demanded: "Who the fuck are you?"

The driver turned from Johnny's light to address the voice in back. "Billy, shut your mouth. I told you we shouldn't have come up here."

Johnny saw there were 5 people in the car. One boy and two girls in the front, and two guys in the back. Billy was sitting behind the driver.

"Up yours," Billy replied. "I want to know just who and what these soldier boys think they're doing."

Johnny addressed the driver. "Sir, this is a restricted area. Start the car and back out."

"No fucking way!" Billy shouted. "This is a free country and we don't have to listen to the army. No siree Bob." Billy opened the rear door and stepped out. Johnny heard the other door open. At the same time, he heard the click clang as Roy ran the slide on his M16.

Johnny stepped back, put his flashlight on his belt, and brought up his rifle.

"Mother of Jesus!" the driver exclaimed. "You're going to shoot us?"

"You fucking punk!" Billy hollered. "I should ram that thing up your ass."

Johnny sized him up. 6 foot 4, 200 pounds, long blonde hair. Somewhere in his late 20's. Aggressive drunk. He heard Roy yell at Billy to freeze. He heard the girls coming up behind him. Linda approached with her rifle aimed at Billy.

"Well damned if there aren't more of them." Billy had his right hand on the car door and a beer bottle in his left hand. He looked at Linda. "Looks like I'm going to have to shove 2 rifles up 2 asses."

If Linda Smith had one fault as a leader, it was a complete lack of tact. She was a fighter, always had been. This school had done nothing to teach her or anyone else the art of diplomacy. Linda looked the situation over and said: "You know what, Billy?"

Billy laughed. "Well I'll be damned! If it isn't a female in a soldier suit- and with a gun, no less. What kind of army are you people?"

"The best kind," Linda answered. "You haven't answered my question, Billy."

"Oh, a thousand pardons, ma'am," he said sarcastically. "Maybe I didn't hear it."

"Well maybe you'll hear this." Linda glared at him. "I'm going to count to 3. If you aren't back in the car when I get to 3, I'm going to shoot your balls off. Is that clear?"

"For Christ's sake Billy, she'll do it!" the driver shouted. "Get in here!"

"One," Linda counted.

"You're bluffing," Billy said.

"Two."

Billy stepped behind the car door.

"Hurry up!" one of the girls shouted.

Billy stepped in and the car door closed just as Linda got to three.

"Now," she said to the other man who had gotten out. "Get in the car."

No counting was necessary.

Johnny breathed a sigh of relief.

Linda lowered her rifle and stepped in closer to the car. She flashed her light in, and saw that they were all in their teens or early 20's. She settled her light on the driver, who looked away. "What's your name?" she asked.

"Dan," he said. "Most people call me Danny."

"Alright, Danny. It's nice to have met you. Now start your car and back down the road. Where you go from here is up to you. Don't come back up this road again."

"OK," Dan said nervously, and started the car. The lights came on.

"Who are you people?" one of the girls asked.

"As we said, this is a military road," Linda replied.

"Congratulations, ma'am. You did a fantastic job of putting Billy in his place."

"Up yours," Billy slurred quietly. Johnny figured that was the only comeback he knew.

Linda stepped away from the car. "Take it easy."

Team 3 watched as the car backed quickly down the road.

"Holy cow, am I glad that's over!" Amanda said.

"That was a close call," Linda said. "Roy, go ahead and relieve Johnny, since it's only 15 minutes till shift change."

The rest of the night passed quietly. Team 4 relieved them at 8 a.m. sharp. They passed on what had happened, then took the Jeep back to camp for breakfast.

Chapter 23

The July days drifted by. The training routine continued with recruits going to class, serving guard duty, and working on the range. In the third week of July, Abel introduced a new phase of training.

The teams constructed a makeshift house. With Abel as a guide they would practice raiding. A different team would occupy the house each day, posing as armed drug dealers, and the others would have to take it.

The recruits enjoyed the practical training. Highly organized plans were created and carried out. Blanks were issued for the weapons. Abel ordered the plans to be carried out with as few rounds spent as possible.

"Any fool can pour hundreds of rounds into a house," Abel said. "It's simple to duck down behind a rock and blast away. There are much better ways to take a house. Besides, when you're out there in the real world, we aren't always going to have the circumstances or time to fight a full scale battle."

The second week of training involved night raids. Abel assigned team 6 to hold the house. They had no idea who would be coming after them, or how many. On this night, it fell to team 3 to take the house.

Team 6 was expecting an attack sometime between 9 p.m. and 1 a.m. The recruits were so invested in the games it became a matter of pride to either take or hold the house, depending on the assignment. They also had a running system of bets.

The one advantage given to team 3 was that 6 had no idea how many people they were up against. Team 3 had elected to attack alone out of pride for themselves. They had come up with a plan, but were not totally confident it would succeed. However, it was the only thing they could come up with that had half a chance, so they rolled with it.

Johnny lay 50 yards behind the house. Beside him, Amanda shifted her position slightly. They were waiting under a full moon. The advantage was with the team in the house. Team 6 had a clear field of fire both in front of and behind the house. Team 3 had tried to make the best of their situation when planning. Rushing the place would've been foolish.

Linda was off to their right somewhere, working her way around to the front. Roy was angling left to approach the house from the east. The plan called for Linda to arrive at the front and create a disturbance to attract the attention of team 6. At a given time, Johnny would work his way around to the west side of the house. When Amanda thought Johnny was in position, she would open fire with a few rounds. The idea was to convince the people in the house that the assault was coming from the front and the rear. Then Roy and Johnny would open up from the sides, and when they had team 6's attention, Linda and Amanda would rush the house. They admitted it wasn't a great plan, but it was the best they had.

Johnny got moving and stayed low while he worked his way to the west side of the house. They agreed it would probably take him 2-3 minutes to make it . He was halfway to his selected spot when he heard a single shot set off by Linda. It was immediately answered by a volley from within the house. Bastards, Johnny thought. They get to blow off all the ammo they want.

Team 3 knew they would catch hell from the others if they didn't take the house. When 3 held the house they successfully defended it from 2 teams.

Amanda fired 2 shots. She was answered with another volley. Team 3 now knew that 6 was expecting them from the front and the rear. Johnny reached his goal and dropped to the ground. He was 50 yards west of the house. He started inching his way forward. Every 2 minutes or so Linda or Amanda would fire a shot. It was answered quickly each time. He moved forward another 10 feet. He had no way of knowing when Roy would reach the house, and vice versa.

Johnny figured if this was a real operation they'd all get killed. However, if this was real they'd have a better system of signals and different circumstances. He inched forward. 20 feet from the house. 10 feet. Finally he stood and charged the house, rifle up.

Johnny reached the window and emptied a clip into the darkened interior. Someone yelled. He saw the flashes as Roy opened up from the other side. It was dumb of team 6 to not cover the windows. Johnny rammed home another clip and scrambled through the window.

Abel sounded his whistle. The game was over.

"I never saw anything so damn sloppy in all my life!" Abel said.

They were gathered in front of the house. The rest of the recruits had come out of their hiding places to listen to the two active teams get chewed out. Abel didn't know it, but the other recruits had placed bets. The odds had been heavily favoring team 3. Who collected how much from whom now depended on how Abel judged both teams.

"I would hate to try and take a house from team 3," Abel said. "However, it would be a cake walk to defend one against them. In this case, team 3 failed miserably. You people will be up here in 2 nights to try this again. This time I expect you to come up with something a damn sight better."

As a consequence for blowing the operation, team 3 had to run the two and a half miles back to the barracks. Everybody else went in Jeeps, and they all made a point to jeer as they passed. The only ones who really meant it were the ones who bet on team 3 and lost. The runners had no choice but to take it and keep moving.

Two nights later, they scored a success. They felt much better as a result. Before the games ended the following week, everyone experienced both defeat and victory. They learned, and that was the point.

On the last day of training, Abel paid the recruits the greatest compliment they had ever heard from him: "I would hate to be in any house that any of you people were after. I would also hate to be in the bunch that tried to take one from you."

Chapter 24

The third week in July was another time of worry for the governor. This morning had done nothing to improve his mood. It was raining, his popularity had slipped by two points, and he had a press conference to attend.

The press conference was a regularly scheduled event. In the old days he used to look forward to them. Now, after nearly 7 years at the helm, he didn't like them much. Reporters were like a bunch of hounds after a fox. They could never settle for a simple answer. They would keep digging until you tripped. Well, today he had a surprise for them. He had decided not to run for re-election.

Paul had told no one. Not even his closest associates had a clue. His announcement would throw the race for his party's nomination wide open. He decided it would be fun to watch the wolves fight.

He looked at his appointment calendar and made a face. In 20 minutes he was meeting the controversial chairman of the Land Conservation and Development Commission. They didn't like each other so the meeting would be short. Then he was meeting with Richard Brownwell. Every time he thought of Brownwell he also thought of the Cleanup Committee. That's about the only thing that's gone right this month, he thought. At least those fanatics had been quiet.

The governor did paperwork until the chairman of the LCDC came in. That meeting took 25 minutes. The chairman was hardly out of the office when Brownwell came in. Brownwell got a cup of coffee and sat down. He looked tired.

"Hey, Rick. Did you ever come up with anything on that guy that was killed last month by Mount Angel?" the governor asked.

Brownwell took a drink of his coffee. "No," he said, "and Paul, that worries me. It isn't easy to hide someone's true identity. Even in cases where people were badly burned from airplane crashes they've been able to make identification. Nothing of any kind has turned up on this guy. That can only mean either he or the people he worked for went to a lot of trouble to cover up in advance."

"So you still think we're dealing with a highly organized, well financed group of people," the governor said.

"Absolutely. I also think that we had better come up with a plan to meet their threat soon."

"What threat? They've killed some people, true. I see them as cold blooded fanatics but I don't see them as a threat to state or national security. Assuming they were behind that shooting in Silverton, they haven't been heard from in a month."

Brownwell got up and started pacing the floor. His head was up and his hands were folded behind him. "Let's quickly review what we have," he said. "First, they admit responsibility for at least 11 killings. All of them have been swift and accurate. Everyone they've killed turned out to be drug pushers. They have automatic weapons and people who know how to use them. They have money. They've bought one car that we know of with $1700 cash. Last but not least, all of their killings have shock value. They're not killing at random, they know who they're after."

"Maybe that dolt Blakely was right," the governor said. "Maybe it is the CIA.

Brownwell returned to his seat and drank more coffee, then looked at his boss.

"You know, the idea is so ridiculous I'm tempted to believe it. Mind you, only tempted."

"I hate to keep bringing it up, Rick, but nothing's been heard from them in a month. Maybe they've shot their wad."

Brownwell said, "I have a feeling that we have only seen the tip of the iceberg with these people. I believe we're going to have hell to pay."

The governor smirked. "You're basing your opinion on a feeling in your bones?"

Brownwell stood up. "Yep, just a feeling in my old tired bones. The feeling is strong enough, Paul, that I'm going to sneak off to my office and see if I can't put an idea on paper for meeting this problem. I can't give you a date or anything, but I know this is going to be a bigger problem in a short while. I'm going to draw up a battle plan."

"Rick, are you sure you don't need a vacation?"

"Yes, I need a vacation badly. It will just have to wait a while."

"Before you go, I have something to tell you," the governor said.

Brownwell looked at his boss. The two men had known each other for many years. Their eyes met and held. "You're going to hang it up, aren't you?" It was more of a statement than a question.

"Yeah, I'm going to hang it up after this term. I doubt I could win again anyway. Best for me to quit while I'm ahead." The governor looked relieved to say it out loud.

"I'm damn sorry to hear it, Paul. A hell of a lot of other people will be, too."

"I know one that won't," the governor said.

"Who do you have in mind?"

"That oaf of a senator from the 42nd district."

Brownwell made a face. "He couldn't get elected as a dog catcher."

"I heard a lot of people say the same thing about Blakely."

"At least Tom Blakely has good sense," said Brownwell.

"Are you sure about that?"

"He's far more intelligent than people think. He's just too smart to let people know it."

"He certainly had me fooled," the governor said.

Brownwell laughed and headed for the door.

"Good luck with your news conference," he said. "I saw the wolves gathering on my way up here."

"I'll give them a real bone to chew on this week," the governor said. He watched Brownwell leave. He hadn't bothered to say so, but he felt the same way Brownwell did. A big problem was heading their way. He hoped with politics off his back he might be better equipped to handle it.

The governor stood and picked up his briefcase. He picked up the typewritten statement he had prepared. He checked it over one more time, folded it, and dropped it into his jacket pocket. He took a look around the office that had dominated his life for years. It's been nice, he thought. He hoped the next governor would get as much hell as he'd been given.

The governor turned off his office lights and walked out to meet the press.

Chapter 25

By the end of July, several things had happened. The governor had announced he would not seek re-election.

The senator from the 42nd district had declared his interest in the job. Privately he told folks it was about time that old man retired.

Rick Brownwell had a plan for meeting the Cleanup Committee when they returned. Others had already started to forget them. Rick never would.

It was hotter than hell at the camp, and the recruits were sweating. They swam at the lake in the evenings, or relaxed next to it. They were still exercising, but running at a slower pace. They were also finishing up Cain's photography class.

Abel had taken his leave on August 2nd. On the morning of his departure he assembled the recruits in the day room to give a farewell.

"You'll be leaving here the morning of August 20th," Abel announced. "You will be returned to the airport near Portland that you left from at the start of camp. Those of you who already had cars will find them waiting for you at the airfield. Further instructions will be given the day before you leave. Thank you all for coming along."

Abel boarded the chopper to cheers from everyone. Cain had lined them up on the road, and they stood at attention until the chopper was gone. The knowledge that training was almost over had a sobering effect on the recruits.

Operating on a reduced schedule gave the recruits more free time than ever. The weather was too hot to get much done after 11 a.m. these days. Teams still rotated guard duty, but there had been no incidents since the 4th of July.

Just after midnight on the morning of August 10th, team 3 was on guard duty again. It was obvious to everyone they were in for a real mean thunderstorm. They sat beneath the large pine tree where they spent many hours and listened to the still distant thunder.

Roy said quietly, "That thunder reminds me of the artillery I used to hear in Vietnam. We'd all go to sleep listening to that sound."

Amanda shifted uncomfortably. They were dressed in the minimum military style clothing Cain would allow, but it was still sticky hot. "I hate thunder and lightning," she said.

The group knew she was really terrified of storms. The last time there was a storm Amanda had cowered like a scared puppy against the wall of the barracks. They were outside for exercise and Abel had not halted the training for weather. The group had gathered around her protectively. Linda got down next to Amanda and spoke to her like a mother would a crying child.

"We're with you, Amanda. It'll be ok.," said Linda.

Johnny didn't like the conversation, or the idea of not seeing these three people anymore. There was no way he would break ties with them. He asked aloud,

"Do you suppose they'll tell us to stay away from each other after training?"

The air was getting heavier. The animals were quiet. Linda's voice seemed unusually loud when she said: "I'd like to see them enforce that rule, if they make it. I'll observe all the rules while on a mission, but when we're on our own time, that's our business."

Whatever anyone else might have said was lost when a monstrous thunderclap shook the world around them. Amanda screamed. The rain hit in pounding drops that bounced off the ground. A brilliant display of lightning lit up the sky. In seconds they were all soaked, but nobody minded. It had been too hot for far too long.

The team remained under the tree. There wasn't a better shelter while on guard duty. Linda was holding Amanda. Between claps of thunder Johnny could hear her broken cries and Linda's soft reassurances. Johnny moved over near Roy. He put two hands up by Roy's ear and spoke through the tunnel his hands created.

"What do you think happened that made Amanda so afraid?"

Roy shook his head and shrugged.

Mother Nature was doing her best to drown the four recruits. Johnny couldn't remember ever being so wet. Neither could he remember seeing a more spectacular light show than the one being presented in this summer storm.

Johnny shouted, "Maybe we should move. What if lightning hits the tree?"

"I don't know about the lightning, kid, but I'm not about to move from here. With luck the lightning would take the tree instead of us," Roy shouted back.

"Makes sense, I guess," Johnny shouted. He moved back over to where the girls were.

"How's Amanda?" he asked Linda.

"She's going to be ok. She's slowly beginning to realize it isn't all that bad."

Johnny dropped to one knee and put a hand on Amanda's arm. "It's ok to be afraid, Amanda. We all are sometimes. If Roy and I can help you in any way, please let us know. We're here for you."

He went back to where Roy was standing and looked out at the lake. Great jagged streaks of lightning shot down from the sky.

"How's Amanda?" Roy asked.

"Linda says she's a little better. Go talk to her, man."

"I don't know what to say to her."

"Anything's ok. Anything at all. She just needs to know we're all here with her."

"How do you know what she needs?" Roy asked.

"Linda told me that once. She said when somebody's scared like that, the best thing is to have people they trust around."

"Makes sense," Roy said, and moved over toward the girls.

Johnny was left standing to watch the light show. The lightning was so bright and so frequent that it seemed to burn right through to the back of his skull. As if Mother Nature was finding new weapons to throw at them, a wind kicked up from the west. The recruits held on to each other, for it was now getting cold.

They figured Mother Nature was trying to topple their pine tree. It was huge, at least 75 feet tall and 3-4 feet thick. The wind couldn't do more than rustle it's leaves.

Finally, around 2:30 a.m., the storm blew itself out. They were left with a gentle rain. The mercury had dropped a good 20 degrees and the recruits' teeth were chattering. They had to stick out the night. Cain would not send a relief team until 8 a.m. Thankfully they'd had enough training to have a clue about such situations.

The team gathered up whatever they could find that would burn. Just when it seemed like it would take a miracle to start a fire, it took. It wasn't much, but it was a fire. Linda had a small jar of instant coffee. They heated the water in their canteens on the fire then dropped in the coffee. Johnny imagined that was what tar tasted like...but it was hot, so they drank it all and it stayed down. When they were finally relieved at 8 a.m., they were tired, damp, hungry, and closer as a team than they had ever been.

There were two Jeeps coming down the road. In the lead Jeep was their relief, team 9. In the second Jeep was Cain. The recruits had nicknamed Cain "The Black Menace". It was meant with almost reverence, not any disrespect. Cain was always turning up in unusual places at unusual times. He moved as silently as any cat. Sometimes recruits would get involved in horseplay or extra breaks, thinking they were alone, only to turn and find Cain watching them.

One he had caught team 3 goofing off during an assignment. Linda had turned to do something and found Cain standing just inside the doorway. They had no idea how long he had been there. None of them had heard him arrive. He hadn't said a word. He just stood and looked at them in that way of his. When he was satisfied they all knew they'd been caught, he turned and walked away.

"Holy crap!" Linda had whispered. "If I thought that man was after me I'd just kill myself."

Now they watched Cain get out of his Jeep and follow team 9 to where they were waiting. It was his policy to be present at the changing of the guard. Cain did not usually allow conversation during the change over, only a briefing between leaders.

Tom Stevens stopped his team a few feet away. The two teams looked at each other. Johnny looked at Paula. She looked bright and fresh like the rest of their team. She was radiant to him. Paula looked back at Johnny like he was a ghost. Her dark brown eyes softened, and he knew she felt sorry for him and the others.

"Good morning," Tom said, "and if you don't mind my saying, you people look like hell."

"I dare say you wouldn't look any better if you'd spent the night under a tree in that storm," Linda replied.

Tom got a look on his face that made Linda think he had seen a spirit rise up before him. Mystified, she looked around, as did the others. "You spent the night under this tree?" Tom asked.

"Yes, where else would we have stayed?" Linda asked.

Cain stepped forward. "You people are lucky to be alive. The last place you want to be in a storm like that is under this tall tree."

Team 3 looked at each other, confused.

"I thought everyone knew about that sort of thing," Tom said.

"That is the mistake we all made," Cain said. "We assumed something was common knowledge. Let this be a lesson in assumptions- it makes an ass out of you and me. Linda, next time remember to get in a ditch or gully, or something low. Don't stand under a tall tree in a lightning storm."

"Yes, sir," Linda replied. "I don't believe any of us will ever forget."

The changeover was made, and team 3 went back to camp with Roy at the wheel. Cain followed. At the motor pool, Cain parked his Jeep behind them and waited while they got out.

"Get breakfast and then hit your racks," Cain said. "Be up at 2 and in for a briefing at 2:30." That was the last time they saw Cain at Summer Lake.

Chapter 26

The past 3 days had moved swiftly. Team 3 had gotten up the afternoon following the thunder storm and reported for briefing as ordered.

Dot was waiting for them, looking fresh as a flower. "Welcome," she said. "Take your seat with the others."

Someone called out "You don't want these bums in our program! They stand around under trees during thunder and lightning storms!"

Someone else said, "Let them in! Maybe their good luck will rub off on the rest of us."

Dot smiled. "Take a seat and relax, 3. If it had been them out in a storm all night, they wouldn't be so mouthy."

Team 3 sat down and were immediately served with coffee by team 6, who had kitchen duty. Johnny asked someone about Cain, but no one had seen him since before lunch. Dot called them to order by taking a seat behind the desk in front. They knew from experience it was time to settle down.

"Thank you," she said. "I've got information for you, and it's important. First, you'll be leaving here in 3 days at 8 a.m. You'll be flown back to the same airfield you left from several months ago. It's safe to say you're all going back better equipped for the world than when you arrived.

Once you've landed you will find your cars waiting for you. Those of you who did not have a car when you joined us now have one. You will be given a packet prior to leaving. In it you will find your vehicle description and license plate number. The other papers are instructions, which you are to read carefully. You'll find your registration and insurance papers in the glove box. Your first 6 months insurance has been paid. For those of you who already had vehicles, you'll find they'll have different colors, different suspensions, and a few other changes for your advantage."

Dot stood up and put a hand on the box that rested on her desk. She looked serious.

"Now we're going to discuss a subject that may not be too pleasant, but is absolutely necessary. This is no Sunday school picnic you're going on. Many of you may be wounded or killed. If that happens we must have some way of knowing who it was, because a lot of assignments will be handled alone. In this box are some identification tags that we want each of you to wear while on assignment."

She opened the box and took one of the ID tags out and held it up to the recruits. It was square and gray, about the size of a military dog tag.

"All this has on it is the number that the Committee has assigned you, and your blood type. If hurt and unable to speak, medical personnel may need to know." Dot picked up the box and walked among them, giving each person their tag.

She continued, "Obviously it's designed to be worn around your neck. If you should be killed, God forbid, someone will find this tag. The Committee has contacts spread far and wide. One way or another, the word will get back to them."

Dot paused to recognize a hand that had gone up in the back of the room.

"What if we're just wounded?"

"Most of the time you will function alone, but you will still be able to rely on your team. For example, if Roy gets an assignment, it will generally not be in his hometown of Salem. Let's say he's sent to Roseburg. Those of you who live in the area will be advised that an operation is going down.

You'll remain close to your phones so that if someone gets hurt, or needs a safehouse, you'll be there to help.

You've been given extensive medical training so that you can treat a fellow team member that comes to you wounded. In the event someone does come to you hurt, you'll have a number to call. It will put you in touch with one of the doctors who work for the Committee. Do exactly what the doctor on the phone tells you. You've also had the training to simply provide a safe space if that's what your team mate needs."

Linda asked, "What if we're thrown in jail?"

Dot expected the question from her, since she'd been in jail before. "In that situation, you'll call your nearest fellow team member and advise them of where you are. Every attempt to get you out legally will be tried. If that fails, you'll be taken out by jailbreak. I hope it never comes to that, but rest assured you'll never be allowed to sit in the bucket for long."

"Why should we let them take us to jail in the first place?" someone asked.

"The majority of policemen will support our efforts. It won't be a public support, it will be passive. Most cops would like nothing better than to do what we're doing. Nobody knows better than they do just how useless the system can be. They know what it means to work for months on a case only to have the jerk they arrest out on the streets before they've finished paperwork. That police support, passive as it might be, will go out the window if we kill one of them. If you are ever faced with the choice of being taken to jail or shooting it out with the police, let them take you."

Dot waited. This was the first time they'd really discussed injury, jail, or death. She knew it was having a sobering effect. She had no doubt they would live up to the

Committee's expectations, and she had told them so. What she left unsaid was that the chance was high at least one of them wouldn't make it out alive.

Next, Dot took them step by step through the details of how the committee was constructed. She used a blackboard to draw a diagram. The diagram had 9 sections. At the head of each section was a controller, a member of the founding committee. That controller could only be contacted by phone. The teams were not to know the identities of their leaders. That person would give assignments, get them out of jail, and arrange for legal and medical services. She drew the rest out, explaining as she went. Finally she turned back to the recruits.

"On your first assignment, you'll be accompanied by myself, Cain or Abel. We'll be with you to advise and cover. After that, you will be mostly operating alone, as stated.

Now, let's talk about where you're going to live and how. The Committee has bought several mobile homes and placed them in your respective cities. They were placed in trailer parks with a mind for security. The houses are owned by "Oregon Homes LLC," a company created by the Committee, so think of yourselves as renters. They spent a lot of money to make the company virtually untraceable. In a few minutes I'll give you your mew addresses.

You will work at jobs the Committee has secured for you. They won't be the highest paying jobs in the world, but of course money won't really matter. When you're settled into your homes, your controller will call you with facts you need to know, including what information has been given to your employer. He will also give you a believable story regarding your whereabouts for the past few months."

Dot turned and erased the blackboard. She then turned back to the class.

"It's time to start getting ready to leave here. Obviously we can't just get up and walk out. I'll give each of you assignments. Most of them will be done at night."

For the 72 hours following, the teams worked to pack or destroy everything. Two teams had retrieved the boats from the lake, and loaded them onto a large truck. The boats were then covered with a huge canvas.

Guns and ammo were packed into Jeeps on their last night at camp. They were being returned to the National Guard armories from which they'd been taken. Doctor Fish had fixed the paperwork so well it was unlikely the Jeeps had ever been missed.

Last minute security checks were made. The recruits were then lined up in the now empty motor pool area for last minute goodbyes and best wishes. Only Dot and Doctor Fish were present.

"Thank you for all you've done, and all you're going to do," said Doctor Fish. "We will do our best to make sure you never regret it. Now, Dot has something for each of you. Board up when she's finished handing them out."

The last few words were nearly drowned out by the helicopter approaching in the distance. Abel got into the truck and prepared to leave with the Jeeps. Dot gave each recruit a packet and reminded them to read the instructions carefully. She also reminded them to destroy the packets after reading them. Then they all boarded up, and that was the last of Camp Summer Lake.

Chapter 27

Luther Sherman was a mile from his hilltop when he heard the helicopter. For months now he'd been hearing and watching that chopper. It always brought supplies and never stayed long. He knew that one day it would be taking out whoever was at that camp. He wanted to be on hand when that happened.

Luther was building a fence this morning. He had wire, nails, wire stretchers, and other tools scattered all around him. It was a job he detested, so when he heard the helicopter he dropped what he was doing to have a look.

He walked over to the Jeep, ducked under the canvas top and reached in for his binoculars. He pulled the case out, slung it around his neck, and walked rapidly up a shortcut toward the top of the hill. He might've taken the Jeep, but decided it would take longer to rearrange all the crap in it than to walk. The morning was slightly cooler since the storm 4 nights ago, but not much. He panted up the hill, and reached the top just as the helicopter was setting down at the base.

Luther had started using caution when observing the people at the camp since he'd been caught. He half expected a visit from the base commander after that day, but no one had shown up. He continued watching, and was convinced that whoever they were, they weren't actually military. He went to his usual spot, took out the binoculars, and brought them into focus. He looked, and whistled. This must be the day, he thought. They're shipping out or I'm a monkey's uncle.

The first thing Luther noticed was that they were in civilian clothes. This was the first time he had seen them dressed that way. They were boarding the chopper. The next thing he noticed was a large truck. It must have been brought up during the night. The truck was working its way down toward the lake road. It had 5 canvas covered units on it. He believed they were the Jeeps he had been seeing all summer. He wondered where the two sedans and the other truck were.

Luther shifted his gaze to the dock where he'd seen the swimmers that day. The dock was there but the boats were missing. There had been 3 boats tied up at that dock for several weeks. Wondering, he looked back at the chopper. The last of the passengers were getting on board.

Luther couldn't say why he believed these people weren't really Army. It was just a feeling. Something didn't fit, but in all those months he hadn't figured out just what it was.

The truck turned right on the lake road. The helicopter's blades were spinning slowly. The sound of its motor didn't reach him. He was so enthralled that wild horses could not have drug him from his spot. What Luther witnessed was the end of a training school, and the beginning of one of the bloodiest chapters in state history. Of course as he stood on the hill that August morning, Luther had no way of knowing that.

He watched as the chopper lifted from its pad. Now the sound of the engine reached him. The blades whirled in the morning sun, and the chopper flew over the lake in his direction. It was so close he could almost count the rivets. He lowered his binoculars, and it passed over his head with a loud rattle.

Luther watched it go south and out of sight. He listened to its sound fading away in the distance. It made him feel a little lonely. He carefully placed the binoculars back in their case and started back down the hill. He hurried because he wanted to get the fence job done and get back to the house.

He also had an unfinished letter hidden in his desk to complete.

He approached his Jeep with his mind on what he was going to do. He noticed the Jeep door was closed. Funny, that was open, he thought. He opened the door and leaned over to put the binoculars back. He saw the rattlesnake a split second before it struck.

Luther screamed and fell back as the snake sank its deadly fangs into his throat. For a moment, man and snake writhed on the ground. Sherman desperately tried to free himself. Hot and tired as he was, panting from the walk, heart beating rapidly, and bitten in the throat, he had no chance. Within 3 minutes, Luther Sherman had passed out. The snake freed itself and coiled again. It lay there with its wedge shaped head moving back and forth.

Cain watched from 20 feet away. He was experienced with snakes and knew it wouldn't be long until nature took its course. Cain had observed this man for weeks after Doctor Fish showed him the photo. He and Fish agreed the man had to die, and it had to look like an accident.

Cain had planned the accident a bit differently. He hadn't expected the snake to get Luther's throat. He thought perhaps the hand. In that case, Luther would have dropped with a precise hand strike to the neck. The snake would have done the rest. Now he took one last look at the situation. The snake would go on its own way. Silently, he thanked it for helping out. It had been reluctant to do so, of course. He had a devil of a time getting that snake into the Jeep. It had been plenty mad by the time the job was done.

Cain turned and walked away. If anyone had been observing, they would have witnessed the big black man seemingly disappear into thin air. They would've seen the snake slowly uncoil and slither away toward some sage brush. Yet no one was watching, except the eagle circling high above. The eagle wasn't impressed by the human falling over. It had only one thing on its mind: breakfast. It dove rapidly, caught the snake in its talons, and carried it away.

Chapter 28

Johnny felt someone shake him.

"Wake up," Linda said. "We're here."

He rubbed the sleep from his eyes. He looked out of the helicopter window and saw the cars and buildings grow larger as they neared the ground. He turned to Linda.

"I'm going to miss all of you," he said.

Linda gave a bittersweet smile. "I'll keep in touch, Johnny. We're not about to lose track. After all, you're on my team."

"That's not it," he said. "I'm going to miss the everyday contact. With you, and the team, and all the others too."

"We're all in that boat," Linda replied. "Look around."

Johnny looked at his fellow graduates. They were part of the best organized and biggest vendetta ever arranged. They were all emotional now, for lives would change and friends could be lost in the coming year. There would be no time to stop for feelings later.

One by one they stepped off the chopper. They formed up in teams out of habit. It was strange not having an instructor telling them exactly what to do. The pilot came off and waved at a building 100 yards to his left.

"Your cars are in there," he said, and walked away.

The first thing they all noticed was the industrial smog. They looked up into a brown muck that let a hot, blurry sun through. After months of clean air around Camp Summerlake, this was discouraging.

"Where's the damn pilot?" Roy demanded. "I'm going to hijack this bird back to camp."

A weak cheer greeted his proclamation, but they continued to stand around idly. Johnny supposed it was the feeling of not seeing each other again. To many of them this was the only family they had ever known. He saw Paula standing alone, looking kind of lost. He walked over and touched her arm. She looked up at him with tears in her pretty brown eyes.

"What's wrong?" he asked. It was a silly question because he already knew.

"I'm going to miss everyone," Paula said quietly.

"I know what you mean. It isn't going to be much fun rattling around by ourselves."

Paula sighed. "I'm supposed to go live in Bend. I don't know anyone there. They got me a job working in a clothing store. The hours are good enough, but it would be a lot nicer if I could have someone with me."

Johnny wished he could be with her. Then he remembered he hadn't looked at his own papers yet. He said, "I wonder why they made all of you guys that live on the other side of the mountains fly back here."

"Probably because of the cars," Paula said. "Easier to get them all in one place."

"What kind of car did you get?"

Paula smiled. "Just what I wanted, a nice new Pontiac Firebird."

"Rad! I didn't put anything down. I bet I'll just get my old Mustang back."

Linda walked up. "We should all go to lunch. It'll be kind of a celebration."

Johnny looked around. "Where do we eat around here?"

"This is Roger's hometown," she said. "He said he'll show us a place.'"

"Are we just forming up a convoy?"

"No, too many cars," Linda said. "We'll ride in teams with the team leaders. After lunch we'll come back here."

Plans were confirmed. Linda looked around and found she had just what she wanted- a Ford LTD. Team 3 got in and Linda proudly took their place in line.

Roy said, "See that sexy Plymouth two door over there? That's my baby."

"I wish they weren't all such boring drab colors," Amanda replied.

"They don't want you to stick out like a sore thumb, honey," Linda said.

Johnny had glanced over his papers, and then found his Mustang in with the others. It had been painted a dull green. In fact, it was the ugliest green he had ever seen. There was a time he wouldn't have been caught dead in a car that color, but now he accepted it as necessary. At least the paint job was done well.

The line moved out. They had their windows down to let in the breeze.

"Damn this place is hot," Roy said. "As soon as I can, I'm going to scat back over the mountain."

"I'll be right behind you," Johnny said.

"Damnit!" Linda swore, hitting her brakes. "How do people live here?" She dropped the shifter into low gear and hit the gas. The motorist that had pulled out in front of her was making her lose her place in line. The Ford's tires squealed as it leapt out and around the slow car.

"Hey, she's got some get up and go!" said Roy.

When they made it to the restaurant, the management was not prepared to take on 36 customers at once. They stood around waiting while the banquet area was prepared.

One thing the group did not lack was money. Team leaders offered to buy lunch for the others. However, that was shot down. In the end everyone gave their part for a 36 person feast. The total bill was around $500.

The mood had improved during lunch. The airport gloom had lifted and been replaced with goodwill. Jokes were made. Laughter was heard out into the restaurant.

The waitresses wondered who this bunch with all the money was. Once the food was served, the team leaders organized their trips. Those with the longest drives decided to leave as soon as possible.

On the way back to the rest of the cars, Roy noted a special compartment built into the door panel of Linda's Ford. "What's this for?" he asked.

"If you had read your packet completely," Linda said, "you would know they're specifically designed to carry an extra hand gun, plus room for ammo."

"That's convenient," Roy said. "Next you're going to tell me they all come equipped with an Uzi in the trunk."

"Not quite, but each car does have special racks for carrying them. The racks are hidden behind the panels on the fenders. If some cop should force us to open the trunk for some reason, they won't find it."

Linda paused for a moment. "All of you should pay attention to your reading material. You won't have much, so read it well and remember what it says."

Johnny figured the instructors knew what they were doing when they made Linda team leader.

When they arrived back at the airfield, people lingered. Addresses were exchanged, tires were kicked, engines were examined, and opinions given on car colors.

Johnny raised the hood on his Mustang and everything looked good. He climbed in to find the interior was stuffy from being closed up for so long. He started the engine and he could tell his 351 had been tuned to its best.

Tom Stevens led the way out, with Paula following in her Firebird, then the rest of team 9. Linda led the way for team

3, followed by Roy, Johnny, and Amanda. Forty minutes later, after fighting traffic and being held up by an accident, they got on the freeway.

Johnny turned his radio on to music that was too loud and too hard. He turned the station until something pleasing found his ears. He looked out at the road going south, and remembered the drive up that same freeway just a few months back. That night had been hell. He was lucky to have made it.

Johnny continued to stay with his team until Salem. When they'd almost reached the city, they pulled over into the emergency lane. Linda got out of her car, walked back to Roy and handed him a leather case with a Browning 9mm pistol in it. She then handed Johnny his and continued on to Amanda. Roy had already pulled back out into traffic. This was where the organization ended, and individual efforts began.

Johnny felt a sense of loss. For months it had been the four of them. Now he was looking at Linda speed ahead. Would they feel the same sense of loss?

Albany came and went with its smelly paper mill. Fields of strawberries, hay, wheat, and other farm goods slid past between small towns. This was the breadbasket of Oregon: rich farmland and prosperous farmers. Slowly the farmland was being infringed on by ever-expanding towns. He wondered if it would someday be one big city from Eugene to Portland, and if so, where the food would come from.

Johnny put the thought out of his head as he approached his exit. He waved at Linda and Amanda as they continued south. As soon as he saw a service station he stopped and went to the men's room. There, he cried.

He had not really cried when his parents died. He didn't have time to mourn for Brenda. Now he cried for all the times he couldn't. He cried because for the first time he was experiencing that which all humans fear the most; he was alone. He was finally completely alone.

15 minutes later he left the restroom. The feeling that something had been taken from him was still there; but he also felt like a weight had been lifted off his shoulders.

Getting back into his car, Johnny made a discovery that jarred him out of his own thoughts. He had left the Browning laying on the seat in full view. Fortunately, no one had taken it. Breathing a sigh of relief, he picked up the gun and set it in the door panel holster. The papers he should have read sooner were lying on the same seat where the Browning had been. He decided it was time to look them over… but this was not the place. Across the street was one of those chain restaurants that offered a reasonably good meal to travelers.

He crossed over and parked between two semis, musing how small his car seemed next to them. The restaurant had its air conditioning on full blast. The place was packed. Looking around, he spotted a booth with only one man seated. He carried his papers over and asked, "Mind if I sit here?"

The guy looked up. He had a boyish face and soft blue eyes. His hair was dark brown and average length. His complexion suggested he was outdoors a lot. He wore a white sports shirt and tan pants.

The man said. "I don't mind. The place is rather crowded. Pull up a chair."

Johnny dropped onto the padded seat facing the stranger, who was finishing off a BLT sandwich. He placed the papers on the seat beside him and waited for the man to speak again, or for a waitress to show up.

"I hope you're not too hungry," the guy said. "Service is a little slow around here."

"I'm not too hungry," Johnny admitted. "I just wanted someplace cool to relax and do a little reading. I'll order a milkshake or something."

The man picked up a napkin and wiped his mouth and fingers. The waitress appeared and Johnny decided on a strawberry milkshake. It was surprisingly good.

Wishing the guy across the table would disappear, Johnny said "This isn't bad."

"These chain joints can surprise you once in a while," he replied.

"Are you traveling?" Johnny asked.

"No, I'm just killing time. I don't have to be anywhere for another 30 minutes, and it's a darn sight cooler in here than out there."

"Do you live here in Eugene?"

"Yeah, you could say that," the man answered. "I've only been here a short time. I'm from a little town in Kansas that most people have never heard of; a place called Coffeeville."

"I've heard of it," Johnny said.

"No doubt because of the Apple Dumpling Gang."

"That's right. I saw the movie a few years back. I watched the movie because my sister had a book at the time called 'Outlaws on Horseback'. It was interesting."

"I haven't read the book, but all kinds of writers came to town for material. I suppose each one wanted to write their version of the story."

"Did you see the movie?" Johnny asked.

"Yeah, if you like violent entertainment, it qualified," the man replied.

"Are you against violence?"

"It depends on a lot of things," the man answered. "Man is a violent animal by nature, so violence is a fact of life. I just don't believe it should be promoted or glorified."

Johnny looked closer at the guy. He figured he might be a head doctor or a minister.

The man smiled at him. "You think I'm some kind of nut, don't you?"

"No, a lot of people nowadays feel the same way you do," Johnny said. "I just don't agree with you. I believe violence should be seen, but it should be constructive, not destructive."

The man made a face. "Constructive violence?" Disbelief was in his voice. "Come now, you don't really believe that, do you?"

"Yes, I do," Johnny answered. His temper climbed a notch. "I believe it's very constructive when a criminal who is a threat to everyone in society is shot. When a bad person is dead they can't hurt anyone else."

"You're serious, aren't you?" the man mused. "How old are you?"

Johnny looked at him. Shrinks jumped around subjects a lot, maybe that's what this guy was. "I'm 18," he answered. "Why?"

"That's mighty young to be packing around as much hate as you have."

"I don't hate anyone!" Johnny said incredulously.

"I think you do," the man said. "I just hope the hate doesn't destroy you."

"Who are you?" Johnny demanded. "Who do you think you are talking to me like that?"

"I'm Father Michael Henry. Pastor of Saint Rose Catholic Church."

The boyish face spread into a grin at Johnny's flustered face. "I'm sorry, man, you're no doubt upset. You probably thought you were talking to someone who just wanted to argue."

Johnny grinned sheepishly. "I thought you were a shrink."

"I am, of sorts," Father Henry replied. "I have a degree in psychology. I counsel people in my line of work."

"How come you don't look like a priest?"

"More and more of us are appearing in street clothes," he said. "People get nervous when they find themselves in the presence of people in uniform, whether it be priests, doctors or police officers. The only time we really look like priests anymore is when we're performing the duties. We say mass, visit hospitals and nursing homes, teach, etc. Besides, it's hot today."

"Well, I'll be damned," Johnny said.

"I certainly hope not," Father Henry replied.

Johnny paused for a moment. "I find this whole conversation a bit confusing," he admitted.

"I'm sorry, the blame for that rests at my door. I fear we're off to a bad start. However, I think we can still be friends. Someday when you have a few minutes, you're welcome to come see me. Saint Rose isn't hard to find."

Johnny did not point out he had attended Saint Rose as a child. That was a lifetime ago.

Father Henry slid a card across the table. "I'd like us to get to know each other better."

"Why?" Johnny asked. "What do I have that you could possibly want?"

Father Henry stood up. "Maybe I have what you need. Think about it." He walked away.

Johnny picked up the card. Something about that man upset him. Pushing his milkshake aside, he picked up the packet and looked through the papers. He learned where his home was, and that his old job was waiting. Mr. Paddock had been given a cover story for his absence. The papers also said to look his house over carefully, and pay special attention to the wall in the bedroom closet.

On the bottom of the envelope there was a savings certificate for $100,000. There was a note attached. 'Place this in a bank box. Destroy the other papers.'

Johnny looked at the certificate in awe for a moment, then realized he should get it back into the envelope and out of sight.

He finished the milkshake and left the restaurant at 3:15. His instructions were to be home by 4:30 as a call from his controller would be coming through about that time. The two semis he had parked between were gone. He was grateful they had not taken any part of his car with them.

Twenty minutes later he found the trailer park that contained his new home. Space 14 was a blue and white single wide. More than enough for me, he thought.

Leaving the Mustang in the carport, he walked to the office as directed. He was given the keys to his house by a plump gray haired woman with a kind face and rapid speech. She advised him to let her know if everything wasn't in order.

Johnny noticed the place was mostly occupied by young families. A lot of kids were running around, shouting and playing. He wondered if he'd ever get used to the racket, and hoped to be back in the quiet high desert someday.

The house had obviously been sitting here for sometime, as it was stuffy when he opened the door. Johnny went around opening windows, and was thankful to find they all had screens on them. He poked one and found it was a heavy wire, not cheap plastic. Looking closer, he saw tiny wires. An alarm system had been installed. While poking around in the kitchen a few minutes later, he found the instructions to the alarm system. He carried them to the living room and dropped them by the phone to be read later.

Next he went over the two bedrooms carefully. He found his clothing in the one at the end of the hall. The bedside table had a lamp, alarm clock and telephone. The clothing in the closet included shirts, pants, suit jackets, raincoats and extra boots. Moving some clothes aside, he spotted a small button on the paneling. Below the button just a couple of inches was a handle. He tried the handle...and nothing happened. He reached in with the other hand and pushed the button while moving the handle. The paneling slid back smoothly. He quickly moved the clothing aside to get a better look.

There was a light switch in the closet. It revealed a light in the compartment built into the closet wall. Johnny found an Uzi 9mm machine gun on a shelf where it could be reached easily. Suspended on a rack above it was an M-16. It was the rifle on the top rack that caught his attention, though. He reached up and brought it down, backing it out of the small area into the bedroom for a better look.

They'd seen pictures of this rifle but had not used one. No explanation had been given about that. It was a Ruger 25.06 model 77. It featured a heavy target barrel and 3-9 variable scope. This weapon could drive nails at 400 yards. Johnny checked the safety, which was on. He released it and ran the bolt. It was as smooth as a knife through hot butter. The live round that had been in the chamber fell to the carpet. Three more times he ran the bolt, and three more rounds fell to the floor.

Gently, he placed the rifle on the bed. He picked up the rounds from the floor and examined each one. They were 95 grain hollow points. These were designed to expand and explode once in the target. They could do astounding damage to anything with flesh. He deduced that this was meant for an assassin's shot over a long distance.

Johnny picked up the rifle, replaced the rounds, ran the bolt and reset the safety. He returned it to its rack and slid the compartment door shut. Then he went back down the hall to the living room and dropped into the recliner. On the end table next to him, the phone rang.

"Good evening," the voice on the line said. "I hope this day finds you well."

"Yes," he replied. "I'm just starting to settle in."

"Did you look over the house and find everything?"

"Yes, everything."

"There's a place not far from you that's excellent for working out with two of the tools we've supplied you with. For the others, you'll need to find a private place to work with them. Is that understood?" the voice asked.

"Yes, I understand." Johnny knew this meant he could practice with his handgun and Rutger nearby. However, the Uzi and M16 were illegal, so practice would have to be secret.

"Excellent. Do you have any questions?"

"Yes. What about the extra parts for the tools?"

"When you need anything, call this number. Do you have your pen and paper handy?"

"I do." Johnny had found a pen and notepad by the phone. He jotted the number down.

"When you call this number you will reach an automatic service. Simply give your personal number, 36, and say what you need. You will be contacted with instructions. Also, I'm going to give you the home numbers of your closest associates. Do your best to commit them to memory. It's best you carry as little as possible regarding your work."

After Johnny wrote down the numbers and acknowledged them, the voice asked: "Is there anything else you need at this time?"

"Not at this time. I seem to be all set up."

"Good, good. You should expect to be contacted by a staff member in a couple of days. They will furnish you with evidence that they are who they claim to be."

"Alright, I'll be waiting for them."

"One more thing," the voice said. "Please remember to follow your written instructions to the letter."

"Yes, sir," Johnny answered.

"Thank you very much. Take care, we'll be in touch."

There was a click at the other end of the line. Johnny dropped the phone back on its hook and sat for a moment. That voice had been familiar. He had heard it somewhere before. Then it hit him….it was Dot's father.

I'll be damned, he thought. Then he wondered what the show had been all about last winter at the mansion. He figured out it must have been for Dot's sweet mother, and the old man was with Dot on the Committee.

Johnny had no idea how close his guess was. It's not that the knowledge would have mattered, for Johnny and 35 others were already on a path of destruction. They had been taught that their destruction would create justice. He believed it completely. So did the others, and they were all committed to the task.

Chapter 29

Two evenings later, Johnny arrived home from work with the late August sun still bright. Kids were playing in the street, and a baseball game was underway in the neighborhood park. Johnny left his car in the carport and walked toward the game. It was nothing organized, just a bunch of people playing ball. Most of the players were teenagers. It wasn't until he was actually seated on a bleacher watching the game that he saw a guy approaching him.

The guy just seemed to amble along, hands in his pockets, looking around with shifty eyes. He was in his 20's, average height and weight. He had a little beard and of all things, a ponytail. Johnny took instant dislike to this guy. It wasn't the guy's appearance. It was the way he looked at the kids. This son of a bitch was a dealer.

He ambled on over to where Johnny was. Uninvited, he dropped onto the bleacher a couple feet to his left and said: "Fine day, ain't it man?"

Johnny glared at him. "Fuck off, jerk."

"My, my, aren't we picky?" the man said. He was sitting with his hands folded in his lap. His legs were crossed and Johnny noted the hole in the bottom of the guy's left shoe.

"What's the matter?" Johnny sneered. "Can't find enough guys to get you some decent shoes?" The man reminded him of Fat Freddy.

"Who needs you, man?" the guy answered. "It's summertime."

Johnny looked at the guy's eyes, expecting to see a dazed look. Instead he saw cool, clear gray eyes that smiled back at him. He looked away.

"My name is Luke," the guy said quietly. "I'm from the organization."

"What organization?" Johnny asked.

"The Cleanup Committee, that's who."

"I've heard of them," Johnny said.

"I'm sure you have," the man said. "I'm sure you've also heard of Dot, Cain, Abel and Boxer."

Johnny looked at the man with more interest. "So you're the guy they told me to expect."

"I must be."

"Funny, I was expecting Boxer."

"That would be rather difficult," Luke replied. "Boxer is quite dead."

"Ok, you pass," Johnny said.

"I'm going to split for the time being, Johnny. When things settle down later, I'll contact you at home. We have a few things to discuss."

"I'll be home all night," Johnny replied. "I've got no place else to go."

Luke got up and ambled away slowly. He didn't look back. He looked like a guy who had just gotten tired of being near someone else. Johnny decided he was cool.

It was 8:40 that night when Luke appeared at the house. This time he was dressed in a business suit, of all things. He was carrying an expensive looking black leather briefcase.

"Can I interest you in some life insurance, young man?" Luke asked with a smile.

"Come on in," Johnny answered, opening the door for Luke. "Where'd you get the suit?"

"I have a lot of different clothes," Luke replied. "Got anything to drink?"

"Like what?"

"Some cold beer would be amazing."

"I've just got water, milk, or Pepsi," Johnny said.

"Pepsi, with ice please," Luke said.

While Johnny got the soda, Luke made himself comfortable in the living room. When Luke had his drink, Johnny sat and asked if this was a social call or business.

"Business," Luke replied. "You're about to help me shoot some people."

"Shoot people?"

"Well, yes. What do you think you've been training for, the Olympics?"

"No, it's just that you say it like it's an everyday thing."

"It is an everyday thing, Johnny. Hardly a day goes by when somebody doesn't get shot. The difference here is, you haven't shot anyone. Well, you're about to. I'm going along to make sure you do it right, and give you support."

"Who are we going after?" Johnny asked.

"We have an appointment at a farm house about 3 miles east of Creswell at 10pm tonight."

"That's not very long," Johnny said.

"Yep, so you'd better get cracking. Start by getting dressed. A dark colored, long sleeve shirt, dark pants, and boots. Bring your M16 and an extra magazine."

Johnny stood up. He felt like a man in a dream. He was getting ready to kill someone in a little over an hour. This guy was talking about it like it was as common as eating.

He went to his room and changed. It was easier to pretend he was changing for dinner. Then he got the M16 out of its rack . His hands were shaking so bad he dropped the extra magazine twice. Finally, he grabbed it up and shoved it into his pocket. He came back into the living room carrying the gun. Luke was waiting for him, looking as cool as anyone could.

"Sit down, kid," Luke said. "We're going to have a word."

Johnny dropped into his chair, the rifle slung across his knees, barrel pointed away from Luke. He at least remembered that much in his nervousness.

"Get your wits about you, boy, and be quick about it. You've spent months getting ready for this. It isn't going to be easy. Killing never is. When it gets easy, that means you're not long for this world. It means you're getting careless and it's just a matter of time 'till you slip up.

I've been at this game for some time. I know what I'm talking about. I'm not looking forward to this job anymore than you are, but it's a job, and by God it's going to be done right. Cain, Abel and Dot are all with other classmates of yours tonight. These others are as scared as you are, but they'll come through. So will you."

"You may have to tell me what to do," Johnny said.

"That's exactly why I'm here. I'll fill you in on the way to the target area. Consider this a training exercise. This job was planned well, but on short notice. Next time you'll help with the planning as well as the execution."

Johnny stood up. "Which car are we taking?"

Luke stood as well. "I've picked one up for the night. We have one quick stop to make at my place. I'll drive, you listen."

They went out into the deep dusk. Johnny set his alarm and locked the door behind him. Luke had broken the rifle down and had it in his briefcase. He carried the thing like it was a case full of air. The car was a tan colored Ford sedan. They both got in, and Luke handed Johnny the briefcase.

"After we've made the stop near my place, take that thing out and put it back in working order."

"What about my side arm?" Johnny asked.

"What about it?"

"Will I need it?"

"I would've told you to bring it along if it were necessary. You won't be that close to these guys."

"How many are there?" Johnny asked.

Luke started the car. "There are 3 targets. Three of the biggest pushers in these parts. They're taking delivery on one big shipment tonight. We're going to surprise them."

Johnny sat quietly and let the evening breeze coming through the window cool him off. Luke drove east but Johnny didn't pay any attention to the streets. He was concentrating on the task ahead. What difference does it make to me? he thought. A lot of difference, fool. If it wasn't for these kinds, Brenda might be alive today. So might several other people. 3 is a good start, he told himself.

"You said there are 3 of them, Luke?"

"At least 3. Maybe more. If our luck is good we'll get their supplier."

"I assume they'll have guns?"

"You're damn right they will. They'll use them if they get half a chance. We won't give them that chance," Luke said as he stopped near an apartment complex.

He turned the motor off and turned to Johnny. "We are not heroes. We are not getting paid to waste ourselves. Hence, we ambush 'em. Murder the bastards in cold blood. In a standup shootout we'd be far more likely to die."

"I see what you mean."

Luke opened his door. "Wait here. I'll be back in 3 minutes."

Johnny sat waiting with the windows down, listening to the sound of far off dogs barking and kids being rowdy. Full darkness had set in. For some reason, this street had no lights. The 3 minutes seemed to take an hour.

When Luke returned he was dressed in different dark clothing, and his hair was different.

"What did you put on that weird hair for?" Johnny asked.

"If I'm seen by a few locals, I'd rather they not see the real me."

"What about me? Do I need to worry about being seen?"

"The targets might get a glimpse of you just before you blast them, but I doubt it."

Luke had the car started and rolling again. He seemed to be hurrying just a bit now. At a stop sign, he paused rather than stopped. He sped just a little as they went toward the freeway. Luke started explaining more.

"As you know, Creswell is about 15 miles south of here. It's a small town, maybe 2000 people. Our target is on what's known as the Enterprise Road. The house isn't really a farmhouse. It's an old place our main guy bought and fixed up for a meeting place. When he takes a delivery of this size, he usually has 2 guys with him. They're his reps in other parts of the state. If all parties are present, a light will be on and two or more cars will be parked near the house. If the shit's arrived there will be a black van with California plates.

Assuming the van is there, we'll get them out of the house by creating a racket. As soon as they come out, gun them down. I'll be going around back to catch anyone coming out that way. When we're finished with them, we'll set the house on fire."

"Why the fire?" Johnny asked. "We're going to make so much damn noise we'll be lucky to have enough time to beat it."

"Listen, kid. There's no one that close. Also, the place isn't going to explode. It'll take a while to get the fire really going. The reason for the fire should be obvious. The delivery they're getting tonight will be there, and God only knows how much more. We won't have time to search. The object is to punish these bastards for dealing and dry up their source."

"I'm not a little kid," Johnny said testily. "I can draw some conclusions myself."

The car made a sharp right, circled and entered the freeway. Luke tapped the case with one hand. "Put that baby together," he said.

Johnny put the rifle together quickly. He and his classmates had all done this so many times over the past months that they could do it blindfolded. When it was assembled he carefully moved it up and over until it was resting on the back seat.

Luke turned the car radio on. Some guy was singing about how he wanted to live fast and die young. Luke sang along and was really into it. When the song ended he slapped the wheel and said "That's my song, boy, that's my song."

"You want to live fast, love hard and die young?" Johnny asked.

"Why the hell not? What's the point in growing old?"

"I don't know," Johnny said. "I hadn't really thought about it."

He sat quietly, listening to Luke singing with the car radio. He thought he might understand Luke a little but reserved judgment. One thing for sure, Luke wasn't like his other instructors. Cain would've hated having him around. He was loud and mouthy.

"You know," Johnny said," this strike doesn't seem very well planned."

Luke turned down the radio. "You're right," he answered. "I only learned about it today. When I told the big boys about it, they told me to take you along. So, I admit it's not as well planned as a normal operation...but fear not, Johnny boy. We'll pull it off with flying colors."

"You seem very confident."

"You will be too when you've been at it as long as I have. I had a good teacher. Old Cain taught me all I know. I covered half of Southwest Asia with that guy."

Johnny was surprised. "You know Cain that well?"

"Sure do. He used to be known as the Black Menace."

"That's what we called him in training, just not to his face," Johnny said. "That guy used to scare me just by showing up."

"Someday when we have time, I'll tell you all about Cain. He's got quite a story." Luke began slowing the car for the Creswell exit. "Won't be long now."

Johnny pressed his shaky hands together. "How are we going to do it?" he asked.

"We'll drive past the place first. If it looks normal we'll turn around and park."

"What did you mean about getting seen by some of the locals? Do we have to go through any yards?" Johnny asked.

"No, I was just trying to be funny," Luke said. "As usual it didn't work."

They left the freeway and headed toward the small town. They crossed Highway 99.

"This will be our road home," Luke said. "We used the freeway coming down for time saving. Going home we can take it easy."

They continued out of town. The houses became fewer and farther between. Fields and trees lined the sides of the road. Luke drove with the lights on dim. The moon was bright so they didn't need their brights on.

The farmhouse was sitting maybe 50 yards back from the road on the left. They drove past slowly.

"Good, they're all there," said Luke. He continued slowly up the road.

"I didn't see anything."

"The cars are parked on the west side of the house near the trees. I saw the black van, a green VW Bug and one other rig. We're going to turn around up here a bit and then come back. I know a place we can park just off the road. We'll then approach the house through the trees."

"What are the odds they'll have a guard?" Johnny asked.

"Pretty damn good," Luke replied. "We'll have to find him and neutralize him."

"This gets dingier by the minute," Johnny said.

"It sounds screwy," Luke admitted, "but we've got the upper hand. The guard won't really be expecting anything. Fear not, Johnny. Old Luke will see you through."

Johnny decided Luke was okay, and that he was also completely nuts.

One mile up the road they turned around and started back. A quarter of a mile from the house, Luke pulled off the road into some trees. It was dark there, with the moon only showing through in spots. Luke turned off the motor.

"Damn it's quiet," Johnny said softly.

Luke smiled. "It'll get noisy enough pretty quick."

He reached over and opened the glove box, removing a small automatic with a silencer on it. "This is our neutralizer. It's a .32 automatic. Does a vicious number on people."

Johnny turned and picked the rifle up off the back seat. Luke checked his .32 while Johnny brought the rifle forward. In the dark he ran his hands over the familiar weapon. All he would need to do was drop the safety and it would be ready to use.

Luke ran the slide on the .32. "Now I'm dangerous," he said, and opened the door.

Johnny got out and let the door close against the first latch. The click seemed extra loud in the quiet night. Luke

was by the back of the car. Walking around there he saw
Luke bringing something out of the trunk.

"My baby," Luke said, and held up an Uzi. "I can carve my
name with this jewel."

"It's a sweet gun," Johnny replied. "I like it a lot."

"Okay kid, it's 9:50. Time to get to work. Follow me."

They moved off through the trees with Luke leading the
way.

"I've been up here a bit and poked around. Do you know
the sound of the crow?" Luke asked.

"A crow? Sure. It's got that funny caw caw sound. Why?"
Johnny asked.

"If you hear a crow," Luke said, "drop where you are and
keep quiet. Don't move until I tell you. Understood?"

"Understood."

Luke chose a path that allowed just enough light from the
moon to see by. If it hadn't been for that little bit of light,
Johnny might've been lost in the first ten feet. Luke moved
silently down the narrow trail that had been made by deer. It
angled right through the trees toward the house in a
northwest direction.

The trees ended about 20 yards from the nearest car.
That's where Luke signalled a halt. Luke dropped to his
knees, and Johnny did the same.

"Wait here," he whispered.

Johnny saw him lay the Uzi down and crawl forward on
all fours. He was out of sight in nothing flat. Johnny waited,
straining to pick up any sound he could hear. Finally, he
heard a car in the distance. It was traveling at a pretty good
clip. It echoed through the trees. It seemed to go on for a
long time. He continued to wait and listen. Somewhere off to
his right, an owl hooted. The sound made him jump. He
discovered he was sweating like a man who had just run the
440 on a hot day.

He wondered how Luke could be so cool. He figured Luke must be a spook. Luke the Spook, he thought with a smile. Luke the Spook is going to get us both killed.

"They have one guard out."

Luke was next to him. The whispered voice made him jump again.

"Damn, you are a jumpy sort," Luke said.

"Sorry," Johnny whispered back. "I'll get over it. I hope."

"Never mind that now. I figure there are 5 or 6 guys in the house. There's a big glass window to the left of the front door. When I was here two days ago it had no covering. Work your way around to the front and keep low. When you're in the driveway behind the van, get down and crawl to a spot where you can cover that window and door. I'll be taking out the guard who is relaxing on the other side of that van. When you hear a crow caw twice, spray that front window. I've decided to take them in the house rather than let them get outdoors. I'll be in the back door 2 seconds after you hear the crow, hitting them from that angle. Stay down until you hear me give the all clear. By that time I'll be able to talk out loud so you won't misunderstand."

"I've got 2 magazines," Johnny said. "That's only about 40 rounds."

"That's enough, and you know it," Luke said. "You're well trained, remember that. Don't get carried away and waste ammo. You should be able to take most of them out with the first burst of fire. Now get going. Time is short."

Johnny stood up and was surprised at the wobbliness in his knees. Luke grabbed his arm.

"You're going to be fine. Breathe. Now get a grip on yourself," Luke whispered.

Luke let go of his arm and headed off, angling left.

Johnny decided to go up toward the highway about 30 feet using the trees as cover. At that point he would leave the trees and cross behind the van. The moon cast a glow over the dirt path in front of him. When he had gone what he figured was the right distance, he stopped and looked. He could see the yard in front of the farm house was covered in weeds.

He started to step forward, then heard a sound to his right and stopped. He listened and heard it again; a thud. Then, he knew what it was. The .32 automatic with its silencer. Not far away, the guard had just died.

Stepping out of the trees, Johnny crossed the road and dropped to his belly on the other side. Crawling forward, he kept an eye on the light that was spilling out the front window of the house. The ground was rocky, and little weeds with stingers pulled at him. He knocked a bug off his neck. He hoped like hell he didn't run across a snake out here.

After what seemed like a month, he reached a spot in the yard where he was in line with the window but well outside of the light it was emitting. Two men could be seen in the front room. They were in full view of the window, apparently unconcerned about the outdoors. The two men were talking. The guy nearest the window had his back to it. Once in a while he would look to his right and speak, addressing someone out of sight.

I sure hope a car doesn't happen along when the shooting starts, Johnny thought. He waited and waited. Where the hell is Luke, he wondered?

He heard a sound to his left and turned to look, but it was too late. The thing was in the middle of his back. His hand flew up and he felt fur. It was a dog. We blew it, Johnny thought. Luke missed the guard dog.

He thrashed about, trying to get the beast off him. He had no idea what he'd do once it moved. This thing would kill him for sure if he didn't kill it first. Then, a shocking fact reached his mind. The dog was licking him. A big old slobbery tongue was lapping at his face.

I don't believe it, Johnny thought. They've killed me. I'm dead and I'm in Hell. This must be Old Scratch's welcoming dog.

He was now on his side, trying to stop the dog from licking him anymore. "Quit!" he whispered. "Go away! Shoo!"

He couldn't believe it. This damn dog thought he was a long lost friend or something. This wasn't a guard dog. It wanted to play. The dog had no idea what was up.

The sound of a crow reached Johnny's ear.

Wildly he turned and the dog fell away. Johnny got back into position and grabbed the rifle he had dropped when the beast found him. Hoping against hope the dog had enough, he brought the rifle up. Three backs were now in full view in front of the window. He squeezed the trigger. Nothing happened. He released the safety and squeezed again.

The rifle bucked against his shoulder. He heard glass splatter and saw the men jerk as the bullets slammed into them. He fired another short burst at a figure he saw pass in front of the window. The bolt locked open, telling him his magazine was empty. Quickly he reloaded the gun and waited.

He remembered the dog, and wondered where it was. No sounds came to him. No one was in sight in the house. Slowly, he saw the door open. Someone leapt through it and started running toward the van. Johnny fired a short burst, and the man pitched forward and lay still.

From in the house he heard Luke call out. "They're all down, boy. Good work. Stay where you are. I'll be with you shortly."

Slowly, Johnny got to his knees and looked around. He saw the dog laying a few feet to his left, its head down on its front paws. At first he thought it might be injured. Then he saw its eyes glowing in the night. Hell, that dog's just frightened, he thought. Don't blame the poor thing.

He started talking softly to the dog.

"You scared the hell out of me, mutt, so if you're scared it's no less than you deserve. Where did you come from anyway? You could've been shot hanging around here."

The dog started crawling toward him on its belly. It crawled up right next to him and laid there. Johnny reached down and scratched its head. From off to his right he heard a low moan.

"My God, dog, that one is still alive. What should I do about that, huh boy?"

Luke called, "Hold your fire. I'm coming out."

He came striding out the door and over to where Johnny was. In his right hand he carried two revolvers. He carried them with his middle finger hooked through the trigger guards. Stopping, he looked down at the dog. "Where did that bag of bones come from?"

"I don't know," Johnny said, then explained what had happened.

"I wondered what took you so long to react," said Luke. "I was in the house with them before you opened up. They were downright unhappy to see me. So unhappy, in fact, that one of them was reaching for his weapon when you got him from the rear."

Johnny pointed right. "I think that one over there is still alive."

Luke turned and walked over to where the guy was. "He's about gone," he called. "Nature will take its course."

Slowly, Johnny got to his feet. He was surprised to find his knees were no longer wobbly. Hardly 3 minutes had passed since the shooting but it felt like hours. Luke came back over and handed him the revolvers.

"Take these and head for the car. Can you find it?" Luke asked.

"I think so," Johnny said.

"Dump them on the floor in the back seat. I'll be along shortly."

Taking the revolvers in his left hand and his rifle in the right, he set off for the car. Halfway to it he realized the dog was following him. He stopped and turned around. The dog had stopped when he did. It was about 5 feet back just standing and looking at him.

"Go home," Johnny said.

The dog dropped to its belly and whined.

"What would I do with you? I don't think Luke would even let you in the car."

The dog stayed on its belly. Johnny turned and started walking again. He kept on, knowing the dog was still following. He started trying to figure out how to convince Luke to let the dog into the car. He'd decided to take the furry pest home.

He was still in the shadows of the trees when he realized there was a policeman standing by the car. The cop was walking around the car, looking in the windows. Johnny could tell by his uniform the officer was an Oregon State trooper. There was a patrol car idling not far away.

Johnny froze where he stood. His heart pounded wildly, and his blood ran cold. What were they going to do now? Where was Luke?

The dog growled. It was a low rumble but resounded plainly in the night. The policeman turned. His hand was on his service revolver. The dog growled again.

"No!" Johnny whispered, but it came out like a choked shout. The officer had his weapon out and pointed it right at him.

"Come forward!" the cop demanded. "Hands in the air!"

For a split second he contemplated running. Then he decided that would invite more problems. This was a poor showing from the start. Now they'd been caught. It never even crossed his mind to shoot the officer, although they could have done so easily. The dog growled again, and Johnny again tried to shush it. A flashlight shone in his eyes.

"You! Come up here!" the officer demanded.

He walked forward. The cop looked him and his guns over. The service revolver was now pointed at Johnny's chest. "Been doing a little hunting?"

"No sir."

"You're as well armed as anyone I've seen in a long time. Put 'em down. Easy."

Slowly, Johnny leaned over and set the guns on the ground. The dog was on its belly beside his right foot. Straightening, he stood with his hands raised.

"This your car?"

"Yes sir, it's mine."

"What's it doing here?"

"I just left it here for a while while we went for a walk."

"By we, you mean yourself and the dog?"

"Yes, me and the dog."

"You're a damned liar. There are two sets of prints here. Where's your friend?"

"He's back over yonder somewhere."

"Why do you have so many guns?"

"We just brought 'em along. Just in case."

"What's your name?"

Johnny didn't answer. It didn't seem like a good idea to give that information out.

"Come on!" said the officer. "What's the name?"

"Look, Officer, I can explain this. It isn't what it appears to be."

"Then just what is it?"

"I think I'd better not say anymore." Johnny's mind was muddled. He couldn't seem to think up what to say. He wanted to stall as long as possible until Luke returned. He was about to open his mouth to say something, anything, when Luke's voice reached him and the officer at once.

"Drop the gun and light, Officer. Turn around slowly. Mind what I say. I don't want to shoot you but I will if you force it."

The policeman started to jerk around. It was an instinctive reaction.

"Don't!" Johnny said. "He'll shoot you!"

"Damned right I will, if I need to. Drop the gun. Now."

The gun thudded to the ground along with the light. The light bounced and rolled away with its beam toward the trees.

"Get that light and turn it off," Luke ordered. "Then get his cuffs out and lock his hands behind him."

Picking up the light, Johnny put it under his left arm and approached the back of the officer, who had turned to face Luke. Carefully, he unsnapped the leather case and brought out the cuffs. They were shockingly cold.

"Hands behind you," Johnny said.

"This will get you guys 30 years each," the officer said, but he complied.

Having no desire to hurt this man, Johnny used care while locking the cuffs. When it was done he stepped back. "What now?" he asked Luke.

"You gather things up and get them in the car. I'm going to take our friend here to his car and leave him in it."

"Don't hurt him," Johnny said. "You know the rules."

"What rules? What are you guys talking about?" the officer asked.

Luke stepped around the back of the car. The machine gun was still in full view and trained on the officer. "I'm going to take a minute for a little P.R. work, even though time is short. You've just had the misfortune of bumping into the Cleanup Committee. We just pulled a job on the other side of those trees."

"You guys are the Cleanup Committee?" the officer asked incredulously.

"We're only two of them," Luke said. "There are more."

"How many more?"

"Sorry, but that's a trade secret," Luke answered. "Look, we just did you a favor. PR time is over, guy. Get moving."

Johnny got the guns into the car, then turned to see if he'd forgotten anything. He saw the dog. He also saw a dull red glow in the trees and remembered the plan for the farmhouse. Quickly, he turned back to the car and moved all the guns from the back seat to the floor. He held the back door open, turned to the dog and slapped his leg.

"In!" he said. The dog jumped in and Johnny closed the door behind it.

Luke returned at a fast walk. "Got everything in?"

"All in."

"Then get in and let's go. That cop will have a friend checking up on him in no time flat."

They jumped in and Luke started the car. As he shifted into reverse and looked to back up, he saw the dog.

"What's that flea trap doing in here?"

"I didn't want to leave him there. He seems like a good dog. I want to keep him. I've never had a dog. Now is as good a time as any to get one," Johnny said.

"Aw Christ, I'll have to have the car fumigated. That mutt smells."

They were out on the road now. Johnny saw the darkened State Police unit where Luke had left it. It was about 20 feet back from the spot where they had entered.

"Will he be alright?" Johnny asked.

"Sure he will."

"What did you do with him?"

"I left him handcuffed in the backseat. I also took the liberty of cutting his mic cord. He had our license number written on a notepad so I removed that too."

The car gained speed rapidly. When they passed the burning house they were doing 70.

"What did you start the fire with?" Johnny asked.

"Some papers and rags I found in the house. Man, they had a bunch of shit in there. This was a big deal. I picked up a bunch of money, too."

"Money?"

"It's gotta be the cash they were handing over for the drugs. I'm guessing it's $80,000."

"Wow. What happens to it from here?"

"I turn it over to our bosses," Luke said. "The money will be used to help finance future operations."

As they neared town, the car slowed to the speed limit. They had just entered city limits when they saw the first fire truck responding to the farmhouse. It roared by them with its lights flashing. An Oregon State Police car was right behind it.

"There goes the help for our friend," Luke said. "In no time they'll have an APB out on this car. We'll have to shed it fast."

"How do we do that?" Johnny asked.

"Just a few miles up the road," Luke said. "We have a house where an extra car is stashed. We'll dump this one and take the other."

"That cop will probably remember this one's plate. It'll be hot."

"A fine lot of good it will do him," Luke chuckled. "The license on this car was taken from a junked out rig in a wrecking yard."

Luke fell silent as he concentrated on driving. He was careful to keep his speed right at 55. Nothing attracts a cop's attention like a speeding car. The last thing they wanted right now was a second look from some patrolman. Five miles from town, Luke turned left onto a country road. One mile further, he turned into a driveway and rolled the car to a quiet stop.

"Get out and open the garage door," Luke said. "The car in there has keys and it's ready to go. Back it out here. I'll move this one over and give you room."

Johnny stepped out. The dog stood up in the back seat and whined.

"Wait here," he said. "I'll only be a minute."

The dog laid back down and was quiet.

"Maybe when you get him cleaned up he'll be a more attractive companion," Luke said. "Right now he looks like hell and smells rotten."

Johnny got a green Datsun 210 out of the garage. They transferred the money, guns and dog. In 5 minutes they were back on the road.

Luke explained, "That Ford will be picked up in a day or two and taken out of the area. It'll be too hot around here for a while."

"What about this one?" Johnny asked.

"Remember that place you went when Dot first picked you up? I'll put it there."

At 10:42 p.m., Luke let Johnny and the dog out a block from their house. Johnny carried the leather bag with his M16 in it, and the dog trailed along behind as he walked the short distance to the house. After dumping the case on his bed, he took the dog into the kitchen and looked for something to eat.

"You are the worst looking, ugliest hunk of dog meat I've ever seen. Tomorrow, you're going somewhere for a bath and a haircut."

Not knowing what else to feed it, he put two pounds of hamburger in a bowl and set it in front of the dog. It gobbled the food like it was manna from heaven. While the dog ate, Johnny looked it over. He figured the dog would probably weigh 90 pounds when fully healthy. It had big feet and long ears. He hadn't met a dog quite like this one before.

"What am I going to do with you?"

The dog had finished eating and was licking the dish. Then it looked at him expectantly. He got up and gave it another pound of meat, and another bowl filled with water.

Chapter 30

Richard Brownwell had no idea how long the phone had been ringing when it finally managed to get through the sleepy fog that filled his mind. He fumbled for the receiver and brought it to his ear.

"Hello," he mumbled. "Brownwell here."

"Sorry about calling you like this Chief, but we have a mess."

It was the voice of Captain Rally, the station commander in Eugene. Brownwell and Rally went back a long way. Rally was a good cop and excellent leader. It would take something big to prompt him to call in the middle of the night.

Brownwell sat up in bed and reached for the lamp. Long years of being woken in the night taught him how to find things in the dark without knocking other things over. His wife Joan slept on, hearing nothing.

"Go ahead, Rally. What do you have?"

"That damned Cleanup Committee has gone wild."

"Well shit," Brownwell said. "I knew it would happen eventually."

"We've got 6 dead people here. Reports of other shootings are coming in by the minute. Prineville has 3 dead men whose truck was ambushed on route 26 near there. Portland office is working a shooting near Sandy involving 3 others."

Brownwell whistled into the phone. "Well, it's happened. I've been telling the governor for weeks this was going to be the way of it. What else is happening that made you call me?"

"We got a man in our office here who got a damned good look at two Committee gunmen who did a number on those pushers near Creswell." Rally sounded almost excited.

Brownwell was now wide awake. "Wait a minute," he said while reaching for his pants. "Which man are you talking about?"

"One of our troopers was on patrol in the area. He surprised one of the two gunmen. Then another one got the drop on him."

"Your guy got a look at them and is still living?" Brownwell couldn't contain the excitement in his voice.

"Yeah, Chief. I think you'd better come to Eugene."

"I'll be there as soon as I can. Is your trooper injured?"

"No, he's shaken up but not hurt."

"Put that man on ice, Rally. Keep everyone away from him. Stick to him like glue until I get there. Go ahead and get a statement from him."

"He's already on ice. See you soon." Rally hung up.

Joan Brownwell was now awake, sitting up in bed and looking at her husband. She had been a cop's wife long enough to not waste time with questions. She waited quietly while he threw on clothes.

While buttoning his shirt, Richard looked at Joan and said: "The Committee struck in force. Sounds like a military type operation. I'm going to Eugene to talk with a trooper that got a good look at two of them."

"Is the trooper okay?" she asked.

"Rally says he's shaken but alright otherwise. I'll be back when I get back," he said.

Brownwell was so excited about the possible break in the case he walked out of the room without kissing his wife goodbye. An hour and 20 minutes later he rolled his official car to a stop in the parking lot of the Eugene patrol office of the state police.

It was 3:02 am when he strolled into the lobby. Most of the staff here were unknown to him. He was known to them, though, and so was the purpose of his late night visit. He waved and nodded while passing through to Captain Rally's office near the back of the building. As he approached, Rally opened the door, clearly told of Brownwell's arrival by the front desk.

Rally was a short guy at 5"7, with gray hair and big green eyes. When he'd first applied to the State Police years ago he'd been refused because of his height. Then World War II happened and Rally was denied service in the military due to a bum knee. After that he had been accepted by the State. Rumor has it that an uncle of Rally's, a Portland industrialist, had managed it for him. At the moment, Brownwell was not thinking about any of that as he stepped into the room and confronted the young trooper who had won himself a place in history.

Rally closed the door and locked the bolt. He asked, "How did you get by the reporters?"

"Somebody must have scared them off," Brownwell replied. "I didn't see any."

Dropping into the chair beside the big desk, Brownwell looked at the trooper. He was a tall kid with red hair. He seemed fairly relaxed, with only a little edge of nervousness.

"Well, trooper, it sounds like you've had a big night," Brownwell said. "Tell me what happened."

"I made a statement to Captain Rally, sir," the trooper replied.

"I'd still like to hear it directly from you."

The trooper held up an empty cup. Rally took it and filled it from the coffee pot in the corner, and brought a second one back for Brownwell. The trooper took a slow sip, then began his history.

"I was returning from an extended patrol west on Highway 58. There's this one spot I always check. I've found numerous violations at that spot. Kids parked smoking a joint, tipping a few, so forth. This time I spotted a car just like I expected I might. Putting the light on the car, I wrote down its plate number. I got out and walked around the car, looking inside. I had been by the car for maybe a minute when I heard something. It was a dog growling. Scared 10 years out of me."

"What did you see in the car?" Brownwell asked.

"Nothing. It was completely empty. I was pondering that when I heard another noise. I turned and put a light toward the direction of the noise. I found a guy looking at me. He was as surprised as I was. He was also armed to the teeth. I pulled my service weapon right away."

"Did you hear anything prior to the dog growling?"

"Not a sound," the trooper said. "In fact, thinking back on it, it was too quiet." The trooper told how he had brought the suspect forward after having him put down his guns. He explained how a second suspect had gotten behind him and forced him to drop his gun and light.

"I want to know exactly what they said to you," Brownwell said. "Try to remember."

The trooper outlined the conversation to the best of his ability. He finished by saying, "The second guy then took me to my patrol car where I was left handcuffed in the back seat. He cut the microphone cord and took off with my notepad. I remembered the plate number, though. Captain Rally had it fed into the computer with no results. The plate came back to a vehicle that's been junked out."

Brownwell questioned the trooper for an hour. He asked for the suspect's descriptions three different times.

"One more point," Brownwell said, "then I think we can let you go home. Are you sure these people have some kind of rule against shooting policemen?"

"That's what the younger one said."

"I think they figure we're allies, willing or unwilling."

"Good point," Rally said. "They harm one of ours and the shit would hit the fan for sure."

Brownwell said, "I'll bust any man who lets the public think we're supporting this gang. I've been at this long enough to know how officers act and think. I know a hell of a lot of cops give private lip service to support this group. The problem being, the damn press will have the public thinking we support them and we'll do nothing to stop them. Captain, make sure no one gives the press any fuel for that idea."

"I think the public supports that bunch," the trooper said. "They see them as saviors, and they think we're a bunch of failures."

"That's exactly what the people running this Cleanup Committee want them to think," Brownwell said. He turned to Rally. "See that this man gets home without seeing the press. I've got some phoning to do. Meet me back here when you're done, Captain."

Brownwell then turned to the trooper. "Say nothing to the press. If they press you, tell them you've been ordered to keep quiet by me. That will make them mad at me, and I haven't seen a reporter yet I couldn't handle. Understood?"

"Yes, sir."

"Good. I want you back down here for more work by noon. I'm going to have some pictures for you to look at. Maybe you can pick out one or both of those guys."

"How are you going to do that?" the trooper asked.

"Don't worry yourself about that," Brownwell answered. "Just get some sleep and be back here by 12. If the press is still hounding you, call in and we'll send a unit to get you. For now, get your rig and you'll have a unit in front of and behind you to escort you home."

Smiling broadly, the trooper stood up. "Wow, the VIP treatment."

"You are a VIP right now," Brownwell said. "Now get going. Rally, see you here in a few."

Brownwell left the room and walked down the hall to the front desk. The pretty female officer looked up as he approached. She was one of twenty women accepted by the State Police in the last class. He had not kept quiet about his feelings regarding women in police work outside of limited ways. The idea of women packing a gun and driving after dangerous nuts didn't sit well with him. However, politics of this nature were not on his mind this morning. The officer stood up as he approached. Her name tag said Trooper L. Dodd.

The radio was chattering, and the teletype in the corner rattled. Two uniformed troopers were just entering with an intoxicated man between them. The drunk was struggling and swearing at the officers. They quickly hustled him by the counter toward the room where a machine was located that would measure the amount of alcohol in his system. Trooper Dodd looked from the officers to the Chief.

"Jerks like that disgust me," she said.

"It disgusts me that they have to be brought through here where the public might be," Brownwell answered. The public was in fact present in the form of two reporters who were sitting off to one side. When they spotted the Chief they immediately stood up and walked toward him, notebooks out.

Brownwell realized he wouldn't be able to speak to Officer Dodd aloud with the press there. He reached toward the desk and pulled a notepad over. He wrote, "Send a teletype to the DMV in Salem. Request that photo files on every white male from 18 to 22 years of age be pulled and made available to me as soon as possible at this office. Get an ETA."

He slid the note to Dodd and turned to face the reporters. They were both young and looked like they'd been awake for quite some time. They did not appear to be very alert. Brownwell wasn't fooled by the look. Some reporters used that look to make officials careless with their words.

They handed the Chief their press cards. One was from the Eugene Register Guard, and the other was from United Press International. The UPI man accepted his card back and leaned against the counter.

"Can you give us a statement, Chief?" he asked.

"No. I don't have anything to say yet." He saw their routine. One would question, the other would write.

"Are you going to let us interview the Officer who saw the Cleanup Committee?"

"Who said anything about a trooper seeing anything?"

Tiredly, the UPI man pushed his press card back into his pocket. "Come on," he said. "We know you've had one of your men on ice for hours. I doubt you were discussing the chances of the Dodgers making it to the World Series."

"You're right, we weren't," Brownwell answered.

A smile started to appear on the UPI man's face. He thought the Chief was giving in.

"We were discussing fishing in the Blue River."

"Come on!" the reporter exclaimed. "You don't expect us to believe that, do you?"

Brownwell looked at his watch. 4:51 A.M.

"Gentlemen," he said. "I'm just not ready to give a statement. As soon as we can give you something of value, I'll see to it personally that you get it. However, you're going to have to be patient."

"I'll accept that," said the man from the Register Guard. He put his notebook away. "Good stories usually require a little sweating."

"Chief," said Trooper Dodd. Brownwell turned to face her. She slid a yellow teletype sheet across the counter to him, face down. He picked it up and started back down the hall. He fell into the chair in the Captain's office and looked at the message.

'Referencing your photo file request: will need until at least 9 am to assemble material.

Tossing the teletype sheet on the desk, he got up and started pacing. He mentally reviewed the events of the past few hours. He hoped like hell the trooper would recognize one of the gunmen in the photos. It was a long shot, but it was the only one he had.

Brownwell was still pacing when Captain Rally returned. He was carrying a tray with sandwiches and coffee. Brownwell thanked Rally, sat down, and picked up a sandwich. He was still thinking about what the trooper had said. Rally was holding a sandwich with one hand and rewinding a tape recorder with the other.

"Let's hear that tape again," Brownwell suggested. "Maybe we'll pick up something we missed."

"My thoughts exactly," Rally said.

They listened and made notes. They didn't catch anything new, though.

Brownwell said. "Well, let's see if any of the lab boys are back yet. Maybe they found something at the scene that will help."

Rally picked up an intercom line. "Seen any lab guys yet?" he asked, then paused to listen. He then said "Send them to my office" and hung up.

He turned to Brownwell. "Whitman and Parkerson just got back. Whitman is a print man and Parkerson's a ballistics specialist."

A minute later two tired plainclothesmen came in. Whitman was the older of the two, having been in the department for 17 years. Parkerson had just hit his 10 year mark. Both had extensive experience in their respective fields and were well respected. Brownwell knew both men by reputation. He shook hands while Rally moved two more chairs to the desk.

When everyone was seated Brownwell said, "Thanks for joining us. We'll try not to hold you too long. I need to know what you may have turned up. Whitman, let's start with any prints you found."

"Chief, by the time we arrived the firemen had pretty well wrecked everything. They mean well but they're thinking about fire, not evidence. Anyway, I did manage to lift some prints off the van. I'll send those prints along to the feds and see if they can match them up."

Brownwell was disappointed. He'd hoped for more. "Well," he said, "Maybe the feds will come up with something. Any ideas why they set fire to the place? That's not like the Committee. In fact, this whole operation is out of gear from what they normally do."

Whitman shrugged. "You got me. I've read the reports, and that business of firing the place up is off beat."

Brownwell looked at Parkerson. He was sitting with his head down, and for a moment it looked like the man had fallen asleep. Then he realized Parkerson was looking at something he had in his hand.

"What've you got there?"

Parkerson handed the chief a business card. "Found it by the van," he said.

Brownwell had seen lots of these cards but each one fascinated him. He often thought that if they could somehow find the printing press used to make these cards, half the battle would be won. He held this one up and looked at the legend on it, which was now well known to all law enforcement officers: *Some garbage for you from the Cleanup Committee.* He flipped the card over and looked at the familiar art- a man standing against a wall with a red paper heart pinned to his chest.

"Is this the only one you found?" Brownwell asked.

"That's it," Parkerson said.

Brownwell looked at Whitman, who shook his head.

"I checked it for prints. There were none."

Brownwell asked Parkerson, "Anything usual about the weapons this time?"

"Mostly the M16 as usual. One dead man was found to have been shot with a .32 automatic. One shot through the back of his head. Two of the stiffs in the house had .32 slugs in them, but the medical examiner will probably find it was the M16 that killed them."

"What are your conclusions about how they did it?"

"Looks like one went in from the back of the house and got their attention. Somebody in the yard shot them in the backs with the M16. Funny thing," Parkerson said, "when I was picking up brass in the yard, the area where the rifleman apparently laid to shoot looked like some kind of struggle had occurred. I called over one of the other guys and he agreed something had happened. We found the tracks of what looks like a dog. We thought maybe a guard had been used and jumped the rifleman."

Brownwell and Rally looked at each other. Parkerson caught the look.

"What is it, does that mean something?"

Brownwell asked, "Do you know about one of our guys being stuck up by those gunmen?"

"Yeah, I heard about it at the scene. No one knew any details."

"One of the guys had a dog with him. It appeared to be a friend of one of the gunmen. It also appeared to be a bum-like mutt. Not a well taken care of dog, so likely not a guard. The thing that doesn't make sense is why a struggle would have taken place. Could you guys have been mistaken on that point?" Brownwell asked.

"Not a chance," Parkerson said. "Between myself and Kaga Rapp, there's no mistake."

Kaga Rapp was a Native American man who had been with the department for four years as a forensic analyst. He had a statewide reputation for finding hikers and escaped prisoners.

Brownwell said, "Well, if Rapp agrees there was a struggle then there was one. Did he track them from the house to the car?"

"He did. He said it looked like the dog was stalking the guy it was following. The whole damn thing is confusing." Parkerson shook his head.

"By the way," said Whitman, "which one of our guys was it?"

"George Henry," Rally replied.

"Well blow me down," said Parkerson. "I'll bet that scared a few years out of him."

"It would have scared anyone," Rally said. "Fortunately he kept his head and stayed alive. He also got a good look at one of the men."

"Well well well!" exclaimed Whitman. "Maybe we've got a break at last."

"It's a long shot," Brownwell said, "but we're going to play it for every ounce of juice we can get out of it."

Chapter 31

Johnny Redwine slept well that night. He hadn't expected to, but he passed out right after getting in bed. The dog had laid down on the rug beside the bed and stayed quiet the whole night. When he woke up, the clock read 6:20 a.m. The dog was looking up at him as though to ask what was next.

"Next we get you to some place that can make you look like a dog instead of a dust mop." He felt a little foolish talking to a dog, but figured the dog wouldn't mind.

Johnny got up, showered, dressed and took the dog out for a walk in the park. When they got back to the house he pulled out the phone book and looked up a veterinarian clinic that advertised having a groomer on duty as well. He called and found they opened at 7:30.

When Johnny brought the dog in, the veterinarian had questions to which he had no answers. He said he found the dog wandering his neighborhood and none of the neighbors knew him. When the vet was satisfied, Johnny started to walk away. The dog started to follow.

"Stay," Johnny said. The dog sat down.

"By the way," the vet said, "what's his name?"

Johnny thought for a moment. "Bummer. His name is Bummer."

Leaving the clinic, he drove back downtown. He looked for a restaurant near his workplace where he could grab a quick breakfast. His car radio gave him the news from the night before. It felt like they were talking about someone he didn't know, and an event that occurred in some faraway place. Then his attention was grabbed by another news story.

"A truck was ambushed on Highway 26 about 4 miles northwest of Prineville, in Eastern Oregon. Police say the truck's tires were shot out. It was forced off the road and crashed. According to a rancher in the area, several shots were fired. He said it sounded like machine guns.

An officer on the scene who asked not to be identified said the 3 men in the truck survived the crash and tried to shoot it out with the ambushers. One of the ambushers was injured but it's not known how badly. State Police found 500 pounds of marijuana in the truck."

Johnny wheeled into a parking lot and shut off the engine. His heart beat rapidly. Paula, he thought. I've got to find out if Paula is okay. He walked quickly toward the restaurant. He was so wrapped up in his own thoughts he didn't even see the tall State Police officer until he practically bumped into him. The officer was just coming out of the restaurant.

Johnny stopped and backed up. "Sorry," he muttered. "I wasn't watching."

Chief Richard Brownwell stood in the door with Captain Rally right behind him. Brownwell and Johnny looked at each other. Neither could tell what the other was thinking.

"Excuse me," Brownwell said. "We weren't watching either."

Johnny stepped aside and let the two cops pass. Without giving them a second thought, he stepped into the restaurant. He didn't notice the long second look Brownwell was giving him.

Johnny's urge to eat had been chased away by the news story and his worry for Paula. However, he took some coffee and a donut before making his way to the phone booth at the back of the restaurant.

Stepping in, he slid the door shut and pulled out all of his change. A minute later, the phone was ringing at Paula's house. It rang 3 times before she answered.

"That'll be $1.30 for the first 3 minutes," the operator said.

Johnny's fingers were shaky as he fumbled to get the coins in. When it was done the operator said, "Go ahead."

"Paula, are you alright?" Johnny asked.

"Yes, I'm fine. You no doubt heard the news story?"

"Yeah, I was scared it was you. Who was it?"

"Kathy from Prineville," Paula said.

"How bad?"

"Look," Paula said, "We shouldn't discuss this here. Where's your sense of security?"

All Johnny felt was relief. "You're right," he said. "Listen, I'll try to get over there to see you this weekend."

"Sounds good. You know the address?"

"I'll call you when I get into town and we can meet."

"See you then," she said, and hung up.

Replacing the phone, he took a deep breath and gathered his wits. Leaving the booth, he crossed the restaurant and headed out for his car. He did not notice the two State Policemen who were sitting in their unmarked car across the street. As Johnny got into his car, Chief Brownwell reached for the microphone on his dash.

Two hours later, Johnny was busy labeling incoming freight in the back room at the store where he worked. Suddenly, he became aware of another person's presence. Instead of reacting instantly, he kept going with his work trying to figure out who it might be. It couldn't be an employee from the main store, or he would've heard all the noise. The loading dock door was closed and locked. Slowly, he turned and looked around. Standing by a stack of boxes a few feet away was Luke. He was just standing there, thumbs hooked in his belt, smiling.

"Damn, you know how to sneak up on people," Johnny said.

"I had the best teacher in the world," Luke answered. "Old Cain himself."

"What are you doing here?" Johnny wanted to ask how Luke had gotten in, but didn't. If Cain had taught him, locked doors would be no problem.

Luke leaned against the packing cases and removed his thumbs from his belts. He reached into his pocket with his right hand, removed a sheet of paper and handed it to Johnny. It was a copy of a police teletype.

"Where did you get this?" Johnny asked.

"Read it."

It was a copy of the teletype sent to the DMV by the Chief of the Oregon State Police. It was requesting all photos on file of white males between the ages of 18 and 22. Johnny felt the sharp stab of fear and looked right and left like he expected someone else was watching.

"We're alone," Luke said. "I made sure of that."

"Man, we're screwed," Johnny said.

"That depends," Luke said. "Do you have a driver's license with your picture on it?"

"No, thank God. When I come up for renewal they'll make me get a mugshot for the new one."

Luke visibly relaxed. "Fortunately, that law is new enough that not a lot of people have their photos on their licenses. I'm not so lucky. They have me on file, but to my knowledge that cop didn't get a good look at me."

"I don't think he did either. He sure got a good look at me though," Johnny said.

"Even so, I'm going to have to get lost for a while. You'll be contacted in a day or so by someone else."

Johnny felt a sense of loss, like he was losing a crazy but cool uncle.

"Damn, that's too bad. Any idea where you're going?"

"I know exactly where I'm going, kid, but it's not for you to know."

"Well, good luck, Luke. I hope we meet again sometime."

"Fear not, kid, we will. Now give me that teletype and get back to work. I'll find my own way out."

Johnny handed Luke the teletype and shook hands with the man he'd known so briefly. Dropping Luke's hand, he turned and resumed marking boxes. He didn't hear anything as Luke left. Christ, he thought, I hope he or Cain never come after me.

At lunch Johnny called the clinic to check on Bummer.

"That's an interesting dog you have," said the Vet. "Where did you say you found him?"

"He was just wandering around the neighborhood."

"Where are you now?"

"I'm calling from work. I'm on my lunch break."

"Do you plan to come by after work?" the vet asked.

"Yes. What's all this about?" Johnny asked. "I just found the dog. Is he really something special?"

"He's special alright," said the vet. "He's a guide dog."

"A what?"

"A guide dog. He's trained for leading blind people."

"Well I'll be damned!" Johnny exclaimed. "How did he get lost?"

"We can talk about it more when you come by later. I'll fill you in then."

Johnny spent the afternoon pondering the dog. He finally got to the clinic at 5:30 that afternoon, then had to wait for

15 minutes for the vet to see him. He was escorted into a private office where the vet was waiting with Bummer.

Bummer saw Johnny and immediately ran to him. He wagged his tail with excitement. Johnny scratched the dog on the head and marveled at how well he'd cleaned up. Bummer was a downright beautiful dog.

"He's a golden retriever," the vet said. "His real name is Ernie."

Johnny walked to a chair and sat. Ernie laid down next to him. The vet slid a paper across the desk, which Johnny picked up. It had a name and address on it. The address was in Junction City, a small town about 10 miles north of Eugene.

"How on earth did this dog get here from Junction City?" Johnny asked.

"What's your name?" the vet asked.

Johnny decided to keep his real name to himself. "Ronnie Stevens."

"Well, Mr. Stevens, this dog was lost a couple of months ago following a traffic accident on Highway 58 near Creswell. As I heard the story, Ernie was lost after the gal's husband rolled the family car. He and their two year old son died in the accident. The gal was injured badly. Ernie was thrown clear and wandered off. The police eventually called off the search, but they sent out a description to all the clinics in the area just in case. I had forgotten about it. I might have missed it completely if I hadn't found the ID marker in his ear."

"ID marking?"

"These dogs are earmarked by the school where they're trained. He's from the guide dog school in San Rafael, California. Ernie's owner Mrs. Rebajo has had him for about 4 years."

"Does she know Ernie's been found?"

"No, Mr. Stevens, she doesn't. I'm going to let you do that. I did notify the cops so they could stop looking for him. I doubt they were looking all that hard, but since he's been found they can notify the other clinics."

"Did the school know Ernie was lost?"

"Yes. They assumed he was lost for good. They've scheduled Mrs. Rebajo to return for training with another dog when she's able."

"Maybe she won't want him back," Johnny said.

"Don't get your hopes up, Mr. Stevens. I'll bet she'll be overjoyed to have him back. I have some guide dogs as clients and I know how their owners feel about them. These dogs are more than just eyes for blind people; they're family. Sometimes the dog is the only family the owner has. With her husband and son gone, Mrs. Rebajo may just be overjoyed to have Ernie."

"I'll take him to her today, if she's home."

"She was released from the hospital 3 days ago."

Johnny stood up and reached for his wallet. "How much do I owe you?"

"$25. You can pay at the front desk. Thank you for caring enough to bring Ernie in."

Johnny looked down at the dog. It was hard to believe this was the same ragged looking creature he had brought in. "I wonder where he lived all that time."

"Who knows," replied the vet. "What's even more amazing is the fact that he got from Creswell to Eugene alive."

If only you knew, Johnny thought. He checked out and the beautifully clean Ernie followed him to the car.

It was just starting to get dark when Johnny found the address with a large green and white house. The driveway was occupied by a brown Pontiac. He parked at the curb and slowly got out. Ernie's ears were perked up. Johnny figured he knew where he was. As soon as he opened the back door, Ernie shot out like a rocket and raced across the lawn to the porch. Ernie looked back at Johnny as if to say 'come on slowpoke!'

"I'm getting there, dog, be patient," Johnny said. He walked up and rang the doorbell. The porch light came on and the door opened slightly.

"Yes, what is it?" asked a tiny female voice.

"I've brought Ernie home," he answered.

The door was pulled wide open and Ernie bounded in, jumping around the living room and barking happily.

Johnny stayed on the porch while the two women in the room fawned over the dog. The girl who had opened the door (and nearly been knocked over by Ernie) was a slender gal of about 23 with black hair. She had dark features that suggested Hispanic heritage. The other girl looked like the first except a few years older. She also had one side of her head bandaged and her left arm was in a sling. She was having a difficult time holding on to the overjoyed Ernie. It was a pretty happy scene, Johnny figured.

He turned to leave quietly and let these people enjoy their homecoming.

"Wait," said a voice, "don't go."

Turning back, he saw the girl who had opened the door watching him.

"I don't want to bother anyone," he said.

"Bother?" she said. "Man, you've just made my sister extremely happy. That kind of bothering can take all day."

"I'm just glad I was able to bring Ernie home," Johnny said. "He's a nice dog. Before I found out he was a guide dog I thought of keeping him."

"Come on in," the girl said. "Tell us all about it."

Johnny followed her into the large living room. The furnishings were nice, but not the expensive stuff he'd seen in other places. At one end of the room a fireplace burned, emitting a comforting heat.

"Please sit down," Mrs. Rebajo invited. She was still down on one knee with her good arm around Ernie, who was leaning against her and panting with excitement.

The girl who opened the door said "I'm Lisa Rebajo. This is my sister-in-law, Donna."

"I'm Ronnie Stevens," Johnny said. "Pleased to meet you both."

"Please sit down," Donna said. "Perhaps you'd like something to eat or drink?"

"Just a cup of coffee, if it's not too much trouble."

"Be right back," said Lisa, and she went to the kitchen.

"Thank you so much for bringing him back!" Donna said. "I thought he was long gone." Donna came slowly to her feet. Ernie stood with her. She moved slowly to a large chair and sat down. Ernie dropped to the floor in front of her, his head on his paws.

"He's a beautiful dog," Johnny said.

"Yes he is," Donna said quietly. "When I found out he was gone right along with Lee and David it was almost more than I could stand. I've cried so many tears the last few months I sometimes wonder if I have any left."

Johnny wasn't sure what to say. After a moment he decided on: "I'm glad that I could at least bring Ernie home."

Lisa came in carrying coffee and cookies on a tray. She set them down on an end table near him, then sat on the carpet to pet Ernie. She said: "Tell us all about it, Mr. Stevens. Don't leave out a word."

He slowly reached out and picked up a cookie. He wasn't hungry but it was a darn good way to stall. This story would have to have some color. The simple one he'd given the vet would not work here.

"I first saw him about two days ago," he began. "He was wandering around in a little park near where I live. Some kids were playing with him. They'd throw a ball and he would bring it back. I figured he belonged to one of them. Then I figured he was just in too ratty a condition. His coat was a mess, and his feet looked sore. After a while I asked the kids about him. None of the kids claimed him, so I took him home. He was hungry, the poor guy. I thought he'd never stop eating. I took him to the clinic this morning to get him cleaned up. The Vet found the ID number in his ear, told me, and here I am."

The room was quiet except for the ticking of the clock. Lisa looked from Johnny to Ernie, then to her sister in law and back again.

"Do you know how Ernie came to be lost?" Lisa asked.

"The vet said there had been an accident," Johnny said.

"Did he tell you where it happened?"

"Yes, he did."

Lisa looked at Ernie, who had fallen asleep.

"I've heard stories about animals coming home after years," Johnny said.

"I've heard about things like that, too," Donna said, "and I guess I had some hope that Ernie would make it home."

Lisa asked, "What do you do for work, Mr. Stevens?"

Johnny was taken aback. He decided to keep that truth to himself. "I work at a gas station."

"Which one?"

"It's a Texaco on Court Street."

"I'm in Eugene a lot," Lisa said. "Maybe I'll come in and see you sometime."

"Sure," he said.

Donna asked, "How can I thank you for bringing Ernie home?"

Honestly, and from the bottom of his heart, Johnny said: " Seeing you and your dog happy together is thanks enough."

He ate one more cookie and chased it with the last of his coffee. "I've got to get back to Eugene. I've got work in the morning." He didn't really want to leave but he felt uneasy here. It didn't make a bit of sense; no one was around but these two women and the dog. Then he looked at Lisa's eyes. They were a dark brown, and plainly skeptical of him.

Standing , he stepped over to Ernie and scratched him behind the ears. "So long. It was nice knowing you. You take good care of Mrs. Rebajo, Ernie."

Ernie looked up at him and thumped the carpet with his tail. He didn't get up.

Donna surprised him with a question. "Did you have a name for him, Mr. Stevens?"

"Before I knew what his name was, I called him Bummer."

"Bummer," she repeated. "I guess he was reduced to that, wasn't he?"

Lisa stood up. "I'll walk you to your car." Her eyes warned him not to object.

"Thank you," he said. "Goodbye, Mrs. Rebajo. Have fun with Ernie."

"You can call me Donna," she replied. "Thank you again."

Johnny and Lisa walked out. They were by the car before she spoke.

"Why the pretending?"

"Well that's not very nice of you. I bring Ernie home and you accuse me of conning you?"

"I'm not accusing you," Lisa said. "I'm stating a fact. I don't know what your game is Mr. Stevens, or whatever your name is."

"I have no game, ma'am. I bought the dog home and that's it. You'll never have to see me again."

"Especially if I stop by the Texaco on Court Street," she said.

"Well, I might be on, you never can tell," he answered.

"There is no Texaco on Court Street." With that, Lisa turned and walked away.

Angrily, Johnny got in the Mustang and started it up. He had ruined his own story. He roared away knowing Lisa was watching him. He assumed she was taking his plate number. After a few blocks he was still kicking himself for acting like a fool, but he'd cooled down a bit. He pulled over to the roadside and did some thinking.

It was 20 minutes later when he slowly cruised down the street intersecting the Rebajo's home. From the stop sign he could see the Lane County Sheriff car parked in front of the house. He eased on through the stop sign and got out of dodge.

Chapter 32

"Damn, damn double damn!" declared a pacing Richard Brownwell.

Captain Rally looked at him tiredly from his seat behind his cluttered desk. Trooper Henry sat by the desk, his head down on his arms.

For hours and hours the three lawmen had looked over the hundreds of pictures delivered by the DMV. Brownwell had received the delivery shortly after returning from breakfast. They'd swung by Rally's place for a quick shave before returning, where Brownwell had borrowed a safety razor. He scraped away at his stubble while he pondered the kid in the parking lot.

Something about that kid triggered his cop instincts. He just couldn't figure out why.

"Maybe he's too clean," Rally had suggested.

They had been waiting in the parking area across the street for the kid to come out of the restaurant. Brownwell drummed on the steering wheel with his fingers. "I'll bet that green Mustang is the kid's," he said.

"That dull thing! You've gotta be kidding, Rick. That kid's probably driving the red Chevelle," Rolly mused.

When the kid came out and got into the Mustang, Brownwell felt rewarded. Once for being right and twice because he'd already committed the plates to memory. Back at the station, the plates came back registered to a Portland PO Box number. That left him with an empty feeling.

Trooper Henry arrived at noon looking restored, and Brownwell again hoped they might be onto something. He and Rolly had gone over the pictures, picking out the ones closest to the descriptions Henry had supplied.

Now, Brownwell stopped pacing and looked at his watch. 8 pm. Rally was now at 24 hours without sleep and Brownwell wasn't much better. Admitting defeat was hard for him. Only this morning, which now seemed like a week ago, he had assured the governor they were on a good lead, the best one yet in fact.

"I sincerely hope so," the Governor had replied. "This situation is getting out of hand."

Understatement of the year, thought Brownwell.

He looked at the young trooper. "Jim, let's have one more look at those you think come the closest."

Rally moaned. "For Christ's sake, Rick!"

Jim Henry said quietly, "they all look the same now, Chief."

Brownwell stepped over to the desk and picked up a handful of photos. He handed them to the trooper. "Look these over again," he said gently. "These are the ones you looked at the longest. Maybe you'll spot something you missed before."

Reluctantly, Henry took the pictures and began looking over them. Rally refilled the coffee pot. Brownwell dropped into a chair. He was tired. The office was hot and stuffy. Without meaning to, he dozed off. He snapped out of it suddenly when he heard Henry's voice.

"That's him! I'm sure of it."

Brownwell got up and took the picture from Henry. He flipped it over and looked at the name on the back. Lucas Gordon Perkins, it said. He handed the picture to Rally.

"Feed this info to the computer. You know the drill." Rally left the room.

Turning to Henry he asked, "Was this the guy with the dog?"

"No, that's the guy who locked me up in the back of the car. I'm sure as can be."

"Okay. Good work. Go home and get some sleep. Don't think about this any more tonight. Tomorrow is your day off, right?"

"Yes, Chief."

"You made this choice under difficult circumstances. These photos are going to be here for a day or two. If at any time you want to have another look, notify Captain Rally. No one but you two are to handle these at any time."

Trooper Jim Henry stood up and stretched. His uniform looked like he'd been wrestling. "Is it alright to attend mass before going home?"

"You want to go to mass, you say?"

"Yes, my brother is the Pastor at Saint Rose."

"Sure," Brownwell said. "Don't forget to drop your weapon in your trunk. I doubt your brother wants guns in his church."

Brownwell suddenly found himself very tired. Dropping into a chair, he put his head back and fell asleep as Trooper Henry left the room.

As the young trooper reached the front door, he met an attractive woman in her late 40's carrying an overnight bag.

"Excuse me, young man," she said. "I wonder if you might've seen my husband. He has forgotten to come home."

"May I ask who your husband is, Ma'am?"

"I'm Mrs. Brownwell," she answered.

"Last office to the left," Henry said. "You'll find him sound asleep."

Brownwell felt himself being shaken. At first, he thought there was an earthquake. With the shaking, he could hear an awful racket.

"Rick, wake up, dear."

Slowly he came out of the fog of sleep and realized his wife was the one doing the shaking. Captain Rally was seated across the desk with his feet up and head back, snoring loudly.

"Good Lord, what a noise! How could anyone sleep near him?" Brownwell asked.

"You were doing a fine job of it, dear. Now, get up and come with me."

Brownwell cast a suspicious look at the zipper bag she was holding. "What's that?"

"Some clean clothes, your razor, and some other things. Come on, I have a motel rented for the night. You need a hot shower, food, and some sleep," Joan said.

"Sleep is for people who have nothing to do," Brownwell replied.

"It seems to me you've done quite enough. You know what the doctor said. Rest."

"To hell with that quack! What does he know about anything? Doctors. Hmph."

"You stubborn old fool," Joan said with narrowed eyes. "If you don't come with me I'll get one of these good looking young officers here to put you in handcuffs and leg irons and I'll drag you out of here."

Brownwell grumbled. "It would take more than one of them," he said, and slowly got up. "Let's go find that shower and food."

"Don't forget the sleep," she replied.

"We'll see."

After getting cleaned up in the hotel room's shower, Brownwell felt much better and set his mind on a plan of action. He got so involved in his planning that he forgot to take into account his wife. She had other ideas.

"You are not going anywhere tonight," she said. "The local police can pick that guy up."

Brownwell was seated on the edge of the bed wearing only his shorts. The telephone book sat on the bed beside him. "I have to be there when they pick Perkins up," he argued.

"Why? Chief Thompson has a good department. They're capable. Quit glory hunting and settle down."

Chief Brian Thompson of the Eugene Police was an old political enemy of Brownwell's. However the two men could, and often did, work together.

"I want to talk to Brian about security for the prisoner after he's picked up. I'm sure his friends will either try to spring him or silence him."

"Alright," she said. "You call him while I get changed. Then we're going to dinner and then you're coming to bed with me. You can pick this business up again in the morning."

Brownwell watched his wife disappear into the bathroom and picked up the phone.

A deep voice answered. "Well, if it isn't old 'everyone should be a state cop' himself! I hear you got one of your boys grabbed last night, Rick."

Rick took a deep breath and counted to 5 before answering. "You could say that, but it worked out for the best. We have an ID on one of the gunmen."

"Do tell!" said Thompson. The man was impressed but would die before admitting it.

"The guy lives in your city, Brian. I think it should be a city pickup."

"My, my," Thompson said. "Aren't you generous? You guys haven't given me the time of day. Now you want me to pick this hot shot up."

"Don't you want to do it?" Brownwell asked.

"In a way," Thompson answered.

"What does that mean?"

"A lot of my men are of the opinion these people should be left alone. They seem to be doing a good job of taking out the trash. The price of weed is going up with the reduced supply."

Brownwell fumed. "I hope that your opinion isn't well known by the public."

"That's public opinion as well, Rick. You know it."

"The public is a bunch of fools. They don't know what's good for them. If this is permitted to go on, pretty soon we'll have another committee to come after this one, and more and more problems. You know that."

"I'll pick your man up, Rick. Don't lecture me or try to shape my opinion. It won't work."

"Thanks, Brian. I appreciate your help."

"So where do I find this hot shot?"

Brownwell gave him the address.

Thompson whistled. "That is a right fancy neighborhood. Those folks are going to be mighty surprised to see a bunch of cops around."

Brownwell said, "My main concern is the security of the prisoner."

"He'll be safe. By the way, what's the guy's name?"

"Lucas Perkins."

"What else do you know about him?" Thompson asked.

"That's it for now."

"You said you're worried about security. Do you doubt the ability of my men?"

"Not at all, Brian. What concerns me is that the Cleanup Committee may try to spring him or silence him."

"Are you going to be there to direct the show?" Thompson asked.

"Nope, this is a Eugene PD show."

"Well I'll be damned!" declared the surprised Chief. "What's the catch?"

"There isn't any catch, Brian. None at all."

"Are your State boys going to let us take credit for the arrest?"

"Sure we will. I'm going to hold a news conference in the morning. The press is busting it's printers to get hands on my man, Trooper Henry."

"Are you going to let them talk to him?"

"Yes, but a lot of what he says will depend on whether or not you are successful in bagging Perkins."

"If that bird has flown, we'd better not get the shaft in any way."

"You won't," Brownwell said. "Take down my number here, and give me a call here when you've grabbed the guy."

"You want to know either way?"

"Yes, please, either way."

"Well, if I didn't know better, I could swear I just heard Chief Brownwell say please."

"Fuck off, Brian."

"I'm not piped right," said Thompson, and he hung up.

Brownwell hung up the phone and realized his wife had come out of the bathroom.

"Do you always talk to other people that way?" she asked.

"No," he said. "Only when they insult me."

Ten patrol cars with two men to each vehicle took up stations near the condos where suspect Luke Perkins lived. Chief Thompson himself, along with 8 other heavily armed officers, moved in. They covered all hallways and stairs. Residents were told to stay inside.

Thompson and two of his best men kicked in the door belonging to Perkins. They found it empty. Completely cleaned out. Not a single thing was found. No hint of when it was vacated.

Afterwards, Thompson dismissed his men and called Brownwell.

"Gone," he reported. "Not a trace of him left."

"Well, you tried, Brian. That's all anyone can do."

The next morning at 10:30, the news conference was held at the State Police office. Trooper Henry was questioned. Brownwell limited what he could say on the grounds of protecting the ongoing investigation. As a result, the press got little information. In anger, they turned on Brownwell, who only echoed what he had allowed Henry to say. When the papers hit the streets that afternoon, disappointed reporters gave the Oregon State Police bad press.

One reporter wrote, "If Brownwell had only notified Chief Thompson sooner, they could have picked up Perkins before he fled town. Brownwell sat on the information rather than let someone else get credit for the arrest."

That night, Brownwell read the review his department was getting from the Salem Statesman. He had returned home with his wife after the press conference. The Statesman was usually kinder than other papers toward the state police, but this time the editor joined the others in criticizing how the situation had been handled. Disgusted, Rick tossed the paper aside.

"These damned newspaper people never know when to thank you for doing something. They sure know how to take half facts and knock the hell out of you with them."

When it was obvious he was not going to get a reply from Joan, he picked up the paper again. Turning away from the editorial page, his eyes fell on a story about the upcoming summit between President Carter, the Prime Minister of Israel, and the President of Egypt.

In the lower corner of the page, another story caught his eye. It was a human interest article, the type that did not usually make the papers. It was about a blind woman getting her lost guide dog back. He read the story twice. After reading it a third time, he slowly lowered the paper and pretended to watch TV.

Chapter 33

The morning of September 10th dawned clear and cool over Summer Lake. It was quiet except for the song of the occasional bird. On the abandoned grounds of what had been the training camp for the Cleanup Committee, birds of all types were now nesting. From out of the north, the morning quiet was split as a flock of geese settled in over the lake. They dropped by the hundreds to rest on the water before continuing their journey southward.

It was the noise of the geese that woke Susan Sherman that morning. She lay in bed and stretched. They sure are noisey, she thought. Sadly, Susan realized she was going to miss this sound. For years the call of the southbound geese in the fall had been a part of her life. Now her life was changing.

She rolled over and hid her face in the pillow. The sound of the geese through the open window reminded her that last year at this time she and Luther had begun gathering an apple crop. That reminded her of the horrible day not long ago that Luther had died.

Luther had told her that morning he was going to repair fencing on the lake side of the property. He'd taken a lunch, figuring on staying with the job until it was done. When he had not returned by 4:30, she began to worry. When 5 pm came and went with no sign of him, she went to the phone. She called Grandma Sherman, who lived only a short distance away, to see if he had stopped there. He had not. Susan got the pickup truck and drove out to the area where Luther said he'd be working.

She honestly figured Luther had forgotten the time, or was just wrapping things up. The thought that he might be busy spying on that camp again touched her mind, but she dismissed it. He had told her once he'd been watching those people and suspected they were up to no good. That nice Major had explained to some of the townsfolk what they were doing, but her husband had not believed it.

"I tell you Susan," he had said, "those people are not real Army."

"Well, you leave them alone. It's none of your business," she had replied. The subject had not come up again.

Susan was totally unprepared for what she found by the fence. She halted the pickup and jumped out. The Jeep was between her and the body that had been her husband. She came around the Jeep and stopped. Her hands went to her mouth, but it did not stop the scream from escaping her lips.

The body was completely swollen. Flies were crawling over it. Poison from the snake and hours in the hot sun had left a sight her mind could not absorb. She had no idea how long she had stood there screaming her lungs out.

Remembering, she pulled the covers over her head to try and block out the picture somehow. It wouldn't go away. It haunted her in her sleep and in her waking hours. It had all but driven her mad.

She didn't know how much time passed on the hill. She became aware that someone was beside her. The man put an arm around her and tried to turn her away.

"My God! My God! Oh, sweet Jesus Susan! Don't look!" By then the picture was burned into her mind.

She had been found by Marlin Thomas and one of his sons. They had heard her screaming from a mile away and came running. They took her back to the house. Marlin remained with her while his son went for help. She couldn't remember much of the rest of that day. At some point a doctor had arrived and given her a shot, then it all went black.

Through the remaining days, Marlin's family, who had been her neighbors for many years, proved how valuable friends can be. With their help, she made Luther's funeral arrangements and contacted all the relatives. Her only sister Darlene drove up from Los Angeles to stay with her.

Now, this morning of September 10th would be her last morning on this ranch. She had sold it to the Thomas family, save for the two acres where Grandma and Grandpa Sherman would live out their days. Susan was going to California. Beyond that, she had no plans.

She didn't know when the idea had first crept into her mind, but she suspected her husband's death was caused by whoever had been at that camp. It was a thought she voiced to no one. It was an idea that seemed totally ridiculous. The idea never really had a chance to develop in the rush of things until a few days back when she had cleaned up Luther's desk.

The letter was dated two days prior to his death. It was hidden under some other papers on his desk. It had been folded but not placed in an envelope. She read it slowly. She then put it down and rubbed her eyes. Any doubt that her husband had been murdered vanished. She had no idea how they got a snake to do it for them, but she was convinced the people at the camp had done it. They found out Luther was onto them and shut him up. It was with considerable fear that she read the letter again.

"Dear Chief Brownwell,

I'm not sure who else to write about this, so I guess you might as well be the one. I might be getting jacked out of shape for nothing.

Something damned funny is going on over here by Summer Lake. For several months, a bunch of people have been at a camp there. They stay to themselves and won't associate with the community. They look like the Army. There was a man in here during the winter who called himself Major Howard. He told my neighbor and some folks in town they were some secret military force being trained to fight in the desert.

I'm thinking you or someone you know should look into it. If they are not who they say they are, then no possible good can come from it. I would appreciate it if you would keep this letter to yourself. Please don't contact me. I don't want them to know I'm suspicious of them, whoever they are.

I get the feeling they're about ready to ship out.

Susan tossed back the covers and got up. In an hour, the Thomases would be taking her to Lakeview to catch a bus. She had decided to take the letter and leave it with the police. They would know what to do with it.

Chapter 34

On the morning of September 11th, the Pacific Northwest received another shock. At 10:30 pm the night of September 10th, three people entered a restaurant in Boise, Idaho. This restaurant had a reputation for being a criminal hangout. Boise police had been watching the place for a while.

The three customers blended in with the crowd. No one paid them any unusual attention. A few minutes after coming in, the trio produced Uzi machine guns from under their coats. They started methodically killing everyone in sight. People screamed and dove for cover anywhere they could find it. Windows were shattered as people dove through them in an attempt to escape the gunfire.

When people lay dead and dying all around them, the three gunmen walked out the back door. The last person out stopped and turned. He tossed a firebomb into the middle of the bodies. It exploded on contact with the floor. The wounded never had a chance. 31 people died in that building. Of the 9 that escaped, 3 died on the way to the hospital.

The next day, a written statement was found on the counter of a Boise radio station. It was read over the air.

Richard Brownwell read the story in the paper like thousands of others. Unlike most readers, his blood ran cold. He had a chilling fear that the system of justice he so firmly believed in was about to fall apart. This fear was a recurring one. He had long ago told the governor that if the committee went interstate there would be a national emergency. He read the article again, and his spirit sank into helplessness. That feeling was still with him when he reported to his office on the morning of the 12th. It remained with him until he got halfway through the weekly reports from the Lakeview office.

He found the letter with no return address. It had a note from an officer paperclipped to it. "Found this on the counter. It was left by a woman who came in while I was busy. She asked that I see to it this gets to Chief Brownwell." The office clerk had simply dropped it in with the other reports and mailed it.

He reached for a letter opener and sliced it open. He read it 3 times before the importance of what he held completely sunk in. After the third reading, he reached for his private phone line to the governor.

The governor was in his favorite place by the window when the phone rang. He recognized it as the private line to Brownwell. He slowly crossed the room to answer it. He didn't want to answer. Brownwell had dropped the ball in Eugene, and since he had appointed Brownwell the papers had been taking some sharp jabs at him. Now, as he reached for the phone, he realized he was afraid to pick it up. It was always bad news.

"Yes, Rick," he said into the phone.

"Paul!" the excited Chief said. "We have a break."

Remembering the "break" a few days ago, the Governor checked his urge to get excited.

"We do?"

"Yes, and this time it's the real thing. I'd like a meeting with you and Attorney General Blakely this afternoon."

"Why does Tom have to be in on it?"

"I agree with you," Brownwell said, "but he is the AG. This will concern him."

"What is it this time?"

"A letter. It came in with the weekly reports from the Lakeview office. You remember where Lakeview is?"

"Yes, I recall it. Pretty little town."

"The letter came through that office from a guy near Summer Lake."

"You find Blakely. Be in my office at 2:30." The governor replaced the phone, buzzed his secretary and informed her of the appointment.

Brownwell was in the governor's office at 2:30 sharp. Attorney General Blakely arrived at 2:35. The governor gave Blakely an exasperated look as the fancily dressed man came through the door.

"You're 5 minutes late," the governor said. "Why don't you ever show up on time?"

The attorney general looked disappointed. "I'm sorry, gentlemen. I didn't mean to keep you waiting."

The hell you didn't, Brownwell thought. Aloud he said: "No matter, Tom, you're here now. Have a seat."

Blakely gave Brownwell a thankful smile and sat down. He packed and lit his pipe.

Brownwell produced two copies of the letter and slid one to each man. He watched them closely for their reactions.

"Good Lord!" declared the governor.

Tom Blakely went white. Brownwell saw it and felt good. It was the first time he had ever seen this dandy lose his cool.

"This...this letter," Blakely stammered. "Where did you get it?"

"It came in the mail with some reports from the Lakeview office, Tom."

Blakely all but forgot his pipe. He stared at the letter in front of him. Both the governor and Brownwell were shocked at Blakely's reaction.

"This letter says they had a camp over there. They camped right under our noses and we didn't know it?"

"Summer Lake is hardly right under our noses," Brownwell said. "It's remote. I checked the map. It's a long way from anything."

Blakely looked down. Brownwell looked at the governor, who was smiling. He found Blakely's shock funny.

"Well, Rick, what's next?" the governor asked.

"I'm going to have a look. Apparently they had a big setup from the way this letter sounds. I'm taking some of my men and flying over bright and early tomorrow morning. With any luck they left some kind of evidence laying around."

"Do you think it could really be the base camp of the Cleanup Committee?"

"I think it's exactly that."

"Maybe they have guards posted," suggested Blakely.

"We're allowing for that," Brownwell said. "We'll be ready to shoot it out with them if necessary."

The governor looked troubled. "I don't like it," he said. "What if you and your men get killed? Then where would we be?"

"I don't think they'll give us any trouble. For one thing, I doubt there's anyone left to shoot it out. I think every man they have is in the field."

Tom Blakely looked at his watch. "This is quite a development," he observed. "If you do find some evidence at the camp it could mean the end of this Cleanup Committee."

"Would that hurt your feelings, Tom?"

It was the governor who asked.

Blakely thought for a moment before he answered. "In a way it would, in a way it wouldn't. I can almost see their points of view."

Brownwell stared at the Attorney General. "Do you have any information about these people that the rest of us don't, Tom?"

"You know I don't!" Blakely replied. "I'd share it with you if I did."

"You were in Eastern Oregon a lot last spring, correct?"

"Yes, I was mostly in Klamath Falls and Bend. That's quite a ways from Summer Lake."

"How do you know it is, Tom?"

"What?"

"You heard me," Brownwell said. "How do you know where Summer Lake is?"

"It must be quite a way. I never heard anyone speak of it around there. You yourself said it was a remote area."

"So I did. It's very remote."

"What time are you leaving in the morning?" Blakely asked.

"About 5," Brownwell said. "My pilot says it's about 90 minutes by chopper."

The governor looked questioningly at Blakely. "Why don't you go along, Tom?"

"Not me," the Attorney General said. "I've got one busy schedule tomorrow." He stood up, and picked up his copy of the letter. Brownwell held out his hand. Blakely looked at the hand, obviously waiting for the letter. He looked at the governor, who was still grinning, and handed the letter over.

"Thanks Tom," Brownwell said. "We don't want anyone finding out we have this information just yet. You have a big office, and someone could pick this up without you knowing it. If this gets to the press too soon, it could be a disaster."

"Sure, sure," Blakely said, and headed for the door. He stopped and turned before exiting. "Enjoy your helicopter ride."

Brownwell watched the door. An idea was moving around in his mind. It was an idea born of years of police experience. His experience taught him that everyone was a suspect until an investigation was cleared. Yet even this idea was too much. Quickly, before it had a chance to develop, he pushed it aside and turned to his boss.

"Well," began the governor, "what do we know about the guy who wrote the letter?"

"I'm having Lakeview do a background," Brownwell replied. "Somebody obviously has something going on over there. I'm assuming a lot by thinking it's a base camp. We'll have to go look. We just might turn something up."

"I hope so," the Governor said. "To be honest, I'd like to leave this office with this dirty business put to rest. By the way, Rick, do you suppose this Idaho bunch is working with ours?"

"No way of knowing at this time, Paul. One thing for sure, they don't seem to have the finesse our people do."

"Christ have mercy! Don't refer to them as our people," said the governor.

Brownwell looked at his boss and grinned. "Well, you know what I've always believed Paul. If it's from Oregon, it's better."

"I agree, but not in this case. I feel no urge to claim the Cleanup Committee as one of our state's better export products."

Brownwell stood and picked up the letters. "See you as soon as I get back."

Chapter 35

Marlin Thomas woke up to the gray light of day showing faintly through the window. The clock on the nightstand read 6:15. The alarm was set for 6:30. He listened. Beside him his wife slept peacefully. Then he heard the sound that woke him up. It was a helicopter.

Getting out of bed, he walked to the window and pulled back the curtains. It was a cloudy morning with no wind that looked like rain was coming. Marlin couldn't see the helicopter, but could tell by the sound it was pretty close to the ground.   Like others in this area, he had gotten used to the sound of helicopters coming and going from the camp across the lake. He walked back by the bed and got dressed. He had an idea of going out to watch the chopper land. He had always been too busy before.

Old Luther, he thought with a shiver, seemed to have lots of time to watch those birds. That poor guy. What a hell of a way to die.

When he had talked about that with the doctor that came to help Susan, the doc said in all likelihood Sherman never knew what happened to him. The doctor had asked if they found the snake. Marlin told him hell no, they weren't going snake hunting.

By the time Marlin was dressed and outside, the chopper was over the lake and dropping fast. He started his pickup and drove along the road to a point where he could watch the helicopter land. The water of the lake was still, and birds flew by looking for breakfast. He saw two deer jump and run when the noise of the helicopter startled them.

He lost sight of it as it dropped behind the trees on the other side of the lake. He started the rig and drove that direction. In a couple of miles he came to the road up to the camp. Where it had been well used in the summer, it was now overgrown with weeds. Funny how nature reclaims things. Marlin ground up the road in first gear. He wasn't sure why he was here, but it was too late to go the other way.

Whatever he expected to find, it wasn't this. Five heavily armed State Policemen were standing near a man who was in uniform but had no gun in sight. The troopers were all looking at Marlin. Behind them sat the helicopter. He had no sooner stopped the truck when the unarmed officer started walking toward him. That's when the other troopers aimed their rifles his way.

Marlin sat quite still, hands on the wheel, and watched the officer with the gold badge approach. He admired the man's obvious cool. His confidence in himself and the men behind him was clear. He suddenly realized who this was- the Chief of the state police- and was glad he came up here.

"Good morning," Brownwell said. "Would you mind turning off your motor and stepping out of the truck please?"

Marlin let go of the wheel with one hand and turned off the key. He looked at the buildings, remembering how much better they looked the last time he was here.

"Step out of the vehicle," Brownwell said again.

Marlin opened the door and got out slowly. He kept his eyes on the Chief.

"What is your name and why are you here?" Brownwell asked.

"My name is Marlin Thomas." His mouth was dry. "I saw the helicopter, thought I would come up and see what was going on."

"Do you live around here, Mr. Thomas?"

"Yes, I have a place yonder across the lake. Why are you here?"

Brownwell's eyes bored into Thomas. "Were you expecting someone else?"

"No, sir. I wasn't expecting anyone. Just curious."

Brownwell relaxed a little. Thomas couldn't, because the rifles were still aimed his way. Brownwell asked, "Do you know Luther Sherman?"

"I knew him," Marlin replied in surprise. "Luther was killed about a month ago when a rattlesnake bit him. His wife and I found him. Poor gal, she was out of her mind."

Brownwell broke in. "He's dead, you say?"

"Yes," Marlin said. "How do you know him?"

Brownwell turned to his troopers. "At ease, men." He turned back to Marlin. "You look like a man who could use some coffee. Our brew is close to crankcase oil, but we'll be glad to share it with you."

"Thank you kindly," Marlin said. "I could certainly use a cup."

Brownwell walked back to his men. One went to the chopper and retrieved the coffee. Brownwell started back toward Marlin, and his men went in different directions.

"I propose that we take it easy in your truck while the others look around. I think you and I have a lot to talk about."

Marlin accepted the coffee and climbed back behind the wheel. Brownwell took the passenger seat. During the next two hours Marlin forgot all the bad things he'd ever heard about the Chief, and Brownwell heard a most incredible story. Marlin talked about Major Howard's story and the weekly helicopter landings, and that the group declined an invitation to the local 4th of July festivities. He also told the Chief about a rumor he'd heard, that some kids had wandered up there and been stopped by armed guards.

"They flew out of here the same day Luther got bit by that snake," Marlin said. "No one's been over here since, until today."

Brownwell handed Marlin a letter. "Read this, Mr. Thomas, and tell me what you think."

Marlin recognized Luther Sherman's handwriting immediately. He read the letter slowly. Then he folded the letter up and handed it back to Brownwell.

"He never said a thing to me about his suspicions. I know he used to watch them a lot. I thought he was just doing it for entertainment."

"It probably started out as entertainment," Brownwell said. "He might have seen something that got his suspicions up. Would you know if he ever said anything to his wife?"

"I doubt it," Marlin said. He wouldn't have wanted to worry her."

"Do you suppose she would be willing to talk with me?"

Marlin explained how Susan had sold him the ranch and left for California a few days ago. "Did she mail you that letter, Chief?"

"Apparently she just left it on the counter at our Lakeview office. It was sent to me with some routine paperwork."

"That must be what she was doing the last few minutes when we took her to catch the bus. I thought she'd gone off to the ladies' room or something. Leaving it on a counter sounds like something she'd do. She's a pretty timid person," Marlin said.

Brownwell put the letter back into his jacket pocket. "Mr. Thomas, I just happened to have a man with me who is a mighty good artist. Do you suppose you could give him enough information about the young people you saw so he could work up a drawing?"

"I sure could describe one girl," Marlin said. "The black girl. She was an absolute knockout."

"Did she appear to be just one of the troops, or an officer?"

"She seemed like one of the troops," Marlin said. He reached for another cup of coffee.

"Any idea how many officers they had?"

"Not a one, Chief. Tell me, if these people are who Howard said they are, then what's the big flap?"

"I don't believe for one minute they were military, Mr. Thomas. I think we'll find this was the base camp for the Cleanup Committee."

Chapter 36

It was a warm fall afternoon, and one of those days when Mother Nature gives the earth a golden burst of colors. Johnny Redwine was halfway through his 18th year. He had seven notches on his gun, and did not notice the glorious autumn display. His gaze at the moment was locked on the marble headstone before him. It bore the legend 'Brenda Marlene Redwine, born June 18th, 1957, died January 1978.

In spite of the warm sun on his back, a chill ran through his wiry body. The old hatred for those responsible for her death welled up in him. His determination to shoot every dope pusher in the world was renewed. Before he knew it he was on his knees, touching the headstone with both hands and crying big tears.

"Brenda, Brenda, Brenda" he cried, over and over.

In a few minutes the tears had passed. He stood and pulled a handkerchief from his pocket. He was drying his tears when a voice behind him made him whirl, his hand darting for the gun that wasn't there.

It was the priest who had spoken to him, the one he'd met in the restaurant after training.

"I'm Father Michael Henry," he said gently. The priest was carrying some red roses.

"I remember you. We met at that restaurant."

"That's right. Again, I'm sorry for bothering you.

"It's ok," Johnny replied. He shoved the handkerchief back in his pocket. "I was just leaving anyway."

"If you don't mind my asking," the priest began, "who were you visiting here?"

"My sister," Johnny answered.

"There's no shame in crying over your sister, son. There's no harm in showing grief for someone you love."

"I suppose not. It's just that I haven't visited her before, and it kind of got to me. You know what I mean?"

Father Henry set down his roses. "I know what you mean. I've shed many tears over friends and loved ones in my day. May I have a look?"

He stepped by Johnny, who didn't object, and looked at the headstone.

"I thought this was the one," he said.

"The one what?" Johnny asked.

"Shortly after arriving here I said a funeral mass for a young lady. It was said at the time she had one brother but no one could locate him. You must be the brother."

"Yeah. I was out of town at the time and didn't find out for a few weeks."

"Well," said the priest, "if it's any comfort to you, quite a few people attended the funeral mass. Apparently she had a lot of friends."

Before he could stop himself Johnny said, "Sure she did. It was those damned friends of hers that killer her. If she had just listened to me..."

Father Henry waited for him to continue. Johnny clamped his jaw shut, fearing that he might have said too much already.

"She died of a drug overdose, didn't she?" asked Henry.

"Yes, she did."

"I don't blame you for being bitter about it. Please don't let it ruin your life, though."

"It won't."

Father Henry picked up the roses. "For a while," he said, "I used to wonder where the so-called Cleanup Committee got its people. After meeting you and some others like you, I can see where many people could be bitter enough to turn to the gun.”

Johnny waited, afraid to speak. His mind jumped around trying to guess where this conversation was going. He decided to be careful before saying a word.

Father Henry walked to a grave a few feet away, set the flowers down, and then said a prayer. Not knowing why, Johnny waited and watched. Seeing the priest gave him recollections of going to mass as a child. It had been years since he’d been in a church. He figured the Devil had him now so he’d never set foot in another one.

Father Henry walked back to where Johnny was standing. “My brother met some of those Committee people a few nights ago,” he said.

Johnny swallowed. “Is he alright? Did they kill him?”

“Scared 40 years out of him and made him come to mass, but they didn’t hurt him. He’s a State policeman. Apparently these people don’t hurt the police. I’m thankful for that, and so is my brother.”

“I heard about that,” Johnny said. “That happened down near Creswell someplace.”

“Once was a time when I was a policeman myself,” the priest said. “I was pretty good at it too. In fact, I’m somewhat of an oddball in the family. All of my relatives are cops of one kind or another.”

“That’s interesting,” Johnny said. “I’m sure glad your brother is alright.” He knew what he’d said didn’t make sense, but the priest was obviously leading up to something.

“My brother got a good look at one of the people,” Father Henry said, smiling. “He even got a good look at the guy’s shaggy dog.”

Again, Johnny waited. He wasn't aware of it but he was holding his breath. Father Henry's eyes bored into his own. Johnny tried to hold the look but couldn't.

Father Henry finally said, "Thank you for sparing my brother."

Johnny felt like he'd been hit in the belly. The air rushed out of him. Cold fear grabbed at his heart. The warm day went ice cold. "You're making a mistake," he stammered. "I don't know what you're talking about."

"Yes you do, son. Don't try to deny it. My brother gave me an excellent description. You fit to a T."

"Are you going to turn me in to your brother and his friends?" Johnny asked, as he took a few steps back. He had no doubt that he could handle this guy in a fight if it came to it. He also knew he could outrace the priest back to the Mustang. Once there he could have the Browning out in the blink of an eye.

"I'm not going to turn you in to anyone," Father Henry said. "I don't know that you have committed any crime. I do want to give you something to think on, though. I don't know how long you've been a member of the Cleanup Committee. If you are even half smart, and I think you are, you should know by now that you can't win. Eventually you'll be caught. When you are you'll have two choices: shoot it out, or run. Either way, you lose. When my brother caught you in Creswell a few weeks ago, you had someone to get you loose. That someone won't always be around."

"How do you know?"

"That's the way of it, and always has been. Figure it out for yourself. You know the police have found that training camp. That was all over the papers. What you don't know, and couldn't know, is that the sister of that girl you returned the dog to is a Deputy Sheriff. She's been trying to convince her associates that you are one of the gunmen from Creswell.

The only reason you haven't been picked up yet is that she can't find you, and everyone else is too busy. Your string of luck has almost run out, son. You'd better come in while you're ahead."

"Come in?" Johnny asked. "Give myself over to be put in jail? No thank you!"

"You'd be treated fairly. You can probably even make a deal for immunity by testifying for the state."

"I wouldn't live long enough. Neither would anyone else," Johnny said.

"You can be given protection."

Johnny looked at Father Henry and remembered how Cain knew no locked doors. He remembered how Luke could materialize in the same room with him, and shook his head no.

"I'm sorry," Father Henry said. "I really am sorry, but if you ever change your mind, get in touch with me first. I'll help you."

"You are a damned fool," Johnny said.

"I've shot 7 people. I don't regret any of them. Before it's over I'll shoot several more. How do you know you won't be next on my list, Father Henry?"

"All of that is between you and God, son. You will account to Him for what you've done and what you will do. As for shooting me, I doubt it. You're not that kind of killer."

Johnny scoffed. "You assume one hell of a lot. For your information, Father, I account to only one person, and he certainly isn't God. For all I know he may be the Devil himself. Whatever he is, he's the man with the money and with the resources. He's also got the knowledge we're going to rid our society of drug pushers."

Father Henry asked, "Then who is going to rid society of the people who got rid of the drug pushers?"

“We’ll go when our job is done,” Johnny said. He turned
and walked away.

Chapter 37

Doctor Fish left the recliner chair and changed the record on the stereo. He took up his pipe and let the sound of the Boston Pops flow over him. Fish was in the basement of the Eugene warehouse hideout. Every few minutes his eyes would wander to the closed circuit TV monitor that showed him what was going on outside.

His presence here was no accident. He was meeting with his 4 field commanders: Dot, Cain, Abel and Luke. The same Luke that had escaped the capture Brownwell had so carefully planned for him would be there. Luke had simply left the apartment he rarely used, and came here. After cooling his heels for a few days, Luke had taken Dot and Abel to Idaho. There, they pulled the raid that had shocked everyone, even Doctor Fish.

The idea of making an out of state hit had been dreamed up by Luke. He was the one who liked to bring in elements to confuse law enforcement. For that reason Luke did things like setting fire to the house in Creswell that made no sense to anyone else.

Fish refilled his pipe and considered the wisdom of ever hiring Luke in the first place. They had badly needed another man after Boxer was killed. Cain had known both men through the service, and had recommended Luke. Fish listened to Cain and never questioned his judgment. Yet after the Idaho raid, Fish felt it was time to serve notice about who was running the organization once and for all.

The last few days were very trying for Fish. Stoneking had called an emergency meeting of the Committee. He had all but had a rebellion on his hands when they heard their base camp was about to be discovered. It had even been suggested that the whole project be abandoned. Fish and Stoneking had finally gotten them settled down enough to listen to reason. They were assured that nothing of any value would be found at the camp. After an hour or so the rest of the group had gone home, leaving Stoneking and Fish alone.

"Tell me," Jonah had said, "how did they find out about the camp?"

Fish explained the letter and how it came to Brownwell's hands.

"You're positive that all identifying equipment has been removed from the camp?"

Fish assured the nervous financier that all was well under control.

"Now what about the girl that got hurt when they ambushed that truck a few weeks ago?" Stoneking had asked.

Fish had informed him that she had died in spite of Dot and Paula's best efforts to save her. They stayed with her, doing what they could until the end came. They had then taken the body out into the desert and buried her. Her disappearance had been explained by a note in her handwriting, which was found in her house.

"We had all the recruits write up a note long ago just in case," Fish explained.

Stoneking then made the sign of the cross and said "That's unfortunate. Make sure her death is avenged."

Prior to that meeting with the Committee, Fish had done a rush job chasing down Cain and Abel. He had dispatched them to the camp for a security check, and then canceled his afternoon appointments. The next 48 hours had been one hair-raising scare after another for everyone.

Obviously they had done a good job of covering their tracks. So far the cops had two things, neither of which were of any real value. Luke had been identified, and they found the camp. These were no more than propaganda victories.

Now, the others arrived one by one. Cain, Dot, Luke, and finally Abel. Fish turned off the stereo. They gathered up coffee cups and took seats, wasting no time on chatter.

"Welcome," Fish said from his recliner. "Thank you all for coming. My main purpose for this meeting is to assure all of you, so you can assure all your people, that all is well. The discovery of our camp is nothing but a propaganda victory for the police. Luke, you are out of reach here. With these things in mind, it's time we get to work. Before we get to assignments, I want it understood that from now on all targets and missions are to be cleared through me first. This is a major policy change, and your people will have to get used to it."

Fish paused and looked around, waiting for objections. He got none. Satisfied, he moved on to the next part of the meeting.

"I have learned through our usual channels of a PCP factory doing a good business near Prineville. Dot, you are to knock that factory out. Leave no one alive."

"It's as good as done," she said. "Do you have the exact location?"

"The map is in my briefcase," Fish replied. "Look it over well. The Sheriff is watching the place, and so are the Feds. Cain, you are to handle a truck that is scheduled to arrive in Klamath Falls tomorrow at 2 pm. It's a van supposedly loaded with furniture. The cops know it's coming and will be waiting. Knock it out before it gets to town."

Cain, silent as usual, nodded his head. Luke and Abel received their assignments next. The meeting then settled down into a generalized discussion. Some ideas were exchanged. A new system of communication was considered. Fish said he would take their thoughts to the Board.

"I have some information on a drug delivery that's to take place in Medford in a couple of weeks," Abel said. "I'd like to send Johnny Redwine on this one. He needs a solo job, and this Medford thing should be a one man operation. If it turns out to require more than one I'll go along."

"Alright with me," Fish said. "You set it up and act as controller on it."

"Be careful with him," Dot said. "He's my pet project you know."

Abel gave her a mischievous grin. "Pet project, eh?"

"Don't you start," Dot replied.

The meeting ended and Fish saw them out. He watched them go to their cars on the TV. When they were gone he started the stereo again, and sat down to do some serious planning.

Chapter 38

October 1st dawned a cold, windy day. It was not Dot Stoneking's type of weather. She preferred sunny and warm. Parking her car on a side street, she walked the two blocks to a clothing store that had a reputation for being one of the finest and most expensive women's stores in Bend. No one would have ever guessed that this beautiful, stylish young woman was a dedicated member of the Cleanup Committee.

Dot entered the store and walked to a rack of dresses near the middle. Several women were in the establishment, but they were too busy to notice the new arrival. Dot feigned interest in a dress, but she was here to contact Paula Davies.

Dot moved around to the other side of the rack. From this point she was better able to observe. Three sales girls were helping customers, but she did not see Paula. She wandered toward the back of the store and found Paula among the stoles. She was doing her best to sell a $5,000 mink to a pudgy older woman who probably had a few just like it.

Paula spotted Dot, smiled at her pain of a customer, and said "Excuse me Mrs. Nolan, I'll be right back. I need to assist with an order pickup."

"Well," said the rotund woman, "I don't know if I like being put on hold when someone else could probably service this woman's account."

The smile Paula had been sporting disappeared. It was obvious to Dot that Mrs. Noland had gone a step too far.

Paula reached out and grabbed the expensive stole away from the startled Mrs. Noland. She tossed it in the general direction of the rack. "You spoiled old pig, I've put up with your shit long enough. You've been coming in here for months wasting everyone's time. You bitch about the service, you degrade the staff, and you complain about the quality. Well, Mrs. Noland, you may kiss my ass. Right smack in the-"

That's as far as Paula got before Mrs. Noland went into a dramatic fit. Her face went red, her tongue stuck out, and her knees gave way. She went to the floor and landed with a splat. From there she started yelling.

"You filthy little black bitch!" she squeaked. "How dare you speak to me that way! I'll have your job. I'll own this store!"

"Let's go!" said Dot. She took Paula by the arm and they went toward the front door.

By now all eyes were turned toward the noise that was being made. Two people had started walking toward the commotion. They didn't notice the girls leaving. Stopping just outside, Dot turned to Paula.

"Your sense of timing leaves a lot to be desired, Miss Davies. It's a good thing for all of us that the Committee owns this store. Otherwise your behavior might have to be explained."

Paula's fire had not died down. She looked back toward the door. "Just let me go back and finish her off. I'll ram the barrel of an Uzi up her fat ass and pull the trigger."

"That won't be necessary," Dot said. "We have far better uses for the ammo. Besides, you won't be going back to that store again. We'll get you a different job. Forget her and forget this store. We have work to do."

The two women walked back toward Dot's car. Paula was still amped up but was working to keep it in check. Dot knew how well Paula liked action. The assignment on the truck ambush had shown that.

"Where is your car, Paula?" Dot asked.

"In the store parking lot."

"Pick it up and meet me at your house in 20 minutes."

"I left my coat and purse in the store."

"Never mind that," Dot said. "They'll be picked up for you and returned to your place. Linda will be at your place too."

"Man! This must be a big job if three of us are on it!"

They stopped for a light at the intersection, and thankfully no one else was on the street to hear Paula's exclamation. Dot gave her a look. The light turned green and they parted ways. Dot found a payphone and called Paula's house, where Linda Smith was waiting.

"On your way?" Linda asked.

"Be there in a few. So will Paula. Everything set?"

"Set and ready to roll. We leave any time you want."

Dot left the booth and got on the road. It had been a last minute choice to bring Linda along. She knew Linda was a good soldier, she just hated leaving Team 3's area uncovered, especially with Abel sending Johnny to Medford. However, Abel had covered that base. He sent Amanda to open a temporary safe house just in case. Linda was here because the unfortunate death of Kathy Price left a gap that needed to be filled.

Dot braked at a crosswalk to let a woman with two young children cross. As she looked at the kids, she had a momentary urge to trade places with the mother. Maybe, she thought, just maybe it would be nice to be bothered with kids and a husband. Maybe it would be nice to sit down and have coffee with friends and just gossip. Yet as she headed for her meeting with Linda and Paula, Dot was fully aware she may never have those simple yet complicated experiences. There was a job to do. The job could be fatal, but she was dedicated to it. As she turned toward Paula's, Dot told herself that her actions today would make the world better for that mother and thousands more like her.

Linda had driven up from Grants Pass last night, arriving in time to catch 4 hours sleep. Dot had driven in from Portland. While they waited for Paula the two looked over equipment. Once satisfied that everything was in order, Dot poured a cup of coffee, sat down and put her feet up.

"You're certainly looking good, Linda."

"Thanks. I feel good too. I'm mostly sleeping well, eating well, and enjoying life."

"Good. I'll brief you as soon Paula arrives," Dot said.

"Meanwhile, I have a story." She told Linda about meeting Paula at the store and the ruckus that followed. Linda laughed long and hard. When Paula arrived a few minutes later, the women spent some time chatting.

Dot allowed the light hearted banter to go on for a few minutes. Then she said, "Sorry to be a wet blanket, girls, but there are plans to be made. We're ahead of schedule. I was going to leave word for you to join us later, Paula, but it seemed prudent for you to leave when I arrived."

She paused while everyone had a short laugh.

"We're here for the purpose of taking down a PCP factory over by Prineville," Dot continued. "Do both of you know what PCP is?"

Paula said,"Deadliest damned drug the pushers have come up with yet."

"Yes. Its effect on people can be highly unpredictable. Several cases of violent behavior have been documented as a direct result of using the stuff. So, before they can do any more damage we're going to knock them out."

Dot spent the next hour going over the plan step by step. They had drawings and plans given to Dot by Doctor Fish.

"It's going to be hard to get there without being spotted," Linda said.

"We're lucky in one respect," Dot replied. "This is the opening day of deer season. 3 women with rifles aren't going to attract any real notice. If luck is with us, we should be able to get right up close to the place."

Linda ran her finger along a line on the map. She was tracing highway 26 from Prineville east to a small town called Mitchell.

"Let me make sure I have it," she said. "We drive east 12.6 miles on US 26, turn left on a dirt road, and drive one mile to where we leave the car. We then circle around and approach the house from the west. We'll look like 3 lost female hunters and play it by ear when we make contact."

"You got it," Dot said. "We don't know who is in that place. Fish says the Crook County Sheriff has the place infiltrated with an undercover cop. We don't know for sure, but the Feds may have pulled out when they learned about it. Nobody can confirm that."

"What surveillance methods were the Feds using?" Paula asked.

"Long range stuff with telescopic cameras."

"What a waste of taxpayers' money!" Paula exclaimed.

"You're forgetting," said Linda, "they have to be careful not to violate constitutional rights against these people, even if they're scum."

Paula demanded, "Since when does anyone have a right to commit such crimes against innocent people? The poor bastards who get hooked have rights. The people they rob and murder to get their fix have rights too."

Dot smiled at Paula, and put a hand on her shoulder.

"That's where we come in."

They started gathering up the papers and ripping them into little bits. Then, dressed in suitable hunting clothes, they carried out the gear they would need for an overnight camping trip. The Uzi machine guns were hidden inside bedrolls. Each of them carried their loaded Brownings in their coats. They each carried a 30.06 rifle with variable scopes that one would expect to see hunters carry. They made the fateful trip in Linda's car.

Chapter 39

Oregon State Game Officer Jack Keever had been having one long day. He'd been knocking around in the hills checking the licenses and tags of the hunters that were everywhere. At this time every year he wondered how they kept from shooting more of each other than the wildlife. To his ears, it sounded like one of the numerous battles he had seen during his stretch with the Army in Vietnam. The hunters had opened up the moment they legally could, and kept at it all day long.

Now it was approaching 4 pm. The wind had picked up and gotten colder. Keever knew from experience the weather was going to get nasty. He stopped his pickup at a crossroad and turned up his radio receiver. He'd been out of contact most of the day in the tall hills. This was one place he knew where he could reach the Prineville base.

Jack checked in, and was advised to clear the area and head out. Breathing a sigh of relief, he put down the mic and started toward town.

Below and on his left was an old ranch. At one time it had been a highly productive cattle ranch, but in recent years it had gone to ruin. From time to time gangs of hippies crashed there for a day, or even a week. It was from that old ranch that he heard the sound of gunfire. He'd been hearing gunfire all day so it took a minute for what else he was hearing to sink in on him. These were machine guns being fired in rapid staccato bursts. They echoed off the hills and rattled around in the canyons.

Jack sped down the dirt road. He picked up his microphone and said, "I have what sounds like machine gun fire coming from the old Steward ranch. It sounds like 3 or 4 going at once. Will check and advise."

He concentrated on keeping his rig out of the deepest ruts in the dirt road. He was so focused it took him a moment to realize his station commander, Lieutenant Todd Bishop was speaking.

"Do not, I repeat, DO NOT approach that property by yourself Keever. Take up a station at the nearest crossroads and wait. Keep this office advised of what you hear. Do not, I repeat, do not attempt to stop anyone seen leaving the area. This may be a Cleanup Committee operation."

Good God, thought Keever, that bunch again. He answered his radio message with a simple "Understood." At the nearest crossroads he listened to a battle rage. It was ten minutes until the firing stopped. Two minutes later, the first of his backup units arrived.

The officers approached the property carefully, from various angles and with weapons drawn. A command was issued for anyone inside to come out with their hands up. There was no response. The team continued toward the house and slowly made entry. Jack Keever couldn't remember the last time he saw so much blood.

Paula was numb all over. Sounds kept coming to her but she couldn't identify them. One sound did get through; it was someone moaning loudly. She wanted to tell whoever it was to shut up. With a shock, she realized the sound was coming out of her. She made an effort to stop and apparently it worked. At one point she heard the sound of someone else crying.

The next sound Paula heard was the voice of a man. She opened her eyes slightly and saw a bright star. Then, she realized it wasn't a star- it was a flashlight.

It belonged to the cop that was leaning over her. "This one's shot up real bad, Dave, but with luck she'll make it." Then everything went black.

Chapter 40

By 10 pm on the night of October 1st, the day's death totals were still incomplete. One police dispatcher in a busy station tore off a teletype message, looked at it, and filed it with the others.

She said to an officer nearby, "I haven't seen figures like this since my days as a military grave counter in Vietnam."

"It does look like a war," he said, and went back to his magazine.

In one bold stroke, the Cleanup Committee had inflicted heavy damage on their enemy. In Caldwell, Idaho, they had blown up a house. A known narcotics dealer and two of his people were killed. The job was so well done that the houses to either side were not damaged beyond minor dings in the plaster or a cracked window. Not long after the house explosion in Caldwell, two other known dealers were gunned down as they left their car near a downtown Boise office building.

When it came to Oregon, the Cleanup Committee committed a statewide massacre. In Medford, 3 people were found shot to death in a motel room. A large amount of narcotics were found under one of the beds. The police were hardly finished with that shooting when they were called to the fashionable home of a well known family. The man's wife and children had come home from an evening out to find that he had been shot dead in the living room. His business partner was gunned down at their office. Medford police finished the evening with 5 dead and no suspects.

Lake County Sheriff Bill Whitmeyer found an airplane at a remote airstrip east of Lakeview. It contained 3 bodies and a thousand pounds of marijuana. The plane and its occupants had been riddled with bullets.

In Salem, two men broke into a house on the northeast side and shot it out with the two men and one woman inside. They killed the people in the house but were surprised by two Salem police officers on the way out. In this case, the Committee had pushed its luck too far. Thinking they could hold a gun battle in a residential area was the worst plan of the day. The suspects tried to run but were shot dead by police 3 blocks from the scene. One of the dead men was identified by some papers found on his body as Roy Errickson. It would be two days before they identified Wesley Keeler.

There were also raids in Ontario, Baker, Portland, Burns, and numerous other small towns. No one in Oregon law enforcement had ever seen anything like it.

Chief Richard Brownwell remained in his office in Salem, hardly even taking time to eat. Like everyone else, he was keeping track of the day's happenings. Unlike everyone else, he had something to put on his sheet besides numbers. He had names. Wonderful, traceable names. Unfortunately, they were all dead.

There was one survivor, a woman whose name he did not know. She was brought to the Prineville hospital in critical condition. Brownwell prayed that she would live and would give a statement.

Officers in Portland had responded to reports of shots fired. It was an estate in an exclusive neighborhood on the east side. After failing to get an answer at the door, they obtained their Captain's approval and kicked the door in.

Jonathan Bernard Stoneking was found dead on his living room floor with a gunshot wound to the head. His wife Beth was found on the sofa, dead of a self inflicted gunshot. No notes were found, and neighbors could give no clue about the reason for the murder-suicide. All attempts to find and notify their daughter Dot Stoneking failed.

Chapter 41

Johnny reached home that night at 10:45. His trip to Medford had been a smashing success. He had found all 5 of his targets and taken care of business. He even brought back a briefcase full of money that he'd taken off the rich guy at the office.

His first stop had been the motel. Abel had researched this one very well. They let him into the room after he gave a password. After being admitted, he had produced the Browning, already equipped with a silencer.

He forced the two men and one woman to sit on one of the double beds. They were here to make a big delivery. Johnny just didn't know if it was here or if they stashed it somewhere else. Johnny questioned them repeatedly. They tried to play coy.

The one named Mike decided to get bold. "You think you're pretty tough stuff, don't you? Suppose you put that gun down and you and me duke it out. I'll bet I can kick your ass."

Johnny felt something snap in himself. The barrel leveled on Mike's chest.

"See you in hell," he said, and fired.

Mike's eyes had gone wide with surprise. Just as quickly, they had closed as the life went out of him.

Johnny's aim was a little high. The bullet had struck the man in the throat. Blood sprayed the air as he was knocked backwards.

The girl, who looked about Johnny's age, started to scream.

He barked "Don't!" and pointed the gun in her direction. She slapped a hand over her mouth, tears flowing down her face.

"You're a murdering pig!" the other guy murmured.

"Ok you two, now where is it?" Johnny asked.

"It's under the other bed," said the girl. "Take it and go!"

"Is she telling the truth?" Johnny asked the remaining man.

"Yes, yes! Just take it and get lost!"

The remaining man shortly realized they were not going to make it out alive. He tried going for a gun he had stashed under the pillow of the other bed. The Browning spoke twice. The first shot caught the man in the left side of his head, right above the ear. It would have been enough, but the second shot went into his chest, just to be sure.

Johnny swung the barrel on the girl, only to find she had leapt off the bed with the idea of finding safety in the bathroom. She died quickly with one bullet through the head. Johnny left his card and departed.

Half an hour later, the trio's intended buyer and his partner were dead. Johnny went home with 5 more notches in his gun.

Upon returning to Eugene, Johnny had dumped the Committee car in a pre-arranged spot, and driven home in his Mustang. He had been in the house about 20 minutes when the phone rang. He was surprised to hear Abel's voice when he picked up.

"Get out of there, kid. Go to the first place you were ever taken. Do you remember how to find it?"
"You mean the place over by the river?"

"That's the one."

"Yeah, I can find it. What's wrong?"

"Go there and wait," Abel said. "Do not leave until you are contacted."

The phone went dead. Johnny stood looking at the receiver in his hand for a moment before grabbing his go bag. It had extra clothes and some ammo. As he tossed the bag into the backseat, he wondered if he would ever see this place again. Discovering he didn't really care, he drove away without a backward glance. If he had taken a look back, he might have found his departure was being watched. Perhaps not, though, as the watcher was being careful about it.

Johnny couldn't help but wonder what had gone wrong as he drove toward Springfield. Thinking back, he was positive he had covered all of his steps as instructed. He turned on the radio, hoping to hear some news that would give him a clue about the panic.

All the radio news had given him was the information that several Cleanup Committee operations had taken place that day in both Oregon and Idaho. The cops were refusing to comment on a report that two gunmen had been killed in a shootout with Salem police.

Turning onto the street where the warehouse was located, he checked carefully for anything unusual. He then turned into the driveway and the garage door slid up for him. He waited until the door had closed before getting out and walking toward the door at the rear of the building.

The door opened when he was 10 feet from it. Abel stood there, holding an Uzi at his side. Johnny stopped and looked at him.

"What the hell, Abel?"

"Sorry, kid. Come on in. I've got news for you."

Chapter 42

Lieutenant Todd Bishop put down the phone in the Prineville Hospital lobby. He turned to a tall man standing nearby. He appeared to be in his late 40's and was dressed in an expensive suit, topped with a lab coat.

"Chief Brownwell will be here in the morning, Doctor. He really wants to see you keep the girl alive."

Doctor Fish tapped the counter where he was standing with his pen and frowned. "Your Chief should be talking to God," he said. "We're doing everything we can here."

Bishop leaned tiredly against the counter. He was exhausted. It was 11:57 p.m. and he had been at it all day. His last meal had been at noon.

"I understand, but I had to give you the message."

The doctor made a note on a chart, signed it, and closed it. He said, "I've left orders to be called if there's any change. The nurse will be with her at all times. Of course we want her to live. I hope your people don't expect us to keep up the special treatment for long, though. We're understaffed as it is."

"We appreciate all your help," Bishop replied.

"Wait until your bosses in Salem get my bill," Fish said, grinning. "Then we'll see how much they appreciate it."

Bishop left the hospital and headed back to his office.

Chapter 43

At 9 a.m. on October 2nd, Chief Brownwell left Salem by car with 4 hours of sleep and no breakfast. By pushing his luck a little, he arrived in Prineville at 2:15. He drove straight to the nearby OSP office. He was greeted by Lieutenant Todd Bishop, who looked like death warmed over. The two men shook hands and retreated to Bishop's small office.

"You look like hell Todd," said the Chief.

"You wouldn't win any contests yourself," Bishop replied.

Brownwell was glad as he faced his Field Commander that it was Bishop handling this end of it. He was a great investigator and just as great a leader.

"Give me what you have."

"It's not much, Chief. We have no identification on the girl in the hospital. Of the 6 dead, we've identified 4. We know them to be the people that were in the house. That house was a PCP factory. It's been under investigation for a while. The sheriff's office had the place infiltrated with an undercover man. Fortunately, he wasn't present at the shooting. He helped us get ID on the others."

Brownwell asked, "How many other people were aware of this investigation?"

"Damn few," Bishop replied. "it's a mystery to me how the attackers would know of it."

"They have a way of finding things out. I'm beginning to think they have someone in State Government helping them."

"You're putting me on!" Bishop exclaimed. "Really? Who could it be?"

"I don't know," Brownwell said. "It's just a theory right now. Have you been able to figure out how things happened up there yet?"

"The attackers were all women, which in itself is something."

"Were any of them black?"

Bishop gave his boss a questioning look.

"Lucky guess. I'll fill you in later. Please continue."

"It appears they approached the house from the west. It was a darn strange direction to approach from if the attack was planned. It's slightly uphill, which makes for bad firing and limited cover.

Our guess is the first girl died instantly. None of her weapons were fired. She died of multiple wounds from an Ingram model 10 machine gun we found in the house. The second gal was apparently hit in the opening blast but didn't die there. She made it to the front door. We found her body on the porch. She had an Uzi with her which still had a few rounds in the clip. An empty 30.06 rifle was found at the bottom of the front step.

All these gals had rifles and bedrolls. I think they were trying to pass as hunters to get into the house. If they'd been successful and gotten in with those Uzi's it would have been all over."

Bishop paused to pour some coffee, then continued. "The one in the hospital was found by a side window. It looks like she tried going in that way. The ground around her was covered in empty brass. She and the gal on the porch poured a lot of ammo in. The gal in the hospital also chucked a couple of grenades through the window. That finished off anyone still kicking in the house. If our survivor makes it, I'd be interested to hear her story."

There was a knock on the door. A uniformed officer came in. He was holding a yellow teletype sheet.

"Got your two gals identified, L.T."

Both Brownwell and Bishop were on their feet at once. Both men reached for the teletype, but Bishop was behind the desk. Brownwell grabbed the paper like a hungry dog might grab a hunk of meat. The grinning officer waited, now forgotten by his bosses.

"Dorothy Marie Stoneking and Linda Joan Smith."

Bishop whistled. "Stoneking! Oh man...."

Down the road, Doctor Fish stood by a hospital bed. He stepped back, looked at the nurse, and said: "I'll be surprised if she lives through the night."

"She keeps calling for Johnny," the nurse said.

"Probably a boyfriend."

Fish took off his hospital gloves and dropped them into a garbage can along with a bloody bandage.

"I'll check back in a couple of hours," he said, and started toward the door. He was halted by the sound of Paula's voice.

"Johnny," she said. "Johnny. Linda. Oh Linda, Dot is dead."

Doctor Fish left the room. The nurse, a girl not much older than the patient, began to pray.

Chapter 44

Amanda Dial had arrived at the Eugene safehouse around 4 the morning of October 2nd. Luke then drifted in, and others showed up at random. They milled around, or slept, or watched TV while Abel, who seemed to be running the show, busied himself on the phone in one of the bedrooms. They were all aware that something was dreadfully wrong, but none of them knew the full scope of what had happened. Chatter was kept at a low tone. It was late afternoon when the Cleanup Committee members became fully aware of all that had happened

Around 1:30 pm, Johnny was stretched out on the living room floor. He had one eye on the security monitor and the other one shut. Amanda sat down beside him.

"Good morning," she said.

He rolled to the side in order to see her better. Amanda was looking good. Her blonde hair was brushed back. She wore blue slacks with a matching pullover. Except for the dark circles under her eyes, she looked fresh.

"I trust you slept well," Johnny said.

"Not worth a damn, actually. I'm too worked up."

"We all are. There's some coffee in the kitchen if you want it."

"I need some," Amanda said. "How about you?"

"Sounds good. I'll help you."

They stepped over some people who were still sleeping on the rug and went into the kitchen. Luke and some others had a card game going at the table. They greeted them, got their coffee and went back to the living room. They found seats on the floor.

Amanda looked at Johnny. "What happened?"

"I don't know," he said. "From what they've said on the TV, we've taken some losses. I don't know who. The cops are being quiet about what they have. I've been worried about Paula. I asked Abel where she was, and he wouldn't say. As soon as they let us out of here I'm going to go find her."

Amanda's pretty blue eyes were cloudy.

"You like Paula a lot."

Johnny could tell by her voice she wasn't asking just to be asking. "What do you know about her?"

"Nothing, really, only that she's with Dot and Linda. I don't know what area they were in."

"I sure hope she's alright."

Amanda fell silent. She was looking down into her coffee cup. Johnny leaned on one elbow, sipping at his coffee, waiting for Amanda to speak. After a minute she looked up.

"This isn't so much fun anymore."

Johnny was taken by surprise.

"Well," Amanda continued, "when all this killing was strictly talk and practice, it wasn't so bad. Now that people are actually dying, I'm not so sure."

"I get it. Remember what they told us, though, Amanda. We're in a war. People are bound to get hurt."

"I guess I thought none of *us* would get hurt. It wasn't so bad when it was just the criminals."

"We've lost someone for sure," Johnny said. "Why else would they have us here?"

"Company coming!" a voice nearby said.

All eyes turned to the security monitor.

"Looks like Doctor Fish," Amanda said. "I'll tell Abel." She got up and went down the hall.

Johnny saw Doctor Fish sitting in his car in front of the big doors. He was just sitting there, patiently puffing on his pipe. Abel came out, looked at the screen and said, "Someone let the man in."

A button was pushed and the big door went up. They all waited quietly and watched. Abel opened the safehouse door by pushing a button on the wall. Fish walked in. He didn't look well at all.

"Welcome," Abel said.

Everyone else mumbled a greeting. Fish nodded his head in recognition of the welcome, walked to a chair and sat down. It was obvious that he had bad news. No one said anything. They all just sat, or stood, and waited.

"I'm sorry," Fish said, "but I have to tell you some things none of you want to hear. When I'm finished I'll have instructions for you. The other members are already informed."

He paused for a breath. "Dot and Linda are dead."

Johnny heard Amanda gasp. People muttered "Oh God no!" or "No way!"

Fish went on. "Paula was on the same operation with them. She is badly hurt and is currently in the Prineville hospital under heavy guard. The best I could find out is that she's in critical condition, and may or may not live."

Johnny felt numb. All he could think about was Paula. He felt his chest tighten.

"Roy and Wesley are dead as well. They did their job but then tried to shoot it out with the Salem police. I thought we taught the poor bastards better than that."

Fish paused and looked around. "As if these losses weren't enough, we have suffered an even bigger loss. The man who has been largely financing and helping direct our operations is dead. I can't explain to you how badly his loss is going to hurt, but it's enough that we'll have to suspend our operations for a while.

None of you are familiar with the upper workings of this organization, but you all know that your recruitment into this force was no accident. It took months of planning and millions of dollars to get this far. This is not over.

The Committee's goal has not been achieved. Until it is, we will continue to fight. For the time being, you are to remain here. Over the next couple of nights you may be able to leave here and return to your homes. Continue to check in with your controller daily. Any changes that are made will reach you through that medium.

Now I'll take questions. No promise I can answer them, but I'll do my best."

No one spoke. They all just looked at each other.

Finally Johnny asked, "What were Dot, Linda and Paula doing?"

"I sent them to take down a PCP factory. They succeeded, but all of us have paid a high price. I don't know what went wrong. Dot, Paula and Linda were all good at their work. I sent them, so I claim responsibility."

Amanda asked, "What's going to happen to Paula?"

"Well," Fish said, "if she lives they'll charge her with murder and put her on trial. They'll try to make an example of her."

"What does that mean?" Johnny asked, an edge in his voice.

"They'll try making a deal with her at first. If that doesn't work they will put her on trial publicly and go for the death sentence."

"They'll pay hell!" Johnny exclaimed. "I'll find a way to bust her out."

Fish gave him a long, stern look. "You will leave Paula to us. We will see that she is taken care of properly."

"Alright, but if I can help please tell me how."

Fish took a few more questions, then left the room with Abel. They spent around 20 minutes out of earshot of the troops. When Fish came out, he walked to the door and then turned to look at those still in the room.

"Abel has your orders," he said. "He will advise when you are to go and where."

Chapter 45

The Prineville hospital wasn't very big. It reminded Abel of the little hospital in his hometown in Mississippi. It had been a hospital for whites. His people hadn't been allowed beyond its front doors. If these people knew what he knew, they wouldn't allow him in this one either. Since they knew nothing, he walked in with no problem.

At 3:45 a.m. on the morning of October 3rd, the hospital was quiet. A gray haired woman was sitting on a stool at the reception desk with a headset on, looking like she'd rather be somewhere else.

As he approached, Abel heard her say: "Just a minute, I got a customer." She turned for the first time and took a good look. He was a tall, well dressed, handsome black man.

"May I help you?"

"Yes. I'm here to inquire after my daughter."

"What is your daughter's name?"

The woman felt stupid asking the question. They had only one black patient in the entire hospital. No one knew her name, though, so by asking she would be the first to learn it.

Abel said in a gentle voice, "Her name is Andrea Jackson."

The woman quickly wrote the name down. "I'm sorry, Mr. Jackson, but your daughter is in police custody. I can't permit you to see her without their permission."

"I am aware of that," he said. "I just want to know how she is."

"I can let you speak to her nurse. Maybe she could tell you more than I can."

"Then please show me to the nurse," he said.

"Oh, I'm afraid I can't do that either, sir. You see, your daughter has a special nurse. She can't leave until her relief comes in at 7 a.m."

"Perhaps I could just talk to her from the door a little. Please," he said, "I've driven so far. I'm extremely tired. I just want to see my baby girl for a few minutes and then I'll get some sleep. I won't cause any trouble, ma'am."

The woman looked uncertain. "Well, I don't know. She's pretty important to the police. They say she was part of this Cleanup Committee."

"I know. They told me all about it when they called."

"The police called you? I didn't think they even knew who she was."

Abel shifted his weight, and leaned against the counter. "You know how the police are, ma'am. They always know things they don't tell the rest of us."

"That is so true, Mr. Jackson. Well, I'm sure that there wouldn't be any problem. She's in room 116, just down the hall to your right. I'll buzz the nurse and tell her you'll be dropping in."

"Oh don't bother her," Mr. Jackson said. "I won't be but a minute, and I'll knock softly so as not to scare her."

His hand came out of his pocket before the receptionist could do anything. He squeezed the bottle in his hand, and a thin spray of gas hit the woman in the face. She went out like a light. He quickly caught the front of her dress and let her slip gently to the floor. He then jammed the hospital switchboard so that the one line on hold remained, but no other calls could go out or come in.

Paula was being very restless. In spite of the Doctor's prediction, she was alive. To the surprise of the nurse she was even slightly improved. Her blood pressure was coming up, and she was breathing easier, but was still a very long way from being out of the woods.

The nurse was writing down Paula's vital signs when she felt a slight change in the room. It occurred to her to turn and see if someone had come in, but that was as far as her thinking got. A large hand shot up to cover her mouth, while the other brought a small can of gas around. One gentle squeeze on the bottle and the nurse was out.

Slowly, Abel lowered her to the floor. She would only be out for half an hour, just like the receptionist out front. This gas, a product he had stolen in North Vietnam, would not harm a person unless they had a heart condition. They would come around with a slight headache that quickly dissipated. To his knowledge, he had the only supply of the stuff in the free world.

Standing by the bed, he looked down at Paula. This job did not appeal to him. This girl had done him no wrong. She was young and could do the organization no real harm. Yet the order had been given, and orders were orders.

To his right, a door opened. He turned swiftly to confront this surprise.

There was a dim light on in the corner. The bright light of the bathroom glared brightly. Officer Jack Keever stepped out, and was shocked to find a visitor in the room. He saw the big black man, then the body of the nurse on the floor. He then observed the man drop whatever was in his hand, and reach for the inside of his jacket.

Officer Keever gave his reactions no thought. He drew his service revolver and fired. The roar of the .38 special filled the room and the hallway. Somewhere, someone screamed. The 158 grain bullet struck the man in the heart, knocking him backward against the bedside table. The room was now filled with the sound of glass shattering and a table tipping over. The IV pole swayed dangerously.

Keever stood, gun still in hand, looking at the disaster in front of him. Then he holstered the .38 and made for the door. He burst into the hall to find two nurses, their faces as white as their uniforms. One of the nurses was speaking, or at least her lips were moving. Keever realized his hearing was not working so well.

"Get in there and see about the patient," he said. "I just had to shoot a man. Don't worry about him, he's dead."

To his surprise, both of the nurses reacted immediately. They pushed right past him into the room. He walked toward the lobby. Keever found the receptionist out cold. It took him a moment to make sure she was not dead. It took another 20 seconds to realize the switchboard was out.

While he was on his way back to room 116 to get his portable radio that he realized there was a problem. Not being able to hear if the frequency was busy or not would make it hard to know when to talk. He came to room 116 and saw the nurses were busy. He thanked God they didn't panic. Finding the portable radio, he asked the nurses to confirm the channel wasn't busy. Then he went into the hall and started transmitting.

The dispatcher on duty at the Prineville OSP office was taken slightly off guard when his radio started chattering. At first, what he was hearing didn't make sense. Then, it sank in that he was hearing Keever, the hospital guard. He must have been using a portable transceiver.

"An unauthorized person came into the hospital. The phone system is knocked out. He was trying to harm the prisoner and reached for a weapon. I had to shoot him. Get Chief Brownwell and the LT here right away. Don't try to reply, I can't hear at the moment."

It was 4 a.m. when Keever made his radio call. It was 4:05 a.m. when the first officer showed up. By 4:15, Keever's hearing was starting to come back. At 4:17, Brownwell and Lieutenant Bishop arrived.

Brownwell pulled into the hospital parking lot behind a car with two doctors inside. They left the car and headed for the Emergency door on a run. Brownwell followed them, silently thanking whoever had called them.

The door opened when one of the doctors pushed a button on the wall. The three men entered a hallway that appeared deserted. Then two State policemen stepped from a doorway, guns drawn and ready. The two doctors stopped so fast Brownwell almost bumped into them.

"Put those guns away!" he ordered. "These men are doctors."

One of the officers said, "And just who might you be?"

Brownwell looked down at his green slacks, mismatched pullover, and brown shoes. As the doctors hurried away, he said "I guess I wasn't too careful about what I was grabbing in the dark."

One of the men stepped forward, looked closer at Brownwell, then holstered his gun. "Sorry Chief, I just plain didn't recognize you."

"At least you men are alert. That's more than I can say for myself. Now, where's Keever, and what exactly happened here?"

The second officer answered. "He's in an examining room with some coffee. I put him there and told him to stay until you or the Lieutenant arrived."

"I understand Keever isn't hearing so well."

"That's right," the second officer said, "but it should get better. I saw a few cases of it in the Army. Guns make a lot of racket. Most people just don't realize how loud it can be setting one of these things off in close quarters."

The first officer said, "Enough of that, Bill. You can give the Chief a firearms lecture some other time."

Brownwell grinned. "Bill, we can get coffee when this is over and talk about guns. Now, one of you will show me to the room. The other can get out to the lobby and intercept the Press. Bad news travels mighty fast. Withhold any comment. I'll speak to them when I'm ready."

The first officer took the Chief to room 116. It was a mess. As they arrived, two other officers were loading a nurse onto a stretcher. A doctor was in the room and seemed to have the situation well in hand. Brownwell stepped aside for the stretcher and saw that the nurse was a bloody mess. He couldn't tell if it was the suspect's blood or her own. Two orderlies were waiting in the hall to take the stretcher from the officers.

Brownwell stepped into the room and looked at his prisoner, then the dead suspect.

"How is the prisoner?" he asked.

The doctor replied, "Thanks to the quick actions of a couple or nurses, she's fine. Her oxygen supply was cut off briefly but they got it restored fast. I'm sure she knows nothing of what occurred."

"Do you have a room with no windows here?"

"Only one," the doctor replied.

"Transfer her to that one, please."

By 6:30 a.m. the patient had been moved. Officers had gotten into the room with cameras to photograph the dead man, make diagrams, and gather evidence. They were especially careful because one of their own had fired the shot. Keever was kept away from everyone but Brownwell and the Lieutenant. The Chief waited in the hall for his men to complete the scientific part of the investigation. He told the first man out of the room to report what they had found.

The officer said, "First he knocked out the receptionist and nurse with some kind of gas.We'll send this off right away for analysis. Whatever it is, it's not fatal." A plastic bag with a small bottle was in the officer's hand.

The officer held up another plastic bag. "This is a Star .25 automatic. Note the neat little silencer it has. This indicates the suspect was not on a social call."

"A logical conclusion," Brownwell said. "Has anyone gotten prints from the dead man?"

"That's happening now. When they're done, the Medical Examiner can have him."

Chapter 46

Doctor Fish woke to his alarm at 5:30 that morning. He had only gotten a few hours of sleep, but he woke instantly. Panic almost got him as he realized the phone call he had been expecting had not come through. Late last night he had a final word with Abel. His instructions were specific.

As Fish quickly dressed, he told himself he was just jumpy. The feeling of doom that crept into his mind was just nerves, he thought. The organization had taken serious setbacks, but not enough to shut down completely. He shaved while his coffee brewed. At the same time, he mentally reviewed the recent events.

First had come the damnable letter that sneaky rancher had written before he died. He kicked himself now for not having Cain take out his old lady too. That had seemed unnecessary at the time, but it was too late now. Brownwell had the letter, and with it knowledge of the base camp. Had he not had that information, Paula's death would not be necessary. They could probably use the knowledge they had to make her talk. Even though she didn't know a lot, her information and descriptions, coupled with what they already had, would be dangerous to the organization. He came to the regrettable decision to have Abel liquidate her.

They had gotten a bad break losing Boxer, but Fish thought they made up for it by finding Luke. Killing was a science to Luke, and he was dedicated. If he had one problem, it was his penchant for throwing in the unexpected.

Fish went into the kitchen and made himself some ham and eggs. He was a firm believer in eating a good breakfast. He thought about the meeting coming up this morning. It was a meeting he did not want to be part of, but it was totally necessary.

He would drive to Portland and meet with the money men. They made up the rest of the Committee. Stoneking had been the man to take care of keeping the money flowing and the others together. Jonah's death, and Dot's, had now made it necessary for Fish to take on that role. He was not well suited for it. He'd never dealt with money men, even during his campaign for Attorney General.

Fish had worked out a new plan for the organization to make it run smoothly again. Specifically for these men, who were businessmen and not soldiers, he had violated his one rule that had never before been broken: he wrote the plan down. He shivered at the thought of it getting into the wrong hands.

The only copy of his reorganization plan was in the safe, which also held several hundred thousand dollars in cash. The money was for various Committee needs. The written plan would be used to sell the idea to men who were scared stiff. After he let each one of them read it, he would burn the paper himself.

Fish brought the paper out of the safe and into his briefcase, which also locked. He made one final security check of the house, and one final pause by the phone. When it still didn't ring he went into the garage and got into his gray 1977 VW Bug. He backed out into a rainy morning and cursed the weather.

By the time he was on the freeway headed north a thick fog had set in. Visibility was cut to 20 feet, sometimes less. In spite of the bad visibility, Fish pushed the little car to go quickly. He was anxious to cover the drive from Eugene to Portland and sell his plan.

Up the road, a car had stopped because the big truck in front of it had stopped. The driver knew that her headlights weren't working. Her husband had told her so, and insisted she get them fixed. However, she had overslept and was going to be late as it was. She was thinking of how mad the boss would get for being late, wishing the big truck would move.

Tom Blakely, aka Doctor Fish, slammed into the back of the stopped car at 65 mph. The driver was slammed forward against the steering wheel. It broke, allowing the steering post to bore through her. Fish died instantly. The woman died before the first emergency vehicle arrived.

The governor was informed of Attorney General Tom Blakely's death via telephone. The call arrived from the Captain of the Eugene OSP office.

"I tried getting hold of Chief Brownwell to inform him," the Captain said, "but he has his hands full in Prineville and will be unavailable for a while."

"What's Rick gotten himself into now?"

The Captain gave the governor what information he had from the teletype system.

"Good Lord!" the governor exclaimed. "Will the killing ever stop?"

The Captain replied in a soft voice, "Maybe, somehow. I certainly hope so. Also, we recovered a locked briefcase from Blakely's car. It may contain state records. I've had it impounded, and it will be delivered to your office later this morning."

"Thank you Captain. I appreciate that. Do you know if Blakely had any relatives?"

"We've located a woman we believe to be his sister. She lives in Utah. We're sending notification at this time. For your information, sir, the Attorney General's body is at the Harper and Sons funeral home in Eugene."

"Very well," the governor said. "If you should hear from Brownwell before I do, please tell him to call me."

"Yes, sir. I'll do that."

The governor set down the phone and finished dressing. While preparing to leave he mentally composed a statement for the press. It was common knowledge that he didn't like the Attorney General, so he wrote something that expressed his "state's grief at the untimely death of one of our most dedicated servants."

Paul then left the home he would occupy for only a short time longer. He drove to his office like many other people. Unlike some of his predecessors, he did not have the big car and driver he was entitled to. He found the press waiting in his outer office, just as he expected. He gave the statement, and asked them to hold their questions until his scheduled 2 pm press conference, where he would also address a particular senate bill.

The Governor then retreated to the safety of his inner office. He closed the door against the din and dropped into his chair. He had just thrown the press a bone to chomp on while he focused on a bill up for vote.

This particular state senate bill had been introduced by his administration with lukewarm support. It had immediately caused an uproar that the press had devoured. The bill came under attack from special interest groups that the governor didn't even know existed. The bill was written by Richard Brownwell. If passed, it would amend the state Constitution to make all county and city law officers part of the State Police. In spite of the strong lobbying against it, the bill looked like it had a chance of passing.

For the next 90 minutes the governor busied himself signing papers and writing statements. He did not get a phone call from Brownwell. He wasn't sure whether to feel upset or relieved.

The governor's intercom buzzed, and his secretary announced that an Oregon State Policeman wished to see him. The man was shown in and presented the governor with a package sporting the state seal and a note. He signed the receipt and the officer left, leaving the governor alone with Tom Blakely's briefcase.

Chapter 47

Johnny came out of a sleep that had been haunted by images of Paula. He dreamt she was swimming in choppy water just far enough from where he stood that she couldn't hear him. He woke himself up by calling her name.

It took a moment for the fear of the dream to fall away. He rolled slowly and looked at the clock. It read 6:45 am. Even with 5 hours of sleep he was still tired. He got out of bed slowly, for this morning his 18 years felt like 80. A shower helped a bit. He dressed slowly and decided to go out and eat. This particular day he had no place to go and nothing special to do.

Once dressed, he looked at the bed and considered getting back into it. The idea didn't really appeal to him, so he walked out into the living room. He refused to turn on any lights, fearing he would lose his night vision if he didn't lose it. For lack of something better to do, he turned on the TV and sat down.

The morning news program showed a picture of Attorney General Tom Blakely. He'd seen the man many times. He had never bothered to listen to the man before, and did not make a special effort to do so now. Johnny didn't know it then, but he'd just caught the first bulletin announcing that Blakely had been killed in an auto accident.

The scene then switched to show the front of a building with some cops standing around. Then he realized they weren't just hanging out. These cops had helmets on and were armed with Thompson machine guns. The camera panned to show the name of the building on a big sign: Prineville Memorial Hospital.

"Paula!" he said aloud. In 3 strides he crossed the room to turn the TV volume up.

The reporter was saying, "Here is Chief Brownwell now. Perhaps he will give us a statement as to what happened here. Chief? Chief, can you make a statement?"

The camera panned in close on Richard Brownwell. It took a moment for Johnny to recognize him as the man he met in the restaurant a few weeks before. He wasn't in uniform this time. In fact, his clothes were mismatched.

Brownwell said, "I can only confirm that an unauthorized person entered the room of the prisoner, Jane Doe."

"Is it true the 'unauthorized person', to use your words, tried to shoot it out with one of your men?"

"The man was shot when he went for a gun after our officer found him in the room."

"Do you know who the dead man is yet?"

"Not at this time."

The reporter was obviously enjoying herself. "Chief Brownwell, are you aware that Attorney General Blakely was killed in an auto accident this morning?"

The question took Chief Brownwell completely by surprise. The reporter knew it would. Her camera crew panned in close to catch the shock on Brownwell's face. The Chief must have realized the trap he had neatly stepped into, so he played the role for all it was worth rather than try to hide his obvious surprise.

"No, I hadn't heard. I'm sorry to hear it."

He turned to officers nearby. "Do you gentlemen know when and where it occurred?"

The camera backed up. One officer answered. "We don't have much information at this time, Chief. It would seem he was one of 2 or 3 people killed in a chain reaction accident near Eugene."

"That's a real shame," Brownwell said. "Blakely was a good Attorney General. He will be missed."

The reporter started to ask about the prisoner again, but Brownwell held up a hand. "Please excuse me, I've got several things to take care of."

"Thank you Chief," the reporter said.

She turned to the camera. "There you have it, ladies and gentlemen. Be sure and stay with this channel."

Johnny lowered the volume and began pacing the room. The interview he had just witnessed bothered him. He had several questions. Who did the cops shoot? Was it someone from the committee? If so, were they in the room to hurt Paula or to help her?

He remembered what Fish had said at the warehouse yesterday about how the committee would see to it Paula was taken care of. What exactly did that mean? During school they were told to sit tight if captured. Someone would get them out. That was before Paula was hurt, though, and before Linda and Dot were killed.

Johnny sat back down, his mind in a jumble. He looked at the TV but didn't really see it. Something he couldn't identify was bothering him. He got up and walked down the hall as if he thought an answer would be waiting there. When an answer did not jump out at him, he decided it was time to get breakfast.

A long time ago Dot had said "Food makes you feel better and think better." Thinking of Dot made him realize what had been bothering him, and he froze.

Sometime back he had figured out that Dot's father was his controller. Then on the news recently he saw a story about a rich guy who had been shot by his wife. Their last name was Stoneking. That was it. Dot's parents. The old man had apparently been financing the Committee.

He started pacing again. With the Stoneking family dead, he thought, that leaves the rest of us in a lurch. Fish had said to keep in touch with our controllers. Who was his controller now? Johnny realized just how little he knew about the organization he worked for. He turned the TV off and headed for the door. He'd decided to get food then pay a visit to the warehouse. Luke might still be around, and maybe he could answer some questions.

It was 8:15 a.m. when he drove up in front of the hideout. He remembered the night months ago when he had first come here with Dot. Those months now felt like years. He was not the same person she had found on the rainy street that night.

The big door slid up. Luke was waiting for him by the door at the back of the warehouse. He was dressed except for shoes. "Morning Johnny boy!" he said.

Johnny noticed Luke's holstered Browning and asked "Why are you carrying openly, Luke?"

"Who's going to see it here?"

"You got a point. If you have a few minutes, I want to talk to you."

"Come on in!" Luke said, backing up. "No one's left here but me, and I'm not going anywhere for awhile."

Johnny followed Luke through the doors. They stopped in the living room.

"Want something to drink?" Luke asked.

"Not now, thanks. Maybe later."

"Alright. Sit down, boy. Tell me what's on your mind."

"Don't call me boy," Johnny said. "I don't like it."

"A thousand apologies," Luke replied. "Now, please tell me what I can help you with."

Johnny sat in the chair Fish had used the day before. Luke sat down across from him in a straight back chair. Johnny noticed that Luke sat so his ability to reach his gun was not hampered. He figured Luke probably sat that way out of habit.

"Who did the cops shoot in Paula's room this morning?"

Luke went rigid, and his eyes widened. "Well I'll be damned! Will surprises never stop?"

"Did you know someone had gotten shot?" Johnny asked.

"No! Damn, damn, double damn. I wonder if Fish knows yet."

"I'd like to know who it was, and what he was doing."

"That cussed Abel," Luke said, then stopped.

He looked at Johnny in a funny way. "What are you doing here, asking me about things that are none of your concern?"

"I was just curious, Luke. It seems like a lot of people are getting killed off lately. It makes me worry a little."

"You've got nothing to worry about," Luke said. "Fish has things well in hand."

"Well, it's more than that," Johnny said. "I told Fish yesterday I wanted to help when it came time to take Paula home from that hospital."

"Abel didn't go to take her out of there," Luke said. "At least not in that sense."

Johnny leaned forward. His heart pounded and he could feel his temper climbing.

"What the hell are you talking about, Luke?"

"Abel was supposed to bump her off."

Johnny jumped up in a rage.

"What in hell kind of organization is this?! I thought you were supposed to help when we got in a fix! Now you're telling me Abel was going to *kill* Paula? Well, fuck this outfit!"

Luke stood up. "Now calm down. Maybe you'd better learn some facts of life. This isn't a game. Paula was a threat to the organization. It wasn't her fault, but she was. When someone becomes a threat you take them out."

"You'd better start shooting, then, because right now I'm a threat."

"I don't think so," Luke said. "At least not yet. You'll cool down. Besides, she was just a Negro gal anway-"

That was as far as Luke got.

Johnny took a long step forward and hit him square in the jaw. Luke stumbled back into the chair. It gave, and he crashed to the floor.

Luke rolled away from the chair and came to his knees. Johnny could tell by the look in his eyes that Luke was crazy mad. He began to back away slowly.

A wild look came to Luke's face. "You dirty son of a bitch, I'll kill you for that."

Johnny stopped backing up as he saw with horror Luke meant to do it. He was actually tugging on the Browning which was in the holster held down by the safety strap. It wouldn't take Luke long to remember the strap was there and remove it. Johnny realized the situation had gone past the point of no return.

"For Christ's sake!" Johnny shouted. "No, Luke!"

Luke was not hearing. Johnny had hoped this crazy situation would somehow right itself, but he had already pulled out the .38 Smith & Wesson revolver he'd taken to carrying at all times.

Luke had just undone the safety strap and pulled the Browning out when Johnny shot him. He fired twice. The roar of the .38 filled the apartment. The bullets slammed Luke in the chest and toppled him backward.

Johnny stood watching the dead man, gun in hand, not at all certain what to do next.

Slowly, he put the S & W back in its place. Luke's gun lay by his lifeless body. Johnny picked it up. He realized several things in that moment. When Fish found out what had happened here he would send Cain for revenge. He had to run, but he had no idea where.

Like a common thief, he removed Luke's belongings from his pockets, for which he felt no shame. All he had was 90 cents and car keys. Johnny then went through the rest of the apartment, and found the safe. It took him 20 minutes to open the thing. Had it been a high quality type, he probably never would have made it, but this one was a cheap model. Johnny counted out $20,000 in hundred dollar bills and left the rest of a large pile of cash.

Chapter 48

Leaving the bedroom, he got a paper sack from the kitchen to hold the money. Then he left the apartment. He didn't bother to wipe away any prints he might have left, for the cops would never know about this crime scene. Fish would have Cain take care of it.

After leaving the warehouse, Johnny drove aimlessly for a while trying to get his mind right. Never in a hundred years had he thought the visit with Luke would turn out that way. He realized he wasn't taking it well. Stopping at a red light, he looked around to get his bearings. When the light turned green he saw the front of the Rainbow's End.

The flashing sign broke through his thoughts. On a whim, he slowed and turned into the parking lot. Johnny placed the Browning he had taken from Luke under his seat and got out of the car.

He had no idea why he was going there. Maybe it was a desire to see the place where it had all started. What Johnny didn't know was the place had been closed down after the killings in January. It's licenses had been pulled and the doors were sealed. It had reopened in July as a coffee shop. The new owners completely remodeled the place, so its history was not obvious.

Johnny pushed the door open and stepped in out of the rain. The sudden change in surroundings jarred him. He looked around and took in the cheerful yet relaxed coffee shop. There were about a dozen people there, business types or shoppers. The sight of people sitting around acting normally made him check his own appearance in the door glass. To his surprise, he looked normal. The reflection showed a young man with no indication that the hounds of hell were on his trail. He smelled coffee, and walked over to the bar, taking a seat on a vacant stool.

The girl behind the counter had one of the nicest smiles he had ever seen. Her name tag said Wanda. She took his order for coffee and pie and went about her work. He looked around again. Nice, he thought, very nice. Hard to believe what it used to be. His order arrived and he enjoyed a very good slice of apple pie.

While sipping his coffee, Johnny felt cold air on the back of his neck. He turned to look and got his third surprise of the morning. Mrs. Rebajo came in. She had a yellow raincoat, and so did Ernie. His harness, which said "Guide Dogs for the Blind", was fitted on over the coat. Johny watched as Ernie led Mrs. Rebajo to a table. She placed her purse on the seat and slid in after it. Ernie laid down under the table on command. He wondered how Ernie knew which table to choose.

Wanda left the counter and approached the table. It was obvious the ladies knew each other. Wanda took her order, then took a look at the dog. She didn't pet him, though. He remembered hearing somewhere that these dogs weren't supposed to be petted while working.

From where Johnny sat, he could see Ernie, and Ernie could see him. The dog didn't show any signs of recognition, but then again he didn't expect him to. It was hard for him to believe this was the same dog that had jumped him in the yard of the farmhouse.

Remembering the farmhouse made him think of Luke. Remembering Luke reminded him he was going to have to leave Eugene for a long time, if not forever. He slid off the stool and reached for his billfold. He dumped a $5 bill on the counter and told Wanda, "Keep the change."

Wanda's eyes widened.

"Your bill is only a dollar. Are you sure?" she asked.

"Yeah. It'll give you something to remember me by."

Johnny started toward the door, but decided to stop and talked with Mrs. Rebajo. She was eating a sandwich. From beneath the table came a low growl.

"May I help you?" she asked.

Johnny felt stupid. "I, well, I just wanted to say hello to you and Ernie, Mrs. Rebajo."

"Well," she said with a look of recognition on her face, "It's Mr. Stevens isn't it?"

"Yes ma'am," he said, glad she had remembered the name he had used.

"Please sit down, Mr. Stevens. Ernie won't mind."

"I was just on my way out the door, but I saw you and wanted to say hi. You are looking healthier."

She smiled. "I feel much better being home, and having Ernie back. If you're not in a hurry, Mr. Stevens, I would certainly like to talk with you awhile. I never got a chance to properly say thank you for what you've done."

Johnny felt out of place, but sat down anyway. "No thanks necessary. As I said, seeing you and Ernie so happy was reward enough."

"I want to apologize for the way Lisa acted that night."

"I don't recall her behaving badly," Johnny answered.

"It wasn't anything she did, at least not in my presence, but I know she was suspicious."

"I've had people doubt me before, Mrs. Rebajo. It hasn't hurt me yet."

"My name is Donna. Please call me Donna. I hear Mrs. Rebajo enough from the kids in school."

"School?" Johnny asked.

"I'm a teacher. I teach 6th grade. I've been off for the past few months because of the accident, but in 2 weeks I'll be back at the grind again."

Johnny didn't know what to say, so he sat and waited for her to say more.

"I get the impression you're much younger than me," Donna said. "Saying Mr. Stevens seems a bit awkward. Do you prefer Richard, Rich, Rick...?"

"Actually, my name is Johnny. Johnny Redwine."

"Oh." Her face went blank.

"I'm sorry about the phony name, Donna. It seemed like the thing to do at the time."

"Johnny, are you in some kind of trouble?"

He mentally kicked himself for giving out his real name. "What makes you ask that?"

"When people use names that are not their own, they are usually trying to cover something up. Of course, that doesn't apply if you happen to be in the entertainment business. They use stage names. I don't think you're an actor, though."

"No, I'm not," he replied. "I'm not in any business at the moment."

"I thought you worked at a gas station?"

He looked at the door. "I should get going. Maybe we'll meet again sometime."

"Don't go Johnny, please." She looked disappointed.

That look, and her tone of voice, made him change his mind. "Alright. I'll stick around for a while."

Wanda came over to the table.

"Will there be anything else Donna?"

"No thank you, this is fine."

Wanda put the check on the table. "Alright, your bill is just to your left. It comes to $1.65."

Donna paid the bill, and Wanda left the table.

"Well," Donna said, "I'm waiting."

"Waiting for what?" Johnny asked.

"For you to tell me about the gas station."

"I don't work at a gas station." Johnny wondered why he was being so honest with this woman. Why didn't he just get up and leave? Something he could not identify held him.

"Do you have any place to be right away?"

"I guess not."

Johnny decided it was time to ask some questions of his own. "How did you get to Eugene, and how do you plan on getting home?"

"I rode the bus to do some shopping. When I'm finished I'll take the bus home."

"Why go shopping when it's pouring down rain?"

"It wasn't raining that hard when I left," she said. "Anyway, it's something to do. May I ask how old you are, Johnny?"

"I'm 18," he said. "How old are you?"

"I'm 27," she said, "but I hope that won't stop us from being friends. I think I can still identify with your thinking. That is, the thinking of 18 year olds."

"Yes, I think we can be friends." He did not mention leaving town.

"It isn't hard to make friends, Johnny. All you have to do is be open and honest with people, and they'll be open and honest with you. Friends also like to be treated well, the way you would want to be treated."

Her words made him remember his childhood teacher reciting the golden rule. It also reminded him of the friends who were now gone. Roy, Linda, Dot, even Luke...all dead. How many more of them would go in pursuit of a cause led by the corrupt?

"I understand all that, but friends haven't been the easiest thing for me to get and keep."

"Well, I think we'll get along just fine," Donna answered.

"Have you finished all your shopping?" he asked, trying to change the subject.

"I haven't even started," she said laughingly. "I've talked myself out of it now. With all this rain I think I'll just head home."

"I can take you home," he said without thinking.

"Well that's very nice of you. Are you sure it's not out of your way?"

"It's okay. I've got no place to be anyway."

They walked out of the Rainbow's End together. He said, "My car is in the parking lot. Turn to your right and walk about 20 feet forward, then the car won't be too far into the lot."

He stayed on her left and marveled at how Ernie worked. Ernie was aware he was around and kept throwing quick glances his way, but stayed on the path to guide Donna. When they reached the spot where they would turn toward the car, Johnny called a halt. "I'm not sure how to tell you and Ernie to get from here to the car."

"Walk in front of us and Ernie will follow you."

Sure enough, he did.

Johnny opened the door and said "Ernie can ride in the back. He's been in this car before."

"I guess he has," Donna replied. "His feet are all wet, though. He'll mess up your seat."

"It'll clean off," Johnny said, and held the seat forward.

When his passengers were in, Johnny went around and got in the drivers' seat. Noticing Donna already had her seatbelt on, and Ernie had laid down in back, he pulled forward then out of the lot. A while later they cleared downtown traffic and were on the road toward Junction City.

Donna had been silent since leaving the parking lot. Johnny sensed she had something on her mind and was building up the nerve to say it. A few minutes later she came out with it.

"Lisa thinks you're part of that Cleanup Committee bunch."

This time, he thought before he answered. This was dangerous ground.

"I've been accused of worse things," he said.

"Do you believe in what their announced goal is?"

"I don't have an opinion," he said.

"Do you use narcotics?" she asked.

"Absolutely not! I've seen what that garbage can do."

"Then you do have an opinion."

"I suppose I do. If it makes them happy then let them have at it." Johnny was paying particular attention to his driving. He didn't want to attract any unnecessary attention, and he didn't want to scare his passenger. It hadn't been too long since her accident.

"Lisa had a visitor that night after you left," she said.

"She called the cops on me, right?"

"How did you know?"

"She accused me of being one of the Committee people when we were out by the car."

"Lisa is a cop too. Lane County Sheriff Deputy."

For a moment Johnny was not sure how to answer. Again he reminded himself to be careful before speaking.

Donna took the need to say anything away from him. "Her visitor was another Deputy," she said. "I was in my room brushing Ernie and they were talking in low tones. I could still hear everything they were saying. Lisa told him she had caught you in a couple of lies. He told her she was making a mountain out of a molehill. They came to my door and Lisa asked if she could bring her friend in to see Ernie. I said yes.

I recognized the Deputy. His name is Larry, and he's very nice. They acted like they were just looking at Ernie because he's fascinating, but when they left I heard Lisa comment about his feet. She said Ernie's feet looked too good, so he couldn't possibly have traveled from Creswell to Eugene. I talked to Lisa the next day and asked her to leave you alone. Lisa is a good sister and I love her very much. She's just too quick to accuse as a police officer. What's worse is she's like a dog that only gets an occasional bone. She gets all the mileage she can out of it."

"Is Lisa at your house now?" he asked.

"No. It's her day off and she left early this morning."

"Good," he said. "I'll drop you and Ernie off then split. Hanging around wouldn't be smart if she is so convinced I'm one of *them*."

"Are you one of them Johnny?" Donna asked. "Would you tell me if you were?"

"No," he said in complete honesty, "I'm not with them." He silently prayed she wouldn't ask if he had ever been one of them. Before she could ask more questions, he changed topics.

"We're coming into Junction City now. Do you have any stops you want to make before going home?"

"No, but thank you," she answered.

"Do you mind if I ask how long you've been blind?"

She giggled. "Since you have already put the question out there, no I don't mind. The answer is since I was 14. It was an accident, but I won't bore you with the details."

"It wouldn't bore me at all," he answered sincerely.

"Are you sure you're only 18? You seem more mature than that."

"I guess I am in terms of experience," he said. "I've had a bit of a hard life."

"Have you no parents?"

"No. All of my relatives are dead, even my sister."

"I'm really sorry, Johnny."

He slowed for the turn onto her street. He was relieved to see her driveway was empty. There weren't any patrol cars parked nearby either. He would get this lady into her house then split. He rolled to a stop in her driveway.

"Please come in for a few minutes," Donna said. "I have something else I need to tell you. It may help you plan what you're going to do."

"Just what do you mean by that?" he demanded.

She drew back a little in what appeared to be fear. Christ, he thought, I hope she doesn't really believe I would hurt her.

"Johnny," she said with a slight tremor, "maybe you're not part of the Committee, but I believe you know someone who is. Sometimes Lisa thinks because I'm blind that I'm deaf too. Two nights ago I heard her talking to a State policeman. They were planning a trap for a young man. I want to tell you about it so maybe you can warn him."

"Why would you do that? Don't you believe in the work your sister does as a cop?"

"I believe in her, but I don't believe in the ability of the law to do its job. I'm blind because of drugs. The accident that took my sight was caused by a man on narcotics. I see kids in my school, 11 and 12 year olds, hooked on marijuana. They get it right on school grounds or across the street. While the methods the Cleanup Committee uses are questionable, I strongly support their goal of stopping the flow of drugs."

Johnny turned the engine off. "Alright, I'll listen."

Once in the house, Donna busied herself with putting her things away and taking the harness and raincoat off of Ernie. She let him out into the garage.

"Ernie has a door in the back of the garage that opens out into a fenced run. It's covered so he can do his thing and keep dry too. He can go out into the yard in the summer when it's dry. In the meantime he doesn't get that wet dog smell."

"That's good," Johnny said. "Nothing stinks like a wet dog."

Donna excused herself to the restroom, and Johnny paced in the living room. He took the opportunity to lay out an escape route in case Lisa showed up. He also checked the room for bugging devices While he was checking behind a picture on the mantle, Donna returned. She was in the middle of the living room before he heard her.

"Looking for something?" she asked in a low voice.

Johnny turned to face her. She was 5 feet in front of him, just standing and looking in his direction. If Donna's eyes weren't blank he would have sworn she could see him.

"I was just looking," he answered.

"Remember what I said about friends trusting each other?" she asked.

"Alright," he grumbled. "I was looking for a bug or something. I thought Lisa might have bugged the place."

"No one knows you're here. There are also no bugs. That's the truth."

"I believe you," he said.

The tension in the air was heavy. For a moment no sound could be heard in the room except the ticking of the clock. When Ernie barked at the garage door they both jumped like they'd been shot. Donna went white.

Johnny stepped forward and quickly took her arm.

"Are you alright Donna?"

"I'll be ok," she said, leaning on him. "I still get weak spells sometimes."

Johnny guided her toward a chair. "Please sit down. I'll let Ernie in."

Ernie came charging in as soon as he opened the door. He ran by Johnny and straight to Donna, where he sat in front of her and put a paw on her knee.

"I'm alright," Donna told him. Ernie laid down on the rug next to her chair.

Johnny shut the garage door and made sure it was locked. He crossed into the living room and sat where he could see everything, particularly the front door. He contemplated Ernie's show of concern toward Donna.

"Would Ernie bite someone if they tried to bother you, Donna?"

"He isn't trained for protection work, but he might because of loyalty."

"I've got a thousand questions," he said, "but they'll have to wait. I want to know about the trap Lisa and the other cop set."

"If I tell you, will you answer some things for me?" Donna asked.

"You scratch my back, and I'll scratch yours."

"Okay. Lisa told the other officer that she had one of the Cleanup Committee members nailed to his residence. She said she was really sure it was one of the guys who had gotten the drop on him in Creswell. She wanted to meet him today and set up a stakeout on the guy's house. Lisa said she knew what the guy looked like, and the officer said he would recognize the guy if they spotted him. I heard him say that Brownwell made him look at so many photos he wasn't sure anymore who looked like who. Nevertheless, he was willing to go along."

"So you think Lisa is watching this guy's house right now?" Johnny asked.

"I'm sure of it. She's ready to bust him."

"Why is Lisa so anxious to get this guy? Why doesn't she let the state police handle it?"

Donna replied, "Her argument is that every cop should be going after these guys. She says our legal system might not be the best, but it's still better than all the others in the world. She thinks that if the Committee is allowed to get away with this it won't be long before people create other groups to wipe out people who drink alcohol, or drive Chevys, or believe in God. I know it sounds silly, but then a few months ago I would've never believed something like the Cleanup Committee was even possible."

"That's horse crap!" Johnny said. "If the system was any good at all the Committee would've never happened. That doesn't matter now. How did Lisa find out where this guy lives?"

"I don't know," she said with a frown. "I never heard her say."

Johnny got up and started pacing. He had to get out of there and do some thinking. There were things in the house he wanted to get, but he'd never get near it with the cops watching. At least not in daylight....maybe at night he would have a chance.

He stopped and looked at Donna for a moment. He realized she was a pretty gal. Her scars from the accident were nothing a good plastic surgeon couldn't fix. She was also smart.

"Suppose I say that I know who you're talking about. Suppose I say that I can warn the guy and that he would escape because of my warning. He might even kill some more people before he's run down. Do you want a killer loose?" he asked.

Donna was silent for a moment. He could see her working up the nerve to speak.

In a low voice she said, "Johnny, it's you we're talking about. Will you admit it?"

Seeing that it was silly to continue the game he said, "Yes. I'm the one your sister's after, but I didn't lie to you about not being part of the Cleanup Committee. Not a complete lie, at least. I was but then I left."

Donna said, "Maybe we'd better start from the beginning. I'd like to hear your whole story. Maybe I can help you in some way."

He sat down on the floor near Ernie, and told her all of it. He talked about being recruited, the training, and how he had really found Ernie. She listened, taking it all in, saying nothing. When he had finished, she sat thinking. Her mind was trying to process the idea that someone so young could be such an accomplished killer.

"That's a fantastic story, Johnny. Do you realize the police really know nothing about the Cleanup Committee?"

"I think it's safe to assume it won't be long until they have something good to go on. If Doctor Fish doesn't get me, he'll tip off the cops. They'll both be after me then."

"You're in a fix," she said. "No getting out of that. I don't think it's hopeless yet, though."

She started to say something else but was interrupted by the phone ringing.

"That will either be my mother or Lisa. I hope it isn't mom, she can talk for hours."

On the third ring she picked up. "Hello? Oh, hi mom."

Johnny stood up and stretched. His legs were stiff from sitting so long. He took a few steps to loosen up then turned and looked at Donna. He found her looking highly excited.

"You're kidding me, Mom! The Attorney General himself?" She listened a bit more then exclaimed "Did you say Doctor Fish? No, mother, it just strikes me as being a silly name."

He wasn't aware until Donna hung up the phone that he was standing at attention. It was obvious something huge was going on. Donna leapt to her feet.

"Johnny! They found a briefcase in Attorney General Blakely's car. It had all of the Cleanup Committee information in it. The governor's holding a press conference at 2:30 to tell everyone. Your Doctor Fish was actually Attorney General Blakely!"

Donna crossed the room toward him then stopped after a few steps. She started to cry.

"Johnny, please give yourself up. They found out about everything in that case."

She then felt his arms go around her. Surprisingly, for the first time in months, she felt safe.

Johnny held her as the sobs shook her frail body. No woman had ever cried like this for him before.

Chapter 49

Every time Lisa took an idea to that son of a bitch Sargeant Stinger, she was met with failure. He would listen, agree to do something, and then nothing happened. Finally, Lisa had found a way to get results from him. Quite by accident she discovered who the Sargeant's latest sexual adventures were with- and it wasn't his wife. She let him know in a roundabout way that if there weren't results, Mrs. Stinger would get a phone call.

An idea came to her shortly after she discovered where that Stevens guy was living. She had no doubt that name was fake, but she had no other name to put on him yet. When the idea came to her, she knew she would have to sell Trooper Henry on it first. He was, after all, the only officer who had ever seen any of those Committee people.

For the twentieth time in as many days, Lisa cursed her luck that it had not been a sheriff's deputy that night instead of OSP. The whole thing would've been much easier if no outside departments had to be involved.

Henry had gone for the idea easily enough, but refused to go ahead with it until he got his department's approval. That high and mighty Captain of his had taken his sweet time, but he finally gave the okay to proceed. Lisa had then gone to Sgt. Stinger.

He listened and said, "We'll see. I'll take it up with the head of Narcotics to see if he'll let you use one of his vans."

Lisa said, "How's Lorraine doing? I haven't seen her in a while."

Sgt. Stinger frowned.

"When do you need the van, Lisa?"

"Day after tomorrow, 8 pm, " she answered.

The van, specifically built for stakeout work, had been delivered on time. Lisa and Trooper Henry drove it to a spot they're already chosen to settle in and watch for Stevens. She got the state trooper to promise that Stevens would be her bust if he was their man.

The hands on her watch crept up to 10 pm, then 11, with no results. The van was stuffy. Rolling down a window was impractical because it was pouring down rain. The rain also made it hard to see. More than a few times during the watching and waiting Lisa had asked herself if it was all worth it. Maybe she should just leave this turkey alone. Maybe she should let that self centered Brownwell have him, and all the rest of them. She decided there was no way she was giving up because it seemed everyone else had already done that very thing.

The State police had been one step ahead of everyone throughout this whole investigation. Brownwell and his people had hogged all the information. The info they did release was of little value....but Lisa had been lucky. At least, it seemed that way at first. An actual committee gunman had been delivered into her hands. Unfortunately, the evidence she badly needed to arrest him had not turned up. The probable cause she needed for a search warrant alse eluded her.

By 11:15 the next morning, Lisa realized she was on a stakeout that was obviously going nowhere. The guy wasn't around. She was kicking herself for not getting there earlier when the tone alert on their portable radio went off.

Lisa picked up the radio from the floor and thumbed the transmit button. "105, go ahead."

The voice of Captain Burke himself came through. "105, pull off and come in. The investigation is over."

"What do you mean it's all over?" she demanded into the radio.

"It will be explained when you arrive at the station."

They wrapped it up and went in. It was there they learned what the governor had found.

A police teletype read: "The Cleanup Committee is a private army put together by a group of Portland financiers. It was initially created and planned by the late Jonah B. Stoneking, and Attorney General Tom Blakely."

It told the officers the rest of the information the public would be given at the governor's press conference. It also carried a message from Chief Brownwell instructing his men to take no action against the individual committee members for 24 hours. His reasoning was that they should be given ample opportunity to turn themselves in. He requested that other agencies do the same.

Now, a disappointed Lisa Rebajo was on her way home. She had the radio on. The governor was telling the public what the police had known for a couple of hours. She wasn't listening to him, though. Instead her mind was on the investigation that had just been pulled right out from under her. She drove through downtown Junction City without really seeing it.

Lisa had made the turn onto her street, and was ready to turn into the driveway when she spotted the Mustang. She was so surprised that she nearly hit a parked car. Stevens wasn't home because he was in her house. A sudden realization came to her. Donna was with him.

Lisa turned left at the end of the block and pulled to the curb. She was shaking badly, her mind stuck on the danger Donna faced. Defenseless Donna. Would Ernie help? She shook her head and told herself, Damnit, Lisa, think!

She turned off the car key. With the motor off and the radio silent, the sound of the rain became loud on the top of the car. She willed herself to look at the situation as calmly as possible. Her police instincts kicked in at last.

Fact 1: Stevens was in the house.

Deduction: He had heard the news that the jig was up. He planned to use Donna as a hostage to secure safe passage out of the area.

Fact 2: It was 3:15. Traffic was heavy. Cars and school buses were all over the place.

Deduction: This traffic would have to be turned away from this area when the backup units arrived. No, she thought, no backups. I stand a better chance alone.

Lisa got out of the car. Her plan of attack was simple. Get as close to the house as possible without being seen. If her luck held she might even make it to the porch. She planned to shoot him on sight. The model 19 S & W Magnum service revolver was in her hand.

Lisa crept toward the house, and couldn't believe her luck when she got to the porch. She stopped at the top of the steps. She pushed her hair back from her eyes with her left hand, the .357 at the ready in her right. She stepped forward and snuck a quick look through the small window in the door. There he was, 15 feet in front of her. His back was turned, and had a hold on Donna.

Chapter 50

Johnny felt the cold October wind. Swiftly as he could, he stepped away from Donna while turning toward the door. He saw Lisa standing in the doorway with a .357 leveled at his chest. Johnny knew by the look in her eyes she meant to shoot.

Donna must have sensed disaster. She yelled through her tears, "No, Lisa, no!"

Johnny actually managed to get the S & W out of his pocket before Lisa fired. The 158 grain round nose bullet knocked him into the TV. He landed on his knees. The gun in his hand suddenly weighed a ton. He heard Donna screaming. It came to him disjointed and sort of echoing. He heard his own breath coming in ragged gasps.

As if in slow motion, the barrel of Lisa's gun leveled on him again. My God, he thought, she means to put me down like a dog. It was the shock his mind needed to give him the fighting spirit, and the last bit of reserved strength in his system, to raise and level his gun.

The roar of the two guns firing at once filled the room and bounced around the walls. Donna was still screaming and sobbing as she fell to her knees. She did not hear Johnny as he fell to the carpet. She did not hear the dull thud of her sister's lifeless body hit the porch.

Sometime later, she had no idea how long, Donna became aware of Ernie whining. He was somewhere nearby. She was on her knees, but did not remember how she got there. The cold wind blew in through the open front door.

"Johnny! Johnny!"

No answer.

She put her hands on the carpet and began to crawl forward, looking for him. She found him shortly thereafter. Ernie was standing by him, still whining.

Donna put her hands in the blood, and tried to find where it was coming from. There was just so much of it. It was no use. There was no way to stop that much blood.

Off in the distance she heard the sound of the sirens. They echoed off the walls and into the canyons of her mind.

In a quiet apartment, tucked safely at the back of a warehouse in Eugene, Cain gathered what was left of the money in the safe. With his brother gone and the Cleanup Committee broken, Cain was on his own with no orders, but also no restraint. He started planning to clean up the drug dealing scumbags himself, bit by bloody bit.

THE END

Acknowledgements

My biggest thanks go to my husband. His unwavering support makes everything possible.

Big thanks to my big brother, who's always been my hero.

Thank you Adele and Rebecca, for giving me perspective.

Thank you my bestie Mela, for always making me smile.

Thank you especially to my readers, for joining me on this journey.